FROM THE ASHES

HEY HONEY'S BARISTAS BOOK #1

KATY MICHELE

For the ones who have been cheering me on since day one —
Stacy, Julia, Vanessa, and Haley

NOTE TO READER

From the Ashes contains topics that may be triggering to some readers. These topics include *explicit* sexual content (chapters 30, 32, 36, 37), domestic abuse (on- and off-page), death of a loved one (off-page), grief, PTSD, panic attacks (on-page), therapy, postpartum anxiety, and brief mentions of abortion.

If any of these topics are triggering to you,
please do what you need to protect your peace. 🩶

PLAYLIST

"I'D HAPPILY LET HER RUIN MY LIFE IF THAT'S WHAT SHE WANTED."

Butterflies by Between You & Me
Always, Everytime by the Wrecks
ATTN. by Beartooth
sleepover by dreamfone
Heavenly by Broadside
Bad Influence by glimmers
Feel Love by Broadside
Try by Fly by Midnight
Please Please Please by Sabrina Carpenter
2 hands by Tate McRae
I Should Have Kissed You by One Direction
Desperate Measure by Marianas Trench
Risk by Honey Revenge
According to You by Orianthi
Untouched by The Veronicas
Gravity by Sleep Theory
Lose My Breath by Stray Kids

CHAPTER 1
JACK

I HATE SUNDAYS.

For me, they aren't for lazy mornings in bed, the smell of coffee ruminating throughout the house, the sunlight peeking in through the shades, the feeling of someone curled up against me.

They're not for rest and recovery, or spending the day doing things that rejuvenate the soul—or whatever the fuck people say.

Sundays are for making the 30-minute trek from my cabin to town to see an old man who gives me a hard time over my choice in nightcrawlers over leeches.

Sundays are for avoiding small-talk with the locals and pretending that being around another human doesn't make me want to peel my skin off.

It's the only day the bait shop is open—it's closed every other day of the week so Banjo, as he calls himself, an old fisherman with an eye patch and a stringy white ponytail, can be out on the lake.

You could use one leech for every dozen of those lousy worms. Be a real fisherman and get the damn leeches.

Without fail, he urges every Sunday, but I don't care enough to argue.

There isn't much I care about these days.

Instead, I just nod and tell him, "Maybe next time", even though we both know I'll be getting two more containers of nightcrawlers when I come back next week.

It's the same routine Banjo and I have followed since my first Sunday walking into his shop five months ago.

My cabin in the Northwoods of Wisconsin belonged to my grandpa, with wallpaper from the '70s and furniture he built in the '80s, not to mention no cell phone service or neighbors within a 25-mile radius.

It's just the way I like it.

No other cabins surrounding the small lake, no other boats out on the water, just me and my thoughts.

Just *solitude*.

When I decided to come up here, the seclusion sounded like a good idea. Too much of home—both the people and the place—reminded me of who wasn't there anymore and how different it was going to be now that he was gone.

"When are you gonna be a real fisherman and get the damn leeches, boy?" the old man rasps around the toothpick hanging from his lip. I set two cartons of nightcrawlers on the glass counter of Banjo's Bait Shop, my hand going to my pocket to pull out a couple bills.

"Maybe next time," I reply as I set the bills on the counter.

"You even catch anythin' with 'em things?" he asks, crossing his arms over his chest, his black and red flannel buttoned up to his neck and tucked into dark blue jeans, his white beard almost as long as his ponytail. "There's no way 'em silly worms get you nothin' more than a few bluegill."

"I do okay," I answer, grabbing the containers and turning toward the door before he can say anything else about my bait of choice. I wave a hand behind me as a goodbye before pushing the door to the shop open, the little bell chiming as I walk into the crisp spring air.

May has been uncharacteristically cool this year, but the cooler weather has pushed off the summer crowd that comes into town for their "upnorth" summer vacation, prolonging the solitude and isolation I've been hiding in. It's also nice sitting out on the lake with a cool breeze or the light sprinkle rather than sweating my balls off in the sun.

A gust of wind greets me, accompanied by the smell of rain from the night before and the fresh pine from the trees. One deep breath of the clear air, and I immediately feel some of the tension in my shoulders release.

While it's possible to fish year-round in Wisconsin, this month marks the beginning of the season for most lakes, and I have been itching for a catch that isn't just the pesky sunfish that eat my worm before I even realize I have a bite. The bass, walleye, along with the loons who keep my company out on the lake, are calling my name.

"Jack!" My name rings out from behind me.

Damn it.

I run a hand through my hair and resist the urge to look at the cloudy sky and let out a groan.

When I'm not overly stealthy with getting my bait and getting out of town, Banjo's wife, Caroline, or her sister, Beatrice, find me—and then ultimately corner me and drag me into their diner for breakfast.

I got out of it the first few weeks I was here, but I got tired of coming up with excuses by the second month. When I finally agreed back in February, I regretted sitting down at the counter within three seconds. Not only did I have to deal with the two of them pestering me with questions, but I had to suffer through the rest of the locals at the diner tuning in to get the 411 on what James Hasting's grandson was doing up here after twenty years.

Since then, I have only had a 30% success rate of getting in and out of town without running into someone other than Banjo and getting trapped into breakfast, running an errand, fixing a sink, or getting a cat out of the tree.

Actually getting a cat out of a fucking tree.

The first time it happened, I honestly thought it was a prank or some kind of asinine joke because the town knows I am—*was*—a firefighter back home, and the stupid motif—or expression, or whatever the hell it is—didn't escape me. Then, it happened again, and I decided it was because the universe likes to laugh at me—along with Beatrice's cat.

I almost don't turn around, but then I hear the voice call my name again—I know it's Caroline. Lake Tomahawk is small enough to drive through and not even see the odometer go up, and her diner is right next door to her husband's bait shop.

"I know you hear me, Jacky Boy." The stupid, childhood nickname makes my fingers clench around the plastic containers of worms at the same time it makes a hairline crack in my annoyance. Technically, I already knew all the locals before coming up here, especially Caroline, but I haven't spent any time here since the summer I turned 16.

My grandparents were a staple here in Lake Tomahawk, but their cabin has been empty since my grandpa died. Even so, their legacy lines every inch of this town—memories of spending summers here with them, my younger sister, Emerson, and all the town locals are etched into my brain—and Caroline isn't afraid of my grumpy exterior, not when she met me as a skinny, sunburnt, braces-wearing kid, only a few years before my grandfather passed away.

I turn to face her, futilely accepting that my chances of getting to my boat within the next 35 minutes are gone.

Caroline's white hair is pulled back in a tight bun with a pencil stuck right through it; her pink, grease-stained apron wrapped tightly around her round waist. She places her hands on her hips and looks at me as if she caught me stealing cookies out of the jar she keeps by the register.

"You snuck out with your bait the last two weeks without saying hello to me," she reprimands, and I almost hang my head in shame like the time she caught me and my sister loosening the caps on the salt shakers in the diner.

"Sorry," I mumble, but it comes out more like a growl.

"*Sorry* doesn't cut it." She deepens her voice to mock my half-assed apology, crossing her arms and taking a step toward me. "You can't be spending all your time holed up in that cabin like your granddaddy did after you kids stopped coming up here."

My annoyance is immediately replaced with a flood of guilt, along with frustration at what she's implying. "We didn't have a choice," I reply through gritted teeth, not wanting to disrespect the woman who has always been nothing but nice to me, but not liking where this conversation is headed. "You know he wasn't the same after Grandma Laurie died." I watch the furrow in her brow turn from one of anger to one of sadness, and it melts some of my anger too.

I don't miss the similarity between my grandpa and me—both of us using this cabin to isolate ourselves after a loss—but I don't let myself sit with the thought for long. I know Caroline made the connection within my first week here.

"Jacky Boy," she starts, her arms uncrossing and reaching out to grab the arm hung at my side, "I'm just worried about you." I feel the warmth of her touch through the sleeve of my jacket, the touch further settling the tension that seems to never fully release from my body these days. "Ever since Ben—"

I stiffen at the first syllable of his name. "Don't," I interrupt before she can say what I know she wants to, and this time it *is* a growl. "I'm fine."

And alive, which is more than I can say about my best friend.

"You've said the word 'fine' so many times, it doesn't even sound like a word anymore."

I shake my head, her words ringing too true and close for comfort. Saying "I'm fine" has become a natural response, and I don't even know what the fuck it means now that I'm living a life without the person who mattered most to me.

But I'm not up here to sit and dissect my feelings.

I'm here to fish and get some fucking peace and quiet.

Before I can say any of this to her, my phone rings. I almost don't register the sound, the noise so foreign after a week of it sitting silently on my kitchen table from the lack of service in the woods.

Caroline lets go of my arm, her eyes misty as she reminds me, "As happy as I am to have you back here, you can't hide up here forever."

I try not to show how deeply her words cut into me, or how jarring it is to no longer feel the tender touch of another human being after so many months alone. I don't need her reminding me of a fact I try to keep as far back in my brain as possible.

Grabbing my phone from my back pocket, I give her a curt nod as I jog across the street to my truck, with every intent of leaving this conversation behind me as I go.

I open the driver's side door, set the containers of worms on the center console, and turn to see Caroline walking back into the diner, her head shaking slightly.

Ignoring the pang in my chest and the overwhelming feeling of grief beginning its slow yet familiar descent into me, I turn my phone over in my hand to see who's calling.

It's embarrassing to admit that I still feel a sense of hopefulness when checking the caller ID, that somehow it's a call from *him*; that somehow the doctors got it wrong, that he isn't gone, and that we didn't bury him six months ago.

A dry, humorless laugh escapes me when I see Arthur Sander's name at the top of my screen. The irony that I'm up here to catch a goddamn break from everything at home yet the reminders of both why I came and what's waiting for me back there punching me right in the face this morning.

"Chief," I say into the phone as a greeting.

The station, the chief of the fire department, and the crew all feel like something from another life—one too good for reality; one so far off and removed from where I am now that it feels like it was all a dream.

"Hasting," he echoes in the same gruff voice he always uses, the sound of my last name hauling me back to the life I left behind. Aside from a few phone calls with my mom and my sister, I haven't heard from anyone back home since I left, let alone anyone from my old job. "Glad I caught you."

Before I can reply, my mind goes to the worst-possible scenario, the only reason the Chief would be calling me right now.

My mom. Emerson.

"Tell me who died," I demand as I feel my whole body tighten, trying—and failing—to keep calm, my voice louder than I've heard it in months. He has no other reason to call me, not since I set my letter of resignation down on his desk before driving up here in the snow back in December.

"Relax, Jack. Everyone's fine here. That's not why I'm calling you." I close my eyes as a wave of relief washes over me. I unclench my fingers holding my phone to my ear, the dull pain bringing me back to reality. But the relief doesn't last long. "I just wanted to check up on you. We're—" He pauses, taking a second to find the right words. "We're all worried about you, son."

Everyone needs to take their worry and shove it up their ass.

"No need. I don't work for you anymore," I snap. The words rush out of me, and it feels refreshing to say something other than "I'm fine".

Anger is easy—in a cathartic, fucked up sort of way.

It's everything else that's hard.

"Watch it," Chief Sanders warns, his no-nonsense personality evident even through the phone. It's the same words and warning he gave me the week before I left, when I refused to go see the therapist the station brought in after losing one of our own.

Chief literally dragged me into the therapist's office across from the station and stood outside the door for the whole session while I had to sit there and listen to the therapist's fuckshit analogy about grief being like a fire—all while holding back the urge to flip the fucking coffee table in his stupid office.

Did he think because I was a firefighter, I could only speak about fire like a goddamn caveman? Did he forget that the whole reason I was even in his office was because my best friend died in a fucking fire? Did he even think to acknowledge the candle burning on his desk made my nails dig so far into my palms that I drew blood?

My chest tightens at the memory, my head feeling like it's going to explode as my anger burns through me, all while my grief threatens to pin me to the ground.

"It's been almost six months." Chief Sanders' voice brings me back to the present. "It's time to quit hiding from your feelings and come home to confront what you lost."

I shake my head even though he can't see me, my thumb and index finger pressing into my closed eyes, pushing until I see spots.

How the fuck did he expect me to heal in the same place—the same *places*—where I used to see my best friend every single day?

Did everyone really think I was going to walk into the apartment we shared or the station we worked at together and *not* feel my lungs constrict with every breath as if my body is actively punishing me for playing a part in how he died? How I couldn't save him?

There is no "dealing" with this.

I'm positive that dealing with it will kill me.

"Jack, it's time to come home. Your job is waiting for you, your crew and your mom and sister too." Chief Sanders has always been like a father to me, the only father figure I've had since my dad left, but it doesn't make what he says any easier to hear.

"I quit, Chief. I'm not coming back." The words come out harsh, and there's something about them that feels like a lie.

"You've been on leave, Jack. Your letter of resignation never made it past my desk."

I shake my head, my hand coming to my forehead.

There's no part of me that is surprised that the chief put me on leave rather than just letting me quit, but it still pisses me off.

"I'm not going back there," I grit out, anger lining the words to cover up how scared I am of where *there* is.

Like I said, anger is easy.

"You don't have to go out in the field. Not until you're ready," he answers carefully. "One of the fire investigators is on paternity leave. We need someone to cover for him while he's out. And that someone is you."

CHAPTER 2
RUMI

I HAVEN'T EVEN HAD time to think about how terrifying it is that I have to push a baby out of my vagina, let alone an almost *ten-pound* baby, since the moment I found out I was pregnant.

My fingers clench the steering wheel, the leather slick from my sweaty palms. "I'm going to need you to stay in there a little longer, baby girl," I grit through my teeth as another contraction ripples through me.

The pressure makes my vision go blurry, and I ignore the alarms going off in my head as I glance at the clock on my dash. "And you're gonna need to give me more than three minutes between these. I refuse to give birth on the side of the road," I add, trying to drive in a straight line.

My insides feel like they're twisting around themselves, but I refuse to stop this car on a road with no street lights.

According to the GPS, I have 22 miles before I'll reach the closest hospital, and I'll need at least that to come up with a story to tell the doctors about why the hell I'm driving to *who knows where* in active labor.

When I left, I didn't really know where I was going—but now? I need to make a decision.

To be fair, when I started driving three hours ago, I didn't know these contractions were the real thing, especially because the Braxton Hicks have been killer the last two days.

It didn't hit me until ten minutes ago that *these* contractions weren't stopping but instead getting dangerously close together.

And I'm less than three days away from her actual due date.

The gushing of liquid between my thighs that I've had the pleasure of sitting in for the last half an hour was another clue that this was in fact the real thing.

I look in my rearview mirror for what seems like the millionth time, but I can't ignore the feeling that Trevor came after me.

I know it's a small chance considering I left him unconscious on the kitchen floor—the pain in my fingers and the dull ache on the left side of my face feeling like tickles compared to the tightening of my uterus—but at least I made it out of there.

Tonight was the last time.

I try to inhale and focus on the road in front of me as I wait for the pain to subside, reminding myself that my whole life has been a plethora of pain, and this is nothing compared to that.

If anything, this pain is beautiful. It means something. It means that I'll meet my baby girl soon. My love, my light, the reason I made it to 25, the reason I left in the middle of the night, the reason for starting all over.

No matter how scary this all feels, it isn't scarier than looking into the face of someone who is supposed to love you as they hurt you in ways you hoped they would never do again.

Or at least *pretended* to hope—part of you knowing they always would.

The thought of running away—fighting back—was inconceivable these last five years. But tonight? Tonight was different.

"Come on. Just give me half an hour," I say through gritted teeth, trying to do the deep breathing that is supposed to help with the pain. One of my hands comes to my stomach, rubbing over the swell in hopes to find some sort of relief.

I let out a shaky exhale, the effects of the adrenaline from earlier tonight finally dissipating to a memory.

"Hold tight, baby girl," I say to my belly as I feel the contraction wane. I know I have a minute or two to breathe before another one comes barreling through, and I take the moment to glance at the GPS on my phone.

It's darker than sin outside, the only light on the road coming from my headlights. The trees of the wooded area I'm in make the two-lane road feel even smaller than it already is, and I haven't passed another car in over an hour.

I take my eyes off the road for two seconds before I feel pain radiate through me—another contraction takes my breath away. The muscle spasms and the squeezing in my stomach make my vision go blurry, and then I'm struck with another type of pain. This one is piercing and hitting me on every inch of skin exposed by my nightgown and accompanied by screeching metal, crumpling impact, and a sudden *thud*.

I thought the road was dark, until I fell into complete darkness.

CHAPTER 3
JACK

FUCK TODAY.

After my conversation with Chief Sanders about his job offer, I finally got out onto the lake. I told him I would let him know my decision in a few days—telling *myself* that I need at least that to think about what the fuck I'm going to do about the looming return home that seems to be becoming more and more of a possibility as the days tick forward.

And I had plenty of time to think today because I didn't get a single catch.

Not even a fucking bite.

It's like the fish were refusing to take the bait of an unemployed firefighter, hiding in a cabin, who can't even light a goddamn match without his heart rate speeding up.

It took one singular nightcrawler wiggling around on my line for six hours for me to come to the conclusion that it was time.

Time to go home.

Time to figure out what the fuck I'm going to do with my life.

Time to be a man, bury these feelings, and get the fuck over it.

"Shit," I mutter to myself, almost veering off toward the side of the road for the third time tonight. The roads in these woods are windy and dark as fuck.

I haven't seen a single car since I left my cabin an hour ago, and I still have a good 20 miles before I'm back in civilization and another three hours until I'm back in Milwaukee.

My cell service is back, but it's the middle of the night—way too late to call Chief Sanders and tell him I'll take the job as a fire investigator but only until Simmons is back from leave.

The all-too-familiar mix of feelings starts to bubble to the surface, making my skin feel hot and cold at the same time.

Anger, sadness, frustration, and emotions I can't even name begin to blend in my gut—the combination strong like the arms that wrapped around me, refusing to let me follow my best friend into that burning house. The same arms that ultimately held me up when I watched the structure collapse on top of him.

"Fuck," I mutter, resisting the urge to bang my head against the steering wheel.

My mind tries to latch on to *anything* but the last moment I saw my best friend alive—the song playing from my truck's speakers, the howl of wind coming in through my cracked windows, the shine of my headlights, the shadows of the trees.

I'm coming up on a curve in the road, seconds away from slamming on my brakes—just to force myself back into the present before this weight in my chest destroys me from the inside or before I crash trying—when I notice light coming from around the bend.

I release the gas, slowing down on the narrow road, hoping the car coming around from the other way is staying on their side of yellow lines, when I see the faint glow of headlights unmoving and illuminating the dark night.

"What the hell?" I whisper to myself, feeling slightly

grateful for a distraction, but quickly feeling the layer of sweat that was forming on my skin turn to ice, and a familiar sense of urgency takes hold when the twisted metal of a car wedged against a tree comes into view; its front crumpled in a mangled mess.

A part of my brain that has been dormant for months comes to life, and I don't hesitate to spring into action. I pull my truck over to the side of the road, parking it as far off the concrete as I can and cutting my engine.

One second, I'm opening my driver's side door, and the next, instinct is taking over, and I'm ensuring the scene is safe and assessing potential hazards—like how if a car comes around this bend a little too fast, we're dead.

The stillness and silence of the night makes the soft hiss of the car's engine seem out of place, along with the crunching sound of gravel under my work boots as I approach the car.

"Hello?" I hear, but it's muffled and distant, the sound struggling to carry.

"Hello?" I echo, a slight crack in my voice.

"Miss, are you still there?" the voice says again, like someone talking through a thick wall.

I'm a few steps away when I freeze.

Shattered glass.

Deployed airbags.

"Miss?" The voice sounds clearer, like a phone on speaker, now that I'm just outside the car, and I can hear the slight panic. It's what brings me back to the moment.

I'm trained for this.

This is my job.

Through the shattered driver's side window, I can see a figure slumped over, a head of dark brown hair at the center of the spiderweb crack in the glass. I go to open the driver's side door, finding it's already opened, as if the driver pulled the handle but didn't push.

I've been in similar situations to this, but the difference

between arriving at a scene with my team versus coming across a car crash while *severely* out of practice does not escape me.

I slowly open the door, careful not to disrupt her position—without properly assessing, I don't want to risk further injury by moving her, and I'm not about to take her out of this car when any vehicle could come around the corner.

We're no more than two feet away from the damn road.

With the position of the car against the tree, the thick grass, and the lack of incline in the road, I don't have to worry about the car moving, so at least we're stable there.

I catch her body against mine as I open the door, pushing it out of the way so I can properly assess her status, and her body melts against me. I grab my phone from my back pocket, turning the flashlight on, and shining it into the car to make sure there isn't anyone else in there.

"Holy shit."

Is that a car seat?

Panic surges through me as I move the phone's light and try to angle my head to see the child—*baby?*—in it. I haven't heard a single sound, no screaming or crying coming from anyone in the car, and it isn't until I see the car seat is empty that I let out an exhale.

Thank fuck.

The woman's head is against my chest, her small body being held up by the seat belt she thankfully had on. Her face is covered by her dark brown waves matted with blood, the skin of her uncovered arms marred with cuts and scrapes.

I reach down to carefully move her, so she's sitting back in the driver's seat, and that's when I notice she's in nothing but a thin satin nightgown, the pink material stained with dark red spots and stretched over a swollen belly.

Fuck.

I need to assess the situation and get an ambulance here as soon as possible.

Reaching over, I feel around for the level to flatten the seat as low as it can go.

"You're going to be okay," I say—a small part of me hoping she responds to my voice but knowing it's a long shot because she's clearly unconscious.

Once she's as flat as I can get her, I tilt her head back and lift her chin, using my phone's flashlight to check her airway, and noting the slight yet steady rise and fall of her chest.

She's breathing.

I let out an audible sigh. "Atta girl," I whisper, my shoulders shrugging with relief.

Her long lashes frame her closed eyes, and the pale skin of her face is stark against the dark interior of the car and the dried streams of blood coming from what is most definitely a head wound.

I carefully move her hair resting over her shoulders, the waves soft against my calloused skin, and press two fingers to her neck, finding her pulse just under her skin—slow and thready but there.

ABCDE

Airway, Breathing, Circulation, Disability, Exposure

One, two, and three are done, and she's clearly a "U" on the AVPU scale—she's in no way alert and isn't reacting to my voice or the pain of her injuries. Her unresponsiveness worries me along with the bruising and swelling around her eye—I don't think the crash caused that kind of damage.

Carefully using my thumb to lift her eyelid, I shine my phone's flashlight to assess her for any signs of neurological damage, and my mind immediately goes blank.

Her blue eyes are some of the brightest I've ever seen, the color reminding me of when the sunlight hits the water, and I wish I was looking at them under different circumstances because I can see myself getting lost in them the same way I do when I'm on the lake.

I watch as her pupils constrict under the light and dilate

when I take the light away; another wave of relief hits me, my own eyes closing for a brief second.

"Miss? Hello?" The voice I heard earlier is much clearer now, and I realize it's probably been asking for a response for the last however many minutes that have passed since I opened the car door. My eyes open, and I finally notice the small stream of light coming from the passenger side floor.

"Hello?" My voice sounds so loud in the quiet of the night.

"Hello? Who am I speaking to?" the voice on the phone asks.

"Jack," I answer. "Who's there?"

"This number called 911 about ten minutes ago, but the caller must have passed out after giving me her name and telling me she's been in an accident. An ambulance is still a few minutes out."

"I found her on the side of the road. She's unresponsive but breathing. Her airway is clear, and her pulse is thready, but she's holding on. She's got multiple lacerations all over her exposed skin, but no obvious head trauma," I rattle off, knowing that this information is more important for when the paramedics get here, but I can't help the rush of protectiveness I have over this woman, wanting the operator to know that I've got her. "And she's pregnant."

"Pregnant?" the operator echos, followed by a muffled curse.

I nod my head before remembering the woman on the phone can't hear me. "Yes, and pretty far along from what I can tell."

As my adrenaline begins to subside, something akin to fear begins to take hold. It's like everything from before I came across this wreck is back with even more strength, and I have to hold onto the hood of the car to stay standing, my legs threatening to buckle with the weight in my chest.

Exposure

I need to make sure she doesn't have any injuries I can't see.

I take a breath, bringing my mind back to the present. *She needs me right now.*

I'm not too worried about the cuts and scrapes on her arms and chest—there's one on her shoulder and across her collarbone that might need stitches and that bruising on her face is concerning.

"What's her name?" I ask the operator as I reach down, muttering an apology for the invasion of privacy as I slowly lift up the pink satin, the sight of her swollen stomach like a sucker punch to the face.

"Rumi. Rumi Matthews."

"Rumi," I repeat, the name feeling familiar on my lips, as if I was used to saying it in another life.

Why the hell is she out driving this late?

She's pregnant for fuck's sake, and it's the middle of the night.

Where's her husband or boyfriend or whoever the fuck knocked her up.

He should be here making sure she's okay, protecting her, driving this damn car.

She shouldn't be out here right now.

She's growing a fucking a *life* in her right now, bringing some fucker's child into the world, and yet she's out here.

Alone.

I pray to all the gods I don't believe in that she makes it out of this, and that her baby is okay, and that the son of the bitch who isn't here to protect her gets his ass beat.

She can't lose this baby.

She won't.

No one deserves to live with the weight of a loss like that.

She'll feel guilty.

She'll blame herself.

I would know.

"Ambulance should be arriving any minute," the operator says, but it sounds like she's underwater with the pounding beginning to grow in my ears.

Why the hell is she barefoot?

Pajamas, no shoes, and nothing but a car seat in the car—aside from the crash, what the hell happened to her tonight?

With no obvious evidence of internal injuries, I carefully bring Rumi's nightgown back down. That sense of protectiveness over her is back with vengeance at how exposed she is, how fragile she looks, how scared she must have been.

The sudden urge to shield her from anything and everything surprises me, considering I don't even know the girl's last name, yet looking at her in this state—bloodied and hurt, pregnant and alone—makes a foreign possessiveness take hold.

I look down at my bloodied hands against the softness of *her*. The contrast is jarring, yet it stirs something inside of me.

Suddenly, I hear the sound of distant sirens, and they bring me back to the last time I was in a situation like this, waiting for an ambulance.

Only this time, the life can be saved.

I feel my lungs constrict with every breath, each coming quicker, trying to get any ounce of oxygen I can, but it's like my body forgot how to breathe.

My chest tightens, and a ringing sounds in my ears, my heart pounding so hard it feels like it might explode. My mind spins in a fog of overwhelming fear—fear that I'm going to lose him.

No, *her*.

Everything around me blurs—the dark forest beyond the car, the pink material of Rumi's nightgown, the red lights coming from around the corner. All of it distorts my reality, and my mind warps the scene in front of me to the one that's haunted my dreams for the last six months.

A screaming mother, looking for her daughter.

A daughter she thinks is still in the house.

The house that is up in some of the biggest flames I've seen in my career.

I see Bennett.

He's running.

Running toward the fire.

I'm shouting his name, but he doesn't turn around.

I'm trying to go in after him, but my body is stuck in place.

I drop my phone, the small thud in the gravel barely registering in my mind as I feel my body falling to the side, catching myself on the car door before my knees hit the gravel.

I can't feel my limbs, my body aching from the lack of oxygen, my skin prickling like I have a fever.

My eyes are wide open, but I can't see straight.

Ambulance sirens, the rush of the hoses trying to put out the fire.

Screaming.

And if it wasn't for the burn in my throat, I wouldn't know it was coming from me.

The house crumbling on top of Bennett.

His body buried.

Hours—minutes?—passing before we find him under the debris.

More ambulance sirens, the squeaking wheels of the gurney, the chatter from the paramedics. They can't find a pulse. His right arm is twisted, his left leg crushed. He's unresponsive. Severe head trauma. Multiple contusions. Third-degree burns. They need to get him in the rig. They're hooking him up. Flatline.

"Ow." A calm voice registers in my ear, but that doesn't make sense. Bennett is dead. I couldn't save him.

He didn't make it.

The scene in front of me fades, but I can't take in a full breath. The sirens are louder, and I see the white exterior of the car in front of me, a red hue falling over it as the ambulance stops on the road in front of us, three people jumping out and coming toward me.

I think I'm having a heart attack.

Can you have a heart attack at 35 years old?

That has to be what this is.

I scramble to my feet, holding on to the car door for support, ready to tell them to save him. Save Bennett. Save my best friend. He's not dead. He's alive.

I bend down, almost losing my balance again, my hands catching myself as I feel around for my phone in the gravel. With the flashlight still on, I shine the light into the car just as a calm, firm voice tells me to step back.

"We got her," another voice says, and I feel a hand on my shoulder, my eyes still adjusting.

Her? No. It's Bennett. But I can't form the words. I let the paramedic walk me a few steps backward while someone else wheels a gurney over, two of them carefully moving the figure out of the car.

No, I want to say. *It's him. They have to save him.*

"Are you hurt?" the paramedic asks me, and I shake my head once, my eyes looking past him as they lay the body on the gurney.

"We heard you found her. You did a great job. Let us take it from here." *Her?*

What is he talking about?

I push past the man in front of me, closing the space between me and the gurney.

I need to see him.

"Sir!" I hear, but I don't care. I grab the side of the gurney, and I freeze.

Looking down, expecting to see the shaggy blonde hair and the navy eyes of my best friend, I see the lake at sunrise.

I see the reflection on the top of the water as it splashes against the side of my boat.

I see the calmness of the waves and the peacefulness of the small ripples when I cast my line.

And they're looking right at me.

Her eyes bring me back.

The accident. The woman.

The *pregnant* woman.

"We have to get her to the hospital," one of them says, but I can't bring myself to let go of the gurney. I hear something about *distress* and *baby* and *labor* as the gurney starts to slip from my grasp.

My lungs are finally filling with air again, and my vision clears.

She needs to be okay.

"She will be," I hear, and I realize I said the words out loud. "Are you riding with us?" the paramedic I ran past asks from behind, and I shake my head, feeling like I just completed a marathon then got hit by a bus at the finish line.

A sense of numbness washes over me as I watch the paramedics load the gurney in the ambulance, closing the doors, and heading back the way they came.

I don't know how long I stand out there on the side of the road before my body moves in autopilot, walking back to my truck and starting the engine—heading back the way *I* came, straight to my grandfather's cabin.

CHAPTER 4
RUMI

ONE YEAR LATER

"I HAVE an iced vanilla oat milk latte and a black coffee for Mia." I set the two cups down on the "Pick-Up" side of the counter, the last order of a very busy morning rush. It has taken me the last six months working at Hey Honey's to get through the hustle and bustle of the morning crowd without spilling at least one drink, and I'm proud to say I've made it through another without having to change my apron.

"Thanks, Rumi," the blonde regular says from behind a double stroller, her twin girls in matching pink jumpers and mini black converse asleep in their seats. She reaches for her two coffees, setting them in the cupholders of the stroller.

"Anytime," I answer, bending down to put away the carton of oat milk in the fridge underneath the counter. Mia is a friend of the owners here at Hey Honey's, so her drinks are always "on the house", but she slips a $20 bill in the tip jar when she thinks I'm not looking.

"Have you thought more about what I mentioned last week?" she asks, as I stand up, bringing her hand back to the stroller to push it back and forth to keep her twins asleep.

"A little," I answer, a slight blush coming to my cheeks. I stick my hands into the pockets of my apron, one of my hands instantly finding the black Sharpie I keep in there. My thumb and index finger mindlessly begin playing with the cap.

"The offer still stands," she says, taking a sip of the iced latte. "Us moms have to stick together. Trust me." Her glossy lips curve in a soft, reassuring smile, and there's something about her aura that feels safe, like I can trust her. "The list is vetted, and I'm happy to share it with you," she adds, alluding to the master list of babysitters and nannies that her friends and her brother all share.

"I appreciate it," I tell her, wishing I could better explain how it makes my heart double in size at the thought of not being so alone in all of this like I thought I would be after leaving Trevor.

I'm still not used to the kindness I've been receiving since moving to Milwaukee, and it's a weird feeling—borderline uncomfortable and very strange.

Mia gives me a small nod, taking my noncommittal answer, before turning to head to the door. I don't know if she senses my trepidation or unease with the attention or her effort to connect, but if she does, she doesn't show it.

"Tell Annie I'll be a little late to tonight's meeting," she says over her shoulder, her blonde waves bouncing behind her.

Annie, the co-owner of Hey Honey's, is due to stop in tonight with her fiancé and co-owner, Luke, for our monthly meeting. Every month, they hold a meeting about the upcoming specials and events happening in the space the coffee shop shares with the neighboring businesses.

Mia always joins as the person who does the marketing and social posts for Honey's. The owners of the bar and book-store next door usually join too, along with the other baristas.

"Will do," I answer as she steps outside the coffee shop.

The warm May air rushes in as the front door closes, and I take a moment to look around the shop. It's pretty empty aside from a couple seated by the windows. The mid-morning sunlight warms the air within the space, the smell of coffee now a familiar, grounding scent to me.

I wipe down the espresso machine, taking advantage of the lull in orders at the moment, thinking about what Mia said about the babysitters—as if I have anywhere to go besides work.

They always say it takes a village to raise a baby, but I was fully prepared to do it on my own.

When I left Minneapolis, I was basically saying "fuck the village", even more so when I felt those contractions on that dark road in Northern Wisconsin and kept driving further away from what I used to call home.

But with no parents or siblings, and not many people I could consider friends, I guess it really never was home to begin with.

This idea of *not* having to raise my daughter all on my own doesn't seem real to me, like I can't trust it. I'm also not used to taking what people say at face value. I'm used to finding hidden meanings and having to read between the lines, saying what someone wants to hear without them telling me.

It's what I did with my father; it's what I did with Trevor.

It's what kept me safe.

I'm lost in my thoughts and barely hear the door to the back office swing open. "Someone wants to say hi," a voice from behind me calls out, and I turn to see the manager of Honey's, Ava, with an *almost* one-year-old against her chest in the baby carrier I got as a present from Luke and Annie when they hired me here.

"There's my girl," I coo, an instant smile coming to my face when I see the head of dark hair and the soft, chubby thighs hanging from the carrier. The thoughts of Trevor and childcare fleeing from my brain for the moment. "How was she?" I ask Ava. My daughter's little limbs wiggle from where they stick out of the carrier; small babbles and little baby noises fill the quiet cafe, mixing with the soft jazz playing over the speakers.

Ava gives me a little shake of her head, as if my question is silly. "You know, asking the same question and expecting a different answer means you're insane," she teases, a smile on her face as she tucks a piece of auburn hair behind her ears.

I close the space between us, giving my daughter a peck on the top of the head, that intoxicating baby smell warming me from the inside out, bringing me back to when she was born.

When I woke up in the hospital, almost a year ago to the day, having no memory of how I got there, I had no idea that it would lead me here. I can still recall the pain all throughout my body—my skin covered in fresh cuts and bruises forming over the ones Trevor left.

It wasn't until a nurse explained to me that I was in a car accident, and the doctors performed an emergency C-section that everything came rushing back.

The dark road.

The impact against the tree.

Calling 911.

Passing out.

I was in labor before the crash.

I instantly forgot about the pain I was in and leaped from my hospital bed in pursuit to find my daughter, to see if she was okay—if she was *alive*. The nurses had to hold me down, and I passed out from the increase in heart rate, the intensity and trauma of both my injuries from the crash and the C-section taking over.

It was when I came to for the second time that my nurse, Phoebe, brought my daughter to me.

There's no proper way to explain what it feels like seeing your child for the first time. A rush of warmth and pure love overwhelmed me, as if time stood still, and every part of me connected to her instantly. Her tiny hands grasping mine felt like the beginning of a bond so deep, so unspoken, that it filled my heart with a joy I had never known before.

She made every iota of pain I ever felt completely and utterly worth it.

It also confirmed to me that I made the right decision leaving that night.

Trevor didn't deserve something as pure and beautiful as her.

And getting her—us—away from him almost killed her.

I made a promise to the both of us that I would never let anything—*anyone*—hurt her.

Ever.

I haven't heard from Trevor since I left, and it's not like I had much of a support system in Minnesota. I doubt anyone has even noticed I've been gone.

Trevor was all I knew, the only family I had.

The hospital staff instantly knew the severity of my situation when all the dots started to connect. A young, pregnant woman, fleeing in the middle of the night alone, bruises of all colors and stages of healing covering her body, fresh injuries that weren't just from the crash—it didn't take much time for my nurses, especially Phoebe, to put everything together.

My nurse introduced me to Ava—her older sister, the manager of a coffee shop in Milwaukee who was looking for a roommate in the duplex she rents in the neighborhood across the street.

Fast forward a year, I went from having absolutely nothing to my name, to a home, a job, a friend, and my daughter.

Evelyn Jade Matthews.

"But, to answer your question, she was perfect. Just like the perfect little angel baby she is. Isn't that right, Evee?" Ava's voice transitions into the baby one she uses when she talks to my daughter. "She is always great company when I do payroll," she adds with another smile, her hazel eyes reflecting the genuine care she has for her.

I didn't think people like Ava and her sister, or Annie and Luke, or Mia and the other people I've met in the last year existed.

People who understand how the universe can completely chew you up and spit you out.

People who do things out of the kindness of their hearts with no mal-intent or ulterior motive.

People who want to help or give you a hand, not because they have to but because they want to.

It's a feeling I've never experienced before.

One I'm still getting used to.

As Ava and I transitioned from co-workers to roommates to friends, I learned more and more about her own history with a toxic relationship, her ex-boyfriend being emotionally abusive, and it made sense why she was so willing to help someone like me—a broke, single mom with nothing but a bloodstained nightgown and a newborn to her name.

She has become a full-on partner for me this last year, letting me bring Evee to work when we're both on the schedule and watching her when I'm here on my own.

"How's it going up here?" Ava asks, her eyes roaming the space behind the coffee bar, doing her usual mental checklist that everything is up to her standards. I can practically see her checking that the drink station is clean and the bakery case is filled; looking at the high top tables and how the chairs aren't pushed in; noticing how the hanging plants by the front door need watering.

"Good," I answer, playing with the cap of the Sharpie in my apron pocket.

Ava turns to look at me, pausing her silent assessment of the coffee shop, familiar amusement in her eyes.

"What?"

"Oh, nothing. Just can't keep up with all that talking you

do. You're really going to have to slow down one of these days," she jokes as Evee's little hands wrap around Ava's red waves. "I can't take in all those words at once." She gives me a smirk that drips with sarcasm, her specialty.

"Ha. Ha," I mock, tilting my head to the side with each "ha", a smile blooming on my face. Ava is the talker in our friendship—she's the one who fills the silence, starts the conversations, asks the questions. It's more her speed.

I'm content with listening.

I think that's why we work so well—an instant balance within our connection.

Ava looks like she's about to say something more, but the chime of the front door causes us both to pause our conversation. I turn toward the door, ready to greet whoever just walked in, but the "hello" rests heavy in my throat at the sight in front of me.

While I'm not much of a talker, I can't remember the last time I was left speechless.

I watch as the man lets the glass door close behind him, his eyes roaming the coffee shop with a sense of urgency, like he's looking for someone. He has strong, chiseled features with a harsh jawline I can still make out underneath his rugged beard. His long, unruly hair cascades around his face in dark waves, and his large frame takes up the entire doorway.

He has on a brown hoodie with a flannel over. His denim jeans look old and worn, and his work boots look like he walked through mud an hour ago—I can already feel Ava resisting the urge to grab the broom and dustpan to clean up the dried dirt specks falling onto the black and white tiled floor.

"Good morning." I hear Ava's voice, but I can't tear my attention from him.

The man snaps his attention to Ava, his eyes going from her to the baby against her chest. If he's confused why there's a baby behind the counter, he doesn't show it. Even from across the coffee shop, I can feel the anxiety and haste he brought in here with him.

"Can we help you?" Ava asks, her voice a little more tense than her greeting.

The man grunts a one-word response I can't make out, and I can't resist the urge to snort at the caveman-like sound.

A hand goes to my face when the noise escapes and the movement causes him to look my way.

I feel a flush in my cheeks, and it only deepens when his eyes fix on me. A part of me wants to look away, but another part of me can't help but stare right back into his green irises, like the prey of a wolf caught in the line of attack—frozen and cautious of any movement. The green of his eyes feels familiar and terrifying at the same time.

His eyes slightly widen, a hint of surprise, and I take in a harsh breath as memories start clouding my vision, passing quickly and fragmented like flashes of lightning in a storm.

Sirens.

Lights.

Voices.

Then just one.

"She needs to be okay."

The memories don't feel like mine, yet the realness of them make my knees feel like they're going to give out.

I don't remember anything from the accident after calling 911 and giving them my name. From then to waking up in the hospital isn't even a blur; it's just gone, as if those moments were scooped out of my brain.

Was someone there that night?

I grab onto the counter in front of me, the cool metal against my palms is a shock to my system.

My eyes open—I didn't even realize I closed them—and I look up to see his eyes again, only this time they're much closer. Close enough I can see the gold flecks caught in the sunlight coming in from the window, like the sun peeking through the trees.

He's right in front of the counter now, and there's a look of concern on his face. I don't have time to really register more when I feel Ava's hand on my shoulder. "You good?"

I nod my head, tearing my eyes away from the stranger in front of me. "Yeah, I'm fine. Just need a minute." I turn to Ava, putting my hands out. "I got her," I say, gesturing to Evee.

Ava unstraps the baby carrier, watching me carefully but not saying anything more. I reach in to take my daughter. Her warm, little body against my chest settles me instantly, my heart rate slowing with every second I have her in my arms.

With one more look at the stranger, I meet those eyes again and find they never left me. A subtle furrow creases his brow, confusion in his features. His face is hardened and braced with uncertainty, like he's looking for something that he can't find, and I have the urge to step behind Ava, hide myself from the intensity of his glare.

It's my body's response to any sort of confrontation, to shrink away from it—make myself a smaller target.

"What did you say you needed?" Ava asks him, an edge to her voice, no doubt sensing my discomfort with the attention.

The man keeps his eyes on me as if he didn't hear her, and I give in to the urge, taking a step back with Evee in my arms, my hand coming to rest on the back of her head, her little fingers tangling the hair coming loose from the braid hanging over my shoulder. Ava sidesteps to stand in front of me.

With Ava coming more in his view, I watch as the man's head shakes quickly, blinking a few times as if coming back to himself. He takes a step back from the counter, a hand running through his dark hair and coming to rest on the back of his neck, his features softening as he turns to Ava. He looks more boyish now, maybe even a little embarrassed, and I feel myself relax.

"I'm looking for Luke," he says clearly this time, his voice low and gravelly, like he hasn't spoken yet today. His hand goes to his pocket, and I can see the slight redness on the column of his throat—*definitely* embarrassed.

I relax further, releasing an exhale as Evee blows a raspberry against my neck, her little giggles bringing a small smile to my face.

Before Ava can respond, I turn to head to the back office, needing to get my bearings after such a weird encounter, so many conflicting feelings running through my system— intrigue and trepidation swirling through my system.

Not to mention the confusion about the snippets of memories from that night all those months ago hitting me out of nowhere.

As I open the door to the office, my brain catching up to my emotions, I hear Ava ask what his name is, so she can pass it on to Luke.

"Jack," he says as the door closes behind me.

Jack.

CHAPTER 5
JACK

GREAT JOB, assface. Your first day back in civilization, and you forgot all social cues and how to behave properly in a public place. Grunting and one word answers worked with Banjo every Sunday, but they're not going to work here unless I want people calling the cops on me.

I'm pacing the parking lot of Hey Honey's, my feet taking me back and forth from the front of my truck to the back, over and over. My body is tight with anxiety and this overwhelming sense of doom, and my neck is on fire with embarrassment.

Marching in there like a complete ass, *grunting* at the two baristas like a goddamn caveman—what the fuck is wrong with me?

After finally telling the redhead I was looking for Luke, I was told she would tell him I stopped by.

I had every intention of seeing Luke when I walked in—I figured coming here would mark my first stop of seeing everyone I left behind a year and a half ago, starting with Bennett's brother and ending at my mom's house tonight to see her and Emerson. I figured there would be time to stop at the station sometime in between the two to meet with Chief Sanders.

I hadn't talked to the Chief since that phone call almost a year ago, screening his calls and ignoring his voicemails asking me to call him back. I thought they'd stop coming after a while, but he was a persistent bastard. I ended up calling him early this morning when I was on my way back to Milwaukee, leaving him a voicemail that I'd be stopping by the station.

I know there's a low chance he still has a position available for me—specifically one that doesn't involve going into the field—seeing as the one he had for me last year was because of a temporary paternity leave, but I've been gone long enough. It's been a year since I tried coming home the first time, and it was safe to say that went like complete shit.

It's time to suck it up, stop feeling sorry for myself, get my job back, and put my life back together.

This last year helped me bury all those feelings that would come up whenever I would think about what happened to Bennett. I can't say I've come to terms with anything or accepted it—I know that day will never come—but I've learned to live with the loss and the guilt I have. It's always there, lingering in the back of my mind, but I've learned to ignore it.

It rarely comes up anymore.

Not since that night on the side of the road when I helped *her*.

The *her* that always finds a way back into my head. The water in her eyes, the same color of calmness I find on the lake.

And eyes that looked alarmingly similar to the girl working in my dead best friend's brother's coffee shop.

With the baby against her chest, the redhead had most of my attention when I walked in—or at least the attention that wasn't stuck on finding Luke, not thinking about how it's been since I was last here and who knows what's changed.

It wasn't until the other barista was trying to hide her laugh at me when I forgot how to speak in complete sentences that I noticed her. Her brown waves, twisted into a messy braid, were so dark I almost thought they were black. If it weren't for the sunlight coming through the windows, I wouldn't have noticed the streaks of caramel framing her face.

The slight blush to her cheeks when we made eye contact was enough to bring a man to his knees, the soft smile she was trying to hide on her face was something I didn't know I needed to see.

Then something shifted between us.

A magnetic pull of some sort, a need for me to be closer to her. And when she leaned forward, her eyes closing as if she was trying to see something hidden behind her lids, my body moved on its own. It was a foreign feeling, considering I haven't even wanted to *look* at another human in over a year.

And then she opened her eyes.

I didn't want to let myself believe what my brain already knew to be true.

It's her.

It's Rumi.

I'd recognize those eyes anywhere. Aside from being on the boat and marveling at the lake, that shade of blue is the only thing that has brought me any sense of peace the last year. Telling myself that she made it to the hospital; that she had her baby; that she made it to wherever she was fleeing to in the middle of the night.

It's what got me through this last year.

I couldn't save Bennett, but I could save Rumi.

And now, the universe wants to fuck with me right when I sort of have my bearings and place her right in my path—

constantly presenting me with the shit I try to keep behind me.

When she took the baby from the redhead, I knew it was hers. I didn't see the baby's face, but I just knew she was Rumi's. It was in the way the baby melted against her as if it was second nature; it was the way that Rumi instantly relaxed when the little girl was in her arms.

I'm not used to babies. Not used to being around them, and they usually make me uncomfortable. It's not any fault of the babies—it's a *me* thing. I'm not a small guy; I was six feet tall by the time I was 16, now standing at least five inches taller than that in my 36 years. The gym has always been a second home to me—aside from the last 15 months I've stuck to running and cutting wood—so the words "gentle" or "soft" have never been words to describe me.

But the way she held her daughter to her chest, made my whole body feel warm—not clammy and feverish like I'm used to, but as if my body was wrapped around hers, mixed with the conflicting yet conceivable feeling of protectiveness and safety that faded as quickly as it appeared when her eyes met mine.

That's when I knew that she didn't remember anything from that accident—she was barely conscious when the paramedics loaded her in the rig.

Uneasiness, distrust, maybe even fear—that's what I saw when she looked at me, no evidence of recognition.

At least she's alive. She's safe. And hopefully, she's happy.

And she better not be alone.

A flare of possessiveness wracks through me, hoping that whatever asshole left her alone in the first place didn't come crawling back—that she found someone better, someone to take care of her and her daughter.

Not that I have any right to feel that way.

My phone vibrating in my pocket halts my pacing and my

thoughts about Rumi, the lack of ringing a relief I didn't know something so small could give me.

I see Luke's name across the top, not surprised that his employees called him right after a strange man ran into the coffee shop, weirding them out enough to call their boss.

"Hey," I say into the phone, my neck feeling warm as the second wave of embarrassment passes through me this morning.

"Jack?" Luke says into the phone, as if he wasn't the one to call me. "I haven't seen, let alone heard from you, in over a year, and the first thing you do barge into my coffee shop like you're about to rob my baristas?"

If I didn't know Luke, I may actually think he's pissed at me, but I've known the Owens brothers since we were kids, Luke being just a few years younger than Bennett and me, and I know that tone in his voice.

He's not mad; he's amused.

"I was looking for you," I answer, ignoring the smirk that I can't see but am sure is on his face.

Luke is a spitting image of Bennett. With blonder hair and lighter eyes, he's the human equivalent of a golden retriever. I didn't know he had a serious bone in his body until he surprised both Bennett and me, taking charge of his own life —standing up against their asshole of a father—and opening up his own business instead of joining his father's law firm.

I also didn't think he was capable of anything aside from his usual happy-go-lucky demeanor until I watched him lose his brother.

Not that I actually stuck around here long enough to see much.

I haven't laid eyes on Luke since Bennett's funeral over a year and a half ago—when he punched that asshole of a father in the face for taking a phone call during the service.

I couldn't even muster up the strength to go to the ribbon cutting ceremony of the coffee shop he opened on Bennett's birthday—I was already holed up in my grandpa's cabin with no intent of coming back.

He says something, but I don't register it at first, my heart skipping a beat at the resemblance his voice has to Bennett's. A beat of silence passes between us.

"You there?" Luke asks.

Before I let the grief take hold, I push it back into the corner of my mind where it belongs. "Yeah, I'm here." I clear my throat, coughing into my fist. My feet start pacing the length of my truck again, needing to do something with this uncomfortable uneasiness coating my skin. "I'm back in town, and I thought I would stop by."

"I was surprised to hear you're back, from Ava no less," he replies, giving a name to the redhead who looked like she wanted to bite my head off when I couldn't take my eyes off her co-worker.

"Yeah," I start, not really sure what else to say—I didn't think past getting a hold of Luke, and now that I have my phone to my ear, and I don't know where to go from here.

"You're going to tell me why you ran into my coffee shop like a bat out of hell? Or, are we going to pretend that's normal?"

I can't help the chuckle that escapes my throat, the noise so foreign in my ears—I can't remember the last time I found something funny, let alone laughed. "Maybe I was looking for a cup of coffee."

"We both know you'd pick an energy drink over a cup of coffee any day."

My lips curl with something resembling a smile—the muscles feeling tight from lack of use. "Maybe I wanted to see if the hard work I put into that place paid off."

Once the words leave my mouth, it dawns on me I didn't even take the time to look at the space Luke created. Bennett and I helped him with the renovations in the months before opening. The realization that the last time I was here I was with Bennett hits me like a truck.

Even though he can't see me, Luke picks up on the thoughts going through my brain—I'm sure he's no stranger to how grief kicks your knees in when you think you have it under control.

I take in a deep breath and exhale in an attempt to recenter myself. "I decided I was done hiding," I say. "It was time to come home and deal with everything."

I don't have to explain what *everything* is, not to Luke who had to deal with the loss of Bennett too. While Bennett was my best friend, he was Luke's brother.

"And when you say deal, you mean what exactly?" he asks, and I can hear the apprehensiveness in his voice.

"I mean, get back to reality," I answer, and I hope it's the right one. The one that he'll accept and not dwell on.

"Sure," Luke says, stretching out the word, and I can basically hear the way he doesn't believe me in his voice. "And by get back to reality, you me—"

"I'm fine," I cut him off, feeling defensive all of a sudden. I've spent the last year trying to get to a place where I can think of Bennett and what happened to him without plummeting into what I accepted as a panic attack—I have trauma response training as a firefighter, but it is much harder to recognize the signs in yourself than it is with others.

What happened on the side of the road, when I heard the sirens of the ambulance while I was holding an unconscious pregnant woman in the middle of the night, was a panic attack—and I refuse to let that happen ever again.

"If it quacks like a duck, right?" Luke says after a moment.

"What?"

"If it looks like a duck, acts like a duck, quacks like a duck, then it's probably a duck." He answers as if I'm the one not making any sense.

"I don't know how to talk to you when you say stupid shit."

Luke sighs dramatically on the other end of the call, and I almost move the phone speaker away from my ear.

"What I'm saying is, it sounds like you believe that if you keep saying you're fine, that you'll actually be fine."

"You're still saying stupid shit."

Another sigh, and I'm reminded of all the other times in my life when Luke wasn't just Bennett's annoying little brother, but mine too.

"It's not my fault you can't understand the idiom."

"Fuck your idioms," I fire back.

Luke's laughter echoes in my ear. "I'm glad you're back, man."

CHAPTER 6
RUMI

"THAT WAS WEIRD." I look up from the playmat I'm sitting on with Evee to find Ava walking into the back office, her hands on her hips as she shakes her head.

"Did you call Luke?" I ask from my spot, surrounded by baby books, stuffed animals, and other toys we keep here.

The back office is always spotless, thanks to Ava. When the door is closed, it becomes a quiet haven amidst the bustling shop. Shelves line the walls, each one neatly stocked with bags of coffee beans, containers of alternative milks, and extra supplies for the machines. There's a polished wooden desk sat against the far wall, clutter-free of course. Behind the desk, we keep Evee's play area—the only part of the neat office that is constantly turning into a mess—and a little fold-able toddler sleeper for when she naps here.

"Yep," she answers, sitting down at the desk chair and letting out a sigh. "Apparently he was a friend of his brother's." I pretend not to watch her move her laptop and her planner an inch to ensure they are straight and proper distance apart before she spins the chair around to face Evee and me. The soft light filtering through the window casts a calm glow over her, making her waves look more orange than red.

"Was?" I ask as I watch Evee grow tired of the book she's playing with.

I grab a stuffed bunny to put in front of her as Ava answers solemnly, "He was Bennett's friend."

I nod, knowing the story of my boss' brother, and how he died in a fire almost two years ago. Hey Honey's opened on his birthday, and Bennett's go-to coffee order—a coffee with cream—is a permanent menu item we call The Ben.

"I'm surprised I've never seen him before," I answer. The man who walked into the coffee shop no more than fifteen minutes ago was a walking, breathing contrast of a man, with his large frame and gruff voice but the softest eyes.

I definitely would have remembered seeing him.

"I didn't realize it until he left, but I've seen him a few times. Today, he looked a little more," she pauses, trying to think of the right word, "rugged. Like he's been living off the land."

"He did look like he could use a haircut," I add with a chuckle.

"It hasn't been since I worked next door at Lenny's though," she explains, talking about the bar next door owned by some of Luke and Annie's friends. "The last time I saw him, I was still bartending there."

"So he wasn't around when Hey Honey's opened?" I ask, wondering why Bennett's friend wouldn't be here for the opening of the shop dedicated to him.

"From what I remember hearing, he headed straight up north to his cabin after the funeral. Quit his job at the fire station, packed a bag, and went remote," Ava answers with a shrug.

I nod my head in response as Evee reaches for the bunny in my hands, a two-toothed smile on her little face as she disregards the book she was holding for the stuffed animal. "Did Luke say anything else about him? Like why he's back?"

"You seem almost as interested in him as he was in you," Ava teases. I look up at her from my place on the play mat to find a smirk on her face, her freckles more prominent with the sunlight coming in through the window.

"He was not interested in me," I reply, avoiding commenting on her statement of my interest in him and trying to deflect, but I feel heat in my cheeks.

"He so was," Ava shoots back as she leans back in the desk chair. "He was looking at you like he wanted to swallow you whole."

I let out a little scoff, looking down at Evee as she tries to untie the bows around the bunny's ears. "You say that like it's a good thing."

"Come on, Rue. You need to let loose a little. Let a big, strong man like that take care of you."

My jaw drops in feign astonishment. "How un-feminist of you, Ava. We don't teach my daughter that she needs a man to take care of her."

Ava laughs. "Not like that, silly. He could take care of you in many *different* ways," she says with a raise of her brow. When I don't say anything, she adds in an all too serious tone, "What I'm saying is you need to get laid."

I bring a hand to my chest as if I'm scandalized by her words. "Ava Dolores Williams, you are going to be the death of me."

She laughs even harder. "One, what did we say about throwing the middle name at me, Rumi Lillith Matthews?" I reach behind me and throw one of Evee's stuffed animals at her. "And two," she continues, catching the stuffed cat before it hits her in the face, "we need to stop pretending that you are not the hottest, most sexiest MILF to ever walk this planet."

My head drops to my hands, my face burning with embarrassment.

"And I know Mr. Caveman was thinking the same when he looked like he wanted to reach over the counter and throw you over his shoulder to take you to his cave where no other man could ever look at you again."

"That's it. You've killed me," I mutter with my face still in my hands.

When I think back to how Jack was looking at me, my cheeks instantly feel even hotter. His eyes bored into me, and it made me feel like he was seeing me and only me—like no one else mattered.

"I'm just saying," Ava sing-songs, and there is a hint of triumph in her voice, as if embarrassing me was her goal with this all along.

I look up to find that triumph written all over her face as she looks down at me from the desk chair. I shake my head. "And I'm just saying, I don't think that's how he was looking at me." It's the only answer I can come up with; the one that helps me ignore the fluttering in my stomach that should definitely *not* be there.

As if I have any business thinking about dating or sex when I have my daughter to think about.

Not to mention how my knee-jerk reaction to Jack's attention was to shrink into myself and make myself smaller, not bask in it like maybe someone without the history I have would.

I don't do well with attention, especially male attention, something my therapist and I work heavily on, and Jack's attention was on nothing but me when he caught me holding in a laugh at him.

The last time I let myself give in to male attention, I ended up finding a man who was exactly like my father, as if I'm solely capable of attracting men who only feel stronger by hurting the women who love them.

Ava must know where my mind goes because her face takes on a look of concern. She slides out of the chair, sitting down behind Evee, reaching toward me, and putting a hand on my knee. "Rumi," she starts, and I know where she's going to go with this. I can feel the emotion already clogging my throat. "Not every guy is going to turn out like—" she pauses, bringing both her hands to cup Evee's ears, "Trevor," she mouths.

I can't help the small smile that forms on my lips at her antics, as if Evee even knows who Trevor is or is old enough to recognize the name of her "sperm donor" as Ava usually calls him.

Evee keeps playing with her bunny as if nothing else exists in the world as Ava adds, "Or, your dad."

"I know that," I reply, reaching behind me to grab the basket of stuffed animals, knowing the bunny will only be entertaining to my 11-month-old for a few more minutes but also needing to do something with my hands. "But the last thing I need in my life right now is a man."

After I got settled into our place and got the hang of the whole newborn thing, I started therapy, and something we often revisit is the night I left Trevor.

I promised myself and my daughter that Trevor would never hurt her, that no one would. And I knew that meant I couldn't let anyone into her life that I wasn't 100% sure wouldn't turn into the monster my father and her father are.

In therapy, I've worked on building self-esteem, learned how to set boundaries, and practiced recognizing red flags, but I still don't trust myself to see past the manipulation and charm that so many abusers hide behind.

"You know as well as I do how—" I pause, hating how quiet my voice gets when I talk about Trevor or my dad. Aside from my therapist, Ava is the only person I've ever told about my past. And she gets it in ways no one ever will after finally leaving a toxic relationship with her emotionally abusive ex with the help of her own therapist. "How *normal* they seem at the beginning."

Ava nods her head but doesn't say anything, her way of urging me to continue, allowing our occasional role reversal of me being the talker and her being the listener.

"I can't risk bringing someone into her life that will turn out to be just like him." I look down at my daughter who, just like I predicted, got bored of her bunny and started pulling out every stuffed animal from the basket in my lap.

Trevor knew exactly how to make me emotionally depend on him when we met in college, and it happened so meticulously, so slowly, that I didn't realize it. He took little pieces from me—pieces I had just gotten back after leaving the hell of a house I grew up in—until massive parts of me were just gone.

"I know you, Rumi. I know how much you love Evee," Ava replies, her eyes never leaving mine. "And because I know those things, I know you would never bring anyone into the life you built for you two that would bring her any harm."

I nod, my eyes stinging with emotion as we both look down at Evee. Her soft, round face framed by a fine layer of dark brown hair that curls ever so slightly at the ends, and her big, curious eyes—blue, just like mine—gleam with a mix of wonder and mischief as she pulls out a stuffed elephant from the basket.

"I know you are so proud to be her mom," Ava continues, "but I also know that you deserve to be happy."

"I am happy."

"You need a life outside of Evee, me, this coffee shop, and our house."

"I don't need to date or have sex to be happy."

"Well," Ava starts, letting out a dry chuckle. "I would disagree on one of those two," she starts, and I toss another stuffed animal at her. It hits her in the chest before it lands in her lap next to the stuffed cat. "Okay, okay. I digress." She puts her hands up in a surrender.

I shake my head, both hating and loving how easily she can lighten a serious conversation.

"Seriously," she continues, "to each their own. But come on, Rumi. You need to do more for *you*. Maybe you could start with making some friends?"

"I have you," I point out, but my voice doesn't have the confidence I want it to.

"Which I wouldn't trade for the world," she answers quickly before adding, "but there is so much to love about you—and Evee—and I'm not enough. You deserve people to love and who love you."

I let out a sigh, taking in my best friend's words.

At the time, I didn't know how Trevor knew I would be the perfect victim, but I've learned from my therapist, Mariah, that abusers know how to exploit vulnerabilities like loneliness, and that's exactly what Trevor found with me.

It's not like I had "I'm so lonely" tattooed on my forehead, but there was something about how I carried myself that spoke to how lonely I truly was.

And I trusted him, more and more with each passing day. I didn't realize he was subtly eroding my sense of worth, my sense of self, and distancing me from the few friends I started to make when I got to college.

It sounds silly, but it was truly as if one day I woke up and realized he was all I had.

And that's when his mask melted away.

He started by criticizing everything about me: my appearance, the classes I was taking, the degree in creative writing I was pursuing. He knew exactly how to make me feel unworthy and inadequate, and I found myself doing anything I possibly could to make him happy.

As our relationship progressed, we moved in together and that's when things turned physical. It started with a push when I dropped the bag with eggs when we were bringing in groceries. Then a grab around the arm when I wore jeans that were too tight, until it eventually was a slap across the face when I asked him why he smelled like another girl's perfume.

And it only got worse from there.

"I'm not good at making friends," I admit, embarrassed by the fact that I can't name anyone besides Ava that I would consider a friend. Not Reagan, the other barista. Not Ava's friends from her women's fiction book club whom I've met a few times when it's her turn to host. Not even the girls I worked with at the restaurant in Minneapolis.

There's only Ava.

"Like you said, I'm your friend," Ava replies. "You made a friend in me, and you can do it again."

I let out a groan. "Yeah, but do you really even count? We're friends because my nurse—your younger *sister*—knew I didn't have anyone else and apparently thought you'd take in a stray."

Ava throws a stuffed animal back at me, tossing it over Evee's head. "Enough of the excuses. You're coming to Lenny's with me tonight after the staff meeting."

"What? No. What about Evee?" The monthly meeting we have at Hey Honey's is always followed by a drink or two at Lenny's, but I always politely decline the invite from Ava, Annie, or any of the others who join the meeting.

"She can come with us."

"I have the opening shift tomorrow."

"Don't act like you don't stay up reading your vampire smut books every night regardless of when the shop opens."

"You said you wouldn't call them that anymore!"

"I won't if you come to Lenny's. And talk to someone other than me," she says. Then, before I can rebuttal, she adds, "or, you can join my book club."

"Hell no. I refuse to read books without a guaranteed 'happily ever after'."

"Then it looks like you're coming tonight."

I hesitate before finally agreeing, knowing she'll drag me there by the hair if she has to. Once Ava sets her mind to something, there's no point in trying to go against it. "Fine."

Ava lets out a little cheer, making Evee clap her hands even though her Auntie Ava is evil in ways she won't understand until she's older.

"I still can't believe you read those and have never read *Twilight*."

I groan. "We're not having this argument again."

CHAPTER 7
RUMI

THE WEIGHT of a sleeping Evee against my chest makes it hard to keep my eyes open as I lean back in one of the chairs at the tables we pushed together to account for all the people at tonight's Hey Honey's meeting.

I take the last sip of my iced dirty chai, the taste of cinnamon and cardamom with a subtle nuttiness from the almond milk never gets old, the bite from the espresso waking me up just a bit—I need to stay awake so I can listen to my boss and his social media manager argue on whether or not we should keep one of our spring menu items on our summer menu.

Luke says yes.

Mia says no.

My eyes volley back and forth, along with our third barista, Reagan, who's seated next to me.

"Lavender is a spring flavor," Mia argues. "And with how nice the weather has been, I think it's time to transition to more summer flavors."

"Our lavender chai was our best seller for March and April," Luke counters.

"Specials are only special if they are available for a limited time. Plus, it makes sense to have something similar to Lenny's specials for May and June. We want consistency with all the shops, right? Isn't that the point with these meetings?" Mia gestures to all of us watching them and solidifying her argument.

Luke and Mia are sitting next to each other across from me, an empty seat on either side of their missing partners— Annie is in the bathroom, and Mia's husband, Eddie, took their twin girls, Nadia and Naomi, for a walk to the park across the street.

"What *is* the Lenny's drink special for the summer?" Luke asks, looking past Annie's empty seat to the owners of Lenny's, Drew and Emmett Ryan.

Emmett looks to his wife, mirroring my position with his sleeping daughter against his chest, his tattooed hands resting on her back.

I met Emmett at my first staff meeting at Hey Honey's, and I have yet to see him crack a smile that isn't at Drew, their daughter, Lennon, or their son, Knox—let alone hear him say more than a sentence or two.

"We're doing a strawberry old fashioned to go with your strawberry matcha and then we're also thinking of some kind of margarita," Drew answers, tucking her red wine hair behind her ear with one hand. She uses her other hand to rub slow circles on her son's back as she tries to relax him to sleep. "I know you guys are also doing coconut syrup for one of your new ones, but Emmett vetoed it for us."

"Coconut sucks," Emmett grumbles in response.

As if against my will, my mind goes back to a different grump of a man who I crossed paths with this morning, and I have to roll my lips together in an attempt to conceal my smile.

Drew looks at her husband, shaking her head with a soft smirk. "So we're thinking pineapple."

"I don't think pineapple is the way to go for you guys,"

Mia says to Luke, twisting her long blonde hair and grabbing a claw clip she had on the strap of her purse, securing the hair in place. She turns to Drew. "I should have the Lenny's social media graphics and new specials menus done and printed by the end of the week, by the way. I just need to stop by and get pictures of the new drinks."

Drew mouths a thank you as Luke nods his head, pondering.

This is usually how these meetings go. Luke and Mia do a bulk of the chatting while Annie and Drew occasionally add their thoughts or ideas. Mia's husband, Eddie, almost always finds an excuse to take their daughters to go do something, and Emmett goes where Drew goes, so he just sits and listens, never saying much. The bookstore owners from next door, Elsie and Sierra, usually come to these meetings too—all the owners of this building wanting to coordinate and support each other's businesses—but they couldn't come tonight.

That leaves Ava, Reagan, and me. We're here more out of obligation and to know how and when the menu changes, and I will admit that it's fun to watch the Lenny's and Hey Honey's people interact.

I've never seen such strong love and friendships before. It's almost healing to watch them all together—seeing what love, both romantic and platonic, is supposed to be like.

Before Luke can say anything, Annie comes out of the bathroom. "What'd I miss?" she asks. She changed from her scrubs she's required to wear as an exotic animal veterinarian at the Milwaukee Zoo into a sky blue sweat set that compliments her long, chocolate brown hair.

Mia answers before Luke can. "Your fiancé here thinks we should keep the lavender chai for summer."

Ava, the unofficial notetaker of all these meetings, chimes in. "So far, we have the coconut caramel cold brew and the strawberry matcha. Luke wants to keep the lavender chai, and Mia thinks we need something else," she summarizes.

Annie nods. "We definitely need something else."

Luke reaches his arm around the back of Annie's chair, scooting his own closer to hers. "You're right, Annie girl. Lavender was a hit, but it's not a 'special' if we keep it around too long."

"Gee, that sounds familiar," Mia scolds, smacking Luke in the shoulder.

"One of the Lenny's specials has pineapple," Drew explains to Annie, both of them ignoring how Luke gives Mia a smile of mock-innocence only for her to flip him off. "But we were saying it might not work for you guys."

"I could make a pineapple butter cake for the summer baked good," Annie offers, her brown eyes roaming over to the part of the counter with all the bakery items.

Even though Annie's primary job is a vet, she's explained to me how she's a stress baker, and she's currently in a three-year externship with the zoo before she becomes fully licensed as an exotic animal vet, meaning she's often *very* stressed and our bakery is often *very* stocked.

"That still leaves one more seasonal drink," Ava says, her pen coming to her mouth as she looks over the notes she's been taking in her planner.

I look down at Evee in my lap as I listen to Luke, Mia, Annie, and Drew ramble off different flavors to go with chai. While it is my drink of choice over coffee or other teas, I prefer it with just some almond milk—nothing fancy. I always try our seasonal flavor, but it's never as good as the original.

Tuning the four of them out after a few seconds, the small cherries embroidered on Evee's pajamas catch my eye and spark an idea.

"Cherry." The word slips from my lips, and it takes me a second to realize that no one is naming random syrup flavors anymore.

I look up and find too many pairs of eyes on me, and I feel my skin prickle from the attention.

"Oh, sorry," I mutter, but then I feel Ava's hand reach over Reagan sitting beside me and squeeze my knee, reassurance that I didn't say something wrong or talk when I wasn't supposed to—reassurance I didn't know I needed.

"Cherry," Luke says with a nod, looking to Annie. "I don't know why I didn't think of that."

Annie rolls her eyes, but there's a smile on her face. I feel like I'm on the outside of an inside joke.

My face must show my confusion because I hear from my left, "You're not missing much." Drew is looking at me with her kind, green eyes. "But if you ever want to get your boss a gift, she can never have enough cherry lip products."

Drew gives me a genuine smile, and I feel myself smiling back. She leans down to press a kiss to her sleeping son's head, and I feel myself tighten my arms around Evee.

Mia's words from earlier this morning come back to me, how us moms have to stick together. Her words and my talk with Ava today mix with all the feelings I have about being an outsider and an observer to this close-knit group of found family members.

I strive to be enough for Evee, but Ava's right. She deserves to be loved and have others to love right back—just like I see with all of the people here.

And finding a friend or two feels like a safe space to start.

"Employee of the Month goes to Rumi," I hear Luke say with a clap of his hands, and it brings me back to the moment.

Annie lets out a sigh. "It's not even worth saying we don't have Employee of the Month." Her voice sounds exasperated, but there's also love—and teasing.

"So it's decided," Ava says, no doubt wanting to make sure the meeting not only ends on time—two more minutes— but that we finish everything we need to. "Three new summer drinks will phase out the spring drinks next Monday, as well as one baked good to replace the carrot cake scones."

We all nod in agreement. "Lenny's will have their strawberry old fashioned and pineapple margarita, and I'll let Elsie and Sierra know, so they can find a book to match each flavor to showcase at their shop."

"Sounds good to me," Luke says. "Thanks, boss," he says, giving her a salute. We all know Luke is the owner, but Hey Honey's runs as well as it does thanks to Ava. "I'll get every-thing ordered tonight, so it can be here by then."

"And I should have the Honey's graphics and menus done by this weekend," Mia adds.

"Go team," Annie says, as she stands, the chime of the door causing us all to turn in that direction to find Eddie pushing two sleeping toddlers in their stroller.

"Just in time, like always, Ed," Luke says, and laughter fills the space.

Eddie pushes the stroller through the door, walking over to Mia, leaning down to place a kiss on her forehead. "You all know how I feel about coffee," he starts, but Mia finishes for him.

"It shouldn't need all the extra shit," she says, lowering her voice to mock her husband's, causing more laughter from everyone—and I think I see Emmett's lips twitch as he stands up.

"On that note," Drew says as Emmett reaches out a hand for her to take, "we'll see you all next door in a few." She turns to me. "You too, Rumi?" she asks, looking over to me as she grabs her husband's hand.

"Um, yeah. I'll be right over."

If she's surprised that I'm accepting the invitation to Lenny's for the first time since I started working at Hey Honey's, she doesn't show it. She lets Emmett help her up from her chair and lead her to the door with his free hand on the small of her back—his other hand holding their sleeping daughter.

"You're going to Lenny's tonight?" Reagan asks as she

stands up, grabbing her purse from underneath her chair. Her dirty blonde hair is braided in two much neater braids than the one that is currently holding my hair after the morning shift, helping Ava reorganize the stockroom, Evee's bath time, and making it back here for the meeting.

"Yeah, you?" I ask, hooking my diaper bag over my shoulder as I stand, holding Evee in my other arm.

"I don't think so, but I need to talk to Luke and Annie before I head home."

"Oh, okay," I say to her. I try to hide the disappointment I have that she won't be there. Ava is my safety blanket, but I can't rely on her tonight, especially when she's making me go in an effort to make friends. I was hoping to spend some time getting to know Reagan—it's not like we have a ton of time to chat during our shift changes. "I'll see you tomorrow then," I offer, knowing Tuesdays are one of the days where she relieves me from my morning shift.

Reagan gives me a noncommittal nod before heading over to where Luke and Annie are chatting with Mia and Eddie.

I glance outside to see the sun has almost set, and I take a deep inhale. Closing my eyes, feeling Evee in my arms and the faint scent of coffee in the air, surrounded by chatter, I try to let go of any doubt from this morning—the doubt of bringing people into Evee's life or making friends for myself.

We're going to be okay, me and her.

I can make it through a drink or two tonight.

Maybe even make a friend along the way.

CHAPTER 8
JACK

ASIDE FROM MAKING myself look like an idiot at Luke's coffee shop this morning, today hasn't been as bad as I thought it would be.

I thought the day would continue to go downhill when I got to the fire station and knocked on Chief Sanders' office door. But the familiarity of the place, the faces, and even the work itself outweighed the reminders of being there without Bennett.

I left the station with my old job back, my first shift starting tomorrow morning. With reassurance from me that I'm fine and ready to be back at work, Chief put me on my old rotation—24 hours on, 48 hours off—and I've convinced myself that it's the only way to move forward. But I'm on an *unofficial* probation until I deliver on the request he made that I start weekly sessions with the therapist I worked with after Bennett died.

As part of my probation, I'm still expected to report to any active fires we get called to, but he said he has our Fire Lieutenant keeping a close eye on me, ready to report back if there are any issues in the field.

I reluctantly agreed to the sessions, mostly because I don't need anyone watching out for me when we go out on calls.

But if even *one* fire analogy comes out of the therapist's mouth, I *will* flip the coffee table this time.

After my meeting with the chief, I went to the gym to burn off some anxiety that formed in my gut when my mind started spiraling. But, after a five-mile run on the treadmill and a killer back and biceps lift, the thoughts were nowhere to be found.

Since I let my lease run out for the apartment I shared with Bennett, I didn't really have anywhere else to go, and I didn't want to keep prolonging the inevitable of going home and seeing my mom and sister.

When I got there, I wished I had come home sooner.

Seeing my mom and Emerson was something I didn't know I needed.

Just like with the fire station, my childhood home, my mother's cooking, and messing with Emerson was like a breath of fresh air after feeling like I've been inhaling smoke the last year and a half.

My mom's arms wrap around me before I can even shut the front door behind me. "I'm so happy you're home," she says as I feel her head rest against my chest.

"Hi, Ma." I hold her close to me, resting my chin on the top of her head.

"We missed you," she says, stepping out of my hold, putting her hands on her hips as she looks at me. I watch her brows raise as her eyes settle on my face. "You need to shave."

I can help the laugh that escapes my lips, my hand instinctively going to my beard, feeling the grown out hair. I make a mental note to shave before I go to bed tonight, needing to get rid of any overgrown facial hair before I'm back at work—it's been a while since I've needed to stay clean-shaven to properly seal a mask or respirator.

"Is Emmy here?" I close the front door and follow my mom further into the house. It hasn't changed at all since the last time I was home—saturated with memories in every nook and cranny—and it settles some tension in my shoulders.

Before my mom can say anything, my question is answered for me.

"I didn't think it was possible for you to get even uglier," I hear as we walk into the kitchen, finding my sister leaning against the counter, a smirk on her face.

"I could say the same to you," I joke with a smile on my face, happy to see her.

Closing the space between us, I pull my sister in for a quick hug, feeling her half-assed attempt to hug me back before we fall into easy conversation among the three of us.

As my mom finishes cooking, refusing any help Emerson or I try to offer, I listen to her discuss all the neighborhood gossip as well as get all of the updates on my sister's life— where she's living, her job, and what she's been up to.

The conversation is easy—easier than I thought it would be.

Neither my mom nor my sister even mention how long it's been since I've been home, and they don't attack me with questions like I thought they would.

At least not right away.

"Are you going to be staying here at Mom's?" my sister asks as she finishes her second piece of french silk pie. Out of the two Hasting siblings, she has a big enough sweet tooth for the both of us, especially when it comes to chocolate—I can't stand the stuff.

"Until I find a place, yeah," I answer, taking a sip of my beer.

"I helped Luke and Annie pack up all the stuff in your apartment. They took Bennett's stuff, and yours is all packed up here in the basement," she says, matter-of-factly, as if we're catching up on the latest news.

"Thanks," I say, knowing that couldn't have been easy for the three of them. Luke and Annie have known each other since they were kids, meaning Annie also lost Bennett. Not only did she have to deal with her own loss, but she had to help Luke with his.

Same goes for Emerson. Although she was younger than me and Bennett, she knew him as my best friend her whole life.

The thought of the three of them having to pack up all of his stuff—and then my sister having to deal with all my shit too—makes me feel nauseous.

Emerson's deep green eyes find mine as she sets her fork on her plate, leaning back in the dining room chair, crossing her tattooed arms over her chest—she's gotten more since I last saw her, and her dark brown hair is much longer than it was a year and a half ago, with blunt bangs hanging just under her eyebrows, hiding the silver piercing she has on the left one.

"What?" I ask, feeling like I'm in trouble. Even though she's eight years younger than me, she has a way of making me feel like she's the older of the two of us.

"You broke her heart," Emerson whispers, her voice tight with anger, and I know she's talking about our mom.

I shake my head, guilt washing over me as I look over Emerson's chair to see her washing dishes in the kitchen, refusing any help we try to offer her like always. "I couldn't be here, Emmy," I say, not able to apologize for leaving. I don't know what would have happened—what I would've done—if I stayed. "I needed time to figure my shit out."

"So you're back for good?" Her voice grows in volume, and anger. "Or until something bad happens and you need to run away again?"

"That's not fair," I grit out, my palms clenching into fists. "I didn't run away, I—"

"You ran away, Jack. Just like Grandpa, just like Dad. You ran."

"I did not run."

Emerson lets out a humorless laugh. "When Grandma died, Grandpa hid in that cabin until he croaked. Dad left and never came back when Mom got sick. And now you? Your best friend dies, and you run."

I bang my fist against the dining table causing my beer and Emerson's plate and fork to rattle.

"Jacky? Emmy?" I hear from the kitchen. "No fighting at the dinner table," my mom reprimands in her calm yet firm tone. The same one she's used since we were kids. The same one she used when she told us about her ovarian cancer. The same one she used when she said Dad was gone and wasn't coming back.

"Sorry," we both say in unison, but our eyes are still on each other.

"You might be back, but you're not fine. You can tell everyone how fine you are, but until you actually deal with losing Bennett, you might as well have stayed up in that cabin." She grabs her plate and stands, walking toward the kitchen, leaving me with her words, ripping all that fresh air I got today straight from my lungs.

I unclench my fists, tension spreading through my fingers, and lower my head into my hands. Stay at the cabin? Drown myself in my grief? Let it completely destroy me?

Doesn't she see that isn't an option?

I sit up, taking the last swig of my beer, and get up to head into the kitchen.

Emerson is leaning on the counter across from where my mom is loading the dishwasher. The yellow walls still glow with warmth, and the familiar hum of the old fridge and the running sink fill the silence. The wooden cabinets, now slightly dulled, still hold the same sturdy charm, and the crisp, citrus scent of all-purpose cleaner lingers in the air.

"Oh, Jacky," my mom starts as she closes the dishwasher and shuts off the sink. "Mr. Lenard from down the street mentioned a property he's looking to sell. It's not too far from the station. It's newly renovated too. I could tell him you're interested?"

She turns to face me, leaning against where the sink meets the counter, and I feel both hers and Emerson's eyes on me. My mom's dark, silver-streaked hair is pulled back loosely. Laugh lines frame her eyes like gentle reminders of all the happy memories of her, Emerson, and me.

She looks smaller than I remembered, but still unmistakably solid—like someone who'd held up the whole world without ever asking for thanks, even as a single mom with a cancer diagnosis and years in a constant state of apprehension on whether or not she'll stay in remission.

It's been the three of us since my mom got diagnosed with ovarian cancer when Emerson was two, and I haven't seen or heard from my dad since—not that he was even around much before that.

I clear my throat, walking over to the corner of the kitchen with the garbage bins, tossing my beer bottle into the recycling. "Yeah, Ma. That would be great. You can give Mr. Lenard my number."

She gives me a soft smile and a nod before asking, "How is it being home without him?"

My mom is no stranger to my friendship with Bennett, having watched it bloom and grow since we were kids. "It's fine," I answer, the word feeling more like a lie on my lips when I say it to my mother. "I think he'd want me to move on."

"I think he'd want you to be happy," she counters. "You mentioned Chief Sanders said you had to see a therapist?"

I nod.

"Good," she says. "That'll be good."

She steps toward me, wrapping her arms around my waist and pulling me in. I rest my chin on the top of her head as I wrap my arms around her shoulders, her body feeling so small and fragile against mine. I sense Emerson's eyes on us.

I don't tell my mom how I think the therapy sessions are a joke, that they'll be a waste of time. The last thing anyone can expect me to do is bring up all the memories or emotions that come with talking about Bennett or what happened the night he died.

I don't tell her that I will never talk about that night, no matter who asks.

"Well," my mom says, tapping me on the back twice before stepping out of my embrace. I pretend not to notice the tear she wipes away with the back of her hand. "It's getting late, and you two both have places to be."

"Mom, it's eight o'clock," my sister says, from where she's still leaning against the counter. Her voice has her usual no-bullshit tone, but there is a layer of worry in her voice. "You're tired?"

Emerson, more so than me, has always had a front-row seat to my mom's cancer, having lived with it since she was two years old, up until my mom went into remission when she was 15. Then there was the recurrence, and she wasn't back in remission until Emerson was 21.

She's been fine ever since, thankfully.

My mom tsks. "I'm fine, Emmy. Just tired after a long day." She waves her hands like my sister is being silly with her concern. "Are you going to the bar with Jack?"

"You said all you did today was pot some new plants outside," I add, my own concern blooming with the way my mom tries to change the subject.

"The sun really takes it out of me these days."

Emerson doesn't seem convinced—and I can't say that I

fully am either—but she lets it go for now. I look passes between the two of us, no words needed.

We need to keep an eye on Mom.

My mom grabs my arm on her way out of the kitchen toward the stairs that lead to the house's three bedrooms. "I'll call you tomorrow after I talk to Mr. Lenard about the house." She pulls me on the arm, urging me to come down to her height, and gives me a kiss on the cheek. "Be sure to wake me up when you get home tonight. I don't care how late it is."

"Ma, I'm not in high school," I complain, especially knowing how tired she is and not wanting her to lose any necessary rest.

"I don't care," she says, patting my cheek. "You know the rules. They haven't changed since you've been gone." She gives me a smile before walking toward Emerson, giving my sister a hug and whispering something in her ear that I can't make out, before heading up to bed.

CHAPTER 9
JACK

"WHAT MADE you want to come tonight?" I ask Emerson as I park the car in front of Lenny's, the bar next door to Luke's coffee shop and the place he invited me to after our phone call earlier today.

She shrugs. "Figured you might need a buffer for your first social outing."

I can't help but let out a laugh. I'm not a complete introvert, but my sister makes me look antisocial with her extroverted-ness, and I can admit that I am a little relieved to have her with me, especially as I get used to being back home and around people instead of fish.

I wouldn't be surprised if my mom told her to keep an eye on me when she whispered in her ear before we left to head over here.

As we get out of the car and walk up to Lenny's, I resist the urge to turn back to my truck and drive back to the lake. My social battery is already nonexistent from my little to no human interaction, and I already know I'll sleep well tonight with how much I've put myself through today.

I could use a night without the nightmares.

Between the coffee shop this morning, the station this

afternoon, as well as the gym with the after-work crowd, and my mom's for dinner, I haven't heard my own voice this much in months.

Not to mention a part of my past I really wanted to leave behind me being thrown directly in my path. I haven't had much time to think about seeing Rumi since leaving Hey Honey's this morning, but I can't help my wandering eyes as they glance at the dark coffee shop, the place all closed and locked up for the night.

Pulling open the door to Lenny's, the familiar beer and old wood greet me. It's a bar I've been to a handful of times, especially when Luke used to bartend here before opening up Hey Honey's, and it's a total dive. The lights are dim, the place only lit from the neon signs lining the walls. The bar takes up most of the space with booths lining the outside with high top tables throughout.

The place looks the same as it did the last time I was here, and that brings a sense of comfort knowing that some things stayed the same.

"There he is!" I hear, and I instantly find Luke in the small group of people standing by the bar. He's standing behind Annie who's holding a small baby, and my stomach drops.

Did Luke have a whole ass kid while I was gone?

Luke makes his way up to me, wrapping his arms around me and pulling me in for a hug.

"You have a kid?" I ask him as I hug him back, not able to hide my disbelief.

"What?" Luke turns to look at Annie. "Oh, no. That's Emmett and Drew's son," he says, pointing to the big, tattooed guy behind the bar and the woman sitting on the chair in front of him. I let out an exhale, my relief evident enough on my face for Luke to say, "Relax, big guy. I know it's been a while, but you didn't miss *that* much." He turns to my sister. "Hey, Emmy."

"Good to see you, Luke."

He gives her a quick hug, lifting her off the ground like he used to when she was little. "Come meet everyone."

Following Luke, Emerson and I walk up to the bar, and my eyes scan all the people as Luke makes introductions for my sister. I recognize most of the people here, not missing the raise of a brow I get from the redhead—Ava—who I met this morning. It isn't until my eyes get to the far end of the bar, past Drew with her daughter on her lap, that I see *her*.

"And this," Luke slaps his hand on my shoulder, "is one of our baristas, Rumi. But I heard through the grapevine that you two met this morning."

Her blue eyes meet mine, and it takes me a second to gather my bearings. Her hair is in the same messy braid I saw earlier, and she's wearing a long-sleeved white shirt, the same one she had on under her apron. Her legs are crossed in the high top chair, her daughter on her lap transfixed with whatever toy Drew's daughter is playing with in front of her.

Clearing my throat before stepping toward her, as if my body knows it needs to be close to her without my mind truly registering. "Not officially," I say, my voice more raspy than I intend. "I'm Jack." I hold out my hand.

Before she can say anything, I feel a little hand wrap around my pointer finger, and my heart instantly stops when I look down to see another pair of those cool blue eyes. They light up, like when the sunlight directly hits the lake—it's almost blinding, and I have to resist the urge to look away to protect my eyes. There's this foreign amazement as her eyes roam my face and then down to where she holds my finger.

My body tenses, and I don't move. Babies make me nervous, especially babies associated with women who make my whole body feel warm and tingly for reasons I don't have the time or capacity to understand right now.

A soft laugh brings my attention back up, and I don't know how I'll ever look away. I'm met with the most beautiful smile, and, for a moment, the world feels quieter, like the curve of her lips have tugged all the light toward her, softening everything around us. Softening me, softening the thoughts in my brain, softening the tension that is constantly holding strong throughout my entire body.

"I'm Rumi," she says, a slight pink to her cheeks. "And this is Evelyn, but everyone calls her Evee."

"Evee," falls from my lips, the name feeling familiar as it leaves, the same way her mom's did all those months ago when I found her on the side of the road. "It's nice to meet you both," I say, still holding out my hand as Evee tugs on my fingers now with both hands.

Looking at Rumi, I can't help the memories that come flooding back. Seeing those dark waves matted with blood against the broken window. Seeing her pale skin covered in cuts and bruises, her swollen belly, the shattered glass, the eerily dark and quiet night.

All alone and probably so scared when she woke up.

Her blue eyes, the color of the lake, the color of my peace and solace.

A part of me wants to know what happened to her after the ambulance took her away. Did she have Evee that night? Was she all alone when she gave birth too?

Who was she running to that night?

Or, what was she running from?

My eyes trail past her, wondering if she's here alone, or if Evee's dad is close by.

"It's just me," I hear, and it brings my attention back to her.

"I'm sorry?" I say, confused.

"Everyone always does that," she answers. "Looks around to find her—" she pauses, looking down at Evee as if she's her entire world. "Someone else." Her voice is quiet, like she's afraid of being too loud.

"Oh, I—" I start, feeling heat rush up my neck. "I didn't mean—"

"No, it's okay," she says, that smile back but a little softer this time, not quite reaching her eyes.

"I just assumed—" I stop, needing to regroup, needing to see those eyes shine again. "I was raised by a single mom after my dad left when I was ten, and it was just me, my mom, and my sister who's over there. Her name is Emerson, and, well, I guess you know that because Luke introduced her, and—"

I notice that smile is back the same time I realize I'm rambling like a moron. I don't know if I strung this many words together in the last eighteen months, but I was talking long enough for Evee to get bored of me and start playing with the cardboard coaster that was on the bar top.

I've never so openly offered information to a stranger, especially information so personal. But it was something about the way she watched me as I talked, as her lips turned up, her eyes on me and only me made the words fall from my lips. There's something about her that feels familiar—safe, even—yet I'm just a stranger to her.

"Sorry," I mutter, my now-free hand goes to the back of my neck, and it's hot to the touch. "All I meant to say was, I didn't mean to imply that you weren't enough."

"Oh," she says, waving an arm in the air, the other holding Evee close. "No, no, please don't apologize. I didn't think you were."

"I don't know what kind of men you're used to, but I'm a man who apologizes when he's in the wrong, Rumi."

Her blush deepens, and I have to will my heart not to stop. She's avoiding my eyes now, looking just past where I'm standing, and there is something about her shyness, her timidness, that makes me want to do everything in my power to make her comfortable.

I circle around her, sitting down on the empty chair on her other side, hoping that she spins her chair to face me, and feeling like I won the lottery when she does.

"Can we start over?" I ask her.

She nods.

"How old is your daughter?" My question feels silly to ask, as if I don't already know the answer, but it's the only one that comes to mind.

"She turns one next week. Her birthday is May 19th," she answers, and it takes a whole lot of effort to not let my jaw drop.

May 19th was the night I found her.

"Are you doing anything for her first birthday?"

"Oh, probably just something small," she answers, eyes darting away as if unsure whether her words belong in the open. "With me, her, and my roommate." I have to lean a little closer to her to hear her answer, her voice hesitant.

"You don't want to do something with all your friends?" I ask her, unsure why she's in the bar surrounded by people yet seems so lonely.

"Um," she starts, still avoiding looking at me. "No, not really."

"It will be special no matter who's there."

"It's just," she starts, and I don't say anything—don't even move. I don't want to stop her from saying whatever she's about to, scared that if I even breathe, she'll keep it to herself. "I don't have many friends."

I look around, confused why she doesn't consider the people she's out with tonight as friends. "What about everyone here?"

Rumi looks around, and I take a moment to look down at Evee whose eyes look heavy, her lids drooping as she leans back against her mom's chest, and my own chest aches at the sight, as if my heart is physically expanding.

She turns back to face me. "Well, Ava's my friend. My manager and roommate too," she explains, pointing over her shoulder at the redhead behind her talking to Drew. "And I don't know Drew or Mia very well, or their husbands.

They're all my boss' friends." She looks down at Evee, carefully taking the coaster out of her clenched hand, removing it slowly from her fingers to not wake her as she drifts asleep.

"They could be your friends too," I say, even though what I really want to do is tell her that I'll be her friend.

At the moment, looking at the sadness clouding those blue eyes, I want to tell her I'll be anything she could ever want or need—her and Evee—but I keep my mouth closed.

"Maybe," she says with a sigh. "And what about you? I hear you're back in town after being gone for a while. What brought you back?"

You.

But I can't say that. I can't tell her that finding her, saving her, was the catalyst for me being in this bar, right here and now.

I can't tell her that thinking about the *happiest ever afters* for her and her daughter were the only thing that got my mind off losing my best friend, pulled me out of my self-pity and wallowing, and kicked my ass back into gear.

Needing to clear the emotion clogging my throat, I cough into my fist. "I needed to get my life back on track." It's a cop-out of an answer, one that I've been telling everyone—including myself—for the last eighteen months yet saying them to Rumi is the first time it feels like a complete lie.

She nods but doesn't say anything. She doesn't need to. There's something in her eyes that tells me she understands the words I can't bring myself to say.

Something that tells me she knows how hard it is to start over after you've almost killed yourself trying to use the burned and broken pieces leftover to rebuild, doing it over and over until you realize there's nothing left.

That you can't keep burying yourself in the ashes, and that it's time for something new.

"And I don't have a lot of friends either," I add, hoping she knows that I understand her too.

"I find that hard to believe," she says, and I watch as a tinge of pink appears on the apples of her cheeks. She rolls her lips together, her eyes slightly widening as if she didn't mean to say the words.

I don't let her dwell on it too long—more for my sake than hers. "It's true. I haven't made a new friend in a while. I think I forgot how."

"I think I never actually learned how." The admission hits me harder than anything else she says tonight, her words loaded with truths that I don't think she's ready to share.

CHAPTER 10
RUMI

I HOPE Ava is too busy with her conversation with Drew right now to hear anything I am saying. I just know if she could hear me, she'd be thinking of all the different ways to tell me how I have no idea what I'm doing talking to this man right now.

When I first saw Jack this morning after he ran into Hey Honey's, there was an instant attraction for me.

How couldn't there be?

I think anyone would see this man and agree.

And he looked good this morning—a little disheveled, but *good.*

Tonight? His dark hair, striking eyes, biceps on display in his fitted T-shirt that I literally want to sink my teeth into—as if I have ever had that urge before—are sitting in front of me, making my head spin and words jumble in my brain.

It's been years since I have had any sort of attraction to a man like this, and I can't even compare the feelings I had when I first saw Trevor to what is circulating through my body now.

And when Evee grabbed his hand, I wanted to climb him

like a tree and cry into his chest at the same time like a complete lunatic.

He's still a walking contrast of a man, and it's in more ways than one. I noticed it tonight the same way I did this morning. With his large stature and gruff demeanor, the softness of his eyes catches me by surprise whenever I look at him.

And just like when I saw the red creep up his neck when he realized he was staring at me. The same happened when he noticed his rambling; he thought I was offended about him looking for Evee's dad. He has a boyish charm that I wouldn't expect from someone who looks like him.

He's dangerous, and not in the way I'm used to.

"I'd argue you're doing a pretty damn good job right now," he says, and I wish I could control the blood from my body rising to my cheeks at the smirk on his lips.

It's ironic that I came here ready to make a friend, and I think I was doing an okay job with Drew. I know she was doing most of the talking because she could tell I was nervous, but her kind demeanor was reassuring. I still couldn't completely wash away the discomfort I was feeling with the attention; I caught myself worried that I'd say something that would offend her, or make her upset.

It's a habit I just can't seem to break.

But with Jack, his attention on me is intense—how he looks at me like I'm the only person in the world. And tonight? I find myself liking it, almost basking in it.

It's comfortable and warm, like sitting out by a campfire.

"I'm glad you think so," I reply. "Because I have no idea what I'm doing."

"Nobody knows what they're doing. Ever. We're all just making it up as we go." He rests his elbow on the bar, leaning his head into his fist, looking at me as if he recognizes something on my face, as if this isn't the first time we've talked like this.

"That's what it feels like with this one," I say, glancing down at Evee. "I had no idea what I was doing when she was born, but we figured it out along the way. Still are."

"We?" Jack asks.

"Me and Ava," I clarify. "She's basically been Evee's other parent since she was born."

Jack nods, and I think he wants me to keep going, but a little voice in my head tells me to be careful not to say too much.

"The night she was born, I was in an accident. I don't remember anything after calling 911 and passing out. I woke up in the hospital the next morning, and they had performed an emergency C-section."

Jack doesn't say anything at first, and I can't help but look away from the intensity I see in his eyes. It's the same way he was looking at me earlier, like he's trying to find something by looking directly into my soul.

I feel the need to fill the silence between us. "Luckily, Evee was okay. Perfect, even." I look down at my daughter, her head is resting against my arms as I hold her against me. She looks so peaceful, even amongst the chatter and music playing at the bar, with her plump cheeks, gently parted lips, and long lashes—the ones that frame the eyes she got from me.

"She really is cute."

"She's the best thing I've ever done," I say, but it comes off as if I'm saying it to her rather than to Jack.

"Rumi," I hear, and I look back up to find those jade eyes, the green looking more emerald in the dim light of the bar. He looks like he's about to say something, and then there's a slight shake of his head, blinking a few times and throwing on a small smile, one that doesn't feel as genuine as the others he's shown me tonight. "Since we're both looking for some new friends, what do you say about being mine?"

My lips part as my eyebrows raise. I know he's talking

about being his friend, but there's something about hearing him ask me to be his that makes my skin tingle.

I quickly school my features to hide my surprise as I watch the column of Jack's throat peeking out from his T-shirt turn a dark shade of red, his face a clear indicator that he did not mean to say the words out loud, or at least in the way that he did.

"Yes," I say before I can think too much about it. I instantly feel responsible for his embarrassment and rush to make it go away. It's one of my worst habits, taking on the emotions of others, as if I have any control over them.

His mouth opens to say something, but I don't get to hear what it is.

"Ready to go?" Ava asks, placing a hand on my shoulder; I didn't even realize she walked over to us.

I turn to see everyone pushing in their chairs, gathering their things to leave. "Here, let me take her," Ava says. "That way, you can say goodbye." She gives me a wink as she pulls Evee from my lap. She turns to Jack. "Good to see you again," she says to him, before turning and heading toward the door.

I look at Jack as I stand from my chair, and he does the same. When we were sitting at the bar, we faced each other, just a few inches between our knees, but Evee was also between us. All of a sudden, I feel like I'm on complete display without my daughter in my arms. I didn't realize how much I relied on her comforting weight against me until it was gone.

Feeling exposed, I cross my arms across my chest, and Jack puts his hands in his pockets. There's an awkwardness between us that wasn't there before, as if neither of us knows where to go from here.

"Well, I, uh," he starts, rocking up on his toes and back on his heels, at the same time I say, "That was—" not knowing how the hell I was going to finish that sentence.

We both let out a little laugh, some of the awkwardness

lifting from the air around us. He tries again. "I better go grab my sister and say goodbye to Luke." But he doesn't move.

"Yeah, same," I say before quickly adding, "I mean, say goodbye to everyone. Not grab your sister. That would be weird considering I don't know her."

He gives me a smile and seeing it is the only thing that stops me from smacking my hand against my forehead.

"I'll see you around, Rumi," he says, giving me a small nod, before heading past me to the group of everyone saying goodbye.

I turn and watch him put an arm around his sister's shoulder, and she turns around to see where he came from, finding me staring at them like an idiot.

Before I can look away, she gives me a small smile and a nod, the same way her brother just did, and elbows him in the side.

I can't help but smile at the antics, watching the two, and then how everyone around them laughs before exchanging hugs and plans for the coming days.

And as I say goodbye to everyone, following Ava and Evee through the front door of Lenny's, I can't help but feel like I accomplished what I set out to do tonight.

I made a friend.

CHAPTER 11
JACK

I'M two hours into my first shift back at the fire station, and it's not as bad as I thought it would be.

My body is only running on about two hours of sleep, but there's an anxious energy buzzing under my skin that has been keeping me wide awake and aware.

Contrary to popular belief or what is portrayed in mainstream media, a firefighter's job is only 10% of actually fighting fires, if not less. It's a fact I keep reminding myself of —one that I learned in my first week at the fire academy—on my way into my shift today.

One that I had to keep repeating in my mind as I threw on my station wear this morning.

The T-shirt with my department's logo and one of the dozen pairs of cargo pants that Emerson had packed up and stored in my mom's basement gave me such an odd sense of deja vu, as if I had gone back in time.

A time when Bennett would've been doing the same before we headed to the station together.

The thoughts of my best friend—and how weird it was to be going into my first shift without him—were harder to push to the back of my mind. Even after a 8-mile run and an hour of lifting weights before the sun was even up, I couldn't think of anything else on my way to the station this morning,

The only thing that helped was telling myself that going back to work was part of putting everything behind me and moving forward—what I promised myself I was going to do when I came home.

When I got here, willing myself out of my truck and focusing on putting one foot in front of the other, the crew at the station offered a couple quick "welcome backs", but, for the most part, they acted as if I was gone for the weekend rather than eighteen months. It made being here much more tolerable—not having to deal with the "how are you?" conversations, or hearing them tell me they're sorry about what happened to Bennett.

While the crew here knew Bennett as one of their own, the loss wasn't the same for them as it was for me, but that doesn't make me feel any less guilty for not being here with the rest of the crew after we him.

After the offgoing firefighters gave us the pass down briefing report about how their shift went, the incoming crew had our briefing about today—discussing the weather forecast, road closures and construction currently in the works, and our schedule.

My luck seemed to be continuing with a light load of inspections and training for the next 24 hours while we're on call, and some of that anxious energy began to dissipate.

After we were briefed, the crew did our daily equipment checks for the vehicles, tools, and other items before we moved to checking inventory and stocking necessary medical supplies for any upcoming calls we'll get. The familiarity of the different duties settled even more nerves I had—the recurring theme of the last two days that I can't seem to escape.

Muscle memory began taking over for me, allowing my

mind to settle into the tasks in front of me to a point where I found my thoughts drifting to a certain brunette who I already know will be occupying my mind in the coming days more than she should be.

And now, with some down time between daily chores and a lull in calls, that certain brunette is at the forefront of my mind and not going anywhere. Not when I recall our conversation from last night, cringing at the way I asked her to be my friend as if we were in Kindergarten—or like I had *This is my first time out after a year and a half of self-inflicted solitude, and I now don't know what to do with myself* tattooed on my forehead.

And to make matters worse, deepening my residual embarrassment from the night, I said goodbye to her in a way that made it look like I forgot how to properly use my hands.

The urge to lean in for a hug or press a kiss to her cheek was so strong that I had to jam my hands in my pockets to avoid the inappropriate response my body had when I knew she was leaving and the night was ending.

It was as if the thought of her not being within a few feet of me brought on the incessant need to pull her close and keep her there—a completely inappropriate thought to have about someone my brain knows I barely know yet my heart thinks I know all too well.

I bring my palm to my forehead, dragging it down over my face, fighting the heat that threatens to ease up my neck, reddening the skin.

The last thing I need to be thinking of right now is last night.

It was nothing special.

Just two mutual friends of a friend becoming...friendly?

Fuck, it's like I'm sixteen again with a crush—one I have absolutely no business having. I shouldn't be thinking about her dark brown hair twisted into a messy braid, or the pieces perfectly framing her cool blue eyes. I shouldn't be thinking about her dark lashes batting as she watched me talk, or her full lips that would turn up into the most beautiful smile, or the timidness she had at first, and how I watched her comfort with me grow as the seconds ticked by, making me feel as if I was being offered the most precious gift.

And I definitely shouldn't be thinking of the way her slender arms wrapped around her sleeping daughter who has the same brown hair and waves in her eyes as her mom and how it made my arms physically ache to be wrapped around the both of them.

"Hasting!"

I'm jolted back to reality, brought back to the kitchen in the fire station, rather than the dark corner of Lenny's last night with Rumi and Evee. I feel a slight ache in my cheeks, and that's when I realize I was smiling to myself like a crazy son of a bitch, and I wish someone would punch me in the face for the ridiculous thoughts taking over my brain.

"Come on, we're in charge of the grocery shopping today," one of the other firefighters, Anderson, says to me.

I give him a curt nod, standing up and following him and two other guys down the stairs toward the truck.

"Who's got you daydreaming over here?" Anderson teases over his shoulder, but I ignore him, hopping into the passenger seat of the fire truck. Anderson rounds the truck, getting into the driver's seat. "Nice to see you smiling once in a while, Hasting," he says, obviously not getting the hint that this isn't a conversation I am interested in having. When I don't respond, he says, more to himself than to me, "Not in a talking mood. Noted." The engine rolls over, the truck coming to life, and we head on our way.

When Anderson, the other guys on grocery duty, and I get back from the store, the hours fly by. Between a handful of routine calls, writing reports, and a couple visits to classrooms at the local elementary school to talk about fire safety, the sun is already setting.

The members of the crew on clean-up just finished tidying the kitchen from dinner, and there's a quietness among the station as the day winds down and we enter into the evening portion of our shift.

There are ten of us currently on shift, our department being more of a mid-size unit, and there is a soft buzzing of conversations from a few guys still sitting at the dining table playing cards.

The TV is playing tonight's baseball game, and the rest of the crew are on the couch watching. I'm in one of the loungers with a book in my lap, a habit I picked back up when I was staying in my grandfather's cabin—having been a big reader in middle school but not keeping up it until I got much older.

Since there was no Wi-Fi or TV up there, my main source of entertainment was the shelves of my grandmother's books —the ones she'd bring out on the boat to read while my grandfather fished.

Most of them were nonfiction books about the different wildlife of the area where they built the cabin, but I got through those relatively quickly. I ended up getting into her cozy mysteries that she kept on the bottom shelf. I didn't get through all of them, and it didn't feel right taking them.

It worked out that there were some to choose from at the grocery store we stopped at, so I grabbed the first book of a new series when we were out on our run.

"Time to go," I hear, looking up from the page I was reading to find Anderson standing in front of where I'm seated, hands on his hips in the same station wear as the rest of us—black Northshore Fire Department T-shirt, cargo pants, and black work boots. His light brown, shaggy hair is swept over his forehead, one of his brows lifted at me as his eyes roam to the book in my lap. *"Murder Over Coffee?"* The title of the book comes off as a question.

I set the book down on the small table next to the lounger and take off my wired reading glasses, putting them on top of the book.

"That's surprising," I reply as I stand.

"What?" Anderson asks.

"That you can read," I deadpan, walking past him, heading toward the stairs.

He lets out a laugh, as if the joke wasn't the lazy one that it was. "Good one," I hear from behind me.

Anderson started a few weeks before I left, so I don't know him too well. He's a few years younger than me, and he still has that excitement about the job that he had when he first started.

I admired it when I first met him, but now I can see it getting old quickly.

"Where to first?" I ask him, as he follows me down the stairs. We were tasked with a few fire inspections at some nearby duplexes and local businesses, and Chief Sanders partnered Anderson and me together for them.

Between this and grocery duty, I think the chief wants me around the most positive, happy-go-lucky guy on the crew—I wouldn't be surprised if it's his way of keeping an eye on me.

"I figured we could do the ones off Bluemound Road first," he answers as we pass Chief Sanders' office, and I don't let myself glance to see if he's in there.

It would be a lie if I said I'm *not* avoiding him today.

I know he's going to remind me about the mandatory therapy sessions I agreed to, and I'd rather put off that conversation as long as possible. I'm technically cleared for calls, having convinced him that I was okay. But I know I'm on a tight leash—not only am I required to start these sessions, but the chief already warned me that if anything happens, he's filing a FFDE—a "Fit for Duty" Evaluation.

I'm also well-aware that anything that happens today is fair game for Anderson to share with him, so I'm glad it's been such an uneventful day.

There's no telling what would happen if we had to suit up right now and run into a fire—the last time I did that, I lost my best friend.

CHAPTER 12
RUMI

"YOU'RE sure you want to go to swim class tonight?" I ask Ava as she throws Evee's diaper bag over her shoulder. "I really don't mind taking her."

Ava rolls her eyes ignoring me as she takes Evee from my arms, her smile big and bright ever since I put her in her swimsuit.

Swim lessons are something I started with my daughter as early as I could.

Mariah, my therapist, offered the idea as a way to focus on something for her safety that I could control to help with my postpartum anxiety—I was constantly spiraling about all the different ways she could get hurt, ranging from being allergic to something I fed her to being stolen right out of her stroller by an over-sized bird.

We also had plenty of sessions discussing rational and irrational thinking when it comes to Evee's safety after that.

"Maybe if you would've called me when Reagan didn't show up to her shift, I would believe you," Ava scolds, and now I'm the one rolling my eyes. "This whole time, I thought you were at the gym and then the mall like you *told* me you'd be until it was time for Evee's swim class. Not working a whole other shift."

I heard from Ava on our way home from Lenny's last night that Reagan told Luke and Annie she found another job. They asked if she could finish out her shifts this week, and she agreed, but then she no-called, no-showed today leaving me to work open to close.

"I didn't want to bother you," I argue, knowing it's a poor excuse for not calling her to let her know Reagan didn't show up, but I didn't want to call with news that I knew would make Ava upset.

"I know what you're thinking, dummy," she says, leaning into a hip as she holds Evee against her. "It's written all over your face."

She's in jean shorts and a hoodie, her swimsuit underneath for when she gets in the pool with Evee for class. Her auburn hair is tied up in a messy bun, her freckles even more prominent on her cheeks after being out in the sun with Evee at the park today.

I cross my arms, still in my black apron, my white long sleeves stained with various brown stains from a solo twelve-hour day.

"You didn't want to piss me off," she starts, and I open my mouth to say something, but she continues, "even though I would've been pissed at the situation—and Reagan—but not at you."

My mouth shuts, and I hate how she's basically learned to read my mind in the last year and a half.

"Remember what we talked about yesterday? You need time for you, and you need to prioritize it," she says, raising a brow at me.

"I had a whole day to myself. You were the one with Evee." I don't mean for the words to come out as a whine, but my voice raises one too many octaves to sound like my normal cadence.

Ava lifts Evee higher on her hip. "You know that's not what I mean."

I let out a sigh. "I do things for myself," I argue, but part of me sees where Ava is coming from. Even though I don't get many nights to myself, I think I do a good job of balancing being a mom and still being *me.*

I'm ready to explain that to Ava, but she beats me to it. "And staying up late after Evee is asleep to read your vampire smut books is not enough."

"They're called paranormal romance."

Ava lets out a sigh. "Whatever they're called, they're not enough."

"So what am I supposed to do for the two hours you're gone?" I ask her, watching as Evee plays with the drawstrings of Ava's hoodie.

"Whatever you want," Ava answers. "That's the whole point. You can literally do whatever you want and not have to worry about Evee, or me, or work."

I tuck the pieces that came free from my braid behind my ears before crossing my arms over my chest. I contemplate her words, my lips curving into a small smile.

The idea of a few hours to myself after such a stressful, busy day sounds better and better the more we talk about.

How long has it been since I read my book on the living room couch instead of under my covers with a book light?

When's the last time I made dinner for myself while blasting my boy bands playlist?

Or actually made it to the gym or mall after a shift?

I can't even remember doing anything that wasn't taking care of Evee, helping out Ava, or going to work since being released from the hospital last year.

"I guess I could find something to do," I conclude softly, but my eyes go to my feet as a trickle of guilt drops into my stomach when the words leave my mouth.

"Hey," Ava says, waiting to say more until I look back up at her. "Don't do that."

"Do what?"

"Feel bad about looking forward to a night all to yourself."

"How bad is it that I can't remember the last time I had one?" The question hangs between us for a few moments. Forget not being able to remember doing anything for myself in the last year —I don't think I can remember doing anything for myself *ever*.

For as long as I can remember, everything I did was for someone else. Whether it was trying to cheer up my mom after she had a fight with my dad, or helping her pack while hoping she'd take me with her when she left.

Whether it was lying to my teachers about where I got the bruises, or pasting the biggest fakest smile on my face so they wouldn't call Child Protective Services, for 18 years, I lived to do anything and everything I could to avoid my father's anger—and his hands.

The only thing I think I've ever truly done for myself is leave that house and go to college, something I did all on my own.

But I ended up leaving one monster to find another.

The first time Trevor hit me, it was like I was thrown back into my childhood, always walking on eggshells, wishing I could make myself disappear, wishing on every star outside my bedroom window to get me out.

I was back in my bedroom where brand new toys and clothes would appear the next day, along with the promise of ice cream for dinner and that he just lost his temper for a split second; that it was the alcohol; that it was an accident; that it would never happen again.

As if his presents and promises were enough of an apology for the abuse the night before.

With Trevor, I was trapped. *Again.* Stuck in the constant

cycle of another man's highs and lows. The highs that made me think it was the last time, and the lows that reminded me there never would be.

Ava closes the distance between us, wrapping her arm that isn't holding Evee around me, pulling me in. My head finds her shoulder, and the embrace brings me back to where I am now. I feel Evee's little hands wrap around the pieces of hair loose from my braid.

I'm not in that house.

I'm not with Trevor.

I'm here with my best friend and my daughter—I'm safe.

"I wish I had the right words to say, but I don't. But I am here for you, Rumi. No one will ever hurt you ever again," Ava whispers, and the words are exactly what I need to hear.

"I don't know what I'd do without you," I whisper back.

"Good thing you'll never have to know." Ava loosens her hold on me. Evee begins to babble, her hands now fisting my hair and pulling.

"Ow," I say with a chuckle, grabbing her hand and carefully helping her unfurl her fists. "Someone's excited for swim class." The emotions begin to dissipate as Ava laughs too, both of us looking at Evee as she tries to bounce in Ava's hold.

"Alright, girlfriend, we hear you. Enough with the heavy stuff," Ava jokes. "But before we go, tell your mom to enjoy her night to herself."

Evee makes a noise that is half-laugh and half-cry.

"Okay then," Ava mumbles, and then walks over to the entryway and slips her feet into her shoes. She turns to look at me. " Remember, you deserve this."

I nod, internalizing the words to push out the guilt.

"Enjoy it, okay? And I'm talking about whatever," she pauses, a little smirk gracing her lips, "*self-care* you decide to partake in." Her emphasis on "self-care" makes my eyes widen.

"Ava!"

She laughs, her head tilting back, making Evee wave her arms and let out a little giggle too. "Maybe I just meant washing your hair or taking a long bath with a face mask. Get your mind out of the gutter."

I shake my head, meeting them at the door and leaning in to give Evee a kiss on the cheek, knowing that Ava is ready to get going, so they can be at least fifteen minutes early to the 6:30 p.m. swim class.

"I'm sure you have a lot of *material* you could pull from for that self-care too, after last night and all. Your new friend cleans up pretty nicely, if you ask me." She winks before turning to open the front door of our house before I have time to come up with something to say back to that.

The whiplash from the last five minutes is enough to make my head hurt, but I should be used to it by now with Ava and her inability to let anyone around her be in any sort of pain. Always needing to be the one to make sure everyone in her presence is okay.

With such a busy day, I've barely had time to think about last night.

I've been running around like a chicken with its head cut off since accidentally snoozing my alarm one too many times, barely making it to Hey Honey's by the start of my shift where there was absolutely no downtime. There was a steady, manageable flow for the entirety of the day that I honestly didn't even notice Reagan didn't show until it was already an hour past when she was supposed to be there.

"Have fun, Mama!" Ava yells over her shoulder, as she heads down the driveway.

The duplex we rent is owned by a leasing company, all the houses in our little neighborhood having been divided into side-by-side units available for rent and walking distance from Hey Honey's, and we're lucky to have our own driveway for the car we share.

"But not too much fun!" she adds.

"Enough, Ava!" I yell, but I feel the heat in my cheeks, and I can't help but grin as she buckles Evee into her car seat. Ava rounds the car, getting into the driver's seat and blowing me a kiss as she backs the car out. It isn't until I watch her turn the corner out of our neighborhood that I close the door.

"A night to myself," I repeat to myself.

It has been a while since I had some *self-care*.

CHAPTER 13
JACK

"THOSE WERE the only two stops in this building, so we'll head to the duplexes across the street to finish up," Anderson says, as we hop back into one of the station's pickup trucks. We've finished seven of our stops tonight, and all seven have been compliant with their fire safety regulations. So far, all of the local businesses had the proper smoke alarms and functional and maintained sprinklers.

I don't mention to Anderson how familiar I am with this particular building, seeing as though I was just here last night. I didn't realize the building that Lenny's and Hey Honey's is in was on our list for stops tonight.

To be completely honest, both times my mind was as far away from anything having to do with my job as possible.

As I tune out Anderson's need to narrate everything he's thinking to fill the silence between us, my mind wanders to what—or *who*—made it so easy to forget the things that usually take up so much space in my brain.

For reasons unbeknownst to me, Rumi has a way of becoming my sole focus when my mind drifts, like she can quiet my mind when she's not even here.

When I think of her, I don't think about how lonely I feel

in the station without Bennett, or how my heart races when someone turns on the kitchen's gas stove. I don't think about how my stomach drops when we get a call, scared that I'll have to gear up and rush into a fire, or how I'm already nervous to come back for my next shift when this one hasn't even ended.

Thinking of her has a way of blurring everything else, and my thoughts only focus on her.

And I can't decide if that's a good thing or a very, *very* bad thing.

When we stopped at Lenny's to do our inspection, I recognized Emmett behind the bar. He's not a man of many words or someone who cares for small-talk, which I greatly appreciate. It made mine and Anderson's inspection quick and painless, aside from the strength it took to stop glancing over at the side of the bar where Rumi and I sat the night before, as if she would be there with her messy braid and her freshwater eyes.

We gave Lenny's the stamp of approval before walking down to the pizza place, the only other of the four businesses in the building that were open after 6 p.m.

Emmett owns the entire building, so I figured if Lenny's was good to go for the fire inspection, the rest would be. We were in and out of the pizza place in a few minutes, but we will still need to circle back to the bookstore and Hey Honey's tomorrow morning before our shift ends, just to be safe.

The tires of the truck hum against the darkening road as we pass identical duplexes, trimmed lawns, and matching driveways under the soft streetlight. The evening sky is painted in soft purples and pinks, and the cool May air seeps in through the opened windows of the station's pickup truck.

Anderson slows to a stop. "I figured we can start here and work our way back toward the entrance of the neighborhood. The members of the crew on for tomorrow can start here and work down the other way."

I give him a nod, grabbing my clipboard and stepping onto the road.

This neighborhood is nice, perfect for couples or small families, and it's reassuring to know these houses are owned by a company that cares for their tenants safety.

People are often surprised when we show up to walk through their apartment or rental house, checklist in hand instead of a hose, and in our station wear rather than full-on fire gear. We often have to explain that nothing is wrong, and we're just here for a fire inspection, requested by the leasing office or property management.

These walkthroughs aren't always what people expect. We're not there to hand out a fine or tear the place apart. We're looking for basic safety stuff—working smoke alarms, clear exits, functioning carbon monoxide detectors, and fire extinguishers on each level of the house. As part of our community's safety program, firefighters are the ones making the rounds, rather than fire inspectors or marshals.

And the goal's simple: make sure the place you live isn't a fucking trap if something goes wrong. I've seen what happens when it is, and a five-minute check can save lives.

I shake the thoughts away, not wanting my mind to go to that dark place, but they come at me faster than I can will them away.

I've spent months wondering if one of these five-minute checks could have prevented the fire that killed Bennett. I can't count how many times I wished I could find out who did the fire inspections in that house, if it was done right.

If it was done at all.

I feel the rush of anger overwhelm me as I think about how preventable a house fire is.

After the smoke clears and the sirens fade, people always ask if there was anything they could've done. And the hard truth is—yeah, a lot of the time, there fucking *was*. Most house fires start from things we *can* control: candles burning near curtains, faulty appliances, bad wiring that's been ignored for years, lint buildup in a dryer, fireplaces left unattended, grills too close to the house.

Or in the case of the fire that killed Bennett, a space heater that was too close to a blanket.

And if the idiot hadn't gone back in—against better judgement, against orders, if he would've waited one minute—he would've seen there was nothing to go back in for.

That the daughter got out.

That she wasn't still inside of the house.

"Jack?" I flinch at the voice that is only mere inches from my face, and it takes all my willpower not to deck Anderson in the jaw. I didn't realize he rounded the truck and came up next to me.

"What?" I snap.

"I said," he starts, carefully, putting his hands up in surrender as he takes a few steps back, "let's start over here." He points to the duplex he parked the truck in front of, a gray sedan sitting on one side of the driveway, the other side empty. It looks like each house is split into two living units, each with its own garage and a shared driveway.

I exhale as we start walking toward the front door. It takes a moment to register, but as we get closer to the door, a faint scent of smoke hits me. I don't have time to question it because the sound of a fire alarm begins blaring loud enough to hear even through the house's closed windows.

I try to take another step, but my feet feel glued to the spot on the sidewalk and my body threatens to freeze. Instinct wants to take over, go toward the smoke and extinguish it, but it's overridden by something stronger.

Fear.

It's like I'm on the side of the road hearing the ambulance all over again, seconds away from being thrown back into the worst moment of my life. The edges of my vision begin to blur, and my legs shake as if they are about to buckle.

No.

This can't be happening. Not again.

"Damn it," Anderson mutters before breaking into a sprint toward the house, banging on the door. "Northshore Fire Department!" he yells. Through the windows, it's evident there are no visible flames. I try to tell myself that, but my body won't listen. I'm still stuck in place.

I close my eyes.

Breathe in.

Breathe out.

What is it that we're supposed to tell people when they're experiencing a trauma-response? I wrack my mind for something to make this weight in my chest subside.

Then, I hear a scream, and it brings me right out of the panic attack that I know is seconds away from taking over me.

Dropping my clipboard, I sprint toward the door Anderson is still pounding on, but I don't hesitate. "Back up," I yell at him, and, to his credit, he does instantly.

Aiming just above the doorknob, I drive my heel into the door with a sharp, controlled stomp—once, then again, until the frame gives with a crack and the door flies inward. The air inside rushes out hot and thick, smoke blurring our vision as I enter the house, the fire alarm blaring even louder now that we're closer to it.

"Go see if we have a fire extinguisher in the truck!" I yell over my shoulder to Anderson as another scream fills the air, but I'm not sure if it's because of the fire or because this person just heard their house get broken into.

"Northshore Fire Department!" I call out, announcing my presence, hoping to eliminate any potential fear. I use one arm to bat away the thin, gray smoke as I enter the house.

"Over here," a small voice says, followed by a cough. I make my way through the entryway and the small hallway leading to the kitchen, the unmistakable smell of something burning filling my nose.

Through the thin layer of smoke, I can see a small figure, one hand throwing a tray of burnt *somethings* outside her back patio door while the other holds a towel around her body.

Her wet, naked body.

I try not to focus on the latter, finding the open oven—no flames, thankfully.

I quickly move toward it, shutting it off and closing it as the screen of the back patio door slides shut, a small breeze coming in and helping with the lingering smoke.

Grabbing a towel I find on the counter, I begin batting the rest of the smoke away as I hear windows being slid open. The smoke alarm finally stops blaring, and I set the towel down, reluctantly turning to the woman in the towel.

And when I do, I can't look away.

Strands of dark wet hair fall over her shoulders, making her blue eyes even brighter against her pale skin—skin that is coated in drops of water falling from her waves, instantly making my throat dry. Her arm is still holding her towel around her, and the rise and fall of her chest matches mine as the chaos of the last few minutes—along with the smoke—settles around us.

"Jack?" Rumi says, the grip on her towel tightening. I can't help the pride that fills my chest that there's recognition when she looks at me, unlike yesterday at the coffee shop.

I quirk my lips to the side trying to fight the smile threatening my lips as I notice the flush in her cheeks, one that could be from the hot water or the adrenaline from the situation. Either way, I'm all of a sudden thankful I was paired with Anderson for these inspections tonight.

I'm about to open my mouth to say something—*anything* —but Rumi beats me to it. "I was making cookies," she blurts out before her eyes dart to the floor, her pink cheeks turning pure crimson as if I caught her doing something that definitely was *not* making cookies. "I went to, um, take a shower, but I guess I, um, forgot to—" She pauses, staring at her bare feet on the dark hardwood, and I can't help but look too, noticing the light pink polish on her toes.

"Set a timer?" I finish for her, hoping she looks back up at me.

"Yeah," she answers sheepishly.

She stands at the edge of her living room, me in her kitchen, and I feel this unexplainable pull, like I need to be closer to her.

I take a step toward her. "Well, what are friends for?" I try to keep my voice light, just like I did last night. Anything to keep her comfortable with me.

Finally, she looks back at me, and her smile is small, but it's there, and I take that as a win.

"This is not how I pictured running into you again," she admits, and I'm embarrassed about how hard it is to forget the fact that this woman is naked in front of me, the only thing between us is that little white towel. A fact I think she remembers that moment because her eyes widen, and she quickly adds, "I'll be right back."

I hold in a chuckle as she runs into one of the connecting rooms and shuts the door behind her, giving me a moment to collect myself. I lean back on the kitchen counter, my head falling back against the cabinets as I press the heels of my hands into my eyes.

The aftermath of the last ten minutes—and the whiplash that ensued—running through my head.

What the fuck just happened?

And how the fuck I'm going to get the image of Rumi wet and naked in a towel out of my head.

I peel my hands away from my face just as I hear footsteps coming in through the entryway, and I recognize the sound of work boots. "Looks like we won't be needing this," I hear

Anderson say, no doubt holding the fire extinguisher we keep in the truck.

Resisting the urge to let out a groan, I answer, "Nope. No need," with an exhale, pushing myself off the counter.

"So what happened?" Anderson asks, setting the fire extinguisher on the ground next to the refrigerator.

I nod toward the stove. "Forgot to set a timer."

Anderson looks around the kitchen, and my brow furrows in confusion.

"Well, what was in there?" Anderson asks.

I point toward the patio door, and Anderson follows with his gaze. He walks over to the door, peeking through the screen door.

"Please don't tell me you're trying to see if the cookies she burnt are still edible," I say, and it comes out more as a growl.

"No harm in checking," he replies, his dopey grin on his face as he opens the screen door. "I'm going to do a quick walk around the duplex to check for clear pathways for emergency access and make sure they have safe placement of any propane tanks," he adds, and it reminds me that he isn't a complete moron.

"I'll do the inside," I mutter, as he closes the screen door behind him, giving me a salute as he heads out to walk the perimeter of the backyard.

I left my clipboard on the lawn out front, but I know the checklist for the inspection like the back of my hand. Now that our little detour is over with, we can get back to what we're actually here for.

And that doesn't include fixating on whose house this is or how it's like I thought of her enough times today to conjure up a scenario where I run into her—again.

I already know the fire alarm works just fine, and there are two clear exits—one of which I completely destroyed—at both the front and back of the house. There's no upstairs, so as long as she has at least one fire extinguisher, she should be good.

And that's when it hits me.

Where is her daughter?

She doesn't seem like the type to put cookies in an unattended oven and take a shower with a baby in the house. I look around the living room, evidence of Evee all over the place. Her toys, books, and stuffed animals decorate the space, making the space feel that much more homey.

I'm not left to wonder alone for long when the door to what I assume is a bedroom opens, revealing Rumi, no longer wet and naked—much to my relief.

And disappointment.

"Where's Evee?" I ask at the same time she says, "So what are you doing here?"

We both let out a laugh, ignoring the awkwardness of our third coincidental meeting in the last two days—fourth if you count last year—and I gesture for her to go first.

Her wet hair is brushed, tucked behind her ears, and she has on a light green crew neck with matching sweatpants, her feet still barefoot.

"What are you doing here?" she asks again before adding, "not that I'm not happy you were here to help with the smoke —and witness my pure, unadulterated embarrassment—but it's not every day a firefighter breaks down your front door after you burn some cookies."

"We were in the neighborhood for an inspection," I answer, and she nods, watching me carefully as I continue. "We were about to knock on your door when we heard the alarm, and then when we did, there was no answer." I look toward the front door, now realizing it was a slight overreaction to the situation, but it was instinct when I heard her scream. My hand goes to the back of my neck, and I feel a warmth to my skin. "I'll fix it."

Her eyes move from mine to my neck and back up to my eyes, her lips curving. "I might take you up on that," she says.

I clear my throat, coughing into my fist. "Where's Evee?"

"Oh, um, she's with Ava at swim classes."

"You started her young then, huh?" With my EMT training, water safety, especially with infants, is something I'm familiar with, and I like that Rumi does all she can to keep her daughter safe.

Rumi nods. "It was a way for me to get rid of some of the worries I had as a new mom about not being able to protect her from everything." Her eyes look almost gray in the dim light coming from her kitchen, the sun now almost set. She shakes her head. "It sounds kind of stupid when I say it out loud."

"It's not stupid," I tell her. I want to say more, but she lets out a humorless laugh before I can.

"Ava offered to take her after I worked an open to close shift today. Tonight was supposed to be a night for me to… relax." That blush is back in her cheeks.

"You burn cookies to relax?"

This time she laughs for real. "Thanks for rubbing it in. At least it brought my new friend to my door, or should I say *through*?"

The smile on my face blooms before I even realize it, and I bark out a laugh. I take a step closer to her. "You think fire safety is a joke?" I tease—*flirt?* I don't know what the hell I'm doing, but I don't want to stop.

Rumi takes a small step toward me, only a few more steps separating us where we stand in her living room. "The same way you think burnt cookies are," she teases back, crossing her arms over her chest. Last night, she crossed her arms to put distance between us. Tonight, the way she sticks out her hip, cocking her head, she's giving me attitude.

And I fucking love it.

I take another step in her direction, and she does the same.

"First thing you need to know about me, *friend,*" the word makes my lips tingle in a not-so-nice way, "I take cookies very seriously." I have no idea what the fuck I'm saying—I don't even *like* cookies, or any sweets for that matter—but it makes her take that final step between us, bringing her bare feet only inches from my work boots, and I think I'd say absolutely anything in that moment as long as she stays right here.

"As do I," she replies, her voice taking on a more playful tone, one I wouldn't mind coaxing out of her more as our *friendship* grows.

I have to tilt my head down to see her the same way she has to tilt hers up to meet my gaze, the top of her head coming to my chest. I fist my hands at my side, resisting the urge to see if the material of her crewneck is as soft as it looks, to see if the skin beneath it is even softer.

This is the closest I've been to her since the night of her crash, and it is everything I didn't know I needed. Her hair smells like vanilla, but there's a hint of smoke—and I don't want to admit how weirdly perfect the scent is on her. Up until tonight, the smell of smoke made my heart rate speed to the point it felt like I was having a heart attack, but right here? Right now?

Mixed with the scent of *her*?

It's like a glimpse of who I was before the fire, before Bennett died, before the only peace I could find was on the lake.

And maybe that's why the words fall out of my mouth before I can stop them. "Then it looks like I owe you some cookies."

CHAPTER 14
RUMI

ALMOST SETTING my house on a fire while masturbating in the bathtub is a secret I will take to my grave.

Along with the fact I was fantasizing about my newest *hot, firefighter* friend five minutes before he *literally* kicked down my front door.

Talk about a fantasy.

It'll be hard to keep the latter to myself—seeing as though Ava will be home any minute and see our front door on the ground and said friend inspecting our home for potential fire hazards—but the former will die with me.

"I didn't know firefighters made cookies in between, you know, fighting fires," I reply to Jack, looking up into his green eyes, my arms crossed over my chest to put at least some space between us.

Last night, I felt like I needed the space.

Tonight, it feels pointless, like my body needs to be near him despite my mind warning me to keep my distance.

Because I know the story of how his best friend died, I knew he was a firefighter. I guess I just didn't know he *still* was. I can't imagine how hard it is to come back to a job where you experienced such a loss.

I wonder if he knows how admirable that is.

"We don't," he answers, and his lips twitch to one side of his mouth, as if he doesn't want to let his smile show. He's let it slip a few times, but it's like he prefers to keep them to himself. "But, we're friends. And friends don't let other friends eat burnt cookies."

"Who's eating burnt cookies?" I hear from my back patio, and I can't help but flinch at the surprise or stop the gasp that escapes. I hate leaving my windows or doors open, especially when I'm home alone, but there was no other way to get the smoke out. Our yard is fenced in, but someone could easily get over it, and with the glass door open, the screen one being the only thing between me and whoever is out there.

"Hey," I hear, and I feel a gentle touch on the side of my face. "It's just my partner," Jack says quietly, and my body instantly relaxes. His palm is calloused and rough against my cheek, but, for a moment, I find myself leaning into the warm touch, the safety I feel in it.

"What the fuck?!" This voice doesn't make me flinch because it's one I've heard everyday for the last year, but it does bring me back to the moment as Jack's hand falls back to his side and we both take a step back.

Ava's home, and I already know she's not at all ready for the scene she's walking into.

As she heads down the hallway that leads to the kitchen from our entryway, I take a moment to look around the space while Jack walks over to the screen door of the patio, sliding it open to talk to his partner. The man has a similar build to Jack, only a few inches shorter, with shaggy brown hair that is too dark to be considered blonde but too light to be considered brunette. They're both dressed in cargo pants and a Northshore Fire Department T-shirt, and it's no wonder firefighters pose shirtless for calendars.

Ava's hair is tied up in the same messy bun she wore when she left, the pieces falling out a little curlier from being in the water. Evee's asleep against her shoulder, exhausted from her swim class. "What the hell happened here?" she asks as she looks around the kitchen. Her eyes blink rapidly as she takes everything in, her mouth slightly ajar.

The smoke has cleared from the night breeze coming in through the opened windows and doors, but the two very large—very *attractive*—men, one of whom she met yesterday, stand just inside our back patio.

"I'm Anderson Jones, and this is Jack Hasting," Jack's partner—Anderson—says, breaking the silence and stepping into the house, reaching out a hand to Ava. Ava's eyes immediately go to the floor where the man steps, no doubt noticing that they didn't take off their boots.

I don't have to see her feet to know Ava took off her shoes when she walked into the house, even with the surprise and confusion I'm sure she had finding our front door no longer on the hinges.

"Rumi," she says, turning to me and ignoring Anderson and his outstretched hand. Her voice is calm—too calm— which makes it even scarier.

Anderson runs his hand through his hair, blowing out a breath.

"Can you please tell me why there are two firefighters in our house right now?" She knows I don't like making her upset, and she always tries to hide when she is, but this unsettling, overly composed thing she does when she's mad always makes me feel like I have to apologize for anything and everything.

"I'm sorry. I accidentally set off the fire alarm," I tell her, and I feel three different pairs of eyes on me.

I hate how quiet my voice is, but I can't help it with all the attention directed toward me.

"Are you okay?" Ava asks, her voice evening out.

"I'm fine. I'm so *so* sorry," I tell her, walking over to the kitchen to grab Evee from her.

"Good," she turns to Jack and Anderson. "But that doesn't explain why my front door is on the floor," Ava says, her voice still calm but in no way polite. She turns back to me. "And stop apologizing."

She passes a sleeping Evee to me, the movement making her open her eyes for a moment before she closes them again, resting her head on my shoulder as I hold her with both arms.

"Sorry, miss. We were here to do a routine fire inspection when we heard the alarm," Anderson explains.

"And it's 'routine' to kick in the door when you do these fire inspections?" she asks him.

"Well, no," he answers. "But, we tried knocking and when—"

"She wasn't answering, and I heard her scream," Jack interjects firmly, and all eyes go to him. "I needed to make sure she was okay."

With a slight raise to her brow as she looks him up and down, Ava nods her head—his answer must be enough of an explanation for her even though it confuses the hell out of me.

He knocked down the door when he heard me scream?

He makes it sound so simple, as if it doesn't make my insides feel warm.

"So it's you who gets to fix it then," Ava says, and it comes out as a statement rather than a question.

"Already promised to do so," Jack replies.

Ava turns to head to her bedroom, leaning in to whisper something to me as she passes. "I'm sure he did."

My cheeks heat as her bedroom door closes, leaving the three of us in the kitchen—four if you count Evee. Her hair smells like a mix of chlorine and her tangerine-scented shampoo, and her soft breath tickles the skin on my neck.

"I just need to make sure you have a fire extinguisher," Jack quickly says, breaking the silence. "Then, we'll be on our way."

"Oh, it's under the sink," I offer, and he gives me a nod.

Anderson's only a few steps away, so he leans down and checks, before standing to his full height and giving a thumbs up. "Then we're good to go," the fireman says. "Thanks for your time." He starts heading toward the front, but Jack makes no effort to move.

Jack watches me carefully, his eyes going from mine to where Evee's head rests on my shoulder, the weight of her bringing the collar of my crewneck down, revealing my collarbone.

After slowly blowing out an exaggerated breath, I hear Anderson say, "I'll just wait in the car." He stretches out the words, and, by his tone, I can tell he knows *something* is going on—even though I couldn't even begin to explain what that *something* is. He bends to grab a fire extinguisher I didn't even realize they brought in before making his escape, stepping over the door on the ground and heading outside.

A few moments pass, and the intensity of Jack's stare begins to weigh on me, making me feel too exposed, like a wide-open book, all the pages on display for anyone to see.

I feel my grip tighten around Evee, the same way it had yesterday morning when Jack was staring at me at Hey Honey's. Something about it feels very *forward*, like he is looking for parts of me I have hidden away.

"Where did you get that?" Jack finally asks, and I don't know what he's talking about at first.

I follow his gaze, looking down at my exposed skin, the raised reddish scar across the front of my shoulder to my collarbone. "It's from the accident," I answer. "The one I mentioned last night."

The scar is a constant reminder of Trevor's palm against the side of my face, my bruised knuckles squeezing the wheel, the contractions making my vision go blurry, the impact of my car against the tree.

"I went into labor while I was driving. It was on this dark

road in the middle of nowhere when a contraction hit. That's how I crashed."

I lift my eyes from the scar, the memories following the call to 911 still gone, aside from the one that came out of nowhere yesterday.

She needs to be okay.

I look up to find Jack has closed the distance between us, his presence warm and solid. He lifts his hand, as if to touch me again, but he lowers it after a second, his hand closing to a fist at his side.

"But you were okay?" he asks, and his voice is no louder than a rough whisper, and I swear I hear a slight tremble in his voice. "After the crash?"

I nod. "There was someone there. Someone who helped me before the ambulance got there. I can't remember them, but I just—" I close my eyes, wishing the memories would flood back to me once again, wishing I could clearly see those eyes that looked down on me and find that voice that told me I needed to be okay. "I just know."

It feels like there's more to say, like this conversation isn't over, but Evee begins to stir in my arms, and Jack slowly takes a few steps back as if his movement could wake her completely. He runs a hand through his thick, dark hair. "I'll be back to fix your door," he whispers, but his eyes are still on Evee.

"You don't have to be so quiet," I whisper back, fighting the smile threatening my lips. "She's a heavy sleeper."

His lips curl, that small smile forming on one side of his mouth, and it feels like some kind of victory that I was the one to make it come to fruition.

"Right," he says in his normal voice. "The door will close for now, but you should probably keep it locked and just go out your patio door if you have to leave at all. Does your fence have a gate you can go through?"

I nod.

"Good. I'll be back after my shift in the morning."

"Oh, no. There's no rush."

"Rumi," he says, his green eyes fixed on me. "I'm not leaving you, your daughter, or your friend with a faulty door for longer than I have to. I'll be back in the morning."

He heads for the door, walking past me, and I watch as he brings his hand to one of Evee's legs, lightly grazing his finger over her little foot covered by the onesie pajamas Ava put her in, and I honestly think I could melt into a puddle right then and there.

"It'll be too early for cookies," he adds over his shoulder, "so we'll have to save that for another time."

"You really don't have to do all this," I tell him, causing him to turn around. He leans on the wall next to him, crossing his arms over his chest, the muscles rippling with the movement causing his Northshore Fire Department T-shirt to tighten around those biceps I'll be dreaming about tonight.

"But I want to," he answers, as if it's the simplest answer in the world.

I try not to show how his answer catches me off guard, and if he notices, he doesn't let on. "Then, I'll see you tomorrow, firefighter."

Jack's eyes slightly widen, and there's a new look to them, one I haven't seen before. His eyes have reminded me of a forest since the first time I saw them, but right now, it's like that forest was set ablaze.

"Looking forward to it," he says, turning to head toward the front of the house. I follow a few steps behind him, watching as he bends to grab a few metal pieces on the floor before he picks up the door as if it weighs absolutely nothing. He puts it back where it's supposed to go, matching up the hinges and stepping outside, holding it up with one arm. "I'm going to pull this close, and I want you to lock it right behind me. Got it?"

"Got it," I reply, some unease beginning to trickle in. "Um, Jack?" I ask.

His head immediately turns toward me. "Yeah?"

"Can someone really easily break down the door?" I try to keep my voice even.

"Do you have a lock on your bedroom door?"

I nod.

"Good. Make sure it's locked. I'm gonna put the hinge pins I found back in which will secure it a little bit more for now. Where's your phone?"

I gather Evee's weight in one arm, reaching into the pocket of my sweatpants to grab my phone, holding it up to show him.

"May I?" he asks, and the politeness of him will never not be a stark contrast to his brooding, overwhelming presence.

I unlock my phone, handing it over to him. I watch as he types a number in, calling it, and hanging it up before handing it back to me.

"I want you to call me if you hear anything. I don't care what time it is. You hear something, you call me. Understand?"

My lips part, and I wouldn't be surprised if my eyes looked like they were about to pop out of my head. The concern in his eyes mixed with the authority in his voice makes my throat go dry.

"Rumi?" The way he says my name with a small smirk on his face, brings me back.

"Y-yes," I manage to stutter out.

"Atta girl," he praises, bringing a finger just under my jaw, closing my mouth for me—because I'm incapable at the moment. His eyes have a sparkle to them that brightens when he glances at Evee, his smirk deepening slightly. "I'll see you two tomorrow with your new door." He breaks his gaze from us, maneuvering the door until it shuts.

The moment it closes, an exhale escapes me, and I feel dizzy.

But not in a bad way.

I turn around, leaning back on the door to get my bearings.

What the hell is happening to me?

It feels like I was just dropped off at home after a first date.

And why does that thought not scare as much as it should?

There's a quiet knock next to my ear that startles me out of my thoughts, and I feel my phone vibrate in my hand. Looking down, I see an unknown number, but I have a feeling I know who it is.

"Forget something, firefighter?" Maybe it's the door between us and the fact I can't feel his eyes locked on mine, but there's a confidence brewing inside of me—one I felt last night at Lennys; one I don't want to let go of.

"I'm not leaving until you lock the door." Jack's voice is low and gruff in my ear, causing goosebumps to pebble on my skin.

A giggle escapes me, and I'm thankful he can't see the embarrassingly big grin on my face. Still balancing Evee against me and holding my phone between my ear and my shoulder, I turn toward the door, locking the doorknob and deadbolt.

"Thank you," I say into the phone, knowing he's still just on the other side of the door. I can't see him, but I know he's there.

I can't explain the feeling—I just know.

"No need, pretty girl." The term of endearment heals a crack in my heart I thought would be one of many permanent scars, and I don't remember the last time someone other than Evee or Ava made me smile this big. "Sleep tight."

CHAPTER 15
JACK

I KNEW I wasn't going to get too good of sleep at the station last night—I don't remember the last time I slept more than three or four hours or wasn't woken up by a fit of nightmares that left me breathing heavily, a sheen of sweat over my skin.

Plus, I was on call.

But last night was the first night my lack of sleep wasn't because of the past that seems to be haunting me no matter how much I try to forget it. Instead, it was because I was stuck thinking about two sets of pretty blue eyes, the smell of vanilla and orange, and a blushing smile.

My new friend is dangerous—I knew that from the second I found her behind the counter at Hey Honey's and again at the bar at Lenny's.

But it was further confirmed last night when pure chance brought us together.

Or, more accurately, a burnt tray of cookies.

I think Bennett would be laughing his ass off if I told him I was up all night thinking about a girl when I'm as emotionally available as rock, but I think he'd agree with me that there was nothing wrong with a *harmless* friendship.

A harmless friendship with a woman whose life was in my hands almost a year ago, the same woman I thought about almost every day as a way to keep my mind off my best friend, the same woman whose scream made me rush into a potential fire without a second thought—something I never thought I'd be able to do again.

But thinking that Bennett would be on my side of this masochistic decision doesn't help my case in the least bit. Not when he was as dumb as me when it came to this shit.

My 24-hour shift ended a few minutes ago—we just finished our briefing with the crew coming on for the next shift—and I'm walking out to my truck to head to the hardware store and then over Rumi's.

I wasn't kidding when I told her that I didn't want to leave her with a fucked up door longer than necessary—and I can't lie and say my lack of sleep was also from not wanting to miss if she called me.

I unlock my truck, reaching for the passenger side door to throw my stuff in, but my name rings in the air.

"Hasting!" The loud, assertive voice causes my arm to freeze midair, ripping me from my thoughts of which hardware store is the closest and needing to stop at my mom's and grab my old toolkit from the basement.

I thought I'd get lucky and make it through my shift without running into Chief Sanders, but I should've known it was too good to be true.

Reluctantly, I turn around. "Chief," I greet, adjusting my backpack strap over my shoulder, switching my weight back and forth in my work boots. I changed out of my station wear after I showered, having had time this morning for a run on the treadmill and lift at the station gym. The warm May morning is bright, the brisk breeze causing locks of my damp hair to fall over my forehead.

"How was your first shift back?" he asks, his hands on his

hips. The Northshore fire chief looks about ten years younger than his 55 years. He's tall and solid with a square jaw covered in gray and white stubble with deep-set eyes, sharp beneath a furrowed brow. His salt and pepper hair is neatly combed, and I can't help but see my future when I look at him.

Or the future I used to picture for myself.

"Good," I answer, not feeling the need to elaborate. I'm sure Anderson will give him a full run-down if he hasn't done so already. I open the truck door, throwing my backpack on the seat before closing it and leaning back against it.

"Glad to hear it," the chief says with a nod of his head. "Well, listen. Before you head out, I wanted to remind you about those therapy sessions. Have you—"

I cut him off. "Sorry, Chief. I got to go. Can this wait?"

Chief Sanders furrows his brows as he watches me carefully. Waiting for his answer gives me a feeling of unease—the way he looks me up and down, cataloguing my current state, adds to my discomfort.

"We'll talk Friday," he finally says. "My office, after the shift change briefing before you leave. Don't be late."

He turns to head back into the station, and my shoulders drop in relief as I exhale the breath I was holding.

Yes, the therapy sessions were non-negotiable when I came back, but I *just* got back. I'm not ready to walk back to that office and watch that stupid candle burn and listen to the stupid grief analogies and talk about stupid shit as if it'll actually change anything.

Therapy is for people who can't handle their own problems—I'm not about to sit in a room and cry to some stranger like that's gonna bring anyone back or change what happened.

I got through my first shift with routine calls—riding into a scene with the lights and sirens got easier as the hours ticked by, but talking won't make the threats of the panic attacks go away.

It won't make having to suit up and head straight into a fire—the job I was trained for yet can't even think about for more than five seconds without feeling like I'm having a heart attack—any less terrifying.

CHAPTER 16
RUMI

WAKING UP THIS MORNING, the scent of berries and sugar literally pulls me out of bed and toward the kitchen.

"Good morning, sleepy head," Ava sing-songs over the audiobook she has playing from her phone as I walk out of my bedroom, having just grabbed Evee from her crib next to my bed. She presses pause on her phone. "I'm making your favorite."

"What's the occasion? You haven't made me blueberry muffins since my birthday last month," I say, setting Evee down in her high chair. I can't help the yawn that escapes as I sit, having been more tired than I thought after an open-to-close shift and the *excitement* of last night as Ava called it when I filled her in after Jack left.

"Don't you think your hot firefighter will be hungry after fixing our new door?" she asks, grabbing fresh blueberries from the colander next to the mixing bowl and throwing in a few handfuls before setting some down on Evee's high chair tray. "I hope he doesn't mind the vegan version. They're definitely not as good as my original recipe," she teases—trying to get a rise out of me when I've barely opened my eyes—the raise of her brows and the too-big grin on her face gives her away. "And we learned last night that you and the oven need some distance."

"You're hilarious. Has anyone ever told you that?" I deadpan, reaching for the mixing bowl and pulling it toward me, taking over the stirring of the batter.

"I figured you deserved a treat after your night of self-care was interrupted." She sticks her finger in the batter, sweeping some off the side before giving it a taste.

I swore I was going to take the whole *masturbating in the bathtub and almost setting my house on fire* debacle to the grave, but Ava saw right through me when I said I was in the shower too long and forgot to set a timer for the cookies.

You may have fooled Jack, but you're not fooling me, she said.

"We're not talking about this anymore," I say, focusing on mixing the batter as Ava starts putting liners in the muffin tray she pulled out. "And he's not my 'hot firefighter'. He's my friend, thanks to you I should add."

"I'll tell you what, Rue. When I said I wanted you to make a friend on Tuesday, I thought it would be Drew, Mia, or even Annie. Color me impressed that it ended up being Jack of all people." I shake my head, passing the mixing bowl to her, so she can start pouring it into the tin. "And who knows where that kind of *friendship* can go," she adds.

I groan. "Please don't start this again," I complain. "I did what you asked. I made a friend. Now, leave me alone."

"Okay, okay." Ava puts her hands up in surrender. "But you can't blame me for being invested."

Before I can tell her there is nothing to be invested in, there's a knock on the front door.

Both Ava and I look toward the sound and then back at each other.

"Speak of the firefighter," she says, nodding toward the door. "Go answer it."

"You go answer it," I retort, more out of instinct than anything else. There are nerves in my belly that I didn't have a second ago, and I suddenly feel embarrassed by my oversized One Direction T-shirt and flannel pajama pants.

Another knock sounds, and Ava's eyes turn to slits. "Go," she whisper-yells. "Don't make me drag you over there."

I groan but concede, finally standing up and rounding the counter to head down the hallway to the entryway.

Taking a breath as I head to the door, I wish I could exhale the nerves away—the nerves that make my insides tickle rather than feel like my stomach is twisting around itself.

Reaching toward the lock, I turn the deadbolt first before twisting the lock on the knob.

"Rumi?" I hear through the door, the low, gruff voice muffled through the door, but it's a voice I've become quite accustomed to over the last couple of days.

"Hi," I say, my lips curving at the way he says my name, how it falls from his lips so seamlessly.

"Let me open the door, okay? Once it's out of the frame, it won't be stable, and I don't want you to get hurt."

There he goes again, saying things I thought only fictional men—or the centuries old vampires in my paranormal romances—say. "O-okay, um, go ahead," I stammer out, backing up from the door, turning over my shoulder to find Ava watching me, the blueberry muffin batter and muffin tray forgotten in front of her. Evee's watching me too, her curious eyes fixed on me, purple stains around her mouth and on her fingers from her morning snack.

Slowly, the door opens, and I see a large hand reach around the frame, pushing it slowly before grabbing on and lifting it to maneuver it and take it outside, setting it against the house.

Then, I see him.

Standing in my doorway, Jack's dressed in a fitted black T-shirt and dark wash jeans. His signature work boots give him another inch or two, not that he needs them, and the morning breeze causes pieces of his damp hair to fall over his forehead, the freshly washed locks having more of a curl to the ends than when it's dry.

He has a tool bag in one hand and a cardboard tray carrying two iced drinks and a small hot one in the other, the familiar Hey Honey's logo catching my eye.

"I wasn't sure what you ordered, but Luke was there and gave me your usuals," he says, and I can't help but notice how his eyes don't quite reach mine.

My heart skips a beat at the thought of this man walking into Hey Honey's and asking for help on what to order to bring over here, the thought alone meaning more to me than any tangible gift.

I'm about to say something, but he beats me to it. "And before you say I didn't have to," he says, my mouth slightly ajar, "I wanted to."

And now I'm left too stunned to speak. This man has known me for less than three days and is already challenging every preconceived notion I've had about letting new people into my life.

"You catch on quickly." A voice sounds from behind me, and I turn to find Ava who probably had enough of watching me embarrass myself, no doubt noticing that I've forgotten how to form coherent sentences, and came to save me. "Come on in," she says, putting her hands on my shoulders and moving me aside, giving Jack room to enter. "Just take off your shoes," she adds before turning to head back to the kitchen.

"Noted," Jack says, more to me than Ava, giving me a smile and stepping inside and out of his work boots, setting his tool bag down next to them.

"Um, yeah, sorry. Come on in," I say, awkwardly gesturing with my arm. The cool morning breeze coming in from our lack of front door does nothing to cool the heat that rushes to my face as I turn to follow Ava into the kitchen, Jack's heavy footsteps following close behind me.

"You're just in time to supervise Rumi with the oven," Ava jokes as she puts the muffin tray in, closing the oven.

I let out a sigh. "One time, I forget to set a timer."

"Don't worry, Rue. I'm sure your mind was a little *occupied*—"

"Jack," I interrupt her, turning to our guest. "Thanks for coming by," I rush out, finding my voice quickly, so Ava can't embarrass me more.

"It's the least I can do," he says, pulling one of the iced drinks out of the tray and sliding it to where Ava is standing by the counter. "Luke said you do a cold brew with honey and cream?"

"If I didn't know any better, I'd think you were trying to impress me, Jack," Ava says, taking a sip of her coffee, more truth to her words than the lightness of her voice leads on to. While Ava has been teasing me about Jack since I got out of bed this morning—or more accurately, since I went to bed last night—she's gathering her own read on him.

She may not show it, but Ava is as apprehensive as I am when it comes to meeting new people, especially men. Because of her own history with abuse, she knows the signs and red flags as well as the charm and manipulation that often covers them up at first.

And she almost *always* keeps them at arm's length.

"Just trying to correct my horrible first impression," he says with a shrug, not missing a beat, and I can tell by the look on Ava's face that it was the right answer. Jack turns to look at me, passing me the other iced drink. "And an iced dirty chai with almond milk for you," he says before asking, "is that right? Luke had to explain to me what it meant to make a chai 'dirty'."

"It's right," I answer with a chuckle, and I swear I can see his shoulders slightly relax. "Thank you." I take a sip, and it's the perfect blend of creaminess and spice with a hint of espresso.

"And most importantly," he begins, pulling the small hot drink out of the tray, "a warm milk for Evee."

At first, I don't think I heard him right. It must show on my face because his face immediately shifts to a look of concern, like he did something wrong. "Is that okay?" he asks. "Should I have gotten her something else?"

"You got a drink for Evee?" I ask, and I can feel Ava watching this exchange like her favorite TV show.

Jack nods. "Is that okay with you?"

"Oh, yes. No, of course it's okay. I just thought—" I pause, looking at how tiny the cup looks in his big hands, the signature Hey Honey's blue stark against his tan skin. "I just assumed that was your drink."

He looks at the cup in his hands, and his brow raises. He looks back at me. "I don't drink coffee."

"We serve other drinks besides coffee," I offer, walking over to the sink to grab a paper towel, wetting it a little bit before walking over to Evee's high chair to wipe off her face and hands.

"Until Luke starts serving energy drinks, I'll stick to just doing the coffee runs." He walks over to the high chair where Evee is now half-eating and half-playing with the dry cereal Ava must have poured on her tray for her when I answered the door. He looks to me as if seeking permission.

"The milk should be cooled enough for her to drink, but here," I say, holding out my hand for him to hand me the cup. "I usually check by pouring a little out on the inside of my wrist, just in case." I tilt the cup carefully, showing him. He watches intently as if absorbing all of my movements. I feel the warm milk on my skin, and it's the perfect temperature.

I bring my wrist to my mouth, licking off the few drops of milk.

Looking up, I find Jack's eyes still on me, but there's a new darkness to his gaze, one that warms my cheeks—but not in embarrassment.

Evee slaps her hands on her high chair tray, reminding me of where we are and what we're doing—testing milk temperature for my daughter in the middle of my kitchen—so I hold the cup out to Jack. "Here," I say quickly—maybe a little *too* quickly if Ava's snort is anything to go by. "It's perfect, and the lids for the hot cups are pretty sturdy." The words string together in such a jumbled mess, I wouldn't be surprised if he couldn't tell what I said.

With my arm held out to him, holding the cup, Jack seems to come back to himself, remembering our audience. He reaches out, but he doesn't say anything.

"You can give it to her," I reassure as he takes the cup from me, and his features go back to how they were before—the moment between us over just as quickly as it began.

Watching Jack now, that slight discomfort is back, like he doesn't exactly know what to do. He carefully sets the coffee cup of milk on the tray, but he doesn't let go.

With something new in front of her, Evee looks up to see who the source is. Her big blue eyes are wide, her mouth open, putting her two front teeth on full display. She looks down back at the cup, but instead of trying to grab it, she grabs Jack's hand, her fingers wrapping around two of his before bouncing her arms like he's her new toy.

"I should've warned you that she's an extrovert—no idea where she got that from," I say with a laugh. Evee has always been a happy baby who welcomes new people with a smile on her face. She's such a curious girl, and she never fails to make a new friend wherever we go—whether it's waving to everyone she sees at the grocery store, or giving that mostly-toothless grin to the regulars at Hey Honey's who come in more for her than the coffee. She's nothing like her introverted mother.

"Probably me," Ava says, grabbing her coffee. "Now, if you two would excuse me, I am headed to my workout class. With Jack's help, I trust that you can handle the muffins without setting our house on fire."

I narrow my eyes at my best friend as she walks backwards down the hallway to put her sneakers on.

"Love you, bye!" she says with a wave, stepping into her shoes and heading straight out the front where our door is supposed to be. "Bye, Jack!" she adds.

Jack's head snaps up in her direction, as if hearing her yell his name brought him out of a daze he was in. "Bye, Ava," he says, giving her a small nod before his gaze goes back down to Evee who has started putting her spit-covered, no-longer-dry cereal in his hand.

"Oh, I'm sorry," I say, readying to grab Evee's wrist and wipe off her hands.

"I don't mind," he says, looking at me. "I'm fine here."

I want to clarify that he doesn't need to be polite and stand there as my daughter puts cereal in her mouth before putting it in his opened hand, but watching him watch her is enough to keep me quiet. I lean back on the counter behind me, taking a sip of my chai.

We both stand there watching her for a few moments, the silence comfortable rather than awkward or loaded. "She likes you," I say, remembering how she also instantly grabbed his hand that night at Lenny's.

"I'm not good with babies," he admits, his eyes still on Evee, a look of awe lining his features as he watches her finally let go of his hand, remembering the cup he sat down in front of her and grabbing it with both hands. The way he's so timid around her is such a difference to the strong presence he carries.

"Well, you could've fooled me," I say, and I don't think I'll ever get him looking down at her out of my head—the image going straight to my ovaries.

Jack's green eyes find mine, and there's something familiar about them. Maybe it's because I've seen them a lot these last few days, or maybe it's because I can't help but think of them long after he's gone, but I don't think I'll get sick of looking at them.

He holds up his hand. "I'm just gonna rinse the cereal off."

I slide over from where I'm leaning on the counter, giving him a clear path to the sink. "You know," I start, "she doesn't share her cereal with just anyone."

"I'm honored to be one of the few," he says, turning on the sink and letting the water wash off the cereal remnants.

I take another sip of my iced chai. "You don't remember spending time with your sister as a baby?" I ask, not sure exactly where the question comes from, but there's something about how nervous he is around Evee that makes me want to make him feel more comfortable.

"I was eight when she was born, and I tried to pretend she didn't exist when they brought her home because I wanted a baby brother, not a sister," he explains, turning off the sink and drying his hands on the towel hanging on the oven. "I probably held her a few times, but I don't really remember."

I nod, thinking of more questions to ask, so I can keep listening to his voice. "Is she your only sibling?"

"Yeah, it's just me and Emerson," he answers, leaning back on the counter next to me, matching my pose. "What about you? Any brothers or sisters?" He looks down at me, his gaze going from my eyes to my lips so quickly, I think I imagined it.

I shake my head, not only to answer his question but to shake away the ridiculous thought. "Just me."

"Did you grow up around here?" he asks, keeping the conversation going. I know he's here to fix the door, but I can't ignore the butterflies in my belly at the thought of him wanting to get to know me, the same way I want to get to know him.

As a friend, I remind myself.

"No, I'm originally from Minneapolis," I say. "I moved here last year after my accident."

He says something else, but it doesn't register. I'm too busy watching his hands come to the top of the counter behind him, causing his muscles to strain against his T-shirt. I can't help the way my eyes move down his arms to where his hands hold the edge.

"Rumi?" I hear, and I shake my head again before looking back up at him.

"Sorry, what did you say?" I find a knowing smirk on his face, but I'm thankful he doesn't comment on the way I was just drooling over his arms like a dog.

"I asked what brought you here," he reiterates.

"It's a funny story actually, " I say, a dry laugh escaping. "Funny" is a relative term—a more appropriate descriptor of the story would be depressing, so I make sure to leave some of the more personal details out. "One of my nurses from the accident was actually Ava's younger sister who lives an hour north from here. She's the one who introduced me to Ava who was looking for a roommate."

"You and Ava have only known each other for a year?" Jack asks, and I can't help but notice the surprise in his tone.

"Yeah, Evee and I moved here after staying at the hospital for a few weeks to recover from the injuries from the accident and bef—" I stop myself, not wanting the conversation to go in that direction.

At the thought of "before", what pushed me to finally leave, it's like all the air in my lungs is stolen, like I was punched in the stomach.

My mind revisits that night every so often, how different it was from nights before, how it finally showed me I had to get out of that house.

It's not that I'm ashamed of my past, but there are parts of it that are hard to admit, especially to someone I'm only starting to get to know. I'm not ready to share those chapters of my story.

Yet.

But the way Jack listens to me, it feels like I've known him much longer than a few days—like he knows parts of me that I don't always show at first.

Or even ever.

It's exciting yet confusing the way his attention makes me feel like I'm basking in the sun rather than hiding in the shade.

Ava always would remind me how not everyone—specifically every man—out there is like my father or Trevor, but I haven't let myself really get to know anyone to see if she was right.

And here's Jack, someone so kind and thoughtful, someone my daughter took an instant liking to, someone who makes me comfortable to be myself rather than the version I think he wants me to be.

Maybe Ava was right.

But maybe it's too soon to tell.

I can't let what happened with Trevor happen again.

"My injuries from the accident," I say before quickly adding, "living, working, and basically raising a newborn together brought us together super fast. I feel like I've known her my whole life."

If Jack caught on to my slight slip-up with my story or where my mind went for a brief moment, he doesn't show it. Instead, he affirms, "I'm glad you had someone there for you after your accident." There's a softness to his eyes as he says it. He watches me carefully, his eyes roaming my face for a moment, and I stay silent, waiting to see what he says—or does—next.

Then I hear the sound of an empty cardboard cup hitting the floor and my daughter half-crying half-wailing. It's the sound she makes since she can't say, *I want to get out of this stupid chair, Mom.*

"I better get to that door," Jack quickly says, turning and heading toward the front of the house at the same time I say, "Sorry!"

I pick up Evee, holding her in my arms, reality settling back in.

CHAPTER 17
JACK

A SHARP, piercing tone blares through the station's speakers, jolting me awake.

I dozed off reading the last few chapters of the book I picked up on my first shift back two days ago. The paperback flies to the ground from where it was laying on my chest, my body jackknifing up at the alert.

All around me, an urgent yet controlled chaos erupts—boots thumping against the hardwood of the stations living quarters; all the guys making their way downstairs where we keep our gear in the garage as a computerized voice rapidly dispatches the unit number, location, and type of emergency we're heading into.

Please be a routine call. Please be a routine call.

I close my eyes, waiting for the voice to repeat the type of emergency as I stand up from the lounge chair, following the nine other guys downstairs, my book and reading glasses forgotten on the floor behind me.

"Attention Engine 12, Tanker 4, Ladder 3 – respond to a structure fire, possible barn fully involved. Address: 4597 County Road 12. Caller reports visible flames and livestock on site. Time out: 03:17."

My vision goes blurry, and it takes everything in me to make it down the last three stairs, tripping over my own feet as I step onto the concrete floor of the garage, the rest of the crew in different stages of suiting up.

Muscle memory and adrenaline take over, my body taking me to my locker. Opening the metal door, my gear stares back at me—gear I haven't put on in over 18 months, not since the night my best friend was suiting up next to me.

The night he died.

I got through my first shift earlier this week without an emergency call involving a fire, but my luck seems to have run out.

I look to my left where Bennett's locker is—*was*—and I can't fight the urge to open it, wishing to find a piece of him where it's supposed to be.

"Get going, Hasting!" someone yells, but I don't turn around to see who.

I open Bennett's locker, finding it empty.

No gear, no helmet, no picture of him, Luke, and their older brother, Caleb, taped to the inside, no stash of gummy bears that he hid in there because he said someone at the station was stealing them.

Empty.

"What's wrong, Hasting? Why aren't you in your gear?" Anderson comes into view, his brown eyes give me something to focus on, my vision clearing, but I can barely hear him over the pounding in my ears and the sound of the engine of the fire truck turning over.

I shake my head. "I'm going. Just give me a fucking second."

Anderson puts a hand on my shoulder, and it takes everything in me not to shove it off. "We keep it empty, as a sign of respect."

He doesn't have to say more. His words are enough.

I blow out a breath as Anderson gives me a nod before he puts his helmet on and turns to head toward the truck.

I let muscle memory take over again, closing Bennett's locker and facing mine, gearing up like I've done hundreds of times before, but the first time since being back.

Kicking off my station boots, I step into my turnout boots already settled in my bunker pants, yanking them on and settling the band on my waist. I snap the suspenders into place, throwing my jacket over my station T-shirt. I grab my helmet and gloves from the top shelf before closing my locker and turning to follow the rest of the crew to the truck.

Lights and sirens blaring, we speed toward the scene. The wind coming through the window is cool against my skin as I scan the streets, watching as the city lights fade and get replaced by open fields. The heat from the truck's interior mixes with the rising tension in my chest, every bump in the road a reminder of the potential danger that lies ahead.

The rest of the crew prepares, focused and silent, their faces set with resolve as we listen for any updates over the truck's radio and listen to any orders from our station's Fire Lieutenant.

As the truck approaches the scene, I can see a bright orange blaze in the distance, getting larger and larger as we get closer. The faint smell of smoke hits me softly at first, and then it punches through me. I feel my chest tighten, and my palms are slick beneath my gloves.

I grip my helmet hard enough to hear the plastic protest as the truck comes to a stop, the crew all filing out without a hint of hesitation, as if they don't care what they're running straight into—doing exactly what we were trained to do.

Once again, my body takes over, falling in line with the rest of my crew. I hop out of the truck, ready to listen to our Fire Lieutenant give the orders.

Putting my helmet on, I try to focus on his raised voice, but once I see the barn, I can't tear my eyes away. The structure is consumed by a towering inferno, flames licking the sky as thick black smoke billows out, darkening the horizon. The wood crackles and groans under the heat, and it's seconds away from collapsing.

No. Bennett's in there.

If that roof collapses, he's dead.

Someone has to get him out of there.

I have to get him out of there.

But I can't.

My feet won't move.

Even as the rest of the crew begin working in tandem on their assigned roles—assessing the situation by identifying hazards, determining the fire's origin and size, evaluating any potential risks to people, property, or the environment, gathering the necessary equipment—I'm stuck.

Frozen in place.

Left to watch as my best friend gets killed by the very thing we are trained to fight.

"Hasting!" Someone calls my name, but the ringing in my ears is too loud. I watch as the roof of the barn crashes to the ground, flames expanding and shooting up in the dark sky, but I can't even scream.

It feels like every bone—every muscle—in my body has turned to ice despite the sweat coating my skin.

It feels like the slightest touch will shatter me.

My chest rises and falls in quick successions, my lungs feeling like they could explode at any moment from the lack of oxygen and the heavy smoke.

"Hasting!" I think I hear my name again, but I can't be sure. It sounds like Anderson, but it could be someone else.

I watch as they bring over the hoses, the water drowning the fire, and, in a matter of minutes, it's like it was never there —the orange hue disappearing, leaving us all with only the lights from the truck and the stars overhead.

I don't know how long I stand there, and I don't know how I make it back to the truck.

It isn't until I'm standing in the station's garage, alone and still in my gear, that I fall to my knees.

————

At some point, I make it back to the station's living quarters, finding my forgotten paperback and reading glasses put on the side table, someone having picked them up from the floor.

The station was quiet when I finally made it up there, the crew thankfully letting me do it on my own, leaving me to wallow in my own self-pity and embarrassment of what the fuck I let happen to myself tonight.

I don't think I slept more than an hour, and I can feel the lack of sleep in every inch of my body during the shift change briefing, barely being able to stand without feeling my eyes droop close and my body swaying to the side.

After last night, the last thing I want to do is linger around the station.

What I need right now is to grab my shit, hit the gym and tire myself out even more, so I can sleep hard enough to avoid the nightmares.

I'm almost to my truck, when I hear my last name being shouted behind me.

The sense of deja vu hits me instantly, along with the realization that I forgot I was supposed to meet the chief in his office after this morning's briefing.

"Hasting!" Chief Sanders shouts again, and I let my head fall back, my eyes closing. Annoyance floods through me, my irritation seconds away from boiling into anger.

I turn and find the chief only a few steps behind me.

"We need to talk," he says curtly when he closes the distance between us.

He didn't come with us on the call last night, having left

the responsibility of leadership in the hands of our Fire Lieutenant, but I'm sure he read the reports early this morning.

"About?" I ask. I never thought I'd be actually hoping to discuss these goddamn therapy sessions, but right now? I'd talk about them for hours to avoid even just a few minutes discussing what happened to me out in the field.

"Have you scheduled your therapy sessions?" Chief Sanders crosses his arms over his chest, his feet wide. He's in cargo pants and a Northshore Fire Department collared shirt. His eyes are fixed on me as he waits for my answer.

"Not yet." The words sound too clipped. "I was planning on doing it today," I lie, softening my voice to avoid a reprimand.

Chief Sanders nods, and his assessment of me makes my skin feel prickly.

"You agreed to weekly sessions," he reminds me, as if I could forget. Between the chief, my mom, and my sister asking me and reminding me about these sessions, it's starting to feel like it would be easier to just go rather than explain to them how they're fucking pointless. "The therapist is available this morning if you want to get started today."

"I don't," I retort, and it comes off harsher than I intend. "I'll give the office a call and set something up for one of my days off next week."

Chief Sanders rolls his lips together, taking a step closer to me. "I have a hard time believing that, son."

"If you're not going to listen to what I say then I don't know what to tell you."

"Anderson told me what happened on last night's call."

I try to hide my reaction to his words, but I can feel the blood rush up to my neck, both in frustration and embarrassment. "You can tell Anderson to mind his fucking business. I don't need a babysitter, Chief." I can't fight the anger rising in my tone, the same anger that is always the first to surface. Anger has always been the easiest to feel—about Bennett, about what happened, and about everything that's followed, including how angry I am at myself for letting something like freezing on the field happen. "I said I'll go to the therapy session, so I'll go. But we're not going to stand out here and talk about what happened."

"And what *did* happen, Hasting? Because from what I understand, you froze. You saw the fire—the manageable, controlled fire with no victims—and you froze."

"I didn't freeze. I—" The words die on my tongue, his question like a bullet shooting right through my chest.

I've seen more fires like the one last night than I can count —fires that were much more dangerous and much harder to manage—but the smell of burning wood, the smothering heat, the crackling roar, the irritation in my eyes from the smoke, even though my gear, was too much.

Seeing the roof collapse, my mind tricking me—telling me that Bennett was inside.

I froze.

"Can you get through that hard head of yours how *dangerous* that is?" The chief's voice hard, but I'm too angry to let his question sink in.

"How many goddamn times do I have to tell you I'm fine?" I grit through my teeth.

"Watch it, Jack," Chief warns, voice low. His tone may sound calm to an outsider, but I know this man well enough to know that I'm toeing very close to a line with my attitude, and he accepts nothing but respect from all of us at the station. "I know you've been through a lot. Hell, I can't imagine how much it hurts to be back here without Bennett, but I refuse to let you keep acting like it doesn't."

My jaw ticks, and I feel a burning behind my eyes. "This isn't about Bennett." But I can't look him in the eye when I say it. Staring at the ground in front of me, my eyes fixate on Chief Sanders' boots.

I don't want to see his face as he tells me everything I don't want to hear.

"You can pretend all you want that you're fine, but you and I both know that all you've done is avoid dealing with what happened and bury everything that comes with it." I feel a hand on my shoulder, and I instantly shrug it off—as if on reflex—but Chief Sanders grips me harder. "I'm sorry Bennett is gone, Jack. His loss wasn't easy for any of us— myself included. Losing one of my people has changed the way I look at this job. Hell, it's changed the way I've looked at my life." He pauses, inhaling and exhaling. "All of that to say, you and I both know he wouldn't want his death weighing on you the way that it is. It's time you talk about it with someone who can help."

I shake my head as the anger fades into what I haven't felt since that night he died—pure agony. A sadness so guttural and so overpowering that I wouldn't wish it on my worst enemy. A raw, aching emptiness so visceral that it steals all the breath from lungs.

"I can't," I grit out. "It'll kill me."

"No, Jack," Chief says. "*This* will." And something in my chest cracks.

Chief Sanders has been the father I never had, the man who I strived to be like from the moment I joined the fire academy, and he was one of my teachers. He's been a mentor, coach, and role model for over a decade, and I should've known that the lies I've been telling myself over the last year and a half don't stand a chance against him.

My shoulders tremble as I try to keep them still, but it suddenly feels so tiresome to stop the inevitable. My knees buckle, and I let myself sink to the ground beside my truck. Tears break free—slow at first, then relentless—slipping down my face in silence, my jaw clenched against the sobs that want to escape.

I can't remember the last time I cried.

The night Bennett died ,and his funeral, I was too numb, having removed myself from my own feelings, shutting them away in the back of my mind, only ever allowing them to escape in pieces.

Now, it's like the lock on that box busted open, and everything is rushing to the surface, faster than I can stop it.

Like a fire I don't stand a chance against.

Chief Sanders doesn't say anything, but I feel his presence standing just a few steps away from where I'm on the ground. He takes a knee and places a hand on my shoulder. With my head in my hands and the comfort of Chief's hold on me, I let all these feelings overwhelm me after months of pushing them down.

I don't know how much time passes, but my lungs start to fill more, and I can take in a full breath. As I open my eyes, lifting my head from my hands, the sunlight makes my eyes burn, and there's a tightness in my temples.

I expect to feel the usual tension in my shoulders as I sit up straight, gathering myself, but it feels lighter. I'm not weighed down as much as I'm used to, and it makes it easier to stand. I meet the chief's gaze and am relieved to not find pity in his eyes as he observes me.

"I wish I could say this was the hard part," Chief says before giving my shoulder another squeeze then rising back to his feet. I follow suit as he continues, "but this is just the beginning."

Not sure what to say, I nod.

I wish I could say that along with feeling lighter, I feel better. But I don't.

If anything, since now all the emotions have come to the surface with no intent of letting me bury them back down, I feel even worse.

My neck heats at the thought of the chief seeing me like this. I wipe my reddened eyes with the back of my hand, shaking my head and putting my hands on my hips.

I blow out a breath. "I'm—" I begin to say but stop myself. He and I both know that I'm not fine. If anything, I'm finally experiencing the feelings from the night of Bennett's death.

"You'll *be* fine," Chief finishes for me. "Eventually."

I cough into my fist, clearing my throat. "It sure as fuck doesn't feel like it," I admit.

"It's like I told you last year. You have to confront what you lost. No more running away."

A few moments pass as I let his words sink in. Up until today, I thought the only way to heal was to move on or least move forward. I knew I'd never recover from losing Bennett. I knew I'd never be able to accept it.

But now? I can't live like this.

The past few days being home have given me glimpses of what life can be like—shooting the shit with the crew at the station, getting a drink at the bar with friends, having dinner with my mom and sister.

Flirting with my new friend.

But they're just moments—moments that never last long enough.

That's all I'll be allowed to have if this continues.

And I can't live with just moments of peace that cease the second my grief sneaks up on me or when it finally becomes too much to recover from.

"I promise I'll call the therapist today," I finally say, and, this time, it doesn't feel like a lie.

Chief gives me a small smile. "I think that's a good start." He reaches out his hand, and I take it. We shake hands, solidifying my promise. "And we're going to go forward with that fit-for-duty evaluation."

With his hand still holding mine, his grip tightens, and I resist the urge to argue with him.

We both know I'm not fine.

I nod, and the chief pulls me in for a hug, his arms tight

around me for a brief moment before he lets go and turns to head back into the station.

I turn to get into my truck when he calls after me again. "And son, remember. Those emotions you're feeling? They don't make you weak. They make you human. This grief for Bennett is that love you have for him not having anywhere to go. It's proof that you're here. You're alive—*living*. Just like he'd want you to be doing."

This time last year, I couldn't fathom being anywhere but the cabin or on the lake—the only peace I could find.

Today, I want to be better.

I know that peace is here somewhere—I saw glimpses of it in Rumi's eyes.

CHAPTER 18
JACK

IN A BLINK OF AN EYE, my first three weeks being back home have passed me by, and it already feels like I never left Milwaukee in the first place, like I wasn't gone for those eighteen months.

Between my shift rotations, therapy sessions, spending time with my mom, hanging out with Emerson, catching up with Luke, and moving into my new place, the time has gotten away from me.

And waking up this morning, I feel a little lighter than I did yesterday.

A pattern that started up a few days ago—one I hope doesn't go away.

Since my humbling breakdown in the parking lot at the station with the chief after my even *more* humbling panic attack in the field, I've started therapy.

I've been going twice a week since the day I promised Chief Sanders I would call.

It's been hell, to say the least, but I'm still alive—I honestly didn't think I would make it through talking about Bennett, but now that I've started, it's like I can't stop.

My first session, we didn't even talk about the night he

died. To be honest, in the last six sessions, that hasn't even come up. We've spent a lot of time talking about who Bennett was and the friendship we had. I didn't realize how much I've avoided thinking about all the good, happy memories from the last thirty years because I've been too stuck on moving on.

And I didn't flip the table when I heard the stupid fire/grief analogy—turns out, it makes more sense to me than any of the other shit Dr. Ramos has said about grief suppression, post-traumatic stress, and emotional avoidance and its ties to toxic masculinity.

"This is the last time I move these damn boxes," Emerson says, coming up the stairs of our mom's basement with a cardboard box of my things, setting it down on the hardwood floor.

"I second that," Luke echos from where he's waiting by the front door, ready to take the box to my truck.

"As far as I know, this is my last move for a very long time," I tell them.

The property my mom's neighbor was looking to sell ended up being a deal I couldn't pass up. Having money saved up from living with Bennett the last couple of years, I put in an offer Mr. Lenard couldn't say no to.

"Where's this place again?" Emerson asks, pushing the box with her foot toward me.

"About ten minutes from here. Down the street from the station," I answer, picking up the box and walking it over to Luke.

"That's not too far from me," Luke says as I hand him the box. "Your apartment with Ben was so much further, so I didn't get to see you guys that often." He looks over my shoulder to Emerson. "Any more boxes?" he asks her, and the way he goes from talking about his brother to something else so naturally hits me right in the chest.

While my therapy sessions have allowed me to think of

Bennett without feeling the need to bang my head against the wall to stop my thoughts from spiraling so tightly that I can't see straight, I'm still caught off-guard by how casually Luke can bring him up in conversation.

Aside from my therapist, I still can't bring myself to talk about Bennett with anyone.

"That was the last one," she answers, wiping her tattooed forearm across her forehead, her cheeks pink from going up and down the stairs with all the boxes. Luke gives her a nod, heading out to my truck.

My sister looks at me. "I gotta admit, I'm surprised you're putting down roots."

"Thought I'd take off again?" I've thought a lot about our conversation at the dinner table my first day back, and it's one of the many things my therapist likes to revisit at our sessions, in between talking about Bennett or strategies to handle the panic attacks that surface when I have to go into the field.

We haven't been called to many fires over the last three weeks, and the ones we have were controlled with no danger to anyone in the vicinity.

I've yet to freeze up like I did that night of the barn fire, and Chief Sanders put me on exposure protection—protecting nearby buildings from catching fire by cooling them with water—which allows me some distance when we get called to fires.

"So you admit that you ran when you went to Grandpa's cabin?" Her hair is pulled back in a bandana aside from her bangs, all her tattoos on her arms, neck, and chest on display in her black tank top. "I never thought I'd hear you own up to it."

I shrug. "I admit that I needed space to process it all, but I can also admit that I didn't do much processing while I was up there."

"And what about now? You're processing?" she asks.

Even though she's my younger sister, Emerson has always been a caretaker by nature. Having had to help me take care of my mom throughout the cancer and remissions, she's learned how to care for others from a young age.

"I'm doing my best." It's the only answer I'm capable of giving right now, and it's a better one than saying "I'm fine". Even though there's a long road ahead of me when it comes to working through my grief and my own PTSD from how Bennett died, I feel like I *am* doing my best. I'm not hiding from the emotions or trying to push them down.

Granted, staying busy helps, along with the early morning workouts and long work days that help me sleep through the night.

Emerson nods. "So the therapy seems to be working?" She rolls her lips together as she fights a knowing smirk—one that has *I told you so* written all over it.

"Shut up."

"I didn't say anything." The smirk now in no way hidden but on full display. "I'm just happy to see you like this."

"Like what?" I ask.

"Like yourself. I know losing Bennett felt like losing part of who you are, but he wouldn't want his death to take all of you away from the rest of us."

Emotion clogs my throat.

Emerson isn't one to get sentimental—she's not afraid to tell it like it is, but I think she learned early in life to tamp down her emotions, especially when she knew my mom didn't like to see her upset throughout her cancer fight.

Conversations with her like these always go straight to my heart, knowing that talking about feelings and emotions isn't the easiest for her either, both of us having our own resistance to it for differing reasons.

I take a step toward my sister. Words fail me, so I grab her arm, pulling her into a hug—one she takes a second to reciprocate, but after a moment, I feel her arms wrap around my waist.

"Now," she says, pushing away from me and adjusting the bandana in her hair, "you owe me coffee. I didn't move all your shit a second time to not get compensated for my hard work."

I shake my head, fighting my own smile.

"Once again, I second that. And I know a really awesome place," I hear Luke say behind me, coming in through the front door. "It's on the way."

"Oh, and I bet your new *friend* is working today," Emerson teases before turning to Luke. "Is Rumi working today, Luke?"

Luke and Emerson exchange a look that has too much scheming for my taste, but I choose to ignore it and not engage with their antics.

It's been three weeks since I saw Rumi—not that I haven't thought about her, seeing as though she's been a constant in my mind since the moment I saw her again.

But today does seem like a great day to rectify that.

"Why, yes, Emmy. I do believe Rumi is on the schedule for this morning," Luke says, his tone way too exaggerated for my taste.

"Stop being fucking weird," I say to the both of them. "I barely know the girl." The words leave a bad taste in my mouth, but I don't want Luke or Emerson thinking anything is going to happen between Rumi and me. I have my own shit to deal with, and I don't want her anywhere near it. She has her own life—her own daughter—to be concerned about, not my bullshit.

"But you want to," Luke sing-songs, and I want to punch the grin off his stupid face. Both Emerson and Luke know about the burnt cookies fiasco as well as my morning fixing Rumi and Ava's door, but I kept the stories short and to the point, leaving out details that could cause them to act like *this*.

Not that there are any details that are worth discussing.

"She really is a great girl," Luke adds. "A resilient little thing too. I don't know all the details, but I know she hasn't had it easy."

I nod my head, feigning indifference as he talks about Rumi—on the inside, a swell of possessiveness overwhelms me at the thought of someone else knowing her better than me. It's a completely moronic and inappropriate feeling sweeping through me—especially considering Luke is my friend and her boss. It makes me clench my fists at my sides, quickly putting my arms around my back before Luke or Emerson can notice.

I don't know how much Luke knows about Rumi's accident, but I know neither him, nor Emerson, know about my involvement with it, or that I was on my way home when I came across it.

As far as everyone knows, I never even thought about coming back before I did.

Which also means that neither of them know that tomorrow marks one year since that night.

"I heard it's her daughter's birthday tomorrow," I hear Emerson say, and I have to school my features to hide my surprise that she knows that. I must not do it fast enough because she adds, "I was at Hey Honey's last week, and the red-head—"

"Ava," I interject. Emerson eyes me wearily, and I feel Luke's eyes on me too, but I ignore both their looks. "Her name is Ava."

"Right," she says, stretching out the word. "*Ava* said they were planning a birthday party for her at the end of the month."

I nod, still feeling their eyes on me. "Cool," I say, and even *I* can hear how hard I'm trying to stay impassive to all of this. "Anyway, we have a coffee run to do. Let's go, kids," I quickly add, walking past the two of them out to my truck.

"Eager now, are we, Jacky?" Emerson says from behind me, and I can hear Luke snort.

"Are you riding with me or Luke?" I ask her, not bothering to turn around, knowing she's just a step behind me.

"I think I'll go with Luke," Emerson answers, and I know both of them way too well to know what they'll be talking about as they drive behind me.

I nod my acknowledgement, rounding my truck, and getting into the driver's seat. The two of them walk across the street to where Luke's car is parked, loaded with some boxes that didn't fit in my truck, and their heads turn toward each other, suspiciously wide smiles on their faces.

I would never admit it to them, but Rumi has that effect on me too.

A smile graces my lips at the thought of possibly seeing her today.

Pulling my truck into an open spot after the short drive to Hey Honey's, I cut the engine and step into the warm May afternoon. Emerson and Luke are already waiting for me, having been right behind me on the drive over.

Walking through the parking lot, I can feel the two of them buzzing with misplaced excitement as they follow a few steps behind me—as if watching me buy their coffee is the highlight of their week.

I know they are just interested to see who I'm buying said coffee from.

My schedule hasn't left much time for more of our accidental run-ins since the morning I fixed her door, and, even though I have her number, I couldn't think of a reason to text her.

I left her house that day with a blueberry muffin and a smile on my face but completely forgot to come up with some sort of excuse to see her again.

I'll never forget how surprised Rumi was when I brought

her chai, Ava's coffee, and Evee's milk. She looked at me as if I had given her the world, not a six dollar drink.

And I'd do it again and again, anything to make her happy—the same way I knew I would for Evee when I felt her little fingers wrap around mine, looking down at her big blue eyes.

I felt Rumi watching me as I watched Evee, but I was too mesmerized by the little girl to think much of it. It was the first time I understood why parents just stare at their kid, even if they're doing absolutely nothing. Evee was playing with cereal, putting it in her mouth and then in my hand; I would've stood there all day if she wanted me to.

There's this innate part of me that feels like I *know* Rumi—like she and I spent time getting to know each other in another life—but there's so much about who she is that is still unknown to me. I've caught glimpses—taking anything and everything she'll give me—but I want the whole picture. Who she was, who she is, and who she wants to be.

And I can't forget Evee, or the way her big blue eyes can bring me to my knees with a single blink of those long lashes.

Between the two of them, I can't help but want to grow this friendship, especially as I start to feel more like myself.

And I still need to know what the fuck she was doing driving the night of the accident.

We're almost at the door when I stop, needing to take a second to think about what I'm going to say to her. I don't want to freak her out like I did the first time I barged into the coffee shop when she was working, and I hope she's thought about me at least a quarter of how much I've thought of her these last three weeks.

This connection—this pull—between us can't just be in my head.

I hear Luke and Emerson ask what I'm doing, but I ignore them, wiping my sweaty palms on my jeans before looking down at my black T-shirt, making sure it's clean.

I feel like I'm a teenager again, unsure of myself and how to properly talk to a pretty girl. I shake my head, feeling embarrassed at the thought.

I'm just here to buy Luke and Emerson coffee and say hello. Maybe ask her how her day is, or what she ended up deciding to do for Evee's birthday. I could ask her what she's doing after her shift this morning, or when she wants me to rectify her burnt cookie fiasco like I promised that night.

This isn't life or death—there's no fire threatening the lives of people I love; there's no emergency that needs me; no distressing call that needs answering.

This is Rumi.

My friend.

"Did you forget how to walk, dummy?" Emerson steps around me, walking toward the door and pulling it open, letting herself in.

"What's wrong, man?" Luke puts a hand on my shoulder. "You okay?"

"Yeah," I answer, but my throat feels dry. I cough into my fist and keep walking.

When I follow Emerson into Hey Honey's, the sharp scent of espresso hits me. There's a hum from the grinders and soft music, and the place is filled with different voices. There's a couple seated at the table by the windows, a group of girls sitting around the round table, and a few people waiting by the end counter for their drink to be called.

It's not too busy, which means I won't be interrupting Rumi in the middle of a rush. My eyes roam the space, immediately landing on her. She's at the register, talking to my sister, as Ava makes drinks behind the counter.

Luke walks past me, waving to a few patrons who recognize him and heading to where the girls are. I watch as Rumi's eyes go from Emerson to him, her lips curved in a small smile, the sunlight from the windows caught in her dark hair.

She's in her usual work attire—a white long sleeved shirt under a black apron. Today, her hair is down, tucked behind her ears rather than braided.

She hasn't noticed me yet, and I take advantage of the opportunity to look at her—notice parts of her I haven't before. There is something so gentle about her, something inherently warm, and though I make no effort to move my feet, some part of me seems to lean closer like my body craves the peace I find when she's near.

Finally, she sees me, and I know I don't imagine that flush on her cheeks, that shyness always being what she shows me first.

She gives me a small wave, her bottom lip going between her teeth in an effort to contain a smile, and I lift my hand in a wave back.

Emerson must say something to her because her attention goes back to my sister, so I close the space between me and the counter.

Up close, I can see the soft freckles that dust Rumi's skin, her long lashes framing those eyes I've thought *way* too much about, her full, dusty pink lips.

She really is beautiful.

And I don't think she has a clue how much so.

Rumi turns to me and says something, but I don't hear it —only see the movement of those lips. Emerson bumps me, breaking me out of my trance.

"Sorry, what did you say?" I ask Rumi.

She lets out a little giggle. "Anything for you?"

"Just the coffees for these two," I say, pointing between Emerson next to me and Luke next to Rumi behind the counter.

She nods, looking down to tap on the iPad in front of her.

"While we're here, I'm going to place that order for more of the seasonal syrups, so we're stocked for the summer." Luke turns to the back office.

"Oh, Evee's napping in the office," Rumi quickly says, her voice slightly panicked, as he walks away. "Sorry, I didn't know you were coming. I can move her," she rushes out.

Luke turns around. "No, no. It's fine. You know I don't mind when she's here."

"Are you sure? I'm sorry. It's just until we find someone to replace Reagan, and Ava and I can go back to alternating shifts."

I can almost see the lightbulb go off in Emerson's head—as a freelance artist, she's developed a good, consistent client base, but I know she's been looking for other jobs to save money for a new apartment.

"I can do it," she says, bouncing on the balls of her feet—both Luke and Rumi's attention goes to her.

"You want to work here?" Rumi asks her.

Emerson nods. "I was a barista in college, and I could use the extra money."

"Hired!" Ava interjects after setting down the last drink she was making at the pickup counter, the lull in customers allowing us all to chat by the register. "When can you start?"

"Hey, I thought I was the boss." Luke crosses his arms, looking at Ava.

"Sure you are," she says, patting his shoulder then looking back at Emerson.

"When do you need me?" my sister asks Ava.

Ava gestures for Emerson to come with her behind the counter toward the back office, Luke following close behind asking Ava if she was being sarcastic or not, leaving me and Rumi to ourselves.

We both watch as the door to the back office closes, and then look back at each other.

"Looks like you just got my sister a job."

Rumi shakes her head. "Sorry, I didn't mean—"

"Why do you always do that?" I ask, interrupting her for no other reason but not wanting to hear her apologize.

"Do what?" she asks.

"Almost every sentence you say either starts or ends with a 'sorry'." I cock my head to the side, watching as she processes my question.

"They do not." She crosses her arms, and the defiance in her makes me raise a brow, wanting to see if I can get more out of her.

"You were just about to apologize for getting my sister a job. How does that make sense?" I put my hands down on the counter, leaning a little forward, wishing it wasn't between us.

"I just meant—" she stops then starts again, "I just wasn't sure if I overstepped."

"With who? Luke? You basically did his job for him," I challenge.

She uncrosses her arms, looking down at the iPad in front of her, her fingers pushing two loose pieces of hair back behind her ears, but they're short enough that they'll untuck if she looks down again.

"I guess I'm just used to apologizing even when I don't have to," she answers before turning the iPad with the total for Emerson and Luke's coffees.

I can tell she doesn't want to expand on that answer, but I file the words away for later. I look down at the screen. "The total says zero," I tell her.

"I just need you to sign, firefighter. The coffees are on the house."

"Rumi, I'm paying for the coffee."

"Luke doesn't pay for his coffee because he owns the place, and your sister is our newest employee, so hers is free. Can you just sign?" That defiance is back, I hope I didn't push her too far.

"If you say 'please'," I tease, wanting to see if she'll give me another smile.

She rolls her lips together, shaking her head, but I know I got her.

"Jack," she says; I love the way she says my name. "Will you pretty please sign for the coffees?" She bats her eyelashes.

I run my finger across the iPad screen before turning it back to her. "Thank you," I say as she rolls her eyes, fighting that smile I wish she'd give to me.

When she turns around to start making the drinks, I pull out my wallet, walking over to the tip jar at the pickup counter and dropping in two twenties before she notices.

I watch her as she moves with ease, her motions so familiar they almost look thoughtless as she preps the espresso for the two drinks. As the machine hisses, she grabs two plastic cups with the Hey Honey's logo, her movements flowing from one to the next, pouring a different type of milk in each cup just as the espresso is ready.

I lean over the pickup counter without meaning to, watching her movements closely. She doesn't rush, doesn't pause, but I notice she bites the inside of her cheek as she works—focused on the task in front of her. She pours both shots of espresso into the cups at the same time, and I watch as her tongue darts out to wet her lips.

The same way it did when she licked the milk from her wrist when she was showing me how to test the temperature for Evee.

When I couldn't stop staring at her lips.

The sound of her scooping ice brings me back to the moment, and I watch as she pours ice into the two coffees, pressing lids to each one before pushing the two cups toward me.

"Order for Jack," she says, looking right in my eyes, a smirk on her face—no doubt because she caught me staring, but I'd let her catch me every time. She's leaned over the counter, almost meeting me where I'm on the other side doing the same.

With her face a few inches from mine, her neck slightly angled up to look me in the eyes, I can smell the vanilla on her skin, mixing with the smell of freshly brewed espresso.

Maybe I am a coffee guy after all.

"Thanks, pretty girl," I say, surprising both her and myself.

I don't mean to call her that, this time being just as much of an accident as the first time, but the nickname comes from my lips so seamlessly, and the catch in her breath makes me thankful for the slip.

She doesn't say anything, just goes back to her station and cleans up, and I think I could spend a whole day watching her, only to fall asleep and wake up to do it again the next day.

"Oh, I almost forgot," I say to her, not sure what I'm about to say but just wanted her attention back on me.

Rumi looks back at me, one brow raised at me, those pieces of her hair untucked, framing her face.

"I—" I start, then the thought hits me. "I owe you cookies."

Confusion mars her face for a moment before understanding dawns, remembering our conversation in her smokey kitchen. She shakes her head, and I know exactly what she's about to say, so I say it with her.

"You don't have to do that," we say at the same time, and her eyes widen before that blush overtakes her cheeks, that shyness creeping back in.

"You can say this next part with me, if you want," I tease. "But I want to." I say it slowly, teasing her a little more. She stares at me, and I can tell by the sparkle in her eyes that she's trying not to smile. Taking on a more serious tone, making sure she hears every word, I remind her, "I like doing things for you, Rumi."

And I'll tell her again and again until she believes it.

She lets out a sigh, but I see the way her lips curve up.

"Well, Ava says I'm still banned from using the oven at the house." It's such a lazy excuse, and a poor attempt to change the subject, that I don't think she's actually trying to get out of the plans.

"Perfect. I just moved, and I'd be honored if you and Evee join me for breaking in mine."

Her mouth opens, but she doesn't say anything, and I'm worried I said something wrong.

"What?" I ask her.

She grabs the towel she has tucked in her apron, wiping down the counter before throwing it over her shoulder, her hands going to the front pocket of her apron, toying with something she has in there.

"You want Evee to come too?"

"Of course," I answer. "Unless, you don't want to bring her?" I frame it as a question, not exactly sure how to approach this.

I figured she'd want to bring Evee, that it'd be easier for her, but maybe not. Maybe it's a pain in the ass to bring a baby to a new place—I don't fucking know. Or maybe she doesn't want to bring her daughter to some man's house who she barely knows. Or maybe I made up this whole friendship and connection in my head, and I'm making the biggest ass out of myself right now.

"I didn't mean to make you uncomfortable," I tell her, hoping I fix whatever mistake I made. "I just want to get to know the both of you."

"No, it's just that—" She stops when her voice cracks, her eyes glistening, and I want someone to come punch me in the face right now because I obviously did something *very* wrong. "That's really sweet," she says, emotion heavy in her voice.

I don't say anything, not wanting to say something else that makes her upset, so I wait.

"I was really nervous to make friends, not only because I've never been good at it, but because I wasn't sure if people would want to be friends with a single mom, so it means a lot that you want to include Evee." She removes her hands out of her pockets, wringing them together before running them down the front of her apron. She seems nervous at the admission, but it makes me release a breath I didn't know I was holding.

"Does Friday night work?" I grab two straws, taking the wrapping off and balling it up between my palms, just to do something with my hands.

Apparently, we're both nervous.

"Friday works for us," she says.

"There's a park not too far from my new house." The thought barely registers in my head before I say it out loud. "Maybe we can take Evee."

"Okay," she echos. "She would love that—the park I mean. She loves the park," she stammers out.

"Great. I'll text you my address." I put the two straws in the coffees still sitting in front of me, tossing the balled-up wrappers in the garbage underneath the counter. "We can figure out something for dinner too."

"Great."

I think she's going to say something else, but we hear the incoming chatter coming from behind her—where I assume the back office is——Ava holding Evee, her little hands rubbing her eyes, her bed head on full display after her mid-morning nap. Luke and Emerson follow close behind her, the three of them talking about a party at the end of the month, but I don't hear much of the details.

"Look who's awake," Ava sing-songs, passing a still-sleepy Evee to Rumi, her small body curling against Rumi instantly, her head falling on her shoulder, her mouth around a pacifier that's clipped to her little yellow onesie. She has white shorts with matching yellow flowers, her feet covered by the same color socks.

"Hi, Evee girl," I say, leaning down to see her pretty blue

eyes—I swear to God, her lashes could blow me away, the same way those eyes could bring me to my knees.

Just like her mom's.

CHAPTER 19
RUMI

"IS 'MAKE COOKIES' code for something these days?" Ava is sitting on my bed with Evee when I walk into my bedroom after taking a shower, my hair freshly-washed, no longer smelling like stale coffee and warm milk, dressed in jeans and a pink baby tee.

I grab the sweater I left on my bed, tying it around my waist to hide the bit of my stomach peeking out above my jeans—while I'm thankful to my body for carrying and bringing my daughter into this world, I'm still working on accepting the softness of my stomach or the scar from my C-section.

"How should I know?" I gather my wet hair, twisting it into a low bun at the nape of my neck. "He probably needs help unpacking and the cookies are bribery."

Ava scoffs. "Yeah, right. Wanting to take Evee to the park, get dinner, and make cookies together is all to get you to help him unpack." She holds one of Evee's sensory books open, letting her play with all the different flaps and attachments. She's in just a diaper, wrapped in her towel, the green frog hood over her head.

I walk over to the dresser next to Evee's crib, pulling out a new onesie, shorts, and some socks for her to wear. "He's just being friendly." Holding Evee's clothes, I lean back on the dresser.

Since Jack came into Hey Honey's three days ago, I haven't stopped thinking about the way he invited me over so casually—and how he thought to include Evee.

I've been open with him about being a single mom lacking in the friend department, so the rational part of my brain keeps trying to remind myself that he's just trying to be a good friend. I shouldn't be surprised he asked to hang out— that's what friends do.

"Do you really think it's code for something?" I ask Ava, suddenly even more nervous than I have been all day.

Ava looks up at me as Evee takes the book from her, flipping to the next page on her own. Ava's auburn hair is twisted into two braids hanging over her shoulders, a few pieces framing her face. She didn't work today, so she's in leggings and a yellow crew neck. She got home just before I did after running errands with Evee all day, having taken over the party planning for Evee's birthday party next weekend.

I can't even begin to guess what all the shopping bags on our kitchen counter are filled with—Ava doesn't do anything half-assed, not even my daughter's themed "Wild One" party her and Emerson came up with yesterday. After one afternoon at Hey Honey's together, the two came up with a whole theme, to-do list, and plan for decorations.

On Evee's *actual* birthday two days ago, Luke and Emerson took the Wednesday shifts to finish up the minimal training Emerson needed, and Ava and I spent the day celebrating Evee.

For her birthday, Ava and I woke Evee up with blueberry muffins—the non-vegan version that Ava argues tastes noticeably different from her vegan ones. I gave up trying to convince her that using almond milk and coconut oil versus buttermilk does *not* make that much of a difference.

The two of us sang her "Happy Birthday" as she stared at us like we had gone crazy before I helped her blow out her candle. She opened the few gifts Ava got for her—a wooden shape puzzle with her name and a pink bunny she's barely let go of the last two days.

Luke and Annie FaceTimed to say happy birthday, telling me they got Evee a one-year ZooPass to the Milwaukee Zoo that we can pick up next time we go—perks of Annie being an exotic animal vet.

Even Mia and Drew sent flowers from both them and their husbands, with a gift card from Elsie and Sierra to their bookstore, Love & Lore, that just recently added a section of children's books.

The day was perfect, and I had this overwhelming joy and pride as we celebrated Evee—all her growth and the precious memories of the past year.

But, at the same time, I couldn't ignore the bittersweet sadness, realizing how much time has passed and how quickly Evee is growing up.

Throughout the day, there were moments that I felt guilty that it was just me here to celebrate her—guilt that I gave her a father who I will never allow near her and grandparents who don't even know she exists—but then I remind myself of all the people who I didn't even know a year ago and how they've become such a huge part of our life.

Evee and I have come so far since the night she was born, and the day truly showed that.

"Doubt it," Ava says, my thoughts darting back to the conversation at-hand. "Jack doesn't seem like the type talk in code." She reaches her hand out for me to hand her Evee's change of clothes. "He actually seems too honest for his own good, like he's incapable of wasting time saying things he doesn't mean."

I nod, taking in her words, thinking about how bluntly he challenged me about my habit of apologizing.

Ava has been trying to get a read on Jack since he barged into Hey Honey's all those weeks ago, and I trust her judgement more than mine. While Jack hasn't given me any reason *not* to trust his intentions or be weary of him, hearing Ava's impression of him settles some anxiety.

I haven't been alone with a man since Trevor—and, just like my father, he never wanted me out of his sight.

Jack's bluntness, although rooted in how much of a grump he can be, is refreshing, like a breath of clean air after years of inhaling smoke. Maybe that's why I feel so comfortable around him—he means what he says.

I'm used to having to read between the lines, staying quiet, and constantly monitoring moods to avoid triggering any anger—tactics I developed over years and years of abuse and living in fear.

Mariah and I have worked on processing my trauma in our therapy sessions. We've discussed the importance of noticing the differences between my safe, respectful relationships to rebuild the trust I have in others—specifically men.

And we've been talking about Jack lately.

Our session yesterday ended up being all about him and my feelings about tonight. I voiced my feelings and fears about Jack and how my initial impression of him is positive, yet my doubts are constantly creeping in, telling me that he could just be putting on a show like Trevor did.

We talked about the different things I could do to feel in control and even empowered tonight—starting with giving Ava my location and coming up with a safe word if I need her to come get me, both of which gave me instant relief.

"Do you think it's okay to bring Evee?" I look at my daughter as Ava sets her down in her lap to put on her socks, having already changed her clothes for me. "Maybe I should go by myself, just in case."

"Just in case, what?" Ava challenges. "I've only ever seen Jack be gentle—maybe even a little scared—when it comes to Evee."

"I know, but—"

She cuts me off. "No 'buts'. That's just the trauma talking."

I roll my eyes. "Yeah. I wish it would shut the hell up."

"It will," Ava says with a smile, holding Evee's hands so she can't take off the socks she just put on like she always does. "Soon."

"Not soon enough," I mutter, pushing off the dresser and holding out my arms for Ava to hand me Evee. "You ready, lovebug?" I ask my daughter, and she gives me that two-toothed grin that you can't help but smile back at.

"It'll be great," Ava says, scooting to the edge of my bed to stand up. "And like you said, you guys are just friends. There's no need to be worried. It's not like this is a date," she says with a laugh.

My cheeks instantly redden at the thought of a date with Jack.

"Right?" Ava prods, standing up, and I feel the flush in my cheeks.

"It's not a date."

Ava eyes me carefully. "Do you want it to be one?"

I shake my head. "No, we're friends. That's it."

"Okay," Ava says, stretching out the word. "Then, you better get going. Don't want to keep your *friend* waiting."

CHAPTER 20
RUMI

THIS WAS A STUPID IDEA.

I should've never agreed to this.

Standing at Jack's front door with Evee in my arms, her diaper bag over my other shoulder, I set the brown paper bag of the carryout order I picked up on the way here. Jack had mentioned dinner, and I don't know if he heard me when I told him I was vegan when we made these plans, so I figured I would pick up food for us.

He texted me his address earlier this week, but we've only sent a few messages back and forth to confirm time and place —I wasn't surprised to find out he's not a huge texter.

I pace back and forth in front of the door, working up the nerve to ring the doorbell.

This is Ava's fault. She's the one who put all that date stuff in my head, and now I'm overthinking every little thing.

What if he already had plans for what to do for dinner, or what if he thinks plant-based burgers are gross? Trevor did.

What if I got the time wrong? What if he isn't expecting me for another hour?

I pull my phone from my back pocket—it's five minutes to 6 p.m.

What if the plans aren't even for today? What if I have the whole day wrong?

What if I missed the text where he canceled? What if he's not even expecting me?

I open up our text thread, needing to settle this anxiety before it swallows me whole, my mind spinning, magnifying each and every bad feeling I had about tonight.

Before I can click on his name in my messages, I hear the front door open.

"You made it."

I look up and see Jack looking at me, holding the door open, and my mind goes silent.

No more thoughts, no more nerves, nothing except for how good he looks in the white long-sleeved shirt and black shorts, short enough to see a few tattoos peeking out on his muscular thighs and trailing down his strong calves, and I let my eyes roam over the skin and back up his tall frame.

His dark hair is damp and brushed back like he just ran his fingers through it; his stubble casts a shadow over his jaw, but it's more prominent above his lips, making them look even more full.

I never paid much attention to a man's lips before—the shape, the color, how soft they look—but there's something about Jack's that makes it hard to tear my eyes away.

A finger brushes just under my chin, gently lifting my head to meet his eyes.

Only a few inches from mine, the green is deeper than I've ever noticed before, like a forest at dusk—lush, untamed, and filled with secrets, begging me to come closer and lose myself within.

"Careful, Rumi," he says, and I can feel his cool, minty breath against my lips—that's how close he is.

I didn't even realize he leaned in.

I should feel the need to take a step back, put some space between us.

But I don't.

"I can't be held responsible for what I do when those pretty blue eyes look at me like that," he adds, using his finger under my chin to close my mouth for me.

And apparently I can't be held responsible for where my mind goes when I see a mustache, thigh tattoos, and five-inch inseam shorts.

Out of the corner of my eye, two little arms reach out, palms opening and closing in Jack's direction, and I come back from whatever fantasy world I was just living in. "Sorry. Hi, thanks for inviting us over."

Jack's smile is subtle, like a whisper of one, but I can still see it. He takes a step back, but Evee's arms still reach toward him. We both look down at her, and I remember the food I brought.

"Oh, and I brought dinner. Sorry, I should've mentioned it before coming," I say, about to reach for the bag.

"Here." Jack reaches his arms toward me. "I can hold her." I didn't think it was possible for my heart to beat any faster, not until he said *that* just inches from my face. "If that's okay," he adds.

"Are you sure?" I ask, but Evee is already leaning toward him.

"Come here, Evee girl," he says to her, and I pass her to him but make no effort to grab the bag of food.

He holds her gently, a little stiff and unsure at first, but the way he looks at her—like she's something fragile and sacred—makes my chest ache in a very dangerous way.

Evee bounces in his arms where he balances her against his chest, one arm under her and the other at her back—he sways back and forth subtly as he looks at her, and I don't think he realizes he's doing it. Her face is curious as she grabs the fabric of his white long-sleeve with both hands, her eyes roaming up and down his face.

Like mother, like daughter.

A cool breeze hits my exposed arms, giving me a little shiver, causing Jack to turn my way. "Come on in," he says, taking a few steps back with Evee, giving me room to enter.

I grab the bag of food at my feet, adjusting Evee's diaper bag on my shoulder as I walk through the door. The smell of fresh paint and clean wood hits me instantly as I enter the space.

Walking in, Jack closes the door behind me, and I take off my sneakers out of habit from living with Ava, looking around at his home. Jack takes the food and the diaper bag from my shoulder, grabbing both in one hand as he holds Evee in the other with greater ease now, getting more and more comfortable by the second.

"Let me give you two the tour," Jack says as I follow him into the living room that leads into the kitchen. He never fails to include Evee, saying he wants to give the two of us the tour instead of me.

It's something small, but it means so much.

Jack sets the food and diaper bag on the kitchen counter, turning to look at me.

He points to where I'm standing just in front of his couch, one of the only furniture pieces in the open living room aside from a coffee table and TV.

"That's the living room." He points from where he's standing with Evee. "This is the kitchen." I follow his gaze as he points to the left. "Bathroom is there. Then there are two bedrooms down that hall, and the primary bedroom and bathroom are upstairs."

"It's beautiful," I say, looking around, noticing the bare walls and random boxes throughout. Although there's not much, the house doesn't feel empty or void—it has a homeyness to it already. "And you've been here since Tuesday?" Emerson mentioned that Jack was treating her and Luke to coffee for helping him move that day they came to Hey Honey's.

Jack keeps moving side to side, keeping Evee moving in his arms as he answers. "Yeah, it's okay. I've never really lived alone before, but I'm really only here to sleep."

"You've never lived alone?" I ask, rounding the couch and heading toward the kitchen. I can't help but ask. I know Jack is at least ten years older than me, putting him in his mid-thirties. Having heard from Luke that he went to the fire academy straight from college, I can't help but wonder why he's never lived alone.

Probably a significant other or something.

The thought is silly and comes out of nowhere, but I can't fight the prick of jealousy—as misplaced as it is—that I feel.

Jack shakes his head as I unzip my diaper bag, pulling out a portable play mat and a few toys and books I brought to keep Evee entertained. "I lived at my mom's when I was going through the fire academy and all my other training, and then I moved in with a friend of mine when we both started working at the station."

"Friend?" I try to ask casually, not wanting to sound *too* interested.

"Yeah, my friend Bennett. We went through the fire academy together and then got jobs at the same station, so we shared an apartment until he—" He pauses, like the word that comes next can't physically come out.

I know the story of Bennett and how he died, and I instantly feel stupid for asking in the first place. I shouldn't have pried, especially now that I made Jack talk about something when he doesn't seem ready to.

He clears his throat, letting the sentence stay open-ended. "Do you want to put that in the living room?" He nods to the playmat and toys in my hands, and I take the hint, letting him change the subject.

Guilt washes over me.

"Oh, sure. That works," I manage to say.

We walk in silence over to the living room, and I lay out Evee's playmat on the carpet.

"Sorry," he says after a moment. "I'm still getting used to talking about him so casually." I bend to set out some toys as Jack sets Evee down.

Sitting next to her, Evee starts grabbing at her toys, and the need to apologize overwhelms me. "No, I'm sor—"

"That's the third time tonight." Jack sits on the other side of the playmat.

Third time?

I don't know what he's talking about.

When I don't say anything, he must read the confusion on my face, so he clarifies, "That's the third time you've apologized for something you didn't need to apologize for tonight, and you've been here for five minutes." His tone is straightforward but not unkind. "I know you said you're used to apologizing even when you don't have to, but you don't have to do that with me." He settles on the floor, laying on his side, holding himself up with an elbow as he puts one of Evee's toys in front of her, and she grabs it instantly.

Part of me wants to say "okay" and move on, but there's another part of me that wants to explain myself—explain why I feel the need to apologize.

Explain why I even asked about his friend to begin with.

But that opens a whole Pandora's box of not only the weird feeling of jealousy that I don't even fully understand, but my past too.

My past that I'm not sure I'm ready to share.

"How come you're only here to sleep?" I ask instead, getting our initial conversation back on track. I criss-cross my legs in front of me, watching as he keeps putting toys in front of Evee for her to grab them from him and play with for a few seconds before repeating the process.

Jack shrugs. "My shifts run for 24 hours, and between

work, the gym, and spending time with my mom, I haven't been home much."

"Does your mom live close?" I ask, a tug of longing pulls at me, thoughts of my own parents—or lack thereof—coming to mind.

"She's not too far from here. I've been trying to see her as much as I can since I was gone for so long."

"You two are close?"

"Very." He smiles when he says it, looking up at me. "I told you she was a single mom, right?" I nod, and he continues. "My dad took off when she was diagnosed with ovarian cancer, so it was just my mom, Emerson, and me since I was ten."

I open my mouth to say something, but he stops me. "And before you say 'sorry', don't. He was a dick, and we were much better without him. And, my mom has been in remission for years."

I roll my lips to hide my smile—Ava's comment about his brutal honesty and no time for saying things he doesn't mean rings truer and truer the more we talk.

"What about you?" he asks.

"What about me?" I counter—more than content to just listen to him talk.

"Are you close with your parents?" He eyes me carefully, like he already knows the answer but wants to hear what I'll say.

"Not at all," I say, taking a page out of his *not beating around the bush* book. "And before you say 'sorry', don't." Throwing his own words back at him earns me a smile, the one that curves to one side of his face. "My mom left my dad when I was five. He wasn't a good guy."

"She didn't take you?"

I shake my head. The familiar crack in my chest at the thought of my own mother leaving me to fend for myself—

something I could never imagine doing, even more so now with a daughter of my own.

The strength it takes to be a mom is unlike any other, but I've learned it's not a strength that everyone has.

My mom didn't.

The words left unsaid leave a lot of room for questions, but thankfully Jack doesn't ask them. Instead, he asks, "Where is your dad now?"

"Don't know, don't care," I say with a sigh. "I haven't seen him since I left for college at 18, and that's when I met her dad." I nod at Evee as she plays with all the inserts of one of her sensory books. Opting to be the one to change the subject this time, I ask, "Are you hungry? I brought burgers from VegOut."

Jack lifts a brow. "The vegan place?"

I nod. "I hope that's okay. I don't know if you heard when I said I was vegan on Tuesday, and I know plant-based burgers aren't for everyone. I also brought vegan cookie dough to bake tonight too. Evee can eat either vegan or not—I don't make her do it just because I do—I don't exactly do it by choice—and I wasn't sure if you had gotten cookie dough or not already." The words tumble out of me, and I barely take a breath before they keep pouring out. "And I won't be offended if you hate it, or the burgers. I know some people think being vegan is stupid especially when you just eat food posing as other non-vegan food."

It isn't until the words leave my lips that I realize a nerve was hit—Trevor's words spewing from my mouth verbatim after hearing them so many times.

"I don't mind," Jack says when I finally stop talking—he doesn't say anything about my rambling or even show he's affected by it. "I've never had plant-based burgers, but I've never met a burger I didn't like." The words are so simple yet negating the insecurity coating my skin. "And I didn't buy cookie dough, but I have the ingredients to make them home-made. I'm sure we can adjust the recipe to make them vegan. I'd love for you to teach me."

"Okay," I say, blowing out a breath before opening my mouth to apologize. The word "sorry" is on my lips, but I see Jack watching me, as if waiting for me to say it, so I close my mouth.

"Atta girl," he praises with a smirk, pushing himself off the ground to stand up.

"My ex would always make comments about my diet." I'm not quite sure why I say it, but the words are out in the open, so I might as well explain. "He thought eating vegan foods that were substitutes for non-vegan, like burgers, was stupid."

"He sounds stupid," Jack deadpans, and I chuckle, the noise escaping me before I realize that he wasn't joking.

I exhale, not wanting to waste this perfectly good night thinking more about Trevor than I have to. "The food might need to be warmed up," I say, pushing up to my knees.

"I got it. You stay with Evee," he orders, but the words make me feel tingly, especially when accompanied with the way his gaze darkens as he looks down at where I'm basically kneeling in front of him. "It's the least I can do after you bought dinner, which will not be happening again, I might add."

"Wow, firefighter. With how confident you are in those short shorts, I didn't take you for a man who struggles with toxic masculinity. *Friends* buy each other dinner." I don't know where the confidence to argue comes from, but I don't regret the words.

Well, maybe one word.

Jack raises a brow, intrigued. He bends down to my level. "True. My mom didn't raise me to be a man who thinks a woman can't buy a man dinner," he explains, picking up on my thoughts, and I notice how he doesn't comment on my mention of us being friends.

I open my mouth to argue more, but he holds up a finger and the words get caught in my throat.

"So," he starts, "even though we both know you're perfectly capable of buying me dinner, tonight was the first and last time because my mother *did* raise me to be the kind of man who takes care of women he cares about."

I cock my head, ignoring the fluttering in my stomach. "I don't need you to take care of me."

He cocks his head, copying me. "I know, but I want to."

And is it wrong that I really, really want him to?

CHAPTER 21

JACK

"ASIDE FROM VEGAN BUTTER, most margarines and oils work as butter substitutes. You can even use applesauce, mashed bananas, or pumpkin puree, depending on the recipe," Rumi explains as she pours flour, sugar, and brown sugar into a mixing bowl.

With Evee in my arms, I watch her mom work and learn more about her—two of my new favorite pastimes. I opted to hold Evee as Rumi took the prepping process for our cookies —something I would have probably done anyway, even if she did have a high chair to sit in right now.

After I warmed up the dinner Rumi brought over, I realized that I didn't have somewhere for Evee to sit. We ended up having her sit on the counter between us as she ate the little pieces of meat and french fries that Rumi cut up for her —explaining that she does something called baby-led weaning for Evee, having started when she was seven months old.

I didn't realize how much stuff you need for a baby, but I'm making mental notes as the night goes on—having added a high chair, a play mat with extra toys she can keep here, extra diapers and wipes as well as a place Rumi can change Evee without having to do it on my small bathroom counter, and something called a pack-and-play that I looked up when I Googled where babies sleep when they're not at home.

I already feel like I've learned so much, not only about how to properly care for a baby or vegan substitutes for baking, but about Rumi too.

"What about milk?" I ask, wanting to learn as much as I can about Rumi's diet. I'm standing next to her, leaning back on my kitchen counter as she pours some vanilla extract into the bowl of batter.

"Cookie recipes don't usually need milk, but for other recipes you can substitute soy, coconut, oat, or any nut milk," she answers. "I've perfected a recipe that doesn't need any egg substitutes either." She rips open the bag of chocolate chips—we checked the ingredients when I pulled them out, and I luckily got a brand that was vegan.

"You need a measuring cup for those?" I ask, grabbing the one next to me to hand to her.

"Nope," she says, popping the "p" sound and pouring the whole bag in the batter.

Rumi begins folding the chocolate chips into the batter—or should I say, the batter into the chocolate chips.

"It's probably too late to say this, but I'm not the biggest chocolate fan."

She freezes, turning to look up at me as if I just told her I killed the person who invented chocolate rather than tell her I didn't like it. "You're joking." Looking down at the bowl, I start to worry that she's going to start apologizing and pick out the chocolate chips by hand.

I've learned a lot about my new friend tonight, and one of those things is she doesn't just apologize because she got used to doing it when she didn't have to.

Someone taught her to.

Whether that's her asshole of a dad who her asshole mom left her with or her asshole of an ex-boyfriend who made her think the way she ate was stupid.

Someone taught her that everything is her fault.

Rumi looks back up at me. The light from the setting sun through my windows makes flecks of gold and amber dance in her irises, like fire flickering beneath the surface of a deep lake, the soft glow casting warm shadows around the edges.

It's like the sky itself has settled inside her gaze.

"I was going to apologize," she starts, "but I can't."

Good, I think to myself.

"Who doesn't like chocolate?" she mocks, her tone playful.

"Then it's probably also not a good time to tell you that I actually don't really like any sweets." I can't help but push her just a little bit more. It's fun to tease her—to see her cheeks blush, her teeth bite down on her bottom lip, her full lips pout.

I've seen a few different sides of Rumi in the short time I've known her, still keeping to myself about the way our paths crossed last year. I've seen her shy and timid, defiant and stubborn, but I think I like this playful side of her best.

Rumi throws her hands up in the air, and it makes Evee do the same in my arms, giggling as she continues to watch her mom with me. "What happened to the whole 'I take my cookies very seriously' when you broke into my house?"

"I did not break in," I argue, fighting to keep the smile off my face.

She ignores me. "And now you're telling me I'm just using your kitchen for you to *watch* me make cookies you're not even going to eat?"

I shrug my shoulders. "I'll have a bite of one."

She lets out a groan. "You know what?" I raise a brow only for her to poke my chest with her pointer finger. "You can finish these cookies while I hold her." She holds her arms out for Evee. "You probably need a break anyway. I know she can get heavy after a while."

I turn away from her, pulling Evee closer to me. "I'm going to pretend you did not just imply that I am not strong enough to hold this 25-pound baby for half an hour." Since my house isn't baby proofed—another thing I had to stop Rumi from apologizing for, as if it's *her* fault that *my* house doesn't have all the necessary things for a one-year-old—holding Evee is the least I can do, so we can keep an eye on her.

But by the looks of it, we might have just broken Rumi's habit of perpetually apologizing.

Rumi rolls her eyes at me. "Relax, firefighter. No one is insulting your strength. I'm sure you're very proud of your big ol' muscles." She's making fun of me, but I see the way her eyes roam to my arms, my long-sleeves rolled up exposing my forearms. I wish I had opted for a short-sleeved shirt today, loving the hungry way her eyes look at me now and when I first opened the front door tonight.

"Damn right," I say, switching Evee from one arm to the other. "I could hold both of you all night without even breaking a sweat."

"With how much you apparently hit the gym, I would hope so," she teases, reaching for Evee again. This time, I relent, passing her daughter to her, even though my arms feel like a part of them is missing the second she's gone.

"Are you one of those metalheads that listens to that screaming music while you lift weights?" she asks as I wash my hands under the sink, switching spots with Rumi and taking over the batter.

"Do I seem like the type?" I ask while I finish folding in her insane amount of chocolate chips.

She eyes me up and down. "I could see it."

"Then, sure. Let's go with that." I lean down to grab some

parchment paper, pulling out enough to line the tray I set out earlier.

Rumi switches Evee from one hip to the other. "That doesn't sound convincing. Don't tell me you're one of those psychopaths who doesn't listen to music at the gym. I'm still not over that you don't like sweets."

"I liked the blueberry muffin you sent me home with after I fixed your door," I say, grabbing some cookie dough and rolling it in my hand to place on the tray. "I finished the whole thing."

Her jaw drops, but the corners of her lips are curved. "Oh my gosh, you are. How can you not listen to music while you work out?" She looks at Evee, grabbing her little hand and bouncing her in her arms. "Did you hear that, lovebug? Our new friend hates chocolate *and* music."

"I don't hate music, but I don't listen to hard rock or screamo when I lift either," I explain, suddenly feeling a little embarrassed. "I listen to—" I pause before finishing, "rap."

She cocks her head, her eyes roaming down my face until she's staring at my throat. "Then why is your neck all red?" she asks, and I look up to find her head cocked as she observes me.

"It's not."

She scoffs. "It is. I'm staring right at it. It's your tell."

"It's not a tell. It's a—"

"It's a tell," she finishes for me. "I noticed it the first time when you barged into Honey's."

"I wasn't lying when I came into Hey Honey's that day."

She laughs. "It's not a tell for lying, firefighter. It happens when you're embarrassed."

My eyes slightly widen at her admission, her perception of me almost as accurate as mine of her, like we can read each other without any words between us and have been doing so since we met.

"And you don't have to be embarrassed that you're a

grump who hates sweets and music. It fits with that brooding image you go for."

"It's not an image, Rumi. It's just how I am." I've been called grumpy, mean, standoffish—almost any other word you can come up with without saying "asshole".

"I think you *want* people to think you are, but you're really not." She looks at Evee whose eyes go from me to her mom before they go back to me again. "Or at least not with us." Her small smile, the way her eyes soften, is enough to make me melt.

"Okay, fine." I feel more blood rush to my neck as I busy myself with rolling more balls of cookie dough, her correct assumption that I'm an ass to everyone but her and Evee hits too close to home, making me feel even more *things* I shouldn't be feeling about my friend. "I listen to Megan Thee Stallion when I work out."

I'd call her music my guilty pleasure, but there's no part of me that feels guilty for needing her music to get in a good run or lift. The embarrassment comes from the "hot girls lift heavy" playlist I found on Spotify that had all her songs.

The first time I clicked on it, it was an accident.

But now, I can't listen to anything else when I'm at the gym.

What can I say? I support women's unapologetic confidence and female strength and sexuality.

The moment of warmth dissolves when Rumi tilts her head back and lets out a laugh. "Not at *all* what I expected you to say when you said 'rap'." She shakes her head as she smiles, her laugh making Evee clap her hands and giggle too. Rumi looks at me, her eyes going from my throat to my eyes. "And no need to be embarrassed. I think more men should appreciate women and their voices to modern feminism." She reaches toward the bowl as I roll another piece of dough and steals some for herself.

"What kind of music do you listen to?" Her hand reaches

toward the bowl again, but I move the bowl just out of her reach, earning a playful slap on the arm.

"My ex was a huge country fan, so I always made sure that's what I had playing at home or in the car," she says—more information about her shitty ex that I file in my brain for later. "But since moving out, I rediscovered my love for boy bands. One Direction, Backstreet Boys, and *NSYNC are my go-to's." She reaches past me to grab more cookie dough for her and Evee, lifting some to Evee's mouth. Evee shakes her head once, her little fists coming up to her face and rubbing her eyes just before she rests her head on her mom's shoulder.

My eyes go to Rumi as she brings her fingers to her mouth. I can't look away as she sucks the cookie dough off her fingers, watching as she licks some melted chocolate off her lips—the thought of being the one to taste it runs through my brain.

The taste of chocolate would be much better if I was tasting it from her fingers.

From her lips.

"Jack?"

I shake the thought away. "Sorry, what?"

Rumi's cheeks redden, and her soft smile tells me she caught me staring, but she doesn't say anything about it. Instead, she asks, "Can I lay her down in one of your extra bedrooms?"

"There aren't any beds in either one of those rooms yet," I answer, reminding myself that I need to order that baby stuff as soon as I get the chance.

"Oh, okay. I'll guess I can just head h—"

"No," I interrupt, not even wanting to think about her going home yet. I can't remember the last time I felt this light, this carefree, this *happy* in months. I'm not ready for it to end yet. "We can lay her down in my bedroom."

Rumi watches me carefully. "Are you sure?"

"Absolutely." There's a crack in my throat at the thought

of Rumi anywhere near my bedroom, even if it's just to lay her daughter down to sleep.

She ponders for a moment before looking toward the living room behind her. "It's actually probably better if I can see her, so I think the playmat is a better idea. She's a pretty heavy sleeper, but we might need to be a little quiet until she's out."

"Of course," I say, and "I'll put these in while you get her settled. We can save the park for another time since she's tired."

"Okay," she answers, heading toward the living room where we left Evee's playmat.

With Rumi putting Evee down, I can't ignore the nervous energy in the air that wasn't there just a second ago.

Up until now, any time I've been with Rumi, we've been around other people or it's been me, her, and Evee. The awareness of it truly just being the two of us with Evee asleep wraps itself around me, causing a flicker in my stomach at the thought.

———

"What happened to only having a bite?" Rumi asks me, reaching to grab another cookie from the plate between us on the couch.

"These actually aren't too bad," I say, finishing the last bite of my second cookie. "Even with all the chocolate chips you added."

"I'm glad you liked them. The burgers too. I know they're not for everyone." She takes a bite of her second cookie.

"What made you decide to go vegan?" I ask, never wanting to stop asking her questions, wanting to learn anything and everything about her.

She chews slowly, her brows furrowed as if she really has to think about the answer. "It wasn't exactly by choice." She puts the rest of her cookie back on her plate, wringing her hands together in her lap.

I watch her carefully, waiting for her to continue. I can tell she's nervous, and that puts me on edge.

"I had to get a kidney removed, and the doctor recommended a vegan diet to reduce my protein load and phosphorus intake, so I didn't strain my remaining kidney since it was damaged too."

This catches me off guard, and I feel a wave of protectiveness for her. "What happened? Was it from the accident?"

"No, it was from before. I had, um, a fall before I got pregnant with Evee. But I'm totally fine now. It's more precautionary than anything."

Her answer gives me pause, the same way she tries to make it seem like getting an organ removed isn't a big deal. "You had a fall?" I ask, hoping she'll tell me what the fuck kind of fall caused enough kidney damage bad enough to need one removed.

Rumi nods. "What about you?" she asks, her tone brighter than it was a second ago, but it feels forced. "Ever broken a bone? Stitches? An organ removed?"

I let her change the subject but just for a moment, leaning back on the couch and crossing my arms. "I broke my arm when I was nine. Bennett pushed me off a table, and I hit my funny bone so hard that it shattered my arm."

"You broke your funny bone? Is that why you barely smile?" Rumi teases.

"Very funny, pretty girl. Tell me what other battle scars you have." I need to know more about what happened to her —there's no way she's just a lightning rod for accidents.

"Well no kidney, and then I have my scar on my collarbone from the crash last year, and then the one from my C-section." I don't think she realizes that she wraps her arms around her midsection as she says the last part, even though she has a sweater already tied around her waist. "But that's pretty much it."

On instinct, my eyes roam her exposed skin on her arms from the tiny pink T-shirt she has on, needing to make sure no other scars adorn her perfect body.

She sits there, body turned slightly toward me, her legs pulled up under her, her denim jeans stretch tight over her knees.

Her shoulders are relaxed, but there's a tension in the way she holds herself, like she's waiting for something to shift.

The way she moves her weight to one hip, then back again, makes me feel like she's trying to make herself comfortable but can't quite settle until I say something.

"Why are you staring at me like that?" she asks, and I meet her eyes.

"You're beautiful." I say it so simply because it's just the truth. It's not what I had planned to say. I think I wanted to ask her more about what happened to her—needing to know why she was driving in the middle of that night, why she was alone, and if she really was running away like I think she was.

"Friends don't call other friends beautiful," she says, but it comes out as a whisper. Her blue eyes glisten in the light coming from the lamp behind my couch, the sun no longer out now that it's past nine.

Three hours with her have passed in what seems like minutes.

Three hours, and it's not even close to enough.

Three hours, and I don't think I'll ever be the same.

"They do when they're as beautiful as you."

Her mouth is left slightly ajar, her eyes wide, like she doesn't believe me.

I'll tell her every day until she does.

But before I can say anything else, a cry from Evee causes both of us to look over, seeing her rubbing her eyes with her little hands as she wakes up.

Rumi stands up quickly, almost knocking over the plate of cookies between us when she does. "I'll get her, and then I need to get her home."

My mind, body, and soul reject the idea as she bends down to grab Evee, and I let my head fall back on the couch.

I knew this friendship with Rumi was dangerous.

Because there's nothing friendly about how I'm starting to feel about her.

CHAPTER 22
RUMI

WHO KNEW a birthday party for a one-year-old could *completely* take over your life?

Evee's party is set to start in less than an hour, and Ava, Emerson, and I are running around Hey Honey's like chickens with our heads cut off making sure everything is prepped.

Luke let us close early today, allowing us to use the space for the party.

"Annie should be here any minute with cupcakes and a cake for Evee," Ava says in between blowing up balloons. "That just leaves this balloon arch and setting up the backdrop for a little photo op."

Emerson is hanging up streamers around the space, offering to help since she opened this morning and was already here. "How many people are we expecting?" she asks over her tattooed shoulder as she tapes the green streamer to the window.

"Not too many," Ava answers. "Probably like 30 people and then the kids of those who have them."

My hands freeze around the plates of snacks I'm preparing. "That many?" I gawk. "I thought it was just us,

Luke, Annie, the girls from Love & Lore, Drew, Mia, their husbands, and—" I pause, my blood rushing to my face before I can even say his name. "Jack."

Ava eyes me, a brow lifting, but I look away before she can say anything.

I haven't seen Jack since our night at his house last Friday, and my mind has been on very little else since. I invited him to Evee's party as he walked me to my car and helped me load a cranky, tired Evee into her car seat.

Spending that time with him, getting to know him, opening up to him, was so *freeing*. I felt more like myself in those three hours with him than I have in years.

Or maybe ever.

But there was a part of me feeling like he was getting too close to everything I try to keep tucked away, and the way he looked at me terrified me, like he wanted to know every part of me, even the parts I don't want anyone to see.

He may think I'm beautiful, but he doesn't know the ugliness of my past.

From a young age, I became accustomed to bending, contorting, even completely changing myself to fit whatever the person I was with needed—and by doing that, I made myself small, quiet, and scared to move... scared to even breathe sometimes.

It started with my father, always needing to predict his patterns, comply with whatever he asked for, and build my own resilience, especially when I knew no one was going to help me.

I did what I needed to do to keep me safe.

But there's something about Jack that already is safe— there's no thought of how I would have to protect myself if I made him upset, no worry that he'll lose his temper, no anticipation of screaming, yelling, or throwing things at a moment's notice.

He makes me feel safe.

"Well it was just them, but then I invited the mom's from Evee's swim class and the girls from my book club," Ava says matter-of-factly. She turns to me, shaking her head at my surprise. "Evee deserves to be celebrated, Rue."

"Yeah, I know that, but—" I look around the space. Decorations are spread throughout the shop, the "Wild One" theme evident with the safari balloon animals, animal print cups and napkins, and fake vines and plants Ava and Emerson placed throughout. There's definitely enough room, food, and drinks to accommodate a party of that size—how much Ava bought all makes more sense now that I know it isn't a party of twelve adults and four kids, plus Evee.

"No 'buts'," Ava reprimands, and I'm getting sick of hearing her say it. "It's a party. It's supposed to be fun."

"Agreed," Emerson chimes in as she hops off the chair she was standing on.

Having worked with Emerson the last week, I've gotten to know her well. She's a lot like her brother—she can come off a little unapproachable at first, but, just like with Jack, I know there's no guessing with her. She's straight up and to the point, and I really like that about her.

"Then, it's settled," Ava says, nodding her head. "Two against one. Now, start having fun."

I groan, going back to setting up the table with all the snacks we bought and prepped.

Initially, I thought Evee's birthday party was going to be just me, Evee, and Ava, but it's turned into a much bigger ordeal. Ever since Ava took over, the party kept getting bigger and bigger every day that went by.

While I don't know the mom's at swim class too well, and I've only met Ava's book club friends a few times, the idea of making connections—making friends—isn't as scary as it was a few weeks ago.

Evee is with one of the babysitters that Mia recommended, and I have been testing her compatibility with Evee on a trial basis—my postpartum anxiety and my past making it hard to trust someone other than Ava around her.

She's taken Evee to the park twice this week for an hour, and today marks the first time she's come to our house to watch Evee for an extended period of time.

"What time is Sadie bringing Evee?" Ava asks as she continues to tie balloons together, almost finished with the balloon arch.

I pull my phone out of my back pocket, finding a message from Sadie that they're on their way over. "They'll be here soon," I answer. I scroll up in our earlier messages, re-reading the updates Sadie has sent me since I left earlier this morning.

"She's good," I hear Ava say. "Sadie seems to know what she's doing. You don't need to worry."

I let out a dry chuckle. "That's like telling water not to be wet." I pocket my phone, bending down to start filling the coolers we have for the drinks we picked up.

"Sassy," Ava whispers under her breath, but I can hear the smile on her face when she says it.

Once Sadie dropped off Evee and Annie and Luke brought the cake and cupcakes, people started to arrive with smiles on their faces and gifts in hand as they greeted Evee and I.

The sound of the Disney playlist Ava queued up mixes with the mingling and chatting of those here, and I look around, taking it all in.

I find some of the moms from Evee's swim class talking with a few of the women with kids from Ava's book club by the food table; I see Drew, Mia, Elsie, and Sierra sitting at one of the tables while Luke, Eddie, and Emmett are chasing after Eddie's twin girls and Emmett's daughter.

By the cupcakes, Annie holds Drew's son and chats with Emerson and Ava, who grabbed Evee from me once most of the guests arrived.

Before I realize, a wave of emotion ripples through me,

and there's a tight swell rising in my throat as my eyes burn with a prickle of heat. I blink a few times, trying to stop any tears from falling, not wanting anyone to think I'm upset.

In reality, the thought of all these people here to celebrate Evee fills me with so much happiness, it seems to be over-flowing. It's like all these missing pieces to a puzzle that I've been trying to find for so long have come together. Some were for the background landscape while some made the picture whole, but all together, they create the perfect image.

I wipe a stray tear from the corner of my eye, just as the front door behind me opens, and it's like the final piece clicks into place.

"You came." I wrap my arms around myself, not sure what to do with them.

Jack leans in, and a hand comes to my arm as he bends down to press a kiss to my cheek. The gesture is small and quick yet natural. Like he didn't think about it—he just did it.

His lips are warm against my cheek, his facial hair tickling my skin as he lightly squeezes my arm with his calloused hand. "I wouldn't miss it," he says just before he stands back up to his full height, dropping his arm to his side. He's wearing a backwards black baseball hat, dressed in a dark green T-shirt and the same black shorts he wore last week. It takes everything in me to school my features, including keeping my mouth closed to avoid drooling at his thigh tattoos and backwards hat. "And I have this for Evee girl." He holds up a leopard print bag with white tissue paper.

I open my mouth to say how he didn't have to bring a gift, that coming was enough—it's more than instinct at this point; it's second nature.

But I fight it, the words, "Thank you," coming out instead, and Jack gives me a nod of approval, like he knew what I was about to say and thought otherwise. I reach to take the gift from him, but he doesn't let me. Taking the hint, I walk him over to the gift table, his hand on my back as we weave through the pods of people talking, Jack giving small waves to everyone he knows.

The gift table is next to where we set up the cupcakes, so Jack sets his gift down to say hi to Ava, Annie, and his sister.

"Thanks for coming," Ava says, passing Evee to him without an ounce of hesitation. "Your turn for baby duty."

Jack takes Evee, holding her against him with ease—all the practice last week paid off, and my heart squeezes as she brings her hands to his cheeks and giggles, showing off her third tooth that recently started growing in.

"Hi, Evee girl," he coos. Jack isn't one to use a baby voice like others tend to do, but he always takes on a higher tone when he talks to Evee. "Happy birthday, sweetheart," he says to her, and I feel my knees threaten to buckle, the urge to faint like a cartoon character with hearts over my eyes is strong, and Ava must know exactly what she's doing to me by giving Evee to Jack.

I can tell by the look she gives to Emerson before they both turn to look at me, knowing smirks on both of their faces.

CHAPTER 23
JACK

IF YOU WOULD HAVE TOLD me five years ago that I would be spending one of my Saturdays off at a one-year-old's birthday party, I would've laughed in your face.

With the way my shifts work, my days off don't always fall on the weekends, and I used to cherish the ones that did, taking advantage of them.

Today, there's nowhere else I'd rather be than watching Evee stare wide-eyed at the cake in front of her, as a room full of thirty adults and a dozen children gather, ready to sing her "Happy Birthday".

The party is bigger than I thought it would be—especially when Rumi had initially told me she was just celebrating Evee's birthday with Ava. When she invited me to *the party that Ava took over*, as she explained it to me last Friday, I assumed it would only be a few people aside from me.

But, even with the room full of people, I only see them.

Rumi's green and white plaid top and short set matches the one Evee is wearing, and it takes everything in me not to grab the two of them and take them home with me, wanting to keep them all to myself.

The more sane, less caveman, part of me is so happy that Rumi has this many people here to celebrate Evee.

I've gotten to the point where a week without Rumi is too long. I've been counting down the days until I got to see her again since I watched her car pull out of my driveway last Friday.

I've been tempted to call her, but I talked myself out of it each time—not wanting to rush whatever is happening between us while simultaneously trying to convince myself that it isn't a bad idea and that it isn't all in my head.

Spending time with Rumi and Evee is everything I didn't know I needed. It's like seeing in color after months of grayscale; like a breath of air after being stuck underwater.

And the way she looks at me—those times I've caught her staring from across the room as she's made her rounds to her guests, the way I watch her breath hitch when I catch her, the way her cheeks blush when I give her a wink—nothing that looks like her could be a bad idea.

It's almost made the eight days I've gone without seeing her worth it.

Almost.

"Wait!" Ava calls out, her phone already in her hand to take pictures of Rumi and Evee. "Where are the matches for the candles?" She looks from Rumi to Annie and Luke where they're standing by the counter who both shrug their shoulders.

My sister, standing next to Ava, reaches in her purse hanging over her shoulder. She pulls out a lighter she always keeps with her—an old school Zippo that used to be our grandfather's. "Here," Emerson says to Ava, dropping the lighter in Ava's hand who passes it to Rumi.

"You ready, cutie pie?" Ava asks Evee, her curious blue eyes roaming all over the space, watching all the people stare at her. Everyone's attention is on her as she tilts her head from side to side, but I watch her mom. Rumi gives Ava a small smile, tucking one of those stubborn pieces of hair that fell out from where half of her hair is tied back with a satin green bow that matches the set her and Evee are wearing. Her dark waves fall over her exposed skin, the top she's wearing falling off both of her shoulders, the sight making my mouth water.

I catch a glimpse of that scar on her collarbone, my heart lurching at the memory of our conversation from last week, the scars she carries with her—the ones I still have questions about.

Granted, I'd probably have questions about everything she tells me about herself—I'm hungry for information, hungry for her, in every way possible—but the way she shied away from telling me about what happened for her to need her kidney removed is still heavy on my mind.

I need to know more about her—need to spend more time with her.

I need *her*.

Out of the corner of my eye, I see Ava bring her phone up to snap pictures as Rumi lights the one candle on the cake Annie made just for Evee—it'll last for a quick song and photo op before Evee sinks her little fingers right into the light green frosting.

I watch the small spark of fire appear in Rumi's hands, and I feel the air in the room grow thin. The faint smell of lighter fluid from the Zippo fills my nose, and I struggle to keep my breaths even and deep as she brings the light closer to Evee and toward the cake's candle.

While therapy twice a week is helpful, the strategies we discuss when it comes to my PTSD from the fire is easier said than done. My adrenaline during calls, along with the familiar urgency and muscle memory that takes over, can often help me stay in the right headspace—as well as keeping my distance from the fire and knowing I'm in the right gear, and no one I care about is in any danger.

Repeating that to myself is what my therapist taught me,

and it has gotten me through the few active fire calls we've received since my panic attack in the field four weeks ago.

But right now, watching Rumi with that flame in her hands and so close to Evee, you'd think this whole building was on fire with the pain in my chest.

I rub my palm back and forth just below my throat, trying to alleviate the pressure building as Rumi lights the candle, gently holding both of Evee's hands in one of hers so she doesn't try to reach for the lighter.

The room of people begin the opening line to "Happy Birthday", but it sounds like they're hundreds of feet away, the pounding of my ears growing louder and louder with every second I watch the candle burn, the orange flame reflecting in Evee's eyes as she stares at it makes my fist clench at my side.

I feel my jaw tick, my entire body tensing as I resist the urge to pull Rumi and Evee into my arms, away from the candle.

An open flame is dangerous, no matter how small.

A spark as small as one from a space heater too close to a blanket is no different than a birthday candle too close to the streamers hanging from the ceiling or the sleeve of Rumi's top getting too close.

All it takes is the smallest spark to start a fire, one that can grow to be unmanageable, one that can eliminate buildings, destroy lives, kill someone you love.

I never heard how the fire inspection here went—did it get done? Does Luke uphold the necessary precautions? Does he even have a fucking fire extinguisher? I look up, seeing the fire alarm and sprinklers, hoping like hell they're up to date and code.

I feel Emerson's eyes drift to me as the song comes to a close, the last "Happy Birthday" ringing out as the people around us begin to clap. Rumi's still holding Evee's hands together, bent behind her chair, her arms wrapped around

Evee as she sways her from side to side along with the song.

My eyes travel up, aching to find some sort of solace in her eyes—the ones that remind me of the calmness, the peace, I can only find when I'm on the lake.

I'm not in the field.

We're not in any danger.

She's okay.

Evee's okay.

I am *okay*.

I have yet to fully let go of all the guilt I have from the fire that killed Bennett. I know, logically, it wasn't my fault—I didn't set the fucking house on fire—but my PTSD, my grief, my anxiety all has a way of mixing together to create this overwhelming panic.

But no matter how many times my therapist tells me that I couldn't have done anything to stop Bennett from running in there—there's nothing I could've done to save him once he made that choice—I just can't get myself to admit it or let myself believe it.

When my eyes meet Rumi's, I'm met with a crease of her brow and a look of concern, her blue eyes filled with confusion as she watches me, no doubt seeing the tension riddling my body.

The crowd around Evee begins to clap, and the noise helps Rumi come back to herself, a smile coming back to her face as she helps Evee blow out the candle, and I finally feel like I can breathe again.

"What's wrong with you?" My sister bumps her shoulder with mine as the crowd around Evee's high chair disperses. People start to grab cupcakes from the dessert table while a few hang back to snap pictures of Evee taking handfuls of her cake into her hands, the green frosting all over her mouth as she eats from her hands.

Tension from my body subsides, and my lungs properly

filling with air again as I watch her. Rumi and Ava both laugh at the sight, pulling the corners of my lips up.

The panic attacks don't last as long, but they're every bit as jarring as my first one on the side of the road a year and a half ago.

Every time this happens, every time I detach from my surroundings—my reality—repeating the same worst-case scenario in my head over and over again, no matter how irrational it is, I'm able to come back to myself quicker.

Emerson bumps my shoulder again. "What?" I snap, more annoyed with myself than with her, but the frustration is in my voice regardless.

"Don't be an ass," Emerson grits through her teeth, her voice low, not wanting to bring attention to us. "You're the one who looked like you were about to strangle someone five seconds ago."

I hesitate for a moment, not sure how to explain myself.

"And I know that wasn't the case because no one was standing too close to Rumi." My sister smirks, her features so similar to mine sometimes. She's teasing me, obviously catching on to my growing feelings toward Rumi, even when I thought I haven't given much away.

I know her and Luke have been rooting for something to happen since they helped me move three weeks ago, but I'm still careful with any details I give my sister, or Luke, when it comes to Rumi.

I told Emerson and my mom about the night they came over, and Emerson—having been a nanny all through college in addition to her job as a barista—was the perfect person to help pick out the necessary items I needed at my house for if —*when*—Rumi brings Evee over.

They tried to hide their excitement over my friendship with Rumi, but my mom's comment about not wanting to be too old of a grandparent one day and Emerson's teasing about putting even more roots down than the house gave them away.

I scoff. "Don't be ridiculous." I try to sound nonchalant, but it comes out forced.

"And don't try to make some shitty excuse," Emerson argues. "I thought therapy was helping." Her voice takes on more of a worried tone, her tattooed arms crossing over her chest. She shakes her bangs out of her eyes as she tilts her head, looking up at me.

"It is." I cross my own arms, feeling defensive suddenly. I haven't told my mom or Emerson much about my sessions, just that I'm going twice a week, and they're helping.

We've started talking more about the night Bennett died, my therapist having created a safe, nonjudgmental space where I finally feel like I can open up without any pressure from anyone else. He's let me do things on my own time which has made the whole process easier—even when I was convinced there was no fucking way talking about that night would ever happen, let alone help.

It's kind of embarrassing to admit how much his low, gentle voice asking structured questions helped me talk through the night at last week's session—how I was able to walk him through what happened and my feelings throughout.

There were moments that I felt myself falling back into the night, the grief threatening to take over and push me into a panic attack, but my therapist knew how to ground me, how to keep me focused on my current surroundings and remind me that I was safe.

I've begun to make sense of what happened, and I never thought I would.

"Are you sure?" my sister asks. "I know you told mom things were going well in your sessions, but you don't have to sugarcoat it for me."

"I said it's helping." I try to keep my voice even, making

sure neither of us raise our voices enough to gather any attention—or more attention than the pretty blue eyes I feel on me.

Turning my head toward Rumi, she's still talking to Ava, but I meet her eyes, giving her a small nod of my head, hoping to ease any trepidation I might have caused her. If Emerson could tell something was off with me, I'm sure I wasn't hiding it well enough for Rumi to not have noticed.

"It's helping, Emmy," I repeat, turning back to her.

Emerson looks toward Rumi, having followed my gaze—not that I've been trying to hide how hard it is for me to take my eyes off her today. "I like her," Emerson says, looking back at me. "I've gotten to know her these last few weeks working with her."

I nod, curious to see where she's going with this.

"But she doesn't need your shit on top of all her own shit," Emerson says, poking a finger into my chest.

I rub the spot with my hand, but I can't fight the smile that forms on my lips. Emerson told me the same things I told myself not too long ago. "Agreed," I tell her.

Emerson pokes me in the chest again, a little less hard this time. "She needs good, solid people in her life. Not people who leave when things get tough."

While Rumi is my friend, and I'm starting to feel better about opening up to her more, the same way I hope she wants to do with me, I'm putting the work in to be someone she deserves in her life.

I'm still trying to put all the pieces together of who she is and the past she comes from, but I'm dying to see the whole picture; dying to be someone worthy of it.

I turn to look at Rumi again, but she's surrounded by more than just Ava as she stands next to Evee's high chair, now completely covered in green frosting. Evee's eyes are starting to look droopy, her sugar high coming down almost as quickly as it came.

I let out a sigh before saying, "I'm not going anywhere."

RUMI

"DO YOU HAVE A SECOND?" The low, gruff voice sounds in my ear, sending goosebumps all across my skin. The warm breath from his lips is such a contrast to the cool early evening air.

"I do," I say before turning around from where I'm loading Evee's presents into the trunk of the car I share with Ava.

Every time I look at Jack, it's like the first time. The butterflies in my stomach are out of control when his jade eyes are on me, or when I imagine running my fingers through his hair, or when I picture those strong arms wrapped around me.

I could go on and on.

"Did you need any more help with packing up?" Jack asks, his arm reaching up to close my trunk for me.

I lean against my car, interlacing my hands together, resisting the urge to grab him and pull him closer, something I haven't been able to stop thinking about since he hugged me and Evee goodbye last week or when he leaned in to kiss me on the cheek earlier today.

The quick moments of touch won't be enough for much longer.

With every one, I crave more in a way I don't think I ever have.

The touch of a man has always been something associated with hurt and fear—part of my story that might be time to rewrite.

"I don't think so," I tell him, tearing myself away from my thoughts. "But thanks for helping us clean up."

Jack stuck around to help me, Ava, and Emerson take all the decorations down and pack up all the presents and leftover food.

"Don't mention it," he says, his hands going to his pockets.

Is he thinking about pulling me closer too?

I don't let myself sit with the thought for too long, letting it go as quickly as it came.

We're *friends*.

"And thank you for coming. Evee loved her gift." I turn to look over my shoulder where my daughter is. Jack got her a plush fire truck with matching stuffed Dalmatian puppies. Looking through the window of Hey Honey's, I can see Evee still clutching the stuffed puppies now, one in each arm, as toddles between Ava and Emerson.

Jack follows my gaze. "Glad she likes them," he says softly before turning to look at me. "Before I head home, there's something I wanted to talk to you about."

I nod. A knot forms in my stomach as thoughts begin to spiral in my head—possibilities of what I did to upset him, what I did wrong. "What is it?"

He lets out an exhale before he continues. "I have PTSD." It sounds like an admission, one that he's been holding close to him for a while now.

A moment passes before I say anything, not sure how he wants me to respond but not wanting him to feel like he made a mistake in telling me something so personal. "Okay," is all that comes out, and I make sure to school my features, keeping them neutral in hopes he says more.

He takes his hands out of his pockets, opening and closing his fists at his sides. "It's from the fire that killed Bennett." His shoulders relax once the words are out, like the sentence was literally weighing on him, and, now that he's spoken it out loud, he no longer has to carry something so heavy.

His eyes slowly blink as he lets out another breath. "I was there the night he died, and I couldn't do anything to stop it." More tension releases from his body, and the slight crack in his voice leads me to believe these words haven't been spoken out loud before.

I reach out to grab his hand, both of mine holding one of his as I hold it between us, the urge to touch him, especially seeing the strength it takes him to say these words, is too strong.

He looks down at our hands. "I couldn't do anything to stop it." He repeats the words once, then again. The third time, he says them more as a whisper, as if trying to convince himself the truth of them.

"You couldn't do anything to stop it," I echo, feeling the need to convince him too.

I know how easy it is to let your mind tell you that you're the one to blame for something that's happened to you; that you could've prevented it; that it was your fault.

Grief and trauma have ways of contorting our reality, making us believe the irrational.

Jack looks up at me, his eyes glistening.

A dry laugh escapes him. "I didn't plan on saying all that." He squeezes the two of my hands with his before he lets go, taking his baseball hat off with one hand and running his other through his hair before putting it back on. "I planned on telling you about my PTSD and letting you know I was in therapy for it because I wanted to explain what you might have seen when everyone was singing to Evee." His eyes drift past me, looking into Hey Honey's. I turn, looking over my shoulder, finding Ava and Emerson talking but they're closer to the window than they were before.

I let Jack's words settle, remembering the look on his face, his body stiff and rigid, his fist clenched, as I lit Evee's candle with Emerson's lighter. "I noticed you looked *uncomfortable.*"

It's partly true—he did look uncomfortable.

Like he was bracing for something, like he was trying to stop his body from fleeing or springing into action—I couldn't tell. But his rigid body, the way it looked like he couldn't keep up with the thoughts circling in his brain, made it look like he was in pain, and that the pain was unbearable.

"My PTSD," he starts, grabbing one of my hands with his as he turns to lean back on my car next to me, interlacing our fingers together between us. He does it so naturally, as if he's been doing it for years. "It's made it hard to be around fire, of any size. When I was staying at my grandfather's cabin the last year and a half, I couldn't even strike a match without my heart rate speeding up. Seeing you with the Zippo and then the flame of the candle so close to Evee—"

He shakes his head, and I squeeze his hand in reassurance.

It takes a second, but he squeezes back then continues. "I thought that time away would help me, I don't know, heal?" He says it as a question, his head shaking. "Then, I came back, and even the gas stove burning at the station still threatened to send me into a full-blown panic. I thought I would just get over it. That I could bury what happened that night until it went away, but then—" He stops again. His hand tightens around mine, his body leaning more into mine as our arms rest against each other.

"Then it all became too much?" I ask, my other hand coming to hold onto his arm. I look up at him, his face hardened as he stares at the concrete just beyond our feet. The sun is getting lower, casting a warm glow over us, turning his green eyes into flecks of gold-laced emerald.

Finally, Jack nods, and I wait for him to continue.

"I had a panic attack in the field. I hadn't had one in almost a year."

The thought hurts my heart, thinking about how scared he must have been.

I've learned through my own trauma that our responses all differ. While some fight, others flee. While some flee, other's freeze. Our body's natural reactions take over, and we are left grappling for any sense of protection, any ounce of safety.

"It was a contained fire in a barn, no danger to us or to the owners, but seeing it sent me back to the night Bennett died, something that hadn't happened in months," Jack explains. "I completely froze."

I lean my head against his shoulder, knowing the feeling of freezing all too well.

The first time I remember my dad hitting me, I was so stunned, too scared to move. He slapped me against the cheek, cutting me in the lip with his wedding ring, and I don't even remember what I did to make him so mad.

I ended up standing in that same spot in our kitchen long enough for the afternoon sun to set—all while my dad drank himself to sleep in front of the TV, my mom having already left him without taking me with her.

I was six years old.

"The station chief, Chief Sanders, made therapy sessions mandatory for me when he gave me my job back. I put them off until it was almost too late." Jack lets out a sigh. "Freezing like that was scarier than any nightmare I could imagine, even scarier than the night Bennett died."

"How come?" I ask.

"The night Bennett died, my whole team had to hold me back from running in after him. I can see now how that wouldn't have helped, how that's not why he died—it was Bennett's decision to go back in against orders—but I didn't freeze." He pauses for a moment, thinking about his words. "What if something like that happens again?" A look passes over his features, one I can't quite read—it's a knowing look. Like he already knows from experience what the answer is. "What if I froze when someone else I love—" he stops, shaking his head. "I wouldn't be able to live with myself if I froze when someone could be saved."

"And today, with the lighter?" I ask, trying to give him space to talk about what happened, how he handled it, how he's feeling about it.

Jack lets go of my hand and reaches his arm behind me, his big hand coming to my hip and pulling me closer to him as we both lean back on the trunk of my car. "I don't know what today was. There was a moment I felt that panic turning into an attack, but I kept trying to tell myself that you and Evee weren't in any danger. But it was different than when I'm out in the field because it was you two."

"What do you mean?" The awareness of how close, how warm, his body is against mine clouds my brain, and it's hard to keep my thoughts straight. I try to focus on our conversation, needing to know what he's about to say.

"In the field, there's no one in the burning house or building. And if there is, I have to trust my team to get them out. There's no one I care about within miles of the fire. But today?" He angles his head to look down to me, using a finger to tilt my chin up to meet his eyes. "Today, it felt like two people I care about were in harm's way, and I was so scared of freezing." His jade eyes bore into me, feeling new and familiar at the same time. Like I've looked into them so many times before but not like this. Not with clouds of emotion making it hard to see his green irises or the gold flecks that only appear in certain light.

"W-we were okay," I manage to say, my mouth feeling dry all of a sudden.

"Logically, rationally, I know that—*knew* that," he answers, his finger still just below my chin, his face so close to mine; it would only take each of us to move forward just an inch for there to be no space left. "But my PTSD clouds my judgement, making me think of any and all irrational, catastrophized outcomes, like that tiny flame turning into an unmanageable one, the alarms or sprinklers not working, Luke not having a goddamn fire extinguisher, the fire burning you or Evee before I could do anything to stop it. It's not probable or rational, but it was all I could think while the candle was burning."

"I'm sorry." I don't know what else to say while he looks at me like this, so much raw emotion that I feel my own eyes pooling with tears that threaten to fall.

Jack gives me a small smile. It's not like the ones he usually gives me, the ones that curve to one side of his face. This one is sad—and a sad smile is the most bittersweet one of all. "What did I tell you about apologizing for things that aren't your fault, pretty girl?"

I grab his hand that's just under my chin, holding it with both of mine as I bring it to my chest. "I'm not apologizing for what happened to you. I'm apologizing because I don't like seeing you hurting."

Jack sighs, and I feel his grip on my hip tighten. "I think I've been hurting for a while now. There's so many pieces of me that broke when Bennett died, but I just kept stomping on them while pretending I would be able to forget and move on. "

"Sometimes it's easier to pretend," I tell him, and my own experiences come to mind. "It's easier to pretend that things aren't so bad, or that they'll get better." I think of all the times I told myself that if I just got through the day doing what my father wanted me to do, I could make it to my bedroom without having a new cut or bruise to hide the next day.

I told myself that once I had the baby, Trevor would stop. I just had to get through this pregnancy, and he would never lay a hand on me again.

"But it's just wishful thinking." The words are for both me and Jack. "In the end, until we actually confront our grief and our trauma, we're just hurting ourselves more." I look out toward the skyline, the parking lot of Hey Honey's basically empty, giving us a perfect view of the sun just starting its slow descent. "I'm sorry you're hurting, Jack. And I'm here for you while you put yourself back together."

I lean my head to rest it on his shoulder. "My therapist used this stupid grief analogy the first time I saw him right after Bennett died." A sound escapes his throat—a mix of a laugh and a scoff. "The chief made us all go to mandatory sessions after we lost Bennett, and I only made it through the one before quitting and heading up north."

"What was it?" I ask.

"He said that grief was like a fire, and it took everything in me to stay seated on that couch and listen to him go on and on about it. It wasn't until I went back a year and a half later, and he told me the analogy again, that it actually started to mean something to me."

I bite the inside of my cheek, trying to understand. "Grief is like a fire?"

Jack nods. "He said that all it takes is a spark for a fire to grow. And, just like grief, once it catches, it gets bigger, spreading faster, burning through everything in its path, not caring what or who it hurts in the process. It has to burn before it can slow down, eventually settling to coals."

"But it never really goes out." My voice is soft as I let his words sink in, understanding grief in a new way.

"It never really goes out," Jack repeats, leaning his head on top of mine. "Once it turns to coals, all it takes is a gust of wind for the fire to spark again—sometimes burning big and tall for hours and hours, sometimes just a little flame that goes out right away."

We sit in the comfortable silence for a few moments as we both sink into our own thoughts. I've never lost someone close to me that I cared about. I was so young when my mom left that I barely remember her to begin with.

And I don't grieve my father—wherever he is these days.

But I do grieve the life I never had, the childhood that was taken from me, the freedom I found that Trevor stole, the family I saw others have—the one I always wanted.

The one I finally have a choice to build on my own for me and Evee.

I bring Jack's hand to my lips, pressing a kiss against the back, wishing something so small could take all this away the pain he must carry after losing his best friend.

His head lifts from where it's resting on mine. "Do that again," he says, his voice gravelly and low. "Please." I look up at him, and he uses his other hand to point a finger to his lips. "Right here."

A wave of confidence mixes in with all the emotions flooding through me—the feeling of being in Jack's arms is addicting, the same way I feel more like myself when I'm with him than I have in years. The way he opened up to me, wanting to share this side of himself with me, makes me feel like it's okay to do the same with him.

From the beginning, Jack has made me feel safe in a way no man has ever done for me. He has done little things—some without even realizing—that have made me trust him more and more, bit by bit.

And learning to trust him has allowed me to learn to trust myself.

I let go of his hand, bringing it to his cheek. His skin is warm, his facial hair rough against my palm as I press against his skin. He doesn't make an effort to lean in, leaving me to do this on my terms, at my speed—something I didn't know I needed, didn't even know I wanted.

But somehow Jack did.

My hand trembles against his cheek, and he must feel it because he brings his hand to rest on top of mine. He turns his head to lightly press his lips to my palm, the heat of his lips sending shivers throughout my entire body, and a sense of want and longing spreads in my lower belly.

This is too soon.

We're just friends, aren't we?

Won't this ruin everything?

My brain is terrified as it tells me yes, but my heart is more afraid of never knowing what Jack's lips feel like against mine.

Gently pulling him to me, I lean in slowly, my heart pounding like a warning and a wish, as I press my lips to his —soft, tentative, wavering with the hope and fear I've been holding on to for so long. My chest aches with the weight of everything both said and unsaid between us, and the worry of what this could mean.

Jack doesn't move as I pull my lips away from his, instantly missing the warmth. I stare up into his eyes, waiting for them to open. When they finally do, it's like he's seeing my past, present, and future all with one gaze, and I bask in the attention.

In this moment, I want to tear myself wide open and let him see every part of me—all the parts I keep buried, the parts I hide away, the parts I forgot were even there.

"Rumi." He says my name like a prayer, like the chorus of his favorite song.

Like a promise.

CHAPTER 25
JACK

"RUMI."

I say her name again, loving the way it feels on my lips.

Almost as much as I love feeling her lips on mine.

The thought of Rumi ever being a bad idea seems so laughable now—this moment with her, opening up to her, just further proved that my feelings for her are developing into something worth exploring. Sure, maybe this kiss will make this friendship between us harder, maybe I'm jumping the gun in assuming she even wants to be more than friends with someone as fucked up as me.

But what I do know, deep in my soul, is I would do anything to make myself worthy of her and Evee. I want to be a man she can depend on, someone who will care for and cherish her the way she deserves.

The person she can trust to protect them and keep them safe—something I'm not too sure she's ever had before.

While I want to be better for myself, I want to be better for Rumi and Evee too. I want to be a man I can be proud of.

A man Bennett would be proud of.

With one hand on Rumi's cheek and the other wrapped around her waist, I hold her close—and I'm already dreading having to let go, knowing how her skin feels beneath my palm. I can see all the questions in her blue eyes as she looks into mine, the same questions that I have but have no intention of asking right now.

What does this mean?

Where do we go from here?

How soon can we do it again?

I smile to myself at the last one ready to lean in and close the distance between us, needing to kiss her like I need air to breathe.

"Jack!"

I freeze, my lips only mere centimeters away from hers when the voice says my name again.

Moments like this make me wish I was an only fucking child.

I let go of Rumi's cheek, watching as that familiar blush appears, my heart stuttering at the way she bites her lip, hiding a smile as we both turn over our shoulders to see my sister and Ava, with a sleeping Evee strapped to her chest, standing just outside the front door of Hey Honey's.

Part of me feels like a teenager caught with his pants around his ankles.

But then I remember I'm 36 years old, and if I want to kiss my friend against the trunk of her car, that's sure as fuck what I'm going to do.

It's taking everything in me not to throw her in her backseat, away from prying eyes, so I can kiss her over and over again. On her lips, her neck, her chest, everywhere and anywhere she'll let me.

With the image of Rumi, laid out and flushed in the backseat of her car—or even better, my bed—now at the forefront in my brain, my answer to my sister comes out much louder than anticipated. "What?" I bark as Rumi pushes herself off from where she was leaning on her car, interlacing her hands behind her back as she walks over to Emerson and Ava. I hear a little giggle come from her as I do the same, following close behind her.

"We wanted to see what you were up to next weekend?" my sister asks. I don't miss the raised brow as she looks between Rumi and me, and I'm sure Rumi notices Ava do the same.

"I'm off Friday but work Saturday." I don't bother asking why, knowing she's going to tell me anyway, images of Rumi under me, on top of me, her sweet skin against my palms, her soft lips against mine fading to the back of my mind. I don't even attempt to not pull her close to me, grabbing one of the hands locked behind her back, using it to bring her close to my side, wrapping a possessive arm around her waist.

Now that I know what it's like to have her in my arms, I have a hard time believing I'll be able to fight the urge to touch her whenever she's near.

"Great." Emerson's eyes, along with Ava's, slightly widen at my public display of affection, and for a second I'm worried I crossed a line—one I'm not sure Rumi was ready to even approach. But then I feel Rumi sink into my side as Emerson continues, my worries melting away. "The drive-in theater is doing a showing of your favorite book-to-movie adaptations."

She waits for me to say something, but I just wait for her to continue.

"You really are a man of many words," Ava mutters, but it's loud enough for me to hear. "Let me guess, not one for small talk either?" she says a little louder.

"Waste of time," I answer.

"Anyway," Emerson interjects, stretching out the world. "Ava and I thought it would be fun for us all to go."

Ava nods, but I don't have time to ask her what movie she's talking about—having no idea what cozy mystery I've read recently has been turned into a movie—because Rumi asks, "All of us?" I squeeze my hand around her waist, fighting a smile at the way her voice raises an octave.

"Yes, all of us," Ava answers matter-of-factly, using a hand to gesture between the four of us. "I'm letting Drew, Mia, and Annie know too because I know how much they love the franchise." She turns to me. "And maybe you can bring your friend, Anderson?"

I can't stop my brows raising at the mention of my co-worker. He's still stuck to me like glue, no doubt keeping an eye on me for the chief, even though I have yet to miss a therapy session or have any issues in the field.

"Anderson?" Rumi questions, but I look down and see the curve of her lips, even with her mouth slightly ajar in shock.

The three of us look at the redhead as she sways side to side to keep Evee asleep against her. "What?" she asks, looking around at us. "He's cute, and I need to get laid."

"And maybe he's a *Twilight*-lover too." Emerson turns to me and realization dawns.

"I am not a *Twilight* lover," I tell my sister, but it's too late.

Rumi turns to me, and I miss the contact of her body the second she's no longer at my side but standing in front of me, her hands on her hips, her eyes wide. "You too?" The way she says it is as if it's the biggest betrayal.

"What do you mean, 'you too'?" Ava exclaims, causing Rumi to turn and face her. "You're the weird one here—the only person on the planet who hasn't even seen five minutes of one of the *Twilight* movies. You didn't even read the books in middle school like a normal person. You skipped straight to the vampire sm—"

"Hey!" Rumi interrupts her, but I know enough about romance genres to figure out what she was about to say.

"Yeah, even Jack read them," Emerson adds, helping Ava's argument but making me want to strangle her in the process, the same way Rumi looks like she wants to do to Ava.

Rumi's eyes get even wider as she looks back at me. "*You* read the books?"

I put my hands up in surrender, shaking my head, ready to explain. "It's not—"

"Of course he did," Emerson answers for me. "He joined my mom's book club during one of her chemo runs when they read the first one—he read it to her because she was so tired from the treatments." I look to my sister, more surprised than upset that she offered the information so willingly to Rumi and Ava, knowing my mom's cancer journey and the impact it had on her isn't easy for her to talk about. "Then, he read the next three on his own."

Ava and Rumi both look at me, and I decide it's not worth arguing. I shrug my shoulders. "I wanted to know how the series ended."

I don't mention that the books were something I talked about with my mom, her having read the rest of the series on her own when she went into remission. We saw the movies together, knowing they weren't masterpieces, but it was something we shared.

Rumi and Ava turn to look at each other, Rumi shaking her head, seemingly already knowing what Ava is about to say. "See, now you have to at least watch the movies."

Rumi's head falls back, and she lets out a dramatic groan.

"That's the spirit," Emerson quips.

Rumi's eyes turn to slits when they land on my sister. "If I knew becoming your friend would result in another person telling me to consume *Twilight* media, I wouldn't have said anything about Hey Honey's hiring in your presence." She crosses her arms, and I have to roll my lips together to hide my smile at her defiance—one of my favorite sides to see of her.

Not that I could ever really pick a favorite.

Emerson brings a hand to her chest. "Aw, Rumi. I love you

too," she teases, making Ava snort, and my smile finally becomes too big to hide.

I watch Rumi roll her eyes, and she's close to accepting her defeat. "What time is the showing?"

"At 7 p.m.," Emerson and Ava say in unison.

With a sigh, she relents. "I'll have to see if Sadie is free to watch Evee."

Ava looks at me. "You'll text Rumi what Anderson says, so she can let me know?" She raises a brow, and I'm not surprised her and my sister get along so well, their scheming tendencies are much too similar for my liking.

I nod, pretending not to notice her eyes flit to my sister who gives her a subtle nod, as if they're two masterminds watching their plan come to fruition. "He should be free."

Anderson works the same rotation as me, and he hasn't stopped asking me about my friend's "redheaded roommate" since the night we did the inspection at their duplex.

"Then it's settled," Emerson says. "You and Rumi can ride in your truck—the back will be perfect for the drive-in theater. Anderson and Ava can ride in his car."

"What about you?" Rumi asks my sister. She's found her place back at my side throughout this exchange, gravitating toward me slowly like she didn't even realize she was doing it. I wrap my arm back around her waist, the smell of vanilla enveloping me.

"Oh, I'm not going," Emerson answers.

"What?" I snap. After this whole ordeal, interrupting Rumi and me, orchestrating this whole plan, scheming with Ava, she's just not going?

"Don't get me wrong. I love the movies—didn't read the books though—but I don't want to be a fifth wheel." She turns to Ava. "If Anderson ditches, let me know. I'll be your date."

"Who said anything about dates?" Rumi exasperates, her

skin goes hot. I can feel it even through the fabric of her shorts.

Emerson and Ava both look at Rumi and tilt their heads as if to say *seriously?* The corners of their mouths twitch with what I can only assume is suppressed sarcasm.

Again, it's no wonder they hit it off so well.

Rumi looks up at me for backup, but even I can't pretend to not see what's happening here. With her cheeks the prettiest shade of pink, she looks down at her feet, and I don't care that we have an audience. "What is it, pretty girl? Don't want to go on a date with me?"

"Are you asking me on a date, firefighter?" she asks, her voice soft and breathy.

"Absolutely not," I answer. "I'm accepting this date that your friend and my sister planned for us."

Rumi laughs as Emerson and Ava walk around us, heading to Ava's car, and I'm thankful for the reprieve of their knowing eyes.

"But, if you'll let me, I'd love to take you and Evee on a date tomorrow."

Rumi's eyes slightly widen. "Are we sure that's a good idea?"

"I've never been more sure of something." The answer comes as natural as breathing, even if I might not be so sure of how to navigate what the fuck is happening between us.

"Can I ask you something?" she asks, her pretty blue eyes shimmering with golden flecks from the sunset.

"Anything."

"Are we sure this is a good idea? It's been a while since I've been on a date, but I'm pretty sure it's not something friends do." The word "friend" makes my skin prickle, the thought of Rumi as my friend—while intriguing when I first met her—now makes me irrationally angry.

Instead of admitting this to her, I say, "You don't sound too enthusiastic about going on a date with me."

"Would you like me to scream my acceptance instead?"

The laugh that escapes me makes her lips roll together, trying to fight a smile of her own. "I'm still waiting to hear it to begin with actually," I tease.

Her smile falls slightly. "Friends don't go on dates." She's trying to keep distance between us, distance that sounded good when we first met but not anymore. Not after I felt her lips on mine, not after I learned what it's like to have her in my arms.

I want nothing between us.

Unless it's Evee.

"Then it's a very good thing I plan to be more than just your friend, Rumi."

CHAPTER 26
RUMI

I'M GOING on a date with Jack Hasting.

I've said it over and over again to myself until I fell asleep last night, continuing to repeat it as I used my day off from the coffee shop to run errands with Evee while Ava was at work.

And it still hasn't hit me.

I thought I was nervous to be around him before?

It's almost laughable compared to how I'm feeling now.

Last night was unexpected in the best possible way, and I would be lying if I said I hadn't thought about kissing Jack before yesterday. But the thought always seemed too much of a dream, something too good for real-life—especially because we established that we were friends when we first met almost a month ago.

Between my focus on Evee and my past relationship and him dealing with his own grief, we both have our own reasons to not be thinking about dating or relationships right now.

But when he told me about Bennett, when he held my hand, when he shared his feelings with me, all thoughts of how I wasn't ready to open myself up to someone else dissipated.

I know Jack still has his own work to do, the same way that I have a lot of my own trauma I'm learning to live with since moving to Milwaukee, but those aspects of us don't feel like reasons to fight this connection between us anymore.

I plan to be more than just your friend, Rumi.

I'm learning to trust myself through trusting *him*, and it's been healing for me, but I can't help but worry that this change in our relationship will stall my progress.

It was easy to trust Jack when he was my friend, but will it be the same now while we're *dating*?

Is that even what this is?

It's been so long since the word has even been in my vocabulary, and the last time I dated someone, it was my abuser.

"What do you think, lovebug?" I ask Evee, holding up the only two dresses I own, hoping one of them looks okay. I've changed my outfit at least seven times—all while Evee has watched me from my bed, barricaded by pillows, playing with the stuffed Dalmatians and fire truck Jack got her.

Evee stares at me for a second before looking back at her toys, leaving me to make the choice on my own.

"I can't wait for the day when you're old enough to give me fashion advice," I mutter to myself, holding each dress up against me as I look into the full-length mirror behind my bedroom door.

I've tried almost every combination possible with my current wardrobe, hating every single one.

Maybe if this date goes well tonight, I'll find some time to go shopping.

Looking at the first dress, I hold it up against me. It's a soft, flowy maxi with a light gingham print. At my height, it will fall to my ankles, with a small slit that stops at my knee. It's not flashy—just casual and comfortable, the kind of dress you could wear all day without thinking about it. It's one I've worn dozens of times.

Holding the second one up in front of me, I try to picture how it will look on. It's short, a more playful cut with a floral pattern of greens, purples, and pinks. The pale color would contrast nicely against my dark hair, and I think Evee has a dress that would match the purple. It's new, still has the tags, a dress I bought when I first moved to Milwaukee, one I wanted to save for a special occasion, but it ended up getting forgotten in the back of my closet.

Without warning, a memory assaults me, catapulting me into the past.

My new dress.

The one I got for his sister's wedding. It was a June wedding, and the dress was perfect.

I didn't realize it was too short, or that it showed too much of my legs.

"You think I want my whole family thinking I'm dating a whore?"

A backhand to the face, a shove against the wall, a push to the ground.

The puffed short sleeves and floral pattern covered with blood from my lip and the cut on my forehead.

I didn't make it to the wedding.

Evee babbling to herself brings me back to reality, my heart racing from the memory. Now, when I look at the dress, I see how the neckline dips too low, and it will put my chest and full cleavage on display, my cup size much bigger than it ever was even a year postpartum. The dress falls just above my knees, and I make up my mind.

It's too short.

I'll go with the other one.

"Is this spot okay?" Jack asks as we walk through the park. He's holding Evee with one arm, the other holding the basket he packed with snacks and drinks. Her diaper bag is over his shoulder as he leads the way past the families enjoying the first beautiful Saturday of June, finding a space in the shade under a big oak tree, our own little private space for an afternoon picnic.

"It's perfect." I splay out the blanket we brought, and the only thing Jack would let me carry after I insisted I carried *something*.

Making sure the blanket is stretched with enough space for the three of us, I sit down, patting the spot across from me for Jack to join me.

He sets Evee down in front of me, smiling in her purple dress and matching sunhat, her sunglasses making me chuckle every time I look at her, the frames too big her face but still the cutest thing I've ever seen.

"You both look beautiful," Jack says, as I kick off my shoes, setting them beside me in the grass.

I look down at the dress I've worn a thousand times, running my palms down the fabric, smoothing it out on my lap. "Thanks," I say, wondering if he would have liked the other dress better.

Jack sets the picnic basket and Evee's diaper bag down before settling down across from me. The sun is warm, our spot in the shade offering a nice breeze, causing a few pieces of his hair to fall on his forehead.

He stretches his legs out on the picnic blanket, his large frame relaxing against the soft fabric, the hem of his shorts revealing the tattoos etched into his tan skin. His T-shirt clings lightly to his broad chest and muscular arms, his dark hair tousled from the wind. He gazes upward, the sunlight peeking through the leaves of the tree above us casting soft shadows across his features.

"So you were saying Evee had what for breakfast?" he

asks, continuing our conversation from our walk to our picnic spot.

Since picking me and Evee up, the conversation between us has been easy, natural, and I can't help but notice how he's much more talkative today than he's been in the past.

I've known from the beginning that Jack is a man of few words—never wasting time with small talk or beating around the bush. It's something I instantly liked about him, wishing more people followed his lead.

But today, there's something different about him. A lightness to his usual broodiness, a happiness to his usual grumpiness.

"She refused to eat anything but her leftover birthday cake," I tell him, explaining how I made the attempt to give her all of her tried and true breakfast options, only for her to throw them on the floor—or at me—until, exasperated and fed up, I gave her a piece of her birthday cake leftover from her party yesterday.

Jack laughs, looking down at Evee. He's gotten so comfortable with her, always eager to hold her and include her in our conversations. "I would've begged Mommy for a piece of birthday cake too, Evee girl," he tells her, always talking to her like he talks to anyone else.

"You don't even like sweets," I argue playfully, remembering how he wouldn't take a cupcake yesterday for himself but took the bite I offered him of mine. My cheeks warm at the memory, how I offered it to him, forgetting he doesn't like chocolate, and how he leaned in to take the bite from my hand, staring at me right in the eyes as he did, as if he knew exactly what he was doing to me.

"Only once in a while." He winks, somehow knowing where my mind went before he nods toward Evee. "But, I wouldn't beg you for a piece for me. It would be for her. I mean, look how cute she is." He plucks one of the small wildflowers from the grass and holds it in front of her. "I don't think I could ever say no to her." Evee grabs the flower from Jack, holding it in her little hand, her round, rosy cheeks red from the warm day. She babbles something to him, and I smile at the noises she makes. They're not quite words yet, but her expressions always give her away.

Jack watches her, and I can't take my eyes off the two of them. The way Evee looks at him like he's the moon in the sky, the way he grabs her other hand in his, her fingers wrapping around two of his fingers and not letting go.

He keeps his eyes on her as she continues to babble, talking in her own little language. He nods along, giving her "mhmm's" and "you're right's", as if they really are having a conversation, and my whole body warms at how good he is with her—how he went from holding her like she was a bomb about to go off to looking at her the way he does.

Evee looks at Jack like he's the sun, but Jack looks at her like she's the entire universe.

"Are you hungry?" I ask, my voice cracking at the last word. I clear my throat, reaching for Evee's diaper bag. While Jack was insistent on bringing the food, I couldn't help but pack a few things—I'm used to always having some vegan snacks on hand, just in case.

Unzipping Evee's diaper bag, I pull out some trail mix I prepped this morning and a bag of vegan gummy bears I impulsively bought at the grocery store.

Jack watches me as I set both down, and his eyes go to the gummy bears. "You want some?" I ask, unsure why he's eyeing them like they might come alive and bite him.

"You like gummy bears?" he asks.

I nod. "They're my favorite. Most aren't vegan, so I was happy to find this brand."

He clears his throat into his fist. "They were Bennett's favorite too."

I don't say anything right away, not wanting to bring too

much attention to how easily he mentioned Bennett—something he said was hard for him to do.

"He always hid gummy bears in his locker at the station because he said someone at the station was stealing them from the drawer where he kept them in the kitchen," he explains, and his lips curl at the memory. "I'm positive he didn't keep track of how many he was eating, so he would run out before he could realize." He chuckles at the memory, and emotion clogs my throat.

To many, it might not seem like a big deal what Jack just did, but, after hearing about his battle with his grief yesterday, it shows the strides he's making.

"What was he like?" I ask carefully, wanting to know more about the person who meant so much to him as Evee makes herself busy with her toys.

There's a hint of sadness in Jack's smile as he thinks about how he wants to answer my question. "He was a lot like Luke," he says. "Not as happy-go-lucky, but he was always so positive and wanted to make the people around him smile." Jack looks off into the distance, the sunlight making his dark hair look less like chocolate and more like caramel. He lets out a sigh. "He was the kind of guy who'd drop everything to help you—loyal to the core, almost to a fault. He had a sense of humor that could pull you out of the darkest place, but he also knew how to kick your ass into gear when you needed it. He made life feel lighter just by being in the room." He speaks with a quiet reverence, eyes distant as he recalls his best friend.

Each word carries the weight of loss, yet also the warmth of a friendship that even death can't erase.

"I think he'd be really proud of you," I tell him, reaching for his hand and giving it a small squeeze before bringing my hand back to my lap. "He kind of sounds like he was your soulmate."

Jack turns back to me and gives me a look, raising an

eyebrow. His lips pressed into a thin line, his eyes fixed on me with a mix of disbelief and amusement. "It wasn't like that."

"Careful, Jack. Don't let that toxic masculinity show."

"Isn't a soulmate who you fall in love with? I loved Bennett, but we weren't in a relationship," he argues. "Even though some people would argue we were," he mutters, and I roll my lips together hoping to hide the giggle that threatens to escape.

"Well, I like to think a soulmate is someone whose soul feels familiar, even after you've just met." I look down at my hands, memories of my childhood coming to the surface—when I wished for a best friend or someone to see through my fake smiles and bandages or my lies of where I got the bruises from. Someone who would be there for me—to see me...*save* me. "It's a bond that doesn't need any explanation. And sometimes it's romantic, but other times, it's platonic. Either way, it's someone who is always with you, the connection never fading." *Even after death*, I want to add, but the sentiment remains unspoken.

Though I think Jack hears it loud and clear.

I look up to find him watching me, as if looking for an answer written on my face. Then, he looks down at the gummy bears sitting on the blanket. "Can you have more than one soulmate?"

"I like to think so."

Jack nods, watching me closely, before he clears his throat with a slight shake of his head. "Bennett and I were friends since we were kids," he says. "There's not a single memory I have that he doesn't play some part of, and we really did know each other inside and out. We went to school together and eventually the fire academy after Bennett dropped out of law school, realizing he wanted to help people, keep them safe—not protect rich CEOs and their big corporations. That's how we ended up at the fire academy together."

"And then to the Northshore Fire Department?"

Jack raises a brow at me. "You studying up on me, pretty girl?"

"Oh, totally," I joke. "It's not like I just happened to notice the logo on the shirt of the firefighter who broke into my house."

We both laugh, remembering how our paths couldn't help from crossing all those weeks ago, how that moment had a way of bringing us here.

"Bennett would have gotten a kick out of that." He pauses for a moment, like the words made him realize something. A small curve graces his lips, even though his eyes are clouded with the grief I know he always carries. "But I think you're right. He is always with me."

"He would've cheered you on when you decided to be my knight in shining armor, huh? Hearing the damsel in distress scream and rushing in to help?" I tease.

Jack eyes me up and down, amusement in his features, his voice taking on a more serious tone. "Something tells me, you're not used to anyone coming to save you."

"You think I need saving?" I challenge.

"I don't think there's anything you can't handle," he answers. "But I wouldn't mind being your knight in shining armor once in a while."

I roll my eyes, but the sentiment hits me right in the heart.

Something about the way he looks at me, how he thinks I'm strong when I've felt weak my whole life, reassures me that I wasn't wrong about Jack—that I was right to trust myself with trusting him, that while I might not need him to rescue me, he sees me as something worth saving.

Something passes over his eyes, and his mouth opens like he's about to say more, but then he blinks, and it's gone. I'm about to ask him what he wanted to say, but Evee lets out an annoyed wail, and I know it's her saying, *I'm hungry, Mom.*

"Me too, sweetheart," Jack says to her, somehow understanding her as if she actually said the words, and our moment fades away, reality settling back in.

Jack grabs the picnic basket next to him. "I hope everything I packed is okay."

I watch as he takes out a few containers, setting them down on the blanket—there's one filled with fresh fruit cut into pieces the perfect size for Evee to eat, another with carrots and hummus, and the last one has peanut butter and jelly sandwiches, one cut into little bite-size squares. He reaches back in the basket, pulling out two bottles of sparkling lemonade, a water bottle, and a sippy cup that looks like one I have for Evee but in a different color.

Looking at the spread, I'm left speechless.

Not only is everything he packed okay, but it's all things I can eat and feed Evee.

He even got her a sippy cup.

"It's perfect," I say, and I hope he doesn't think I'm crazy for how much emotion I'm showing over packed and prepared food.

How else can I say *my standards for men are at the bottom of the ocean?*

Jack smiles, running a hand through his hair. "I made sure everything was vegan. Oh, and—" He reaches back into the basket, pulling out one last container. "I used the recipe you taught me, one whole bag of vegan chocolate chips and all," he teases, uncovering the container of chocolate chip cookies. I can't help but notice the skin peeking out from the collar of his T-shirt reddening, his features softening with a shyness I'm not used to seeing on him.

"Thank you," I say, proud of myself for not even thinking about saying how he didn't have to go through all this trouble —knowing that he did it because he wanted to.

And that makes it all the more meaningful.

"This is a first for me, so I hope I'm doing an okay job," he admits, and I never—not in a million years—thought I would use the word "cute" to describe Jack Hasting.

"Don't worry," I say. "It's a first for me too."

"Your first picnic date?"

"My first date," I clarify, and the admission makes my cheeks redden. The urge to shrink into myself is strong, but I keep my head up, refusing to give in to the temptation to shy away from his attention on me.

Jack nods, his brows furrowed before he asks, "You've never been on a date?"

"Not a real one." The words slip out, and I don't realize how pathetic it sounds until my brain registers what I just said. "I mean, it's been a while," I add, but it's not exactly the truth.

Sure, at first, Trevor took me to nice dinners or to the movies but he was putting on a show. He was biding his time, sinking his hooks into me and gaining my trust. He told me everything I wanted to hear, listened intently to when I talked, and made me feel seen for the first time in my life.

Little did I know, the dates were a performance, one to bring my walls down and give me that dangerous sliver of hope that my life was finally turning around. That the years of abuse at the hands of my father, the abandonment of my mother, the way I learned to trust no one but myself, were worth it because I finally found someone who cared about me.

"You've never been on a real date," Jack repeats, and it almost sounds like a question.

I nod, shifting in my seat on the grass, my fingers twisting in the fabric of my dress.

Jack looks down at Evee as she reaches toward the edge of the blanket to pull at the grass, his hand and the flower he gave her now forgotten.

He seems to be contemplating whatever he wants to say, and I wrack my brain with a way to change the subject, coming up empty aside from everything I don't want to talk about—everything that will ruin this date, this whole entire *day*.

Jack's eyes stay on Evee as he asks, "Her dad never took you on dates?" His voice is hard, like it took effort to push the words out of his mouth, and I fight the urge to apologize for upsetting him, even though I don't know why he would be so mad about something like that.

I give myself a moment to ponder his question because it does give me room to figure out how much I want Jack to know about Trevor, especially since he seems to want to know the answer but is already anticipating one he isn't going to like.

"No." I decide to go with the simple answer, seeing where it will take us. I reach for Evee's diaper bag, pulling out her new favorite toy—the fire truck from Jack—and a few of the sensory books I brought for her, and some bubbles. Jack leans on his back, reaching for Evee and seamlessly grabbing her, picking her up and holding her up above him, making her giggle. He looks up at her, a grin on his face as he moves her through the air before setting her down by the toys I laid out on the picnic blanket.

"What about before him?" he asks as he settles back on his elbow, his eyes moving to me. The way he gazes up at me is tender, that contrast of his strong features yet soft eyes. Some of the anxiety swirling in my stomach settles, like the green in his eyes is a hidden forest I've only dreamed of, warm and welcoming, as if they had been waiting just for me to find them—get lost in them.

I uncap the bottle of bubbles, slowly blowing a few, making Evee look up and giggle. After a moment, opening a door I always thought would be better off closed, I answer, "Trevor was my first and only relationship."

Mariah has explained in our therapy sessions how it's important to open up about past domestic abuse, especially if it affects my boundaries, triggers, or trust and how sharing that part of my past can help build understanding and emotional safety in the relationship.

I made a promise to myself—and Evee—that I would never bring anyone into our lives that would hurt her, and Jack has never done anything to make me believe that he would ever jeopardize our safety.

But this is a step I've never taken with anyone other than Ava.

I blow a few more bubbles before twisting the cap back on, watching them float away—reminding me of the life I used to picture for myself, and how it floated away from me, slowly at first, before disappearing all together.

"Why did you leave him?" Jack asks, and I can't fight the intake of breath, like just the thought of that night can send me back to it, trapping me in the place where I risked every-thing to escape.

I close my eyes, slowly letting out an exhale, reminding myself that I'm not held captive there anymore.

While Trevor never told me I couldn't leave, I was too isolated to feel I had anywhere to go. I was convinced that no one would understand or believe me, not after years of us together and Trevor never taking off his mask until we were home, alone, behind our locked doors.

He didn't tie me up or lock me in a bedroom, but it truly was no different. I didn't feel like there was a way out, and every part of me was convinced that it was what I deserved—it was what my life was meant to be like.

It wasn't until he almost killed me while I was on the verge of giving birth to our daughter that I finally found the courage to leave.

I look at Evee—my precious, little girl doesn't even realize how much strength she gave me. How I wouldn't be here if it wasn't for her. "Because of her."

CHAPTER 27
JACK

WHAT THE HELL happened to this girl?

I want to ask her flat-out, finally hear the answer to the question that has been on my mind since finding her unconscious on the side of the road, but I don't know if now is the right time to tell her about when we met last year.

Rumi fled in the middle of the night from Evee's dad because of Evee? There's more to that story, more that I'm not sure I can handle hearing without getting into my truck, driving to Minneapolis, and bashing the guy's head into the ground.

It takes everything in me to wait—wait for Rumi to say more. She looks like she wants to, like she's trying to figure out what exactly she wants me to hear. She makes herself busy, using one of the lids of the containers I brought to put some fruit and the sandwich I cut up for Evee, setting it down in front of her, the bottle of bubbles forgotten next to her.

I want to tell Rumi that she can tell me anything and I'll listen—that I would sit here for as long as she wanted to talk, that I would give her anything she asked for, that I would happily let her ruin my life if that's what she wanted, but I also recognize we really haven't known each other for that long, even though it sometimes feels like we have.

Is that what she meant when she talked about soulmates?

Regardless, I don't want to push her.

She takes in another breath, and I recognize the deep breathing, knowing how much you need it when it feels like your mind is taking you back to the place that ruined you—how something as easy, as *natural*, as filling your lungs, becomes the hardest thing you could ever imagine doing.

Instinct, as well as how I'm sick of resisting the urge to touch her that I've had since the moment she got into my car this morning, brings my hand to hers, the one resting on her knee.

Wanting to ground her, help her remember that she's here with me, not back in whatever place her mind is threatening to send her back to, becomes my sole focus.

When she looks at me, her eyes look less worried, less frantic, than they did a moment ago—like the moment the waves settle and the water calms again.

"The night of my accident, when I was in labor, was the night I left Trevor," she explains. She looks down at the blanket we're on, just past where Evee flips through one of her flappy books before reaching for the food Rumi placed next to her.

I watch Rumi carefully, noting how she seems to become detached from herself, like she's about to tell a story that happened to someone else, not to her.

"I never thought I would get out of the relationship, but something happened that night that gave me the push I needed to get out of there, to leave him."

Processing her words, fighting the assumptions that begin circling my brain, not wanting to make up scenarios about what this fucker did to make her feel like she was trapped in a relationship because it'll make me start planning how to kill him before I even hear what she has to say.

I barely register that she slips her hand from under mine, settling her hands in her lap, my hand still on her knee. I give it a gentle squeeze before interlacing my fingers in front of me, wanting nothing more than to keep my hands on her but giving her the space she needs.

"What happened that night, Rumi?" I try to keep a hold on my patience.

I need to know why she almost died on the side of the road with nothing but her unborn baby and her pink satin nightgown.

"It was almost midnight, and I was already in my pajamas, brushing my teeth in the bathroom. I had just gotten home from my 10-hour shift at the restaurant I worked at, and I had been looking forward to laying down since waking up that morning. I had been having contractions because Evee's due date was only three days away."

The scene forms in my brain, only it's in my bedroom at my house; the image of Rumi getting ready for bed in her nightgown, stretched around her swollen stomach, comes so naturally to me—the thought of her so domestic, so comfortable, so *safe*, in my space.

She continues, "Trevor was getting drunk or high, or probably both, while watching whatever was on the TV. Usually, I knew when it was coming. I could feel it in the air, sense it in his demeanor—skills I had acquired growing up with my dad —but there was nothing that night."

The image in my head rips down the middle, the fantasy shattering into a million pieces, and a slow heat creeps up my spine. I can feel the sharp edges of my patience fraying as my interlocked fingers tighten around themselves to the point of pain.

I try to keep my features schooled, but Rumi is still staring at the same spot on our blanket. Fighting to keep my voice even, I ask, "Knew *what* was coming?"

"Trevor wasn't spewing his normal insults about my

weight gain or how no man would want to fuck a 'pregnant slut', which he said to me almost every night. He didn't even say anything," she says, ignoring my question—I don't even think she heard me—her voice almost robotic. "I heard him get up from the couch, walk over to the bathroom, and then saw him come up behind me in the mirror above the sink."

A small part of me wants to put my hands over my ears, not ready to hear what I think I know what she's about to say.

The other, stronger part of me, is anxiously waiting for her to say the words—waiting for her to give me just one reason to bash this bastard's head into the ground right next to her dad's.

"I rinsed out my mouth and put my toothbrush back in the glass next to the faucet, and was about to ask him what he needed. I assumed we were out of beer or he wanted me to make him something to eat, but, before I could say anything, he grabbed me by the back of head, tangling his fingers in my hair, and shoved me to the ground."

There it is.

This fucker is dead.

"I didn't even have time to scream," she explains indifferently, her voice just as detached as the rest of her. "I scrambled to my feet, ready to stand my ground and take it—like I always did. I felt the familiar smack of his hand against my cheek, the bloom of pain in my hip and crack in my elbow when my body met the tiled floor, angling myself to protect my stomach from the impact."

Each word hits harder than the last, and I feel the anger rising like a slow-burning flame, tightening my chest and clouding my thoughts—I watch as she closes her eyes, wishing she would look at me. Maybe, just maybe, the water in her eyes would settle this blaze growing inside me, but she keeps them closed.

"All of it was to be expected, and I already knew that he would apologize for it all in the morning, the same way he always did—so I got up again, bracing myself for whatever was coming next. A slap, a kick, maybe even a punch, but none of it came."

She opens her eyes, and she shakes her head as she looks at her hands in her lap. "He reached for me, and for a second, I thought I saw his eyes soften." Her voice lowers, cracking, making my anger melt away for a moment—my sole purpose no longer making this son of a bitch pay for what he did to Rumi.

I watch a tear fall down her cheek, and my own heart unravels—helpless and aching, wishing I could take her pain away, pile it on top of mine, and carry it for her.

"His face looked like it did when he would wake me up in the morning and run a hand down my cheek, ignoring the cuts or bruises, and apologize for letting his anger get the best of him."

Another tear falls, and I push myself up, moving to sit next to her—wanting to be the comfort she needs.

"For a moment, I thought maybe I'd get off easy." Her voice is no more than a whisper. "I wasn't naive enough to think he would actually ever stop. I knew the cycle of abuse— I knew enough to know I was tumbling through—but his eyes drifted from mine to my belly, and I thought maybe he was going to let me off easy because I was so close to giving birth to our daughter."

Rumi's eyes lift to Evee, her daughter so engrossed with the scene just a handful of yards beyond us as she munches on her PB&J—the kids running in the grass and through the colorful playground, trees swaying in the warm breeze, the sun shining overhead.

"I wanted to reach for him. At that moment, I wanted to hold him and tell him it was okay." She looks at me, her eyes clouded with tears, more escaping down her cheek that I can't help but wipe away with my thumb, my hand finding its rightful place on the side of her head as she leans into my touch. "Isn't that ridiculous? He beat the crap out of me, and I wanted to comfort *him*." Her shoulders shake with a sob, and I pull her into me, her face warm and wet against the side of my neck, my arms wrapping so tightly around her with no intent to ever let her go. "Then, it all happened so fast," she whispers after a moment, the words followed by a sniffle.

"Tell me what happened, baby," I say before pressing a kiss to the top of her head.

A small sob escapes from her, and I tighten my hold around her.

"He—" She starts but then stops, her face burying further into my neck.

"I got you," I tell her. "You're safe with me. I promise."

CHAPTER 28
RUMI

I NOD against Jack's neck, his skin warm and soft against my cheek, and I internalize his words.

He's got me.

I'm safe.

Reliving this night is unlike anything I've experienced—while Ava knows I fled because of Trevor that night, I've never told her that he tried to kill me.

Until this moment, I've never told anyone exactly what happened.

I sit up, taking in a breath and letting it out, meeting Jack's gaze. "His hands wrapped around my neck, and I couldn't breathe. It felt like my eyes were going to pop out of my head. I clawed at his hands until my fingers went numb, but he wouldn't stop. My lungs burned, and all I could think about was how my daughter was going to die before she even got a chance to live."

And through it all, Trevor never said a word.

He just stared at me, apathy lining his features, and I knew he was going to kill me.

Having a baby was never the plan. It wasn't even a

consideration when it came to what kind of life I pictured for myself, not after my sorry excuses for parents.

And especially not after Trevor.

I was so careful with birth control—taking my pill religiously every night and making sure they were hidden, so Trevor couldn't find them. I was deliberate in avoiding sex as much as I could, knowing that pregnancy was always a possibility with Trevor never wanting to wear a condom.

I had to get tested almost weekly because I knew I wasn't the only person he was sleeping with, and it was on one of my trips to the clinic that I found out I was pregnant. I realized I had missed a pill a few weeks prior after I came home exhausted from a shift at the restaurant and rushed to bed when I heard Trevor get home, too scared to find out what kind of mood he was in.

When the nurse told me, I knew I couldn't go through with the pregnancy. I wasn't prepared, wasn't ready, to bring a baby into my life—not the one I was trapped in, not with the father he or she was doomed to have.

Six weeks into my pregnancy, I was set on terminating—access my right to choose, the same way I believe every person with the capacity for pregnancy should be able to do —but there was a small part of me that felt like maybe this is what had been missing from my life.

My parents were never my family, and I never had any siblings. I didn't have friends or people in my life that made me feel like I wasn't alone.

The night before my appointment for the abortion, I couldn't shake this feeling that this pregnancy was my chance at a real family, one that I had longed for my whole life; one that was mine to grow and cherish; one that would be the beginning of me rewriting my story.

I reach for Jack's hand, craving his touch but also his comfort. Holding his hand in both of mine, I bring it to rest in my lap. "One second, his fingers were squeezing into my neck, the next, my leg was kicking forward, my bare foot connecting to his groin." I can almost feel the air that rushed into my lungs the second his hands went loose around my neck, and I'll never forget the strained howl that came from his lips when he bent over in pain. "And before he could crumple to the floor, I clenched my fist and swung as hard as I could, aiming for the temple."

It was something one of the waitresses at the restaurant taught me after a shift where one of the regulars got too handsy with us when we were walking to our cars.

They go out like a light, she had told me.

And so did Trevor.

"He was out before he hit the floor."

"Atta girl," Jack praises, but I shake my head.

"It was a lucky shot."

"Don't sell yourself short, baby. You did what you had to do." The words warm my whole body, bringing me back to myself a little more. I've told myself that it was the night I had enough, that I mustered the strength to leave because of Evee—and while that's true, I think I also found strength inside myself that night.

"Without a second thought," I say, remembering how I didn't even hesitate to leave—how I knew it was my only option the moment Trevor fell to the ground. I couldn't even let myself take a moment to feel the relief that I was okay, that he didn't kill me, that he wasn't going to get back up and try again. "I grabbed my keys off the hook by the front door, and with nothing but my nightgown, took off."

"That's incredible," Jack breathes, the adoration in the words making my skin warm. "You're incredible," he adds. "I just wish you didn't have to do it all alone. I wish—" He stops again, shaking his head before looking at Evee, the words on his lips forgotten as she turns over her little shoulder to look at us, a playful squeal escaping her lips.

I reach for her, pulling her away from her sensory books,

snacks, and strands of grass she tore from the ground and on to my lap. She looks up at me from under her sunhat, and I can see her blue, curious eyes through her sunglasses gleaming in the sun.

I chose to have Evee and give her the life that wasn't meant for me but was meant for *her*. The thought of her life being in the hands of a monster before she was even born gave me power I didn't even realize I was capable of. That's how I did it. That's how I broke the cycle.

And not a day goes by that I don't thank my lucky stars that I was able to when so many others aren't as fortunate.

"I'm so fucking proud of you, Rumi." I turn to look at him, his arm coming behind me, giving me the perfect space to lean back against him, my head falling into the crook of his neck.

"I'm proud of myself," I whisper, letting myself bask in both his words and mine, feeling pride wash over me as I hold my daughter close to me, her sticky fingers grabbing on to my arms as she wiggles in my hold.

"Is he—" he pauses, his face hardening. "Is he the reason you lost your kidney? You didn't fall did you?"

I exhale, the memory of when Trevor pushed me down the stairs at my college dorm. We were fighting, and at the time, he really did convince me it was an accident, that I tripped and fell, and he couldn't reach me in time.

But rose-tinted glasses only work for so long.

I nod.

Jack shakes his head, rolling his lips together. I can feel the anger radiating off him, but he manages to hide it well. Clearing his throat, he says, "Thank you for telling me your story." I open my arms, letting Evee crawl back over to her half-eaten lunch and her toys. "I know it couldn't have been easy."

Feeling lighter than I have in years, I look up at him,

aching to get lost in the forest of his eyes. "Thank you for listening."

We both sit in comfortable silence, watching Evee as his head rests on top of mine.

"Where is Trevor now?" Jack asks after a moment.

I shrug my shoulders, leaning more into him, loving the warmth of his body.

"You haven't heard from him?"

I shake my head, blowing out a breath. "Nope," I say, popping the "p". "And I probably never will."

"He hasn't tried to contact you since you left?" His voice becomes more hard, his tone rising in tension. "Not even to ask where you are? To see if Evee was born, that she's okay?"

"He doesn't even know Evee's name," I say, letting out an exhale. I sit up, crossing my legs and looking over my shoulder to meet his gaze. "I didn't put his name on her birth certificate."

"He shouldn't be able to just get away with what he did to you."

I can tell Jack is trying to keep his anger tamped down, but the way his jaw tics gives him away.

"Most abusers never get arrested because survivors don't report it, not with the possibility of retaliation or lack of support. I didn't report the abuse because I didn't think anyone would believe me. Even when abuse is reported, the legal system can fail." Whether from a lack of sufficient evidence or failing to take any action, it was too much of a risk for me—and for so many others.

"What about child support?" Jack asks, and I raise a brow. "You've never thought about it?"

"Honestly, no," I answer, the idea never crossing my mind. When I didn't put Trevor on Evee's birth certificate, it was my way of making sure he never had any ties to her. I knew that leaving him meant starting over and raising my daughter on my own.

I'm lucky with my situation that I can support Evee in all ways, especially financially, and have Ava to help me, so I never thought of child support as something I needed to do.

"When my dad left and didn't want to be part of our lives after my mom's cancer diagnosis, my mom decided to file for child support, not because she couldn't do it all on her own—raise Emerson and me, work, her cancer treatments—but because she knew it would help us," Jack explains. "She was already holding everything together, but that support meant the three of us didn't have to worry."

I absorb Jack's words, admiring how much he loves and values his mom and the obstacles she overcame as a single mother of two. The sentiment makes sense, and there's part of me that agrees that, while I have been raising Evee all on my own and doing a damn good job of it, there would be a sense of comfort from having financial help.

The other part of me is scared.

"It'll piss him off, that's for sure," I tell Jack, thinking about how the smallest things set Trevor off, remembering how hot and cold he would be when it came to my pregnancy —sometimes, he was the doting, loving partner who was so excited for our baby to be born. Other times, he would question if the baby was even his, even though he was the only person I ever had sex with.

And throughout my entire pregnancy, his physical abuse never stopped.

"Fuck him." The simplicity of his response makes me laugh. "He doesn't deserve either of you, and I'd prefer if you continue having nothing to do with him, but we have to think about what's best for Evee."

We.

He said *we* have to think about what's best for Evee.

Like we're in this together.

He kisses the top of my head, and I lift my head to meet his eyes.

"You're right," I say with a sigh. "Even if he's not around, he still should have some sort of responsibility in providing for Evee. I just don't want anything he can hold over my head."

"I promise you this, Rumi," his eyes bore into me, his lips just an inch or two from mine, "I will do everything in my power to make sure he never hurts you—or Evee—ever again."

His promise wraps around me, healing pieces of me I thought were forever broken as he leans down, closing the distance between us. His lips meet mine, and the world stops. His kiss is gentle, tentative, so unlike what I would picture from someone like Jack—but it's perfect.

His lips softly move against mine, as if he doesn't want to move too fast and scare this moment away. There's a gentle urgency, like we're on borrowed time—and a little squeal coming from just beyond my lap reminds me that we are.

Jack pulls away but only enough to press his forehead to mine for a moment, before we both turn our heads, finding Evee clapping her hands with her mostly-toothless grin.

"And one for you, Evee girl," Jack beams, reaching for Evee and pulling her into his arms. He settles her between us, and we both lean in pressing a kiss to each of her cheeks, her giggles warming my heart and soul, just like the man who has completely set my heart ablaze.

CHAPTER 29
JACK

"WHAT MOVIE ARE WE SEEING?" Anderson asks as we head up the driveway to Rumi and Ava's door.

When I told him about the double date Ava suggested during one of our shifts this week, he eagerly accepted, not asking any details aside from what time.

"The first *Twilight* movie," I answer, knocking on Rumi and Ava's door, not able to help myself from eyeing it up and down, making sure it still looks secure and stable like how I left it a month ago when I replaced the one I kicked in.

"I remember dropping my younger brothers off at the theaters when those movies came out. They always took their dates to see them," he explains, going into more detail about how he's never seen them but has heard all about them, but I tune him out as I wait for one of the girls to answer the door.

I've been counting down the minutes until I get to see Rumi again—even if I did just see her on FaceTime last night and talked to her on the phone this morning. While I'm still not the biggest texter, I got into the habit of checking in with her after our picnic date last Saturday, and the few texts quickly turned to phone calls by Sunday afternoon and Face-Times by Monday night.

Ever since she opened up to me about her ex, the temptation to be near her is a million times worse than it was, so I've started taking any chance I have to see her this week, whether it's stopping by Hey Honey's during her shifts to give her a quick kiss over the counter, or bring her lunch during her break; I make the time whether I'm on a shift or not.

I wasn't kidding when I told her that I think there isn't anything she can't handle, but I also made a promise to myself that I would never let anything happen to her or Evee.

Since our picnic date, Rumi has kept me updated on her journey with obtaining child support from that piece of shit she and Ava call Evee's "sperm donor"—a term I prefer *much* more than Evee's father, a man like that not deserving of the title—and I'm proud of her for taking the step.

With the help of the local child support enforcement agency, a court-ordered paternity test was sent to the address of the home Rumi shared with Trevor, so now we just wait. Once the court establishes Trevor as Evee's biological father, the process of filing for child support can start.

The door finally opens, Evee's babysitter, Sadie, letting us in, telling us that Rumi and Ava are just finishing getting ready. I remind Anderson to take off his shoes, knowing the house rules even after the few times I've been here.

"Hey, Evee girl," I say when I find Evee in her high chair, spaghetti sauce all over her face. I lean down, pressing a kiss to the top of her head.

Sitting down at the chair next to her, Sadie cleans up around the kitchen as Anderson makes conversation with her, never one to sit in silence. Through my half-listening as I watch Evee play with the noodles on her high chair tray, I learn that Sadie is a sophomore at a nearby college, is majoring in marine biology, and has a pet cat named Meowth like the Pokemon.

"Jack, Anderson," I hear from one of the bedrooms, turning to find Ava. "Do you guys want a drink or something? Rumi is almost ready to go." She walks into the kitchen, her red hair slicked back in a bun at the nape of her neck, her freckles on full display. She's wearing a yellow sundress that compliments her hazel eyes—the one's locked on Anderson as she walks into the kitchen.

"Nice to see you, again," Anderson drawls, giving Ava a quick once-over, his eyes sparkling as he takes her in, and I instantly feel like I'm interrupting something.

"I'm going to go check on Rumi," I announce, stretching out the words as I stand up from my chair, turning to give Sadie a raise of my brow, noticing that she's trying to hide a smile of her own as she makes herself busy helping clean Evee up as Anderson and Ava make heart eyes at each other —I don't even think they register that I said anything by the way Ava laughs at something Anderson says, lightly touching his arm as he subtly flexes in his T-shirt.

I knock on Rumi's door, and she opens it quickly, like she was standing on the other side of it.

"Hi." Her blue eyes wide with surprise, obviously not expecting me to be the one who knocked.

"I need you to save me." I don't want to enter her space unless she wants me to, so I reach my arms up on the top of the door frame, leaning in just enough to press a kiss to her cheek.

"From what?" she giggles, leaning into me as my lips meet her skin.

"Ava looks like she's two seconds away from mounting Anderson on the kitchen counter." The smell of vanilla washes over me, and it takes all my willpower to pull away from Rumi, wishing I could kiss every inch of her skin, feel her body on top of mine, hear the noises she makes when I—

And I'm no different than Ava.

Rumi laughs, taking a step back, so I can walk into her bedroom.

The space is exactly what I would expect, neat but not

overtly so, with a bed for Rumi and a crib for Evee. The walls are painted a pastel green with a pink and sage green comforter to match. There's a big dresser against the wall with her TV softly playing a playlist I see called "guilty pleasures: boy band edition", and piles of clothes on her bed with a book flipped over with a loose sock sticking out as a bookmark.

"Sorry, it's a little messy," she apologizes.

"Um, what was that?" I ask, my way of reminding her she has absolutely no reason to apologize. I pick up the book on her bed, my eyes roaming over the cover. There's two men, one looking sharp with fangs and the other rough and wild—almost like a half-turned wolf. They're standing close in a dark, moody setting, staring at each other like there's some serious tension between them—and definitely the sexual kind.

Before I can flip the book over to read the back, it's torn from my hands.

"Now is not the time for reading," Rumi says, throwing the book back on the bed, and I can't help but notice how she's not meeting my eyes as she makes herself busy moving clothes from one pile on her bed to the other, as if she doesn't know what to do with her hands.

I raise a brow, now even more intrigued. "Is this what Ava meant when she mentioned vampire smut?"

"How did you—" she starts, no doubt remembering how Ava was about to mention it after Evee's party when we made these plans. "You know what," she says instead, "I don't comment on your reading choices, Mr. Cozy Mysteries."

I put my hands up in mock surrender. "Of course you don't," I tease. "You're too busy admiring my reading glasses."

If I knew the way to Rumi's heart was a man in reading glasses—in addition to the five inch inseam shorts and thigh tats—I would've suggested late-night reading dates over FaceTime much sooner than two nights ago.

"That," she starts, pointing a finger at me before lowering it, accepting defeat. "I cannot argue with."

"See? This is why dating is so fun. Learning new things about each other, like how you don't like *Twilight* because Edward and Jacob don't end up together."

Her eyes widen as if I just flashed her, and her cheeks turn the richest shade of red.

"That is not—"

"Do your cheeks get numb from blushing at me, Rumi baby?" I can't help but tease, wishing I could spend the rest of the night finding all the different ways I could turn those cheeks pink. "No need to be embarrassed, but I promise your secret is safe with me." I close the distance between us but stop with just enough room to admire the outfit she's wearing, one I didn't notice until this moment while taking in her space—and her reading choices.

When she opened the door to her bedroom, I, of course, noticed how breathtaking she looked, her long lashes framing her pretty blue eyes, the dusting of freckles on her pink cheeks, her devastatingly full lips begging for me to taste them, but I didn't notice her full look.

Half of her hair is pulled back in two little ponytails with ribbons wrapped around them, the color of them perfectly matching the pink in her floral dress. The fit of it perfectly compliments her insane curves, accentuating her mouthwatering chest and toned, tan legs.

Beneath the hair falling down her shoulders, I can see the scar on her collarbone—the one that reminds me of how much she has changed since that night of her accident, the night I found her.

She rolls her eyes, sick of my antics. "If I knew dating you meant *another* person commenting on my reading choices, I would've just dated Ava," she says exasperated, but I hear the attitude too. Her spark, that defiance, is intoxicating.

Gone is my shy, timid Rumi who sat in the corner of the bar, holding her daughter close to her chest, in need of a friend yet wishing she could fade into the background of everyone else.

Here, and here to stay, is my strong, confident Rumi, who doesn't have to take shit from anyone—even me.

And I'll never get sick of hearing her say how she's dating *me*.

"But I can't wait to hear all about the vampire/werewolf epic love story on our next late-night reading date." I reach for her hips, pulling her into me. She wraps her arms around my neck as I press my forehead to hers. "You almost ready to go, pretty girl?"

"Almost," she answers, going up on her tiptoes to press a quick kiss to my lips, as if she's been doing it her whole life, as if it doesn't make my heart feel like it'll beat right out of my chest.

As if it doesn't leave me wanting so much more.

She pulls away from me to grab her purse on her bed, and I take the moment to admire the dress from the back. The dress has a playful mix of greens, purples, and pinks—the pale colors contrasting perfectly with her dark hair, making her look effortlessly beautiful.

She turns to look at me, catching me staring, and I feel blood rush up to my neck as I bring my eyes up to meet hers.

"Is it okay?" she asks, her face falling, and it's not at all what I expect. I thought she'd tease me again with one of her flirty remarks, but the confidence I saw in her a moment ago is replaced by worry—worry I've learned she gets when she thinks she's done something wrong.

"It's perfect," I reassure. "But it doesn't matter what I think. Do *you* think it's okay?"

She looks down, wiping her hands down the front to

smooth the fabric. "It's a little short," she admits, and it's like she's looking for something from me.

Permission?

"If you feel like it's too short, then you should wear something you feel more comfortable in," I tell her, wanting her to know that what she wants to wear is up to her and only her. I don't tell her that the only problem I see with it is that she might get cold when the sun goes down, not when that has such an easy solution—either my clothes on her or my body wrapped around hers.

Or both.

"N-no. I like it," she stammers, her rosy cheeks matching the pink in the dress. "I just want to make sure that—" she stops, shaking her head. She squares her shoulders and lifts her chin. "You know what? Nevermind. I'm ready."

That's my girl.

CHAPTER 30
RUMI

IT'S BEEN over a month since Jack barged into Hey Honey's, yet it feels like we've known each other for so much longer. When I was explaining the idea of soulmates to him last weekend, I was really just sharing the thoughts I've always had.

But something about that part of our conversation has stuck with me this last week, something that I can't seem to shake.

I've always thought of a soulmate as someone you feel like you've known your whole life, even after just meeting.

And there's something about Jack that makes me feel like I've known him before, maybe in another life—or maybe our souls just understand each other in ways no one else does.

"We'll meet you guys there!" Ava yells to me from the passenger seat of Anderson's car just before he closes it for her before giving us a quick wave as he rounds the car to get in the driver's side.

Both Jack and I wave back as we walk to his truck. The sun is still high in the sky, and the warm June evening is a little humid from the rain this morning. Jack steps ahead of me, opening the passenger side of his truck, his hand on my back as I step up onto the bar on the side.

The drive to the drive-in theater is similar to our dozens of phone calls and FaceTimes this week—both of us catching each other up on our day, allowing the conversation to ebb and flow toward different tangents, resulting in us getting to know each other more and more every time we talk.

When there's a lull of comfortable silence, the music playing from the radio the only sound aside from the air rushing in through the cracked windows, I take a moment to admire the man in the driver's side—the man I could listen to until my ears bleed; the man who lets me walk him through what I'm feeling, patient every step of the way; the man who makes my knees weak when he runs a hand through his hair before setting in on my bare knee.

The warmth of my skin makes an unfamiliar tension rise in my lower belly, a feeling I don't remember ever having when Trevor touched me.

A feeling I'm wanting to explore more and more.

I find myself wrapping my hand around his arm, the fabric of the flannel he has on over his T-shirt soft against my palms. I sneak a peek at the ink on his muscular legs, finding a bunch of different black and gray designs that somehow look like they were made to be together on his skin.

"We're here," Jack says, the car slowing down, falling into line behind Anderson's car. I see the big white screen at the edge of the open field, cars already lining up, backed into parking spots in the grass, couples and groups of friends setting up their spots before it gets dark and the movie begins.

"I still can't believe I was talked into this. My fun fact about myself was how I've never seen *Twilight*," I admit with a sigh.

"That's not a very fun fact," Jack says, looking over at me with a grin as he squeezes my thigh.

"I don't have many in my arsenal," I retort as the truck inches closer to the ticket window.

Jack scoffs playfully. "I can think of at least three right off that bat."

"Yeah, right."

"One, you can recite One Direction's *Up All Night* album tracks in order from beginning to end. Two, you can tell the difference between gummy bear flavors just by taste. Three, your eyes are the exact same color of North Two Lake."

As he lists off the first two facts, I can't ignore the flip in my stomach at the thought of him noticing those tiny things about me from our random conversations this past week, but it's the last fact that gives me pause.

"North Two Lake?" I ask, having no idea what that is.

"It's the lake my grandfather's cabin is on," Jack answers, his eyes on the car in front of him as he slowly releases the brake to move us through the line before stopping the truck again.

"In Lake Tomahawk?" I ask, remembering how he mentioned the small town a few days ago when he was telling me a story about the owner of the diner up there and how she caught him and Emerson loosening all the salt shakers on her tables and made them be her bussers for the whole week they were visiting their grandparents.

Jack nods his head. "I noticed it the first time I saw you— how your eyes are the same color of the lake when the sunlight hits the water."

"The first time you saw me, you grunted like a caveman and then got embarrassed and left," I tease, giggling at the memory.

I expect Jack to say something more, but he doesn't. He smiles, but it's one that doesn't quite reach his eyes. He seems to go into his head for a moment, almost zoning out, but before I can ask what he's thinking, it's our turn to pull up to the ticket counter.

Sending his reaction to me bringing up the first time we met in the back of my mind to revisit later, we get our tickets and pull into our spot next to Anderson and Ava, the sun just starting to set as the screen begins projecting old trailers for the five *Twilight* movies.

Jack cuts the engine, hopping out of the truck and jogging around the front to open my door, holding his hand out to help me down. "I brought a couple blankets to make the bed of the truck a little more comfortable," he says, opening the back door and grabbing more than just a couple, tucking them under his arm. "Emerson might have mentioned that this was all necessary for this kind of date." I can't help but smile at that boyish charm he gets when he's embarrassed. "There are pillows back here too," he says, and I can't believe I didn't notice the four big pillows he had tucked back here when I got in the truck.

"If you want to grab some snacks from the concession stand, I can set up the bed." My cheeks heat instantly as the words leave my lips, and I can't help but clarify, "The *truck* bed."

Jack notices, both of us fumbling through the actions like we're on a first date.

And I guess we kind of are.

It's our first date without Evee—just the two of us.

"Anderson can go with you," I hear from behind the truck, turning to see Ava and Anderson coming into view, a look passing between them, and I can already tell that Ava sucked Anderson into her silly antics when it comes to Jack and me, always looking for a way to push us closer to one another.

Jack nods at Ava, throwing the blankets on the bed of the truck before turning around to give me a quick kiss on the lips, as if it's something he doesn't even have to think about— as if it's instinct to do so.

As Jack and Anderson head to grab snacks, Ava and I set

up our areas, Ava using the trunk of Anderson's car, making it bigger by pushing down the backseats, as I climb onto the truck bed, laying out the blankets and setting up the pillows.

"You and Jack seem to be getting close," Ava says. Her sentiment may seem harmless, but I can read between the lines just as easily as I can read the smirk on her face.

"I think so," I answer nonchalantly, watching as she splays out the last blanket she packed with her on the pile she already meticulously laid out in Anderson's trunk.

"And you like him?" Ava asks, still not looking at me and making herself busy aligning all the pillows she brought, as if trying to make light conversation rather than dig for information like I know she wants to.

"I think so," I repeat, careful not only with my words but with that dangerous thing we call hope that I feel in the way my heart beats a little fast thinking about how I feel about Jack.

I'm so used to hope being the lie we tell ourselves to keep going, and I learned at an early age that reality often falls short of our hopes.

Almost always, the letdown can feel worse than if we hadn't hoped at all.

Ava lets out a groan, walking over to the truck and hopping up to sit on the edge. "You know, you two really are perfect for each other. Such conversationalists. I swear, you both must fight over who gets to talk first on those late night FaceTimes."

"Okay, fine," I exasperate, sitting down next to her now that both our areas are ready for the movie. "Yes, I really like him. He can come off so grumpy and mean, but he's truly just so sweet and gentle, and I love seeing both sides of him. He's responsible and patient, has a great relationship with his mom and sister, a stable job. I'm sure he even has a headboard and separates his whites from his colors when he does laundry."

The words pour out of me—talking about Jack is as seamless as talking *to* him.

"And don't even get me started on when he's in his station wear—God, Av, I don't know what I would do if I saw him in his full gear." The thought of Jack waltzing into Hey Honey's with Anderson when they were on a grocery run, stopping to bring me a smoothie bowl from a place I mentioned to him I wanted to try—I had to literally pick my jaw up off the floor at both the act and the way he looked in his station's collared shirt and cargo pants. "And him and Evee? They're literally best friends, and he treats her like she's the most precious thing in the world. I swear, he's too good to be true."

"Oh, no. Don't start that," Ava protests, shaking her head at me. "You can talk about the good stuff without the doubt, Rue." She bumps me with her shoulder before adding, "And by the way you just talked for the longest I think I've ever heard you talk in my entire time knowing you, I'd say there is a lot of good stuff when it comes to Jack."

I can't help but laugh. "I know, I know," I tell her. "But I'm serious. It's like I'm waiting for something to go wrong because things are going so well."

"So enjoy it." Ava wraps an arm around my shoulder, pulling me in. "I told you, you deserve to be happy, and it really looks like Jack makes you happy. And opening up to him like you told me you did last weekend? That's huge."

"He makes me feel so protected, but not in a way that is overbearing or that makes me feel like I can't take care of myself. It's like he's there in case I need it, and it makes me feel so safe."

Ava nods, absorbing the words. "I can't imagine how healing that must be."

I wrap my arms around her waist, pulling my best friend into a hug. "He makes me really happy, Av."

"Good because I'll kill him if he doesn't," Ava says,

making us both laugh as she wraps her other arm around me, squeezing me tight. "And I know all of this can feel scary. You and I both know that finding love after being with people who fucked us up feels impossible—the universe knows I'm still trying to figure it out—but *you* are going to do it." She loosens her grip around me, both of us sitting back to look at each other. "You are going to let yourself fall for this guy because I honestly believe that he will catch you every single time."

Emotion clogs my throat. I've felt so sure of myself and my decision to trust my developing feelings for Jack. Trusting him has been so healing for me because it's allowed me to build back trust in myself and my ability to know what's best for me and Evee, all while putting myself together after Trevor nearly broke me beyond repair.

But Ava's reassurance is something that makes letting myself fall for Jack, knowing I'll survive whatever that outcome is, not seem so scary.

"Snack delivery!" Anderson's voice booms, snapping both our attention to the two men coming our way. Anderson carries a tray of every candy you could possibly think of while balancing two sodas and a huge bucket of popcorn. Next to him, Jack carries a tray of his own, the two sodas and a much smaller popcorn, not as precariously perched.

The sun has set now, the dark sky lit with a ten-minute countdown and the dimming high lights surrounding the open field, giving everyone time to get settled before the movie starts.

"I'll see you after," Ava says, giving me a wink as she hops off the truck bed, helping Anderson carry all their snacks into his trunk before the two of them get settled.

Jack carries his tray over, setting it down before turning around to push himself up onto the truck. Goosebumps cover my skin as his warm leg presses against mine, and I can't help the shiver that takes over my body at the contrast of the cool night air and the heat of his body.

Without hesitation, Jack shrugs out of his flannel, draping it over my shoulders before wrapping his arms around me. "I had a feeling you'd get cold," he whispers against my temple as the countdown projecting enters its last minute. "Let's get you under one of the blankets."

He scoots back, leaning against the pillows I set up. "Come here," he says when I look over my shoulder and find him holding the blanket up, waiting for me.

I stand up on the truck bed, walking over to him, stopping between his legs as he taps the space between his thighs. "Sit."

Blood rushes up to my cheeks, and I watch his eyes darken as he looks up at me, waiting for me to do as he says —the snacks now long forgotten.

I slowly sit, turning so my back is against his front, my body fitting perfectly between his legs, feeling every inch of him against me. He settles the blanket on top of us, but I no longer have the need for one, not with the heat radiating off him, warming me inside and out.

Although there's hundreds of people parked in this open field right now, the sides of the truck and the darkness of the night make it feel like it's just us.

There's more privacy than I thought there would be, and I wait for the nerves to assault my stomach as the countdown reaches zero, the movie about to start, but I'm met with a wave of anticipation low in my belly, like we're on the precipice, on the edge ready to freefall.

As the movie begins, I can barely focus on the opening line. Something about her never giving much thought to how she would die, but all I can think about is Jack's arms around me, the smell of his cedarwood body wash making me dizzy, the feeling of his heartbeat against my back as he holds me against him, my body pressed against his—it all might kill me.

I couldn't tell you what happened in the first thirty minutes of the movie, too engrossed with this unfamiliar awareness on my skin—like every nerve on my skin is exposed. I keep shifting in my seat, trying to find any source of relief, but it's useless.

Shifting once again in Jack's lap, his arms around me tighten, and he holds me still.

His mouth comes to my ear, his breath hot against my skin. "I'm going to need you to stop moving," he whispers. His voice is strained, like his patience is wavering.

"Just getting comfortable," I whisper, both of our eyes on the screen, a blue hue mixing with the darkness.

"You've been trying to get comfortable for half an hour," he whispers back.

I shift again, and an unmistakable groan escapes Jack's throat as my ass accidentally pushes further back into his lap, meeting the hardness of *him.*

"And it makes it really hard to be a gentleman when you rub that pretty little ass all over my lap." His voice sends a literal shiver down my spine, and the air is stolen from my lungs as desire pools in my belly, his dirty words lighting a fire in me I didn't know was there.

An apology is on the tip of my tongue, this feeling like something worth apologizing for, but Jack stops me before I can form the words.

"Don't make me fuck the word 'sorry' right out of your mouth."

I can't stop the moan that escapes my lips, and I immediately bring a hand to my mouth. With the speakers placed all over the field, the movie is loud enough to not even hear the people in the car next to you talking, but who the hell do I think I am?

Moaning in public?

At nothing but his *words*?

Jack and I have barely kissed, and here I am falling apart over him whispering dirty nothings in my ear?

It's not that I'm against people fooling around in a truck bed at a drive-in theater, but it's not something *I* do. I've only had sex with one person and the only orgasms I've ever had were from my fucking vibrator.

And I've only had it for a year.

Everything I've learned about sex is from reading romance books, for fuck's sake.

I don't realize I move again until Jack lets out another groan in my ear, and there's something about the effect I'm having on him that melts away the thoughts in my brain. I move again, and this time he whispers in my ear. "Now, you're doing it on purpose."

"I don't know what you're talking about," I whisper back.

"Two can play at this game," is all he says as he snakes one of his hands under the blanket, finding the hem of my dress. Slowly, he gathers the fabric in his fists, pulling my dress up just a few inches until the bottom reaches the top of my thigh.

I feel his calloused hand rest on my thigh, lightly gripping my bare skin. "You're so fucking soft," he growls in my ear, his other hand finding my other thigh, and I can't control how heavy my breathing is. The feeling of his hands on me is intoxicating, but every time he moves his hands up, I'm left wanting more when he brings them back down.

"More," I breathe, and I don't even know what I'm asking for, barely understanding what's happening to me. All I can think about is how badly I need him to touch me.

"More what, baby?"

"I want—" I stop myself, feeling self-conscious all of a sudden, my newfound confidence evaporating as quickly as it formed.

"Don't get shy on me now. Tell me what you want."

"I don't know how," I admit, and I hope he doesn't ask me what I mean because how do I explain I've never done this before? Trevor is the only person I've ever been with, and sex with him isn't even comparable to whatever *this* is with Jack.

"How does this feel?" Jack asks, his hands gently kneading the skin of my inner thighs, getting *devastatingly* close to my center—I can already feel how wet I am, and he's barely touched me.

"Good," I breathe.

"And this?" he asks, moving his hands further up, gripping my hips and pulling me even closer to him, so I can feel how hard he is.

"*So* good."

His fingers tighten around the fabric of my underwear. "Is this okay?"

I nod eagerly, and I feel his lips press against my neck as he slides my underwear down my legs.

His hands find my thighs again, but this time, he uses his grip on them to open me up, my legs falling on to his, completely exposed under the blanket.

"If you want to stop, you tell me, and we stop. Got it?"

I nod.

"Words, Rumi."

"Yes," is all I can manage to say as his fingers inch closer and closer to where I'm aching for him to touch me.

"Atta girl," he praises the same way he has so many times, but it hits me differently when he breathes it into my ear, holding me open as he uses a finger to part me, causing a spark to ripple through my body, and he groans. "You're so fucking wet."

"More," I plead, and he lets out a sigh, but I can feel his lips curl against my neck.

"My greedy girl." His finger parts me again, pressing two fingers to my clit with the most perfect pressure. "Is this what you want?" he whispers against my skin before pressing his lips to my neck, finding a spot so sensitive that my eyes fall closed, my hands finding his knees and squeezing hard as the sensations overwhelm me.

His tongue swirls around the sensitive spot as he begins to move his fingers in slow circles, making me see stars behind my lids.

"Jack," I moan, trying to stay quiet but quickly losing myself in his touch.

"I got you," he assures me before he pushes a finger inside me.

He moves it in and out of me slowly as I get used to feeling, as if he knows I need a second to adjust before he adds a second finger, the delicious stretching sensation almost sends me over the edge.

My head is resting back against his chest, and I feel his other hand snake around my stomach and up to my chest, his big, calloused hand squeezing my breast, finding my peaked nipple through the fabric of my dress.

As he pumps his fingers in and out of me, he uses his other hand to tease my nipple before grazing his hand across to find the other. The stimulation is world-altering, and I'm seconds away from falling apart.

"Don't stop," I breathe, not capable of stringing more than two words together.

"Just for a second, baby," he says, and it sounds like he's in pain.

He pulls his fingers from me, and an embarrassing whimper escapes my lips. "No. Why'd you stop?" I'm too turned on to even be embarrassed about how it comes out as a whispered whine, my skin so hot and prickly that it feels like I'm on fire.

I'm about to say more, but any and all protest dies on my lips the second I feel Jack bring his hand from underneath the blanket bringing it to his mouth. My mouth parts as I watch his eyes close as he tastes me on his fingers, and I honestly feel like I could come just from watching him.

"You taste so fucking good," he growls before he leans down, his lips crashing into mine. His mouth moves against mine, his tongue swiping against my bottom lip, demanding access. Our kiss deepens—slow and hungry—and nothing matters except for what it feels like to have Jack's lips on mine, tasting myself on his tongue.

His hand drops below the blanket again, and he swallows my moans as he pushes two fingers inside me again, his thumb circling my clit as he pumps into me.

"Fuck," I breathe against his lips, my teeth grazing his lower lip, gently biting down as he brings me closer and closer to the edge.

"You look so good fucking my fingers." More of his dirty words, and I don't know how I went this long without hearing them.

The combination of his fingers working me and the way he whispers into my ear is enough to make the world around us—the whole universe—melt away. "I need you to come for me, Rumi baby."

And I do.

My orgasm crashes into me, and Jack kisses me as he works me through it, capturing each and every moan I make, keeping them all to himself.

"Holy shit," Jack breathes as I slowly come back to myself, blinking my eyes to find Jack's on me, his chest rising and falling, causing me to rise and fall with it..

He presses another kiss to my lips, and I wrap an arm around his neck, holding him close to me, already craving more.

"The movie is almost over," Jack says, breaking our kiss, and my lips curl, smiling against his.

"So I guess I can still say I've never seen a *Twilight* movie," I joke, and we laugh together, our foreheads pressed together.

"The first one isn't that great anyway," Jack says, and he kisses my nose before leaning back on the pillow behind him. "At least you can say you saw how it ended, so you're not lost when we watch the second one." He pulls his legs from around me, settling next to me and pulling me into his side.

"Wait," I whisper. "What about you?"

"What about me?" he whispers back.

"You didn't—" I'm too embarrassed to say the word, which seems so silly considering what just happened between us.

I watch as Jack rolls his lips together to suppress his smile. "Trust me. I'm fine," he says, pulling me against him, so my head can rest back on the front of his shoulder, but I can't help but notice he isn't as comfortable as he was before.

"You don't seem fine," I argue, noticing his spine is up straighter, and he isn't holding me as close to him as he was before. I start to feel like I'm going crazy, imagining this distance between us, but there's something nagging at me. "Did I do something wrong?" I ask him, suddenly wracking my brain for how I messed this up.

I've never done anything like this before, and maybe that was obvious to Jack. I'm used to sex being almost transactional—at least that's how it was with Trevor—so I'm confused why we're stopping when I haven't even touched Jack.

"What? No." Jack presses a kiss to my temple. "That was perfect."

"What about you?" I try to ask, but Jack stops me.

"I promise. I'm fine, Rumi."

"But—" I protest.

"I came in my pants."

I slap a hand against my mouth. "What?" I say, but it comes out muffled behind my palm.

"I came in my pants," he repeats, and it comes out so matter-of-factly, I still don't think I'm hearing him right.

"Don't you want to, I don't know, change?" The question is stupid, even more so when I hear myself whisper it, but what else am I supposed to say to *that*?

Not when the only thing going through my mind is how unbelievably good it feels to have made this man come without even touching him, a new confidence blooming that I've never had when it came to sex—just another way this man has healed a part of me without even trying.

Jack sighs. "Well, I wasn't going to advertise to you and everyone else that I came in my pants watching *you* come all over my hand, but now that it's out in the open—" He moves the blanket off of him, scooting to the edge of the truck bed and rounding his truck.

Getting into the backseat, I can see his shadow moving for a minute before he steps out of the car and joins me again just before the end credits of the movie start.

"Glad I decided to keep my gym bag in my backseat today," he says, sporting a mesh pair of black shorts rather than the cotton ones he had on before. Movement begins around us, reminding me that it was never just the two of us —no matter how much it felt like it.

People around us start hopping out of their trunks and truck beds as the lights surrounding the open field turn on.

"So?" I hear Ava say as she walks over, glancing at the tray with the untouched popcorn and sodas at the edge of the truck bed. I quickly make sure the blanket is still on top of me, not having grabbed my underwear yet.

"It was great," I say, and it comes out a little too enthusiastically, almost like a squeak.

My best friend eyes me carefully before her eyes roam to Jack.

"Nice shorts," she tells him before giving me a wink and walking back over to Anderson's car.

CHAPTER 31
JACK

"SHE'S GOING to love you, I promise." I press a kiss to the top of Rumi's head just before opening the front door to my mom's house.

With Evee in my arms, Rumi is holding the vegan blueberry muffins Ava made for her to bring over, Rumi being too nervous to prepare anything this morning after I invited her to brunch with my mom last night when we grabbed dinner together—even when I told her there was no need to be.

My mom has called me at least a dozen times since I told her I wanted her to meet Rumi and Evee, and she offered to host us for brunch today. When I told her that Rumi was vegan, she immediately took it upon herself to convert all of her tried and true recipes into vegan ones.

"Does she know we're bringing Evee?" she asks, her eyes darting from me to her daughter in my arms as she shifts her weight back and forth on her feet.

"Of course, and I brought over her stuff last night." I wanted to make sure Rumi had nothing to worry about, so I brought over the high chair, play mat, and the Pack 'n Play that I bought for my house.

Rumi's shoulders relax as she exhales. "I still can't believe you got all that stuff for her."

"And I'd do it again and again," I say, gently bouncing Evee in my arms. She's tired from her morning nap, so her head rests against my shoulder. She's wearing a white onesie with blue and yellow flowers with blue shorts that match her mom's baby blue sundress. Evee's hair is finally growing in enough that Rumi can give her two little pig tails that she tied baby blue bows in—the sight going straight to my heart when I picked the girls up this morning, their outfits accentuating their matching eyes.

"And you said Emerson will be here?" Rumi asks, my sister and her growing closer over the last month working at Hey Honey's together.

I nod. "She should be here." Emerson texted me last night asking if Rumi had a certain coloring book and crayons that are meant to help Evee's fine motor skills at this age, so I assume she's still planning on coming.

Rumi sighs. "I don't know why I'm so nervous," she admits, but I think we both know why. Rumi doesn't have the best track record with parents, and I don't think she's entirely sure how to handle them, rightfully so.

"My mom has been talking about meeting my girlfriend for days now. I promise, there is nothing to be nervous about."

Rumi turns to me, her brows raised. "Girlfriend?"

Oops.

"Too soon?" I ask her, wanting to punch myself for letting the word slip out.

I can't help but think of Rumi as my girlfriend, even though the word doesn't feel important enough to use for how I feel about her.

"I just wasn't aware I was your girlfriend," she says, her head cocking to the side as she watches me closely.

Blood rushes up to my neck, and I already know I'm

doing this all wrong. "I don't know if on my mother's front porch is the right place to have this conversation."

Rumi's eyes turn to slits, but I see the blush in her cheeks. "We'll put a pin in it."

"Deal," I say quickly, reaching for the door handle and pushing it open.

At least my royal fuckup got Rumi thinking about something other than how nervous she is to meet my mom.

The warm and comforting atmosphere instantly envelopes us as we walk through the door. The smell of savory spices and sweet aromas fills the air of the house I grew up in, allowing the thoughts of my conversation with Rumi going to the back of my mind.

For now.

"Jacky?" I hear from the kitchen as we toe off our shoes in the entryway—my mom having the same rule as Ava when you enter her home. I set Evee's diaper bag down, so I can place a hand on Rumi's back to lead her through the house and into the kitchen.

"Hey, Ma. We're here." Her back is turned to us as she bends to pull something out of the stove. She's wearing the apron she's had since I was a kid over the casual dress she's wearing, her dark hair streaked with gray twisted back in a clip.

Before she turns around, I grab the muffins from Rumi, knowing my mom is a hugger. And, just as expected, my mom turns, her eyes immediately going to Evee in my arms and then to Rumi as she claps her hands in front of her chest. "Rumi," she exclaims. "It is so good to finally meet you two." She rushes over, pulling her into a tight embrace.

Rumi looks surprised at first, but then she quickly recovers, wrapping her arms around my mom's waist. "Thank you so much for having us," she says as my mom finally lets her go. "This is my daughter, Evelyn," Rumi says, introducing the little girl in my arms. "But we all call her Evee. She just woke up before Jack picked us up to come over here, so she's still a little tired."

"Well, look at you," my mom says, her hands coming to her mouth. I can see the way her eyes glisten as she looks at Evee. "She is the cutest darn thing I have ever seen." She gives Evee a little wave. "Hi, honey bun."

Evee twists her head more into my neck, playing shy like her mom all of a sudden. And even though I can't see her, I know she's looking at my mom with those pretty blue eyes, making my mom fall more and more in love with her.

"Oh, I could look at her all day." My mom turns back to the kitchen where dishes line the counter, and I keep to myself how truly I know the feeling. "I hope you two are hungry. Emmy should be here any minute too, so we'll wait for her to eat." My eyes roam everything my mom prepared —a tofu scramble, sautéed vegetables, a loaf of banana bread, fresh fruit, and a pot of coffee. There's more that I can't see, and it warms my heart to see how she went above and beyond for Rumi, wanting to make sure she had options to choose from even with her dietary restrictions.

"We brought these too," I say, handing the muffins to my mom.

"My roommate made them," Rumi interjects, and I twist my lips to the side to hide my smile at the way her nerves are showing.

"They look wonderful," my mom says, taking the container from me and setting them down next to all the other food.

"Can I help you with anything, Ms. Hasting?" Rumi asks my mom, but she just waves her hand.

"Please, call me Angela. And no, but thank you. Please, sit. Let me get you something to drink. Jacky, your energy drinks are in the basement fridge." My mom turns to Rumi. "I don't know how he drinks those things in the morning."

"Right," Rumi agrees. "I could never drink one of those cold, bubbly drinks right when I wake up."

The two go back and forth, sharing laughs at my expense, but I don't care. I grab Evee's high chair from where I put it at the dining table last night when I stopped by, pulling it to the counter where Rumi is sitting. Setting Evee down, I head downstairs to let my mom and Rumi chat.

While it's been a few weeks since the drive-in movie date—the one that resulted in way less movie watching than I had initially anticipated, not that I'm complaining in any way, shape, or form—Rumi and I have really found our routine with one another.

June is slowly fading with July just around the corner, but we both find time to see each other within our work schedules—spending time at each other's houses, hanging out with Ava and Anderson, Emerson, and Luke and Annie and their friends, but we are taking things slow.

Knowing we both weren't necessarily looking for a relationship when we found one another, we're both on the same page that we aren't rushing this.

I think we both know that whatever this is between us could be the real thing, so we want to let it happen naturally as we continue finding out footing—something I royally fucked up by announcing to her that she's my girlfriend when we have yet to talk about this transition from friends to something more.

I'm still going to my therapy sessions twice a week, and I've really noticed a difference in myself. I'm slowly rediscovering what I loved about my job, even without Bennett here. Making more of an effort with Anderson and the other guys on the same shift rotation as me has helped, and Chief Sanders mentioned to me yesterday that he's noticed a difference in me too.

Going into the field isn't as scary as it felt when I first came back almost two months ago. Instead of the anxiety and dread, there's just the adrenaline and urgency that make me good at my job as both a first responder and firefighter.

We haven't had any massive fires, but there's been a few that I feel the familiar threat of freezing overwhelm me. I've been able to use the strategies for my PTSD I've learned in my therapy sessions to help me overcome them.

Grabbing an energy drink from the fridge, I make my way back upstairs, hearing that my sister has arrived.

The morning goes perfectly, and I find myself looking around the table and feeling my heart grow exponentially at seeing my mom, my sister, and Rumi getting along so well.

I don't even try to get a word in, wanting the three of them to talk as much as they want. I make sure Evee is eating and has what she needs, so Rumi can focus on the conversation and not have to worry about her.

Before I know it, two whole hours have gone by just listening to the three of them chat.

"How's the child support filing going?" Emerson asks Rumi. I reach a hand behind Rumi's chair, knowing that she has talked to both my sister and Ava about her decision to file for child support for Evee, but Trevor is not her favorite thing to talk about.

"Okay, I guess," she says, explaining to my sister that there's been little movement with the process since the local child support enforcement agency sent over a court-ordered paternity test to Trevor's last known address. "We're still waiting for the court to prove paternity."

"The whole process can really be a headache," my mom says, speaking from her own experience of having to file for child support when my dad left.

I've told my mom very little about Rumi's past, mostly because I didn't think it was right to give her details that were Rumi's to tell. She's aware that Evee's birth father isn't involved with her and how Rumi plans on keeping it that way, and she knows there's a history of domestic violence.

"Has he tried to contact you at all?" my sister asks as she helps clean Evee up, wiping her face with a wet paper towel and grabbing her one of those flappy books she loves from the basket of toys my mom bought for her and setting it on the tray of the high chair.

I was pretty much holding my breath when Rumi saw that my mom bought Evee toys, waiting for her to say how my mom didn't have to do that. But she surprised me when she thanked her, telling her how excited Evee would be to come visit her again.

"Thankfully, no. I was already nervous for the paternity test to be sent, but luckily it's from the court," Rumi explains.

It's been a concern of hers from the beginning that Trevor might be able to find her if she decided to file for child support, but, as far as we know, her address and other information is protected. But, since paternity cases are localized by county, there is a chance Trevor would be able to figure out where Rumi is.

She is adamant that Trevor won't bother trying to contact her in any way, but it's something I keep in the back of my mind, knowing that there's a chance.

"And you'll let me know if you ever need anything?" my mom asks Rumi. They're seated next to each other, so my mom rests her hand on top of Rumi's. "I'd be happy to help with Evee or anything else you might need."

I press my leg against Rumi's under the table, knowing this can't be easy for her. As someone who missed out on a chance to have a mother and isn't used to being part of a family, I know this all might be overwhelming for her.

Rumi flips her hand, holding on to my mom's. "Thank you, Angela."

That's my girl.

CHAPTER 32
JACK

"THIS IS DEFINITELY *NOT* what we should be doing in the library right now," Rumi whispers against my lips.

I have her trapped between my arms in a dark corner of the Northshore Public Library, having stopped by when she texted me that she and Ava were bringing Evee to an event with a local author of a popular children's book.

I've been feeling like a teenager lately with how much I want to get into her pants, reminding myself that we are taking things slow, but the memory of the night in the bed of my truck, feeling her fall apart on my fingers, seeing the way she looked when she comes, has been on my mind for weeks now.

The two of us have yet to get past what I can only consider as heavy petting—steamy makeout sessions in the car, teetering on the edge of second base, and me going home with no other choice but to jack off in the shower.

But tomorrow night is the night. My mom is watching Evee overnight, and Rumi is spending the night at my place.

"We're going to get caught," she whispers, but I press my lips to hers, feeling her moan against me as I grip her hips tight, pushing against her so she can feel how much I want her. "I have to get back to Evee and Ava."

And I need something to hold me over until tomorrow—the anticipation is killing me, and I know it's killing her too.

"What you need to do is stay quiet." I've been coming to this library since I was a kid, and I know no one ever comes back into this section of government documents, right next to the microfilm and archive room.

I kiss along her jaw and down her neck, my hands begging to lift her sexy little sundress up to see what she has on underneath.

Are they the white lace panties, like the ones I snuck into my back pocket when we were folding up the blankets after the drive-in movie?

Or are they like the pink ones with flowers that she wore to bed last night, giving me a naughty sneak peek during our reading date on FaceTime when I asked what she was wearing under the T-shirt of mine.

"How am I supposed to go back and listen to the read aloud of *When The Sun Sets* all hot and bothered?" Her voice is breathy, and I know by the way she fists the fabric of my station T-shirt that she doesn't want me to stop.

"You just need something to take the edge off," I say, lining kisses along the scar on her collarbone.

"You know, I was going to talk to the author about what I told you last weekend."

Rumi mentioned having an idea for a children's book about a chameleon that teaches kids about different emotions, and I'm happy to hear she's still thinking about it and not writing it off as a "silly dream" like she tried doing with me.

"Are you, now?" I whisper as I bend to kiss across her chest, sliding my tongue against her soft skin.

I may or may not have mentioned Rumi's idea to Ava, along with this author event I saw on a flyer posted on the bulletin board at the fire station.

I've realized with Ava's scheming that if I can't beat her, then I might as well join her.

"I thought you'd be more surprised," she whispers, running her fingers through my hair, pulling lightly at the ends, causing me to look up at her.

"By you? Not at all." I kiss her nose. "I can read you like *my* favorite book, which will be the one *you* write. You're going to go talk to that author to get this ball rolling with publishing your own children's book." I nip at her lips, fisting the fabric of her sundress. "But I need to make you come first."

She gasps, but I swallow it, kissing her hard before sucking her bottom lip into my mouth. Every time I taste her, I'm hit with the highest high—one I never want to come down from.

I lift her dress, not having time to tease her like I did at the drive-in—or how I plan on doing tomorrow. Right now, I just need my fix of her, quick and dirty.

Feeling her through her panties, I groan at how wet she already is just from my mouth, both the way I'm kissing her and the dirty things I whisper into her ear.

"So wet for me," I whisper, her head leaning back on the shelf behind us as I circle her clit through her underwear.

"You do that so well," she praises, and it hits me right in the cock, loving her praise as much as I love praising her.

Pulling her underwear to the side, I push two fingers inside of her, eliciting the most beautiful gasp. She bites her lip as I continue to circle her clit with my thumb, trying to stay quiet. I kiss down her neck, sucking on that sensitive spot just below her ear.

"Don't give me a hickey. Not after I teased Ava about hers." I chuckle against her skin.

Rumi and I quickly learned we weren't the *only* ones fooling around during our double date to the drive-in theater.

"I can't make any promises," I say just before I bite at the spot before soothing it with my tongue.

Pumping my fingers in and out of her, she begins to move her hips with me, bringing one leg around my waist as I grab her ass, keeping her steady.

"I'm gonna come," she breathes as she rides my fingers, and I kiss her hard, sending her right off the edge.

She moans against my mouth as she rides out her orgasm on my hand, and it takes everything in me to not embarrass myself like I did at the drive-in. "That's my girl," I say, pressing a kiss to her lips as she comes down, her lips moving against mine slow and languid, like we have all day.

She pulls back, her teeth sinking into her bottom lip. "Your turn." There's a pink flush to her cheeks and mischief in her eyes as she drops to her knees.

"Rumi, baby. You're going to be the death of me." My head falls back, and I can barely contain the buzzing just below my skin. "Not here."

"What happened to fucking the word 'sorry' right out of my mouth?" she repeats my words from the drive-in as she looks up at me, and the dirty words on her lips may be my undoing.

"You didn't apologize for anything." It's a poor excuse, but it's all I can come up with after hearing those words come out of her mouth.

"But I'm so, *so* sorry," she coos, her full lips pouting.

"For what?" I ask her, a grin on my face as she puts on this show, one I am more than happy to be an audience for.

She ignores me, undoing the button of my pants, bringing the zipper down. "I've never done this before," she admits quietly, but she moves as if she knows exactly what she's doing—the confidence radiating off of her is the sexiest thing I've ever seen.

"Rumi," I start to say, wanting to tell her that I don't want her to do this because she feels like she has to reciprocate. I want her to do it because she wants to.

God knows I fucking do.

She ignores me again. "So you're going to have to tell me what to do."

And that's all it takes to have me convinced, not because she has me in the palm of her hand and wrapped around her finger all at the same time, but, even though she's the one of her knees for me, I'm at her complete and utter mercy.

She lowers my pants and my boxer briefs just enough for my cock to spring free, the relief instant with how hard it was pressing against my zipper. Her eyes widen, like she likes what she sees, and I can't lie and say it doesn't boost my ego.

"You're so big," she says, lightly grabbing me by the base, her light touch sending a shiver through my entire body.

"It's nothing you can't handle," I grit through my teeth, already seconds away from blowing my load, and she's barely touched me. I wrap my hand around hers, showing her what kind of pressure I like, moving her hand with mine, up and down, as we stroke me together.

"Like that?" she asks, watching our hands move in tandem, and I can barely manage to nod, concentrating so hard on making this last.

"Yes, baby. Just like that," I manage to say, slipping my hand from hers, gripping the shelves behind me with both hands to try to remain in some semblance of control.

I'm about to tell her I'm already so close, but I forget how to form words when she looks up at me and says, "You're going to have to guide me through it." She presses a kiss to the head of my cock, and my knees threaten to buckle. "We're in a library, the perfect place to learn." The way her eyes are looking up at me like this could have me come right now. "So, teach me."

Before I can say anything, her lips wrap around my dick, tentatively at first, her tongue swiping off the pre-cum leaking out of my slit, and one of my hands instinctively goes to the back of her head.

She carefully works me into her mouth, adjusting to my size and the feel of me, and I resist moving my hips, letting her find her own rhythm.

My fingers tangle in her hair as I fight the urge to take control, my eyes closing as she takes me further in her mouth.

"Fuck," I hiss as her tongue lines the underside of my shaft. "Yes, just like that," I tell her, and she does it again, and I can't stop the groan that escapes my throat.

With my fingers in her hair, I gently start to guide her rhythm, seeing how far she can take me. "Relax your throat for me, baby," I manage to tell her through heavy breaths, and she does, taking me almost to the hilt. It's almost too much.

I don't want to push her too far, but her hands come to my thighs, gripping me tightly as I continue guiding her with my hold on her hair. When my grip tightens, a moan escapes her lips, vibrating against my cock, and I almost lose it right then and there.

My hips begin moving on their own, thrusting into her mouth, and she takes it in stride. I pick up speed, feeling her moan around me as I tell her how well she sucks my cock.

"You're gonna make me come," I warn, but her grip on my thighs tightens, her pretty blue eyes hazy with lust. I thrust into her mouth, faster and faster, chasing my release as she watches me.

Her eyes on me are what send me over the edge, coming into her mouth as she sucks me dry, and it honestly feels like I've died and gone to what people call heaven.

"Stand up and don't swallow," I growl as she slowly drags her lips over me one last time.

She does what I say, as I come down from my high, already knowing that I will never, ever, have enough of this girl.

"Show me." I bring my hand to her chin, forcing her to look directly in my eyes.

Her eyes slightly widen before she carefully opens her mouth, my cum on her tongue eliciting a wave of possessiveness throughout my entire body—my mind already thinking of all the different ways I plan on claiming her.

"Swallow," I order, and she does.

I press a kiss to her forehead, wishing I could throw her over my shoulder and lock her in my bedroom for the rest of our days—the caveman part of my brain threatening to take over my entire being.

So instead, we make ourselves presentable before I give her a pat on the ass and tell her, "Now, get back to the read aloud."

She bites her bottom lip, suppressing a smile. She gets up on her tiptoes to press a small kiss to my lips before turning around and heading down the long passage back out toward the light.

I follow close behind her, grabbing her hand as we walk down the few flights of stairs and back to the first floor where the author has just started reading her book to all the children and their grown-ups.

Squeezing her hand, wishing I didn't have to let go and walk back over to the station, I lean down to whisper in her ear. "See you tomorrow, pretty girl."

And tomorrow can't come soon enough.

CHAPTER 33

RUMI

IF AVA WASN'T the manager of a successful local coffee shop, she would make a very impressive detective.

The way she is interrogating me right now makes me feel like I did something much worse than fool around with Jack in the back corner of the library.

"Rumi Lillith Matthews, I swear, if you had sex bent over a dusty shelf in that library, I will never let you hear the end of it. Tell me what you were up to when he showed up and whisked you away from me and the Pilates Moms."

I cover my face with my hands, lucky that we don't open Hey Honey's for another five minutes and there are no customers to hear my best friend give me the third degree.

I avoided Ava's accusatory glances during the author's read aloud, and she let me off the hook long enough to chat with the author, Lauren, about her process and experience in publishing, telling her about the idea I had for my own children's book. After giving me her card with plans to get coffee and chat more next week, Ava and I headed home with Evee.

Ava had to get ready for her date with Anderson when we got home so she didn't sit me down and ask what I was doing when I was supposed to be sitting with her and Evee in the Children's Corner of the library.

But sadly, that luck ran out this morning when I walked out of my bedroom to a whirlwind of Ava's questions.

"We didn't have *penetrative* sex," I say, the words muffled from behind my hands.

"And what the hell does that mean?" Her hands are on her hips when I peek at her through my fingers.

"Oh, I think I hear Evee crying," I say, dropping my hands and trying to run past her, but she grabs my arm, spinning me around to face her.

"You and I both know she is dead asleep in that Pack 'n Play. Tell me." Her grip on my arm tightens, reminding me how scary my best friend can be.

I groan. "Fine."

Within the five minutes before we have to unlock the doors, and the various lulls we have in our morning shift together, I tell Ava all of the details from my little rendezvous with Jack, and I don't think I've ever seen my best friend *this* proud of me.

By the time Emerson and Luke come to finish the afternoon and early evening shift, Ava is bursting at the seams to share with her co-conspirators that all their hand work is paying off.

"I'm sick of all of you," I tell the three of them as I take off my apron, hanging it on my hook behind the office door. But, in reality, I can't explain how happy it makes me to have friends that care about this relationship with Jack as much as I do. I've never had friends, let alone friends who wanted to see me—and him—happy and cared enough about us to help make it happen.

"Yeah, yeah," Emerson says from next to me, grabbing her apron off her hook, and Ava shakes her head at me as she holds Evee and her diaper bag, already ready to drop her off at Jack's mom's house tonight for me.

"Who would've thought?" Luke chimes in. "Our first Hey Honey's couple. This might be the start of a Hey Honey's crew."

The three of us look at him, raised brows and cocked heads, having no idea what he's talking about.

"What?" Luke asks, crossing his arm and leaning against the door frame of the office. The mid-afternoon rush has come and gone, so the four of us are taking advantage of the lack of customers to talk.

"Are we just going to pretend what you said isn't stupid?" Emerson asks, always the first one to say something, especially when there's an opportunity to call out someone not making any sense.

"Sometimes I forget how much you're like your brother," Luke says with a sigh. "What I meant was, you know what Mia's brother calls me, Annie, Mia, Eddie, Drew, and Emmett? The Lennys' crew? It all started with Drew and Emmett, the first Lenny's couple. From there, it all just bloomed into the family we are now."

"So?" Emerson says, the three of us still trying to make sense of what he's saying.

"So," Luke says, stretching out the word. "The three of you are so close, and now Jack and Rumi are a couple. It's like you guys are following in our footsteps."

I open my mouth to correct him—seeing as though Jack and I have yet to discuss him calling me his girlfriend when we went to his mom's house—but I decide against it, liking the sound of the two of us being a couple.

"Why are you making this so weird?" Emerson asks, and Ava and I laugh, which causes Luke to throw up his hands in frustration, but I can see the grin he's trying to hold back.

"All I'm saying is, this could be the start of something special. Mark my words." He turns to head back to the front just as the chime to the front door rings.

The three of us look at each other and let out another

laugh, but there's something about what Luke says that sticks with me, something I can't stop thinking about on our way home or on my way over to Jack's for the night.

Maybe this all is the start of something special.

———

"Wow, you look awful."

It's the last thing I expected to say when Jack opened his front door for our first night together, the one we've been looking forward to all week is.

His skin is pale and clammy, and dark circles hang beneath his sunken eyes. He clutches his stomach, as he leans against the door, his eyes bloodshot. "I'm so sorry."

"Now who's apologizing for something that isn't his fault." I hadn't brought anything over after Jack suggested we could go out before coming back to the house for the night, but, by the looks of it, I don't think he's in any shape to leave.

"I meant to call, but I fell asleep on the couch after I got home from my shift this morning." He runs a hand through his bed head, the dark strands messy and sticking out at odd angles. "I really wanted to spend time with you, but I don't want to get you sick."

I wave a hand, stepping through the front door. "I trust my immune system, and you look like you could use some *help*." My eyes assess him up and down, his clothes are rumpled and damp from what I can only assume is a fever.

With how sluggish he is as we walk toward his kitchen, he looks like he's seconds away from falling over.

"Have you eaten?" I ask him, and he shakes his head as he sits down at the chair at his kitchen counter.

"I wasn't sure if I'd be able to keep anything down." His eyes roam to the empty high chair at the edge of the counter. "Did Evee make it to my mom's?" he asks, and I'll never get over how he is always concerned with Evee, making sure she's good and taken care of.

"All good. Ava texted me that Em was there when she dropped her off, and I wouldn't be surprised if Ava is still there. She texted me how much she loved your mom, and they met literally half an hour ago. She sent me a picture of the four of them from outside on your mom's patio." I pull out my phone, pulling up the selfie that Ava sent me to show to Jack.

"Good," Jack says, looking at the picture, but he looks like he's in pain when he tries to smile.

I set my phone on the table, walking over to the sink to fill up Jack's water bottle he has drying next to the sink. "Let's start with getting you hydrated, and then we can revisit the food."

Handing him his water bottle, he brings it to his chapped lips, taking a few big sips. I see the cold medicine he must have taken when he got home today and push that over to him too. He takes the pills with a couple more sips of water.

Looking down at my dress, I feel overdressed to be a caretaker for the night, so I ask Jack if I can raid his dresser for something cozier to wear. I brought pajamas over, as well as anything else I needed to spend the night, but I don't think the tiny silk shorts and tank top fit with tonight's new agenda.

"You're telling me I have to look at you, in my clothes, in my bedroom, when I'm too sick to even touch you?"

"Relax, firefighter. You'll be asleep in half an hour after taking those pills. Hopefully you'll sleep this off and feel better in the morning." I turn to head up the stairs to his headroom, but he grabs my hand to stop me.

"I really am sorry about our night." His voice is soft, his eyes sad, and I don't like it.

"Things happen. Not to mention, I have a one-year-old

daughter. Better get used to our relationship having interruptions," I tell him, running a hand through his hair, feeling his too-hot skin against my palm. "I'll be right back." I give his hand a squeeze before heading upstairs.

Not exactly sure what to expect, I walk into Jack's bedroom and am pleasantly surprised with how nice it is. I've seen glimpses in the background on our nightly FaceTime calls, but this is my first time seeing the whole space.

In the two months Jack has lived here, he's done a lot of unpacking and making the house much more of a home—even though I thought it felt like one the first week he moved in.

His bed is neatly made with a sleek gray duvet, and the simple wooden headboard gives the room a clean, put-together feel. The dark furniture is a nice contrast to light blue walls, a big TV hung just in front of the bed—one I plan on taking full-advantage of tonight while Jack sleeps.

After finding one of Jack's T-shirts and a pair of his sweatpants in his surprisingly organized dresser, I throw his clothes on, my sundress forgotten in a pile on the floor. His T-shirt is soft and smells like him, but his sweatpants barely stay above my hips, even with pulling the drawstrings as tightly as they go.

I pull my hair up in a ponytail, wanting it out of my face and head into his bathroom to wash off the little makeup I have on.

I thought I'd feel more disappointed with the night taking this sort of turn, but it's nowhere to be found. I'm just happy to spend time with Jack, no matter what it looks like.

There's this part of me that feels like we have all the time in the world. We're taking things slow; there's no pressure to rush anything.

And with all the time that passes, it feels more like this is something that is built to last.

When I head back downstairs, I find Jack laying down on the couch, the cold medicine already kicking in.

"Hey, let's get you upstairs." The sun is still high in the sky, the mid-July evening looking like the middle of the day with how bright it is, but he needs to sleep this off.

Jack mumbles something against the couch cushions, but he makes no effort to move. Grabbing his arm, his skin is hot to the touch. I press the back of my hand to his forehead, and he is burning up.

Heading into the kitchen, I find a cloth and wet it with cold water, bringing it back over to Jack and gently placing it on his forehead. He hums as the cool cloth meets his skin, and I dab it on his cheeks as he closes his eyes. "That feels good," he says quietly.

I shush him, continuing to move the cloth to the hot skin on his neck, but he opens his eyes.

"Look at me," he whispers, so I do, meeting his gaze. His hand comes to cup my cheek from where he's laying down, and I settle beside him sitting on the couch. "I could look at you forever," he says, but his eyes have a glaze to them that tells me he's barely conscious right now, the cold medicine taking effect no matter how hard he tries to fight it.

"We have to get you up to bed," I tell him.

"The first time I saw you, I knew you were going to be okay. You had to be." The words seem odd, random even. The first time he saw me, we were in the middle of a coffee shop.

"Okay, firefighter." I stand up, setting the cloth on the coffee table, trying to reign in my smile at his gibberish. He probably has no idea what he's saying, maybe isn't even fully awake right now.

"And I knew I was going to be okay," he adds as I grab his arms, helping him sit up. "I saw it in your eyes. The peace I only ever found on the lake."

There he goes again about my eyes. It reminds me of what

he said on our way to the drive-in, how my eyes were the same color of the lake he fished on.

"I saw it when I found you."

When he found me?

He makes running into each other by complete chance at Hey Honey's that day seem like an act of the universe, like something so simple was bound to happen.

Then again, maybe it was.

Pulling him by the arms, he finally sits up from the couch, slowly standing, so we can head to the stairs.

With an arm around my shoulder, I help him up each stair, holding onto him with one arm and the railing with the other to keep us both steady.

It takes a while, every step Jack puts more and more weight on me, but we finally make it up to his bedroom.

"There we go, " I say, pulling back the comforter and sheets and helping him to bed.

"I was planning on asking you to be my girlfriend tonight," he says as his head hits the pillow. I barely hear him with how heavy my breathing is, completely out of breath from helping him up those stairs.

Lifting his tree trunks of legs with all of my strength, I help him under the covers. "Don't worry about that right now," I reassure him, grabbing his comforter and pulling it over his body.

"Will you be my girlfriend?" he asks, his voice thick and hoarse and slightly muffled from how he's laying on his pillow.

I can't help but laugh. "I'm not sure now is the time you want to have this conversation."

"Please," he begs, and the way he says it is something I know he'd be embarrassed about if he was going to even remember this conversation. "I promise I'll be the best boyfriend you've ever had."

"That's not really helping your case right now." I run my

hand through his hair as I sit beside him, feeling how hot his forehead is—his fever definitely hasn't broken yet.

He ignores me, continuing to speak as if I didn't say anything. "And then I'll be the best husband, and, if you let me, the best dad to Evee." His words trail off as the cold medicine takes effect, his eyelids closing as if they weigh a thousand pounds.

What the hell did he just say?

CHAPTER 34
JACK

WHEN I SAID last weekend was the night Rumi and I finally got a whole night alone, little did I know the universe was going to say "fuck you" and kick me in the balls.

I don't think I have ever been that sick in my entire life, and I blame Anderson for coming to the station sick after going to his nephew's birthday party.

I'm thankful Rumi stayed healthy, even after coming over and spending the night.

While most of the night is a blur, I do remember Rumi taking care of me, pressing cool towels to my head, running her hands through my hair, and wrapping her body around mine when she was looking for heat in the middle of the night.

By the morning, I was much less groggy and out of it than I was the night before, but Rumi couldn't stay long, having to pick Evee up from my mom's.

I ended up sleeping the rest of the day, and now I'm back at the station—it feels like I never left.

"How were your days off?" Anderson asks me, sitting on the couch next to me.

"Shitty," I answer, not even looking up from my book.

Rumi and I recently swapped reading material—she's reading my favorite cozy mystery series about a young investigator using her grandmother's diaries to help solve her small towns mysteries, and I'm reading what Ava calls her "vampire smut books", specifically starting off with the one that looks like an Edward/Jacob fanfic.

Rumi explained that the correct term is "paranormal romance", and I'm enjoying myself either way. Sure, the sex scenes are entertaining—-some giving me plenty of inspiration when I finally get my re-do of a night alone with Rumi this weekend, but it's the forbidden love between the vampire and the werewolf that I'm really enjoying.

"And why is that?" Anderson asks, and I look up at him over the frames of my reading glasses for a moment, finding his bright brown eyes and huge grin extra annoying today.

"You got me sick," I tell him before going back to my reading, tuning him out as he explains to me how it wasn't his fault that one of his nephew's friends came to the birthday party after just getting over the flu.

The rest of my 24-hour shift is uneventful aside from a few routine calls and having to gear up at two in the morning when some nosy neighbor thought the house down the street was on fire—turns out, the owners were just having a big bonfire and the old woman who called it in didn't put on her glasses when she saw a "humongous orange flame" coming from the back of the house.

By the time we do our shift change after briefing the incoming guys about the last 24-hours, I'm ready to head to the gym before stopping by Hey Honey's to visit Rumi at her morning shift.

We have a date to the zoo with Evee scheduled for tomorrow, and we're supposed to have our books read, so we can talk about them as we walk around.

I'm almost to my truck when I hear my last name boom

from behind me, the deja vu hitting me square in the jaw when I turn to find Chief Sanders.

"Chief," I greet with a nod.

I haven't had much time to talk with the chief, not with how busy my shifts have been filling in for our Fire Lieutenant, James, while he's helping out at the station nearby as interim chief.

"I wanted to catch you before you head out," Chief says, crossing his arms over his chest. "How are your sessions going?"

"Great," I answer. "He switched me to just once a week because of my progress."

Even though neither the chief nor my therapist has told me, I know they have eyes on me in the field, and that they are in conversations with one another about my progress.

Before starting therapy, it probably would have pissed me off. But now? I know it's to help me and keep me moving in the right direction, both professionally and personally.

"Glad to hear it," Chief Sanders says. "And I've heard from some of the crew how smooth things have been running in the field recently."

As the Fire Lieutenant in the field these last few weeks, it's my job to coordinate the team during our emergency responses. It's my job to make sure everyone follows the safety protocols and operates efficiently.

It's a tough job, one that James makes look easy. Assessing the scene, making quick decisions, and being the one in charge of directing resources to control the fires, search and rescue, and managing any other situations that arise means I'm the one everyone puts their trust in, and it's vital that I have a handle on my PTSD.

"The crew thinks you're a natural leader, and you've made huge strides in the last three months. It's not easy keeping communication clear and organized and being the point of contact between the frontlines. I'm proud of you, and I think Bennett would be too."

While I'm still not ready to get too close to the active fires—and with my new role as interim Fire Lieutenant, it's my job to stay back and assess the situation as a whole rather than be on the frontline—I've been able to prevent any other panic attacks or freezing in the field.

"Thank you, Chief." The pride that blooms in my chest warms my entire body, the thought of making not only the man I look up to but my best friend proud fills me with confidence in my recovery and in the work I've been putting into myself.

"With that being said," Chief Sanders continues, "it sounds like James will be taking over as chief at Southland's station at the end of next month."

I nod, taking in his words, the ones both spoken and unspoken. James was supposed to be back at the beginning of August, so I figured I'd only be covering his role for one more week, but that doesn't sound like the case anymore.

"And if all goes well, his position is going to you."

"Me?" I can't hide my disbelief. While his praise at my ability to fill in for James is one thing, actually being promoted to Fire Lieutenant is a whole other beast. "Sir, it's an incredible opportunity, but I don't know if I'm ready."

Like he said, I've made progress with my grief and PTSD the last three months, but I still have a long way to go.

I still have yet to get back on the frontlines for fuck's sake.

"Give yourself some credit," Chief Sanders says, clapping an arm to my shoulder. "You passed the FFDE with the psychiatrist your therapist recommended, and you were already next in line for the position before you left. It's not a decision I've made lightly."

He turns to head back to the station, leaving me with his words.

Hopping into my truck, I immediately call Rumi, needing

to tell her the news. Glancing at the clock, I see it's time for Evee's morning nap, so hopefully I can catch Rumi just after she puts Evee down.

She answers on the second ring. "Hi, firefighter," she whispers into the phone, and I can hear a door close on her end of the line.

"Hey, pretty girl."

"How was the rest of your shift? Did you get time to finish the book?" she asks, her voice going back to a normal volume.

I clear my throat. "It was good, nothing crazy, and almost. Planning on finishing tonight. Hey, listen," I say, the words coming out slightly rushed. I run a hand through my hair. "I just got done talking with the chief."

"Is everything okay?" she asks, knowing from different conversations we've had throughout the summer that my talks with the station's chief these last few months haven't always been a walk in the park.

"Yeah, actually. Everything's great. You know how I've been acting as the Fire Lieutenant in the field the last few weeks?"

"Yes," she says, but it comes out wearily.

"Chief wants to promote me to the position permanently."

She squeals in excitement for me. "Oh my gosh! Jack, that's such great news. How do you feel?"

"Good, I think. I just hope I'm ready."

"Of course you are. As long as you keep up with your sessions and are honest with your therapist and the chief about your progress." Her reassurance grounds me, her faith in me making my doubts from a moment ago fade. "I'm so proud of you."

"Thank you, baby."

I'm proud of me too.

CHAPTER 35
JACK

"CHANGE OF PLANS," Rumi says when she answers the door, immediately handing over Evee to me as I walk in. "We're not going to the zoo." Rumi has on a blue and yellow sundress today, and I'm learning with every one she owns that sundresses are my literal kryptonite when it comes to her.

"Aw, but I was so excited to talk to you about your vampire sm—" Her eyes turn to slits, waiting for me to say the words. "Your paranormal romance," I say with a wink.

"Nice save. But no, that'll have to wait."

"Okay," I say, pulling Evee into my arms. "What's the new plan?"

"Remember how I told you about that coffee date I had with Lauren McKinely? The author from the read aloud we went to at the library?" Rumi asks over her shoulder as I follow her into the kitchen.

"Oh, I remember the library," I tease, and she turns around to slap me playfully on the arm, and it makes Evee giggle.

"Yes, I remember your coffee date. You said it went well." She had also said that Lauren thought Rumi's idea for a children's book was exactly like something her agent was looking for, and that she would connect the two. Since the meeting, Rumi has completely brought her idea to life, and with the help of Emerson, not only does she have her story, but she also has rough sketches for illustrations.

"Really well," Rumi says, bouncing on her heels with anticipation, like she can barely contain herself. "And you'll never guess who just called asking to represent me!"

My jaw drops. "Shut up." I grab her by the material of the dress she has on, pulling her to me and hugging her against Evee and me. My cheeks hurt with how hard I'm smiling, my skin buzzing the Rumi's contagious excitement. "Lauren's agent wants to work with you? Rumi, that's amazing."

"I know! Can you believe it? I still have to look over everything, and the whole process is a big commitment, both with time and money, and I'm still waiting to hear an update about the child support, but I really want to make this work."

"We will. We'll make it work. I'm so proud of you." I press a kiss to her lips and then one to Evee's cheek. "Mommy's going to be an author, Evee girl," I tell her, and she claps her hands at the excitement radiating off both me and her mom.

"Ma-ma, ma-ma," she babbles, and we freeze, both Rumi's and my eyes turning to her.

"Did she just—" Rumi asks, her eyes wide.

"Did you just say your first word?"

"This is the best day ever!" Rumi exclaims, grabbing Evee and lifting her high in the air, repeating "mama" back at her in hopes she says it again.

I watch the two of them, my own eyes prickling at the sight.

To think how far Rumi has come in the last year—I don't even think she thought she'd ever be spinning her daughter in the air, smiles on both their faces, in her own house, with a job she adores, and another that marks her dream coming true.

I'm just thankful I get to be part of it.

Rumi looks back at me. "So much to celebrate," she says with a smile, walking over to press a kiss to my lips. "Congrats on your promotion, firefighter."

"*Potential* promotion," I correct, pressing another kiss to her lips. "And congrats on becoming a published author."

She kisses me one more time. "*Potential* published author," she echos.

"And congrats on your first word, sweetheart," I say to Evee, both Rumi and me pressing a kiss to her check, making her squeal.

Looking at Rumi, I ask, "So what are our new plans?" I take Evee back from her so she can sit down at the kitchen counter.

"Well," she starts, her cheeks blushing, "Ava and Emerson offered to take Evee to the zoo this afternoon and then watch her overnight, and I was thinking we could, maybe, go to your place to, um, *celebrate* all of our good news."

My shy girl is back, and it takes everything in me not to kiss that blush right off her checks—*or kiss her until her whole body blushes.*

"I like this new plan. Why don't you show me the new changes to your book while we wait for them, and then we pack you a bag to head over to my place."

Or your entire house, I think to myself, but I quickly let the thought fade to the back of my mind, a much more important question coming to the forefront.

"And there's something I've been meaning to ask you," I tell her, and the way she bites her lip tells me she knows exactly what I'm about to say. "Rumi baby," I start. "Will you be my girlfriend?"

She nods, throwing her arms around my neck and kissing me hard on the lips before pressing little kisses all over my face, squishing Evee in the process and making her laugh a full-on belly laugh. "Third time's the charm, huh?"

she teases, but I can only think of one other time I asked her.

Either way, I'm just happy she said yes.

"And Evee girl," I say through her mom's kisses, "I have a question for you too." Rumi leans back, a confused look on her face, this time having no idea what I plan on saying. I look down at Evee's pretty blue eyes, feeling her mom's on the both of us. "Can I be your mom's boyfriend?"

CHAPTER 36
RUMI

WHOEVER CAME up with the saying, "the anticipation is killing me", had to have been a woman on the brink of her sexual awakening, moments away from having a night alone with the man who showed her the true meaning of sex.

No wonder Ava always talks about needing to get laid.

I've been thinking of being in Jack's bed since the last time I was in it, but I'm thankful that this time he isn't running a fever and speaking nonsense.

The drive over to his house after Ava and Emerson got home to take Evee to the zoo was excruciating. I was already buzzing with the news of Lauren's agent, Joanna, wanting to represent me, not to mention just how anxious—in a good way—I get whenever I'm about to see Jack, the butterflies in my stomach being absolutely menacing when it comes to him and my ability to focus on anything else. And then adding the anticipation of finally getting our night together, *alone*? I feel like I'm seconds away from my nervous system completely shutting down.

And then he had to go and include Evee in asking me to be his girlfriend after she decided she wanted in on all the celebrating and said her first word?

I don't know how I'm still standing.

"Are you hungry?" Jack asks as he pulls into his driveway, his hand on my thigh as he cuts the engine and turns to look at me.

I shake my head, words failing me. With so many thoughts racing through my brain, I can't trust myself to string together any comprehensible sentences.

Jack's eyes darken, and his hand on my leg tightens. I hope he can see that I am in no way thinking about eating, not when we have an empty house just outside his truck and a whole night with just the two of us.

Jack hops out of the truck, before coming over to open my door. He holds his hand out for me to take, helping me hop down from the truck, my feet barely hitting the ground before his lips crash into mine.

He kisses me with a sense of urgency, like he's been waiting to get his mouth on mine all day, all week, his whole life. His tongue dances with mine as he lifts me against him, and my legs instinctively wrap around his body. He holds me tight as he shuts the car door and walks us to the house, never breaking our kiss.

It's early afternoon, the sun still high, and his neighbors probably think we're insane, but none of that matters. Not when I can feel his strong arms wrapped around me, his hard body pressed against mine.

He breaks our kiss just long enough to unlock his door, taking a couple tries as I kiss along the stubble on his jaw and down his neck.

"I need you in my bed." His lips find mine again as we walk into the house, and he kicks the door shut behind him. I feel his steps stutter as we get closer to the stairs before he changes his mind and walks us into the kitchen.

"What are you doing?" I ask him as he sets me down just in front of the counter.

He doesn't answer at first, kissing me hard before he turns

me around. "Bend over for me," he growls in my ear, his voice thick.

I turn over my shoulder to see his green eyes clouded with lust, like fog over the forest, a beautiful yet dangerous sight. I feel one arm hook around my waist while the other gently pushes me down, my exposed chest from my sundress and arms meeting the cool granite of the counter.

"I need to taste you."

A moan escapes my lips at his words, and I feel him fist my dress, bringing it up over my ass that's on full display to him.

"Here?" I ask, but it comes out too breathy to sound even remotely similar to something other than a plea.

"Yes, right here. Right where I watched you lick that chocolate off those lips the first time you came over," he says, hooking his thumbs under the waistband of my underwear, bringing them down slowly—the way he slows down gives me whiplash, my chest rising and falling quickly against the granite.

"You don't even like chocolate," I argue. Not seeing what he's doing makes this all the more hotter, the feeling of him lowering my underwear inch-by-inch making me go absolutely crazy.

"I would if I was licking it off *you*. What do you think, pretty girl?" With my underwear now around my ankles, he grips my ass with both hands. "Should I keep you bent over with your ass out while I melt some chocolate to pour all over your sweet skin?" His hands move up my body, palming my breasts as a groan leaves his lips. "And all over those amazing tits?" He presses kisses down my neck and over my shoulder. "Would you let me lick my way down all the way to this greedy, little pussy?"

He runs a finger down my slit, parting me, and I can feel how wet I already am. The picture he paints in my head, in addition to all this waiting we've done for a night alone, is enough to already have me on the edge.

Jack hums, as he lazily draws his finger over me, spreading my wetness all over my clit and my entrance, pulling a moan from me.

"You'd like that, wouldn't you?" he asks, bending over me and pressing my body more into the counter. The weight of him on top of me and the lazy circles he draws over my clit with his finger is enough to have me seeing stars.

He takes me right to the edge before he pulls away, leaving me breathing heavy against the counter.

"Really?" I say, but it comes out more like a whine. "You really know how to work a girl up, huh?" I start to push myself off the counter, but I feel his hand press on my back, keeping me down.

"Stay right there," he orders, and it sends a bolt of electricity through me.

Turning my head, I watch as he saunters over to the cabinet, pulling out a bag of chocolate chips before reaching into another one for a bowl.

"Are you actually about to do this?" I ask him, feeling silly that I'm still bent against the counter with my ass on full display.

He shushes me, working as if he has all the time in the world—pouring some chocolate chips into the glass bowl before setting the bowl into the microwave. He sets the timer for thirty seconds, and I already know it's going to be the longest thirty seconds of my life.

I let out a groan. "This is ridiculous." I move to stand up again, but Jack is back behind me before I can even sit up an inch.

"What's so ridiculous is how I'm going to make you come before that timer runs out." I don't even have time to register the words before he pumps two fingers inside of me, finding the spot that instantly makes me scream out his name. The stretch is delicious, his thumb finding my clit with such precision, it's like he knows my body better than I know it myself.

He works me fast and hard, whispering dirty promises of what's to come until I'm falling apart in his hands with seconds to spare.

The microwave beeps just as I start coming down, and I don't even have to lift my hand from the counter to know that Jack has a smirk on his face.

"That," he says, walking over to the microwave and pulling out the melted chocolate, "was just the beginning."

"What?" I ask, sitting up on my elbows, finding that smirk I knew would be on his stupid, beautiful face.

"I'm nowhere close to being done with you," he warns, but I'm not scared at all.

CHAPTER 37
JACK

I THINK Rumi is the most gorgeous thing I've ever seen, but seeing her bent over my kitchen counter? I can now die a happy man knowing that I've seen a sight as stunning as this.

Bringing the melted chocolate over, I can almost see the anticipation buzzing on her skin. Grabbing the fabric of her dress, I pull her body up to meet mine, feeling her mold against me as if she's right where she belongs.

She turns around, facing me, her cheeks flushed from her orgasm, her full tits begging to be free from that sundress—the one I'm surprised I held myself together enough to not rip to complete shreds once we were through the front door.

I knew I was being a bit of a tease when I made her wait for me to melt the chocolate, but I was a fool to think I would ever be the one in control here.

I don't know where to start with her, on full display for me.

Setting the bowl down, I grab her by the hips, helping her on to the counter. "As much as I love this dress—every dress you wear for that matter," my admission makes her teeth sink into her bottom lip, hiding her smirk, "I think I'll like it even more over there on the floor."

"I don't know," she whispers, and I can hear the nerves.

"Don't get shy on me now, baby."

She hesitates a moment before her hands go to the hem of her dress, slowly bringing it up her body before dropping it onto the hardwood.

Holy fuck.

Her full tits make my mouth literally water, the way her dusty, pink nipples beg to be sucked. Her toned legs and soft stomach are a fantasy turned to reality, and I honestly feel like I could spend the rest of my life just standing here, looking at her.

My eyes roam, taking in my fill, noting the scar on the side of her stomach from where she got her kidney removed— after that sorry son of a fucking bitch put his hands on her. Seeing the scar adorning her perfect body, causes a wave of possessiveness to take over, my whole body vibrating with the need to claim her in every which way, to prove to her that she's mine to protect.

Her stomach is also decorated with the scar from her C-section, the one that makes my heart ache thinking about how it got there, how that accident prompted an emergency to save her daughter. The pink, raised skin matches the scar on her collarbone—the one that reminds me of how far she's come.

"How are you so fucking perfect?" I ask, but it's more to myself. I close the space between Rumi and me, settling between her legs as I crash my mouth to hers. There's not enough time in the universe for how long I want to kiss, how long I *need* to have her lips against mine.

She wraps her slender arms around my neck, tangling her fingers in my hair. I press kisses to her jaw, her neck, the scar on her collarbone all the way down to the one on her side before finding the one on her stomach.

"Jack," she breathes, and I stop, pausing to look up at her.

Her eyes glisten, and I can almost see every thought in her pretty little head.

"I'm obsessed with this," I say, kissing her scar, gripping her legs tight.

"No, you're not," she says, and I feel her slipping away, shrinking into herself like she does when her self-consciousness takes over.

"I am," I say, looking up at her. "This scar is one of my favorite parts about you. You know why?" She shakes her head. "It's because it shows me, and everyone else, how fucking strong you are, your resilience, and your growth. It shows the world how good of a mother you are and how there is nothing you won't do for your daughter." I press a kiss to the raised skin.

She reaches for me, saying my name again, as she pulls me to her, kissing me hard and with everything she has.

When she says my name, it's like a promise—a promise to overcome our pasts so we can get the futures we deserve.

My chest swells with emotion, wishing there were words to convey what I feel for this woman.

Kissing her deep, she moans against my lips, and I roam my hands all over her body, wanting to feel every inch of her soft skin.

We kiss until our lips are swollen.

Until I'm so hard I think I might die.

"Lean back," I tell her, and she does, her obedience—her trust in me—going straight to my heart.

And my cock.

I reach for the bowl that was forgotten on the counter until now but now at the perfect temperature. Dipping a finger in the warm chocolate, I swipe it over Rumi's peaked nipple and hear a rushed inhale in response.

Leaning down, I take her nipple in my mouth, swirling my tongue over the sensitive skin covered in chocolate before adding some to the other side and doing the same.

I want her to be a writhing mess in my hands, so I take my time teasing her, swiping the chocolate over her perfect tits before licking it right off.

"Fuck," she moans, and it's music to my ears. She's breathing heavily, her eyes closed as I work her. "Jack, touch me. Please."

And I happily oblige.

Licking the rest of the chocolate from my fingers, I run my hand down her body, stopping when I get to her clit, circling my fingers slowly.

"Yes," she breathes, but I know she needs more.

"I got you, baby," I coo, kissing down her stomach until I'm inches away from tasting her—something I've been dreaming about for weeks now. She moans at my words as I continue circling her clit, and I let out a chuckle. "Always such a greedy girl," I whisper just inches from her center before I lower my mouth all the way to her, groaning at the taste of her mixed with the sweetness of the chocolate still on my tongue.

Maybe I do like chocolate after all.

"Oh my god," she moans as I slowly drag my tongue up her slit, circling it around her clit before lightly sucking it into my mouth, her back bucking off the counter as her hand goes to my head.

She presses me closer to her, and I grip her legs, my fingers digging into her skin hard enough to leave bruises. Her taste is addictive, and I don't know how I'll ever get enough.

I pump two fingers inside her as I tongue her clit, moving in the slow circles that drive her crazy, until she's screaming my name, her fingers gripping my hair as she falls apart.

Scooping her up off the counter, barely giving her time to realize what's happening, I carry her upstairs to my bed. She squeals with laughter as I throw her onto my bed, stripping off my T-shirt and shorts in record time.

"I need to be inside you," I plead. "Now."

"I'm clear and on the pill," she says quickly, her cheeks flushed and her eyes hazy with lust.

"I'm clear too, but I have condoms if—"

"No," she interrupts me. "I don't want anything between us."

She doesn't have to tell me twice.

I lay down next to her, pulling her on top of me, *dying* to be underneath her. I pump myself a few times, just to take the edge off, knowing I won't last long but also knowing I won't survive if I'm not inside her soon.

"Ride me, baby," I tell her, as she settles on her knees, hovering just above my aching cock.

"I don't know how," she says in a whisper. "It's never been like this before."

Rumi opened up to me about not being with anyone since Trevor, and I know she's in the process of discovering what sex is to her, so I remind myself to slow down.

"We don't have to do anything you don't want to do," I tell her, grabbing her hands from my chest and holding them tightly in mine.

"No, that's not it," she says, shaking her head. "I really want to. I think that's what makes it so different."

I stare up into her pretty blue eyes, feeling like my sole purpose in life is to be underneath her. "Do you trust me?" I ask her, bringing her hands to my lips and pressing a kiss to her knuckles.

"I trust you."

Hearing her say it takes all the air from my lungs, but I'd happily give up my ability to breathe if it meant she'd feel safe with me.

"And you know I got you?" I ask, hoping she doesn't notice the crack in my voice.

She nods, and I let go of her hands so she can place them on my chest.

"We'll go slow, and on your terms, okay? Just do what feels good," I tell her.

"What about what feels good for you?" she asks, her blush deepening as she sucks her bottom lip into her mouth, biting it hard as she looks down at me.

"You don't have to worry about me, baby. Just the thought of being inside of you has me on edge."

She smiles just before she gently lowers herself on my cock, and the urge to grab her ass and slam her down when I feel that first bit of contact is strong.

But I hold off, fisting my hands in the sheets.

She's the one in control.

"Fuck," I hiss as she lowers a little more, adjusting to my size, taking it like a goddamn pro.

The anticipation is literally killing me, the saying holding more truth in this moment than any other moment of my life.

I watch as her tight pussy swallows my dick, inch-by-inch, until she bottoms out, both of us groaning at the sensation.

"That's my fucking girl," I grit, resting my hands on her hips, helping her find her rhythm. "There you go. Ride me, Rumi baby."

And she does.

I watch as she takes me over and over again, her dark waves falling over her shoulders and down her chest, her blue eyes hooded as she looks down at me.

"You're doing so good," I praise, watching her with pure captivation as her look of concentration fades as she finds what feels good, her eyes closing as she rides me.

"I didn't know it could be like this." Her voice is breathy, and I can feel her tighten around my cock. I reach up, grabbing her full tits, massaging them before lightly pinching her nipples, making her eyes close.

Her head falls back, and I feel her inner muscles tighten as another orgasm crests, and my hands are back on her hips to hold her steady as I fuck up into her, hitting that spot I know drives her wild.

"Jack," she moans, and neither of us could care less about how loud she is—if I had it my way, I want everyone hearing what she sounds like when I make her come.

"Come for me," I order as I reach my own orgasm, both of us falling apart together.

CHAPTER 38
RUMI

I'M NEVER LEAVING this bed.

After tearing ourselves from each other, we took a shower and cleaned up, having to remind each other to keep our hands to ourselves multiple times before Jack bent me over and fucked me against the glass shower door.

By the time we got dressed, we were both starving.

We ordered a pizza and ate in bed, talking about everything and anything until I couldn't keep my eyes open any longer.

With the sunlight peeking through from under the shades, I look over at the sleeping man next to me, wondering if the butterflies I get when I see him will ever go away.

The way he makes me feel is unlike anything I ever thought possible, and last night was so much more than sex. It was hard to not get in my head when it was about to finally happen—I couldn't stop the self-doubt and nerves from taking over, making me feel like I didn't know what I was doing.

But he knew exactly what to say to ground me, to remind me that I was with him—the man I trust—not with the man who almost broke me beyond repair.

I brush a few pieces of his hair off his forehead before curling up against him.

"Good morning," he says against my hair, his voice rough and ridden with sleep.

"Shh," I tell him. "Go back to sleep. We still have two hours before I told Ava I would be back, and Sundays are for rest."

I try to lay on his bare chest but he wraps his arms around me, murmuring something about how maybe he doesn't hate Sundays after all; I don't have time to ask him what he means because he's pulling me on top of him. "I don't need rest. I need you," he says, his hands gripping the tops of my thighs as they settle on either side of him.

"Didn't you get your fill last night?" I tease, already feeling desire pool in my lower belly.

"Never." I lean down to press a kiss to his lips. "Now, hold on to the headboard," he says against my lips.

"What?" I ask, not sure that I heard him right.

"I said, hold on to the headboard," he repeats.

"Why?" I ask.

"Because you're going to need something to hold on to while you fuck my face."

———

"Mia, Drew, your drinks are ready." Setting down the iced vanilla latte and a coffee with cream at the pickup counter, I exhale as the last of my orders for the morning rush are finished.

"Thanks, Rumi," Mia says, grabbing her coffee as Drew gives me a smile and grabs hers. They're both in athletic wear, out for a walk and on their way to meet Annie for her lunch break.

Chatting with them has become a weekly routine when

they stop in, and it's nice to feel like my roots here in Milwaukee have solidified as more friendships bloom.

"Luke mentioned that Sadie was working out well for Evee? I'm glad I finally annoyed you enough to take my list of babysitters." Mia smiles before taking a sip of her coffee.

"Oh, she's the older sister of one of my old students. She's great," Drew adds as I cap my Sharpie, putting it in the pocket of my apron.

"Evee loves her. I'm so sad her schedule won't be as open now that her college courses start at the end of the month, but she's been such a big help this summer," I tell the girls.

"And how did your meeting with your agent go yesterday?" Mia asks, tucking a piece of her blonde hair behind her ears. "Did you decide on your title?"

"We're officially waiting for the final proof of *The Rainbow of Emotions*," I announce with pride, gaining smiles from both Drew and Mia who have been nothing but supportive since hearing about my new, *potential* career change. "With Emerson's new rendition of Callista the Chameleon, everything is finally feeling complete," I tell them.

I never thought I'd get used to having such a big circle of people interested in what I'm up to and happy for my success. The last month of meeting Lauren at the library and then meeting with her—and my—agent, Joanna, has been such a whirlwind I never expected.

But between the help of my friends, Sadie with Evee, and Jack's constant support whenever I need him, I finally understand why they say it takes a village—not just with raising a child, but going through life.

I don't know why I ever wanted to do it alone.

I think it would've been possible, but I just don't think it's what life is meant to be like.

"You should be so proud," Drew says, her green eyes shining, contrasting against her red wine hair. "We can't wait to get the girls and Knox a copy. You'll have to sign them for us too."

"Oh! And I'm sure Annie would love to throw you a release party here. And you have Ava to handle all the party planning," Mia adds, having begged Ava to plan her twin's birthday party back in June.

I can't help but laugh, my cheeks blushing at their excitement for me. I'm about to tell them how I don't want to get too excited—there's still a lot up in the air, and I shouldn't be getting my hopes up yet—but there's a part of me that instead decides to say, "I can't wait."

After Mia and Drew leave, the next hour of my shift drags, causing my mind to wander back to my night with Jack, wishing that our nights together weren't so few and far between.

Leaving my toothbrush there and a change of clothes is a promise for more nights and mornings together, but it's only been a day since waking up with Jack, and it already feels like an eternity.

My lease with Ava is up next month, and we are set on renewing it because how nice it is to live in the duplex and be just across the street from Hey Honey's. The house I brought Evee home to from the hospital, the place I found my best friend—the place where I healed into a better version of myself, the *me* I didn't even realize I was capable of being.

But maybe it's time to move forward.

I don't want to go back to staying because it's comfortable or because I'm too scared to find out if the grass is greener on the other side.

I want to continue to heal and grow.

And I want to do it while going to sleep, wrapped in Jack's arms, and wake up to find his lazy smile and sleepy, green eyes before grabbing Evee to snuggle between us.

"Hi, pretty girl." The voice pulls me from my thoughts, and it's like my mind summoned him here.

"Hey, firefighter," I say as Jack leans over the counter, pressing a kiss to my lips. Dressed in his black station wear that hugs his strong frame, he leans back, crossing his arms as he asks me about my morning so far. His easy, grounded confidence is something that was missing the first time he walked into Hey Honey's, but he's a new man compared to then.

He looks so sure of himself, like he's exactly where he needs to be. His radio is strapped to his belt, the one he's responsible for now as interim Fire Lieutenant before he's officially promoted.

"I wanted to come see you while we were out for the grocery run," Jack explains, and I look over his shoulder to see Anderson waving from the truck parked in the lot. "And see if maybe I could come by after I'm done with my shift tomorrow? There's something I wanted to talk to you about."

"Oh?" I say, and the lack of anxiety surprises me. I expected to feel my smile drop, or my mind try to conjure up everything I've done wrong, but there's nothing.

"It isn't anything to worry about," he adds quickly, and I'm still thankful for the reassurance. "I promise, it's good. Just something I've been thinking about since you left on Sunday." He smiles.

"You're not even going to give me a hint?" I ask him, and he laughs. and I cross my arms, trying to hide my smile. "I'm serious."

"So am I." He leans in again, giving me a quick kiss before he turns to head out the door.

"You're mean. Who dumps *that* on someone and then leaves?"

"Bye, baby," he says, turning around to give me a wink before he's out the front door. I watch him hop into the truck and throw on a pair of sunglasses with a wide grin on his face as Anderson pulls out of the parking lot.

I shake my head, smiling to myself as I watch the truck

disappear from view, and I'm left wondering if maybe it's not too soon.

Maybe Jack is thinking the same thing as me.

We've known this was the real-thing for a while now, probably since before we even started letting ourselves act on the feelings we were developing for one another.

My gaze returns to the parking lot, mostly empty in the early afternoon—my Tuesday shifts always experiencing this same lull—and I'm ripped from my thoughts when the front door to the shop chimes, and I see familiar tattoos and dark hair adorned with a patterned headband.

Emerson waltzes in, bringing my attention back to my surroundings, thoughts of Jack and moving in together floating to the back of my mind for now. "Hey, hot stuff." She rounds the counter and asks me about the morning, but I don't really register her question. Not when I see a familiar car, one I haven't seen in months, back out of one of the back parking spots.

I noticed it pull in this morning, but I don't remember seeing anyone get out. The only reason I gave it any thought was because of the plates.

They're Minnesota plates.

I'm trying to make out the plates when I hear my name. "Rumi?"

"Yeah?" I say, but my eyes are still on the car as it exits the parking lot, but it's too far away now. I squint, trying to see who's in the driver's side, my heart beating faster and faster every second that passes, but I can't see who they are. "What did you say?"

Emerson follows my gaze, and we both watch the car disappear in the opposite direction I watched Jack head just minutes ago, and I take in a shaky exhale.

It can't be him.

It's been weeks since the court issued Trevor a paternity test, and if he doesn't respond by the end of August, the court will most likely default judgement and legally declare him the father. From there, the plan is to go ahead with the child support order, since my circumstances allow for us to go forward without a hearing.

What would he be doing here?

And how would he have found me?

"Who was that?" Emerson asks, and I feel her eyes on me as I begin to busy myself with cleaning the already spotless counters before taking off my apron and folding it over my arm.

"No one," I answer, shaking my head. "I thought I saw someone I knew, but I don't think it was them."

Emerson knows a lot about my past—Jack giving her some details but allowing me to tell her the rest on my own time—but I don't want to worry her over nothing, not when I'm positive this was just my head playing tricks on me.

Almost positive.

CHAPTER 39
RUMI

BY THE TIME I get home, the afternoon has faded into the early evening, and I'm fully convinced that I was overreacting to seeing the black car in the parking lot. After leaving Hey Honey's, reassuring Emerson that I was fine, I went for a walk, needing to clear my head, before circling back home, knowing Evee was taken care of with Ava.

With the situation forgotten, I walk through my front door to find Ava on the other side, Evee in one arm and her diaper bag in the other. I'm surprised to see her, having gotten a text from her that she was going to drop Evee off at Jack's mom's house for me—Tuesday evenings having turned into Angela's night with Evee since she watched her the weekend I took care of Jack when he was sick.

Ava's auburn hair is curled in loose waves, and her freckled cheeks are dusted with bronzer and a light pink blush. She's dressed in a tight black dress that accentuates her slim build and long legs.

She's dressed for a date.

I cock my head and give her a smirk. "Where are you off to?"

I know she's been seeing Anderson, but he's working

today—on the same shift rotation as Jack—and doesn't get off until tomorrow morning.

Holding my arms out toward Evee, she reaches back to me and settles in my hold. She babbles her version of "mama" a few times—her first and only word since she first said it a few weeks ago. She smiles, showing off her fourth tooth that has grown in at the bottom as she tangles her little hands in the loose strands from my braid.

Ava squares her shoulders, schooling her features, never one to not own up to her decisions or actions. "To drop Evee off at Jacks' mom's. I texted you."

"Dressed like that?" I ask, eyeing her outfit one more time.

"Yep," she says, a little too cheerfully. "I'll let Angela know you'll pick Evee up at 8?"

I nod, rolling my lips to hide the smiling threatening my lips. "Then where are you off to?"

Even though she's been seeing Anderson, it's possible they haven't made things official or both are seeing other people. But, from what she's told me, Ava seems completely smitten with the firefighter.

"I'm meeting Jett."

My eyes widen, and I feel my whole body tense with anger. "The hell you are." The volume of my voice surprises Ava, her brows lifting in surprise.

Jett is her emotionally abusive ex, the one who turned her into a shell of a human until she left him last year, weeks before my path crossed with hers.

She's gone no-contact with him since, but she's mentioned a few times how he still has some of her things. He's basically holding a few boxes of hers—the ones she couldn't fit in her car when she left one morning when he was at work—hostage to get her to talk to him, but she's held strong.

Until now, apparently.

"I thought you had him blocked." My hold on Evee

tightens—just the thought of Ava seeing Jett, possibly putting herself in harm's way, makes me hold my daughter closer.

"I unblocked him two weeks ago," she admits, and I wished she was more embarrassed over the admission—that she felt some semblance of guilt for going back on all this progress she's made.

"And what? You guys are talking now?"

She lets out a humorless laugh. "I don't remember needing to answer to *you*."

Her words sting, and I have to resist the urge to step back. The way she says it, laced with malice, catches me off guard.

This doesn't sound like my best friend.

We've never fought, barely ever disagreed, so to hear her say something with such distaste rears me silent for a moment.

I inhale, trying to calm the frustration bubbling under my skin. "Do you really need that stuff he has?"

She shakes her head. "It's not about the stuff. It's about closure."

"What closure? You and I both know that men like him don't change." She of all people should know that best, having been the one to tell me time and time again whenever I doubted my decision to leave Trevor at the beginning of moving here.

"It's none of your business," she says, taking a step toward me.

"Okay, who are you and what have you done with my best friend?"

Ava rolls her eyes. "If you'll excuse me, I have to get her to Angela's." She reaches for Evee, but I instinctively hold her closer to me, and Ava looks like I slapped her across the face.

But the look of hurt is gone as quickly as it came, and she shrugs her shoulders, walking past me toward our car in the driveway. "Suit yourself," she says without even turning to look at me, and I don't wait to watch her get to the car.

Instead, I storm into the house, throwing the door shut behind me, turning the lock, and leaning back against it.

How could she be so stupid?

Going to see the person who constantly put her down, called her names, made her feel guilty for anything that would allow him more control over her.

Jett messed with her head to the point she started doubting herself, and she's the most confident, headstrong, fearless person I know.

And now she's going back to him?

I know how easy it is to get stuck in the cycle, no matter what the person has done or how much time and space you put between them, but what the hell is she thinking?

And she couldn't at least talk to me about it?

She's putting her guard up, and that scares the shit out of me.

I'm still leaning back on the door when the doorknob wiggles, and then I hear a knock.

I'm too mad to hear her explanation or apology or whatever she's coming back for. *If* that's what she's even coming back for.

Maybe she just forgot something.

Without turning around, I turn the deadbolt, kick off my shoes, and head into the kitchen with Evee. I hear the door open behind me, but I don't turn around, not even wanting to look at her right now.

I set Evee down in her high chair as I hear Ava close the door, but she doesn't follow me into the kitchen right away.

And she doesn't say anything.

So neither do I.

Grabbing a pot, I fill it with water, turning on the gas stove and setting the pot on the burner. It's immature and petty to ignore her, but I can't help it—focusing on making a quick dinner for Evee and me, pulling out a box of pasta.

Finally, footsteps slowly approach.

That's weird.

No matter how pissed Ava is, she wouldn't keep her shoes on in the house.

The footsteps quicken, and they sound heavy, not like the heels she had on.

But before I can turn around, I feel a large, cold hand grip my shoulder hard enough to make me yelp in pain.

The person turns me around, and I feel a sudden, shocking jolt of pain in my cheek. A sharp burst of pressure knocks me back, causing my vision to blur, and I stumble, catching myself on the edge of the counter. Whoever it is—*a man?*—is yelling at me, but I'm too disoriented to register what they're saying.

I hear Evee wail over the bellowing as I try to blink away the tears forming in my eyes, but, before I can even register it's happening, another punch comes, and then it all goes silent—and black.

CHAPTER 40
JACK

"THAT'S NOT YOUR USUAL BOOK," Anderson says as he flops next to me on the couch. The clean-up crew for this week just finished tidying up after dinner, the lemon and lavender scent from the all-purpose cleaner still lingering in the air. "And why do you have a pen to read? Taking notes on scenes you want to act out with a *certain* someone?" I turn to see him wiggling his brows.

I set my pen and the book I'm annotating down on my lap, lifting my reading glasses off my nose before looking right at Anderson. "Why don't you tell me what exactly you're implying, so I can be sure you deserve it when I punch you square in the jaw."

Anderson puts his hands up in surrender. "I'll shut up."

I nod, appeased, and put my reading glasses back on, picking my book and pen back up.

I'm currently rereading the *Twilight* books, having mentioned to my mom how Rumi has never read them. She was so excited to dig up her old copies for me to give to her.

Initially, I thought about just bringing them over when I go see Rumi after I'm done with this shift tomorrow morning; however, my curiosity got the best of me—wondering if I'd enjoy the books as much as I did when I read the first of the series for my mom's book club and then the rest on my own.

With some down time today, I picked up the first book and immediately knew Rumi would like it. I've read a few of her paranormal romance books in the last few months, and this is right up her alley in young adult form. I thought it would be fun to put my thoughts in the margins and underline my favorite lines in hopes that it'll make the books she's refused to read even more enjoyable.

Her refusal started off with the argument against Ava that there were other books she wanted to read *more*, but ever since finding out both Emerson and I have ample *Twilight* knowledge, I think Rumi's refusal is more out of stubbornness and not letting Ava win.

Anderson joins another conversation with the other guys on the couch, and I go back to my reading, trying to not let my mind wander the same way it has since seeing Rumi this morning.

The world's toughest feat.

I think about her the moment I wake up, only taking a break when I fall asleep, and every single moment in between.

Waking up next to her on Sunday was a dream.

I hated Sundays, until I woke up that morning with her in my bed.

The only thing missing was a baby monitor on the bedside table, knowing Evee was just in the next room over.

I want that—*need* that.

Having the two of them with me is a need, the same one my lungs have for clear air to breathe.

And that's why I'm going to ask her to move in with me.

Fuck taking it slow.

I've known from the moment I laid eyes on Rumi that she would be my peace. She would be the solace I so desperately ached for.

And now that she's mine, I refuse to not have all of her.

I want the lazy Sundays, tired Mondays, busy Tuesdays, and all the days that follow.

I want to come home to her after my shift and be waiting for her when she comes home from hers; I want to decorate a room for Evee and do it all over again in a few years and then again a few years after that.

I want this house of mine to be *ours*, along with the life I got back this year.

Never in a million years did I think I would live a life that wasn't just going through the motions—I didn't think I was capable of having one after losing Bennett.

Whether or not he was my soulmate like Rumi said, I was missing part of myself for so long—a part I've realized I might never get back.

But in this process of healing, I found Rumi and Evee, the two that make me feel whole again, like this life is worth living, not just for Bennett but for me too.

I realize I'm just staring at the opened book on my lap, not registering a single word when the familiar chaos of a call erupts, the computerized voice dispatching the emergency we're being called into.

As we all file down the stairs, we hear it's a routine call—domestic dispute, called in by a neighbor. It sounds like the caller heard yelling and a baby crying in the house next door to hers. Since it's a smaller emergency, and we don't know what else we'll get hit with tonight, I give orders to those I want headed to the location—an address I don't quite make out over my own voice booming through the station.

I decide to stay back with Anderson and the rest of the crew in case we get another call.

"Think it'll be a busy night?" Anderson asks as we watch them leave in the truck, sirens blaring, and the lights from the truck mixing with the low sunlight as sunset slowly approaches.

"I hope not," I say, turning to head to the gym, wanting to blow off some of this adrenaline in case we get called into something else.

A domestic dispute is never an easy call to get, especially knowing the kind of monsters that are out there and the victims they endanger.

They are the types of calls that have recently started to hit a little closer to home for me.

CHAPTER 41
RUMI

I CAN HEAR movement around me, but I can't get my eyes to open. I try to peer through the darkness that has taken over, but I can't see.

It isn't until I reach my hand, touching my face, that I realize that one of my eyes is swollen shut, the other burning the moment I finally open it—something dripping into the corner of my eye.

Blood.

A loud cry sounds, and it's coming from right above me.

Evee.

It all rushes back—opening the front door thinking it was Ava, footsteps behind me, a hand on my shoulder, him throwing two punches directly at me.

Trevor.

He's here.

He's found me.

I try to focus on my surroundings, needing to know where he is before I even think about getting up. The smell of scorched air and warm gas is faint but there from the pot of water I put on the stove before I was knocked out.

Right now, he must think I'm still out—I need to use that to my advantage.

Evee's cries are hoarse, like she's been crying for hours, and it makes my heart physically crack—knowing how scared she must be but also knowing I can't do anything to comfort her right now.

I really hope I haven't been out that long.

Footsteps sound on the other side of the kitchen, but I don't want to risk moving to try and see them.

If he's still here, it means he must want something.

Evee? No, he hasn't given one single fuck about her, not even since she's been conceived. And why now? We've been gone for over a year.

Me? But that doesn't make any sense. Why aren't we in the car halfway back to Minnesota now if he came for me.

Which can only mean one thing.

He's here to finish the job he couldn't do all those months ago—the night I left.

He's here to kill me.

I try to angle my head up to see if Evee can see me and hoping I'm enough under the tray of her high chair that she doesn't have to live with the image of her mom, passed out and bloodied on the floor, for the rest of her life.

The movement sends a shooting pain through my jaw and the back of my head, causing me to let out an involuntary whimper, and I hear the footsteps stop.

"Get up, you stupid bitch." Trevor walks over to me, I can sense his presence even with barely being able to see through my swollen eye and the blood in the other.

I muster all the strength I have, pushing myself up and ignoring the pain begging me to stop moving. It must take me too long because I feel a kick to my side, the crushing blow knocking the wind out of me.

Forcing my mind into survival mode, I get up, and it feels all too familiar. It's like muscle memory takes over, my brain taking me back to the place it used to take me when Trevor or my father would put their hands on me.

But there's something more—I don't know if it's adrenaline or just sheer willpower that I feel deep in my bones.

A strength I didn't have the last time this happened, or at least didn't have until I got in the car and fled.

A strength that comes from being a mother, knowing your child needs you and doing everything in your power to get to them.

Standing up, I wipe the back of my hand against my eyes, swiping the blood so I can finally see through it. I feel my bare feet ground into the hardwood floor, and my fist clench as I look Trevor in the eyes, forcing him to see me in a way I've never made him do before.

If he's going to kill me, he's going to stare me right in the eye as he does.

My body moves to the side, shielding a crying Evee, and it takes everything in me not to turn and hold her close to me, to protect her from all of this, but I can't risk having her in my arms when Trevor inevitably hits me again.

"What are you doing here?" My voice is scratchy and rough, but I keep my shoulders square and my eyes on the man I thought I loved.

His dirty blonde hair is cut close to his scalp, his dark brown eyes almost black in the lowlight of the kitchen, the only light coming from the sun slowly setting through the windows and the lit burner on the stove.

"What am I doing here?" He lets out a chuckle, one free of any humor. "I'm here because I woke up on my kitchen floor to find my *slut* of a girlfriend left in the middle of the night."

The admission is anything but sincere, and it still doesn't answer my question.

"And it took you over a year to find me?"

I don't have time to brace for the slap against my cheek, the one already swollen from the first punch, and my vision goes blurry once again, the sting of his palm against my skin a familiar type of pain.

"Watch your fucking mouth," he spits. "I thought when you didn't come running back, that I was finally free of you and your fucking kid that won't shut the fuck up." He yells the last part, and I resist the urge to flinch, the volume and cadence causing me to momentarily forget that I'm not back at the house.

Evee's cries have lessened to a soft whimpering, no doubt tiring herself out, and I wish I could do something to comfort her, but there's no telling what Trevor would do to her if I wasn't the one between them right now.

"Then, I get your stupid little court-order," he says, and it takes me a second to realize he's talking about the paternity test. "You think you're going to get money from me? For a kid who might not even be mine?"

"If you don't think she's yours, why not take the test?" It's stupid to push him, but I can't help it. Not when there's so much anger inside of me that I feel like I'm about to explode.

Anger that he found me.

Anger that I let my hope get the best of me. Again.

Anger that he made my daughter cry, and that he's still standing in my kitchen.

This time, I brace for the slap against my cheek, and I don't know what pisses him off more. My words, or that I barely flinch.

"It wasn't hard to find you, you know." He smiles, and it makes my stomach twist. He looks like a predator, locking in on his prey, but I refuse to tear my eyes from his. "When I saw the address was for Milwaukee, it wasn't hard to locate the child support agency you were going through. From there, it was just laying low and hoping our paths crossed."

"You've been stalking me?" The question comes out before I can stop them. The thought of Trevor going through those lengths to find me, having no idea he's been so close, terrifies me to the core but angers me even more at the same time.

And it doesn't sound remotely like him.

Trevor isn't someone who waits for his chance to strike—he acts on impulse.

"Don't give yourself that much credit, babe. I just happened upon you today. It was more luck than anything else. Or, what bullshit did you used to say? How soulmates find each other no matter what?" He knows exactly what he's doing as he grins, throwing words back at me—the ones I used to tell him when we first got together, thinking I had found the person I was meant to find, only to figure out I had to wait a little longer until I would.

"You just happened to find the place I worked?" I grit through my teeth, furious that Trevor had to come and infect my home, my place of work, my *life* that I worked so hard for.

"Actually, I was driving by, headed more into downtown near the agency when I saw the bar next door and thought I'd stop for a drink." He crosses his arms, leaning against the counter next to the stove, reminding me of the lit burner.

Has all that water already boiled?

"And then," he continues, "I was just about to get out of my car when I saw a firetruck pull up, one of the firefighters hopping out and literally skipping into the coffee shop as if he was a little school girl." Trevor laughs, and I suck in a quick inhale. "Then I saw him lean over the counter and kiss a girl who looked oddly familiar and happened to be exactly who *I* was looking for." He smirks at me. "See? Soulmates."

Bile rises in my throat, the thought of Trevor watching me today when I didn't have a clue makes me sick.

"I should've known a slut like you would leave me and find some other man to take advantage of you. I'm sure you threw yourself right into his bed the first chance you got. How's a man like that taste, you whore? One that only wants you for the one thing you're good for."

I take a step toward him, leaning against the counter to keep my balance, my head spinning from both my injuries and trying to stay calm. Trevor tries to hide the surprise on his face when I don't cower and cry the way he's used to—the way I used to when he'd say shit like that before throwing me to the ground.

With just the length of the stove between us, and a smirk of my own, I say, "Like you, but so, *so* much sweeter."

His cocky, disgusting smirk falls, a familiar look of fury taking over as he looks at me, and I take advantage of his impulsivity to reach for the pot of boiling water, lucky to find it's still as full as I had it—a rush of relief washing over me that I wasn't out for as long as I thought.

Grabbing the handle, with one hand, I lift the pot quickly, aiming it toward Trevor, causing the water inside to splash out toward him.

"Fuck!" he screams when the boiling water hits his chest, causing him to stumble back, giving me time to turn and grab Evee, my plan to escape through the glass door the only thing on my mind.

But, before I can get to her high chair, I feel a hand grip my braid, pulling me back with such force that it feels like he's tearing every piece of hair from my head.

I scream, reaching to grab the counter but I fall to the ground.

Holding my arms up to my face, I try to block his fists as he drives them toward me, but it's no use.

The last thought I have before I pass out is of my daughter's cool blue eyes, and the jade green eyes I wish I could see one more time.

CHAPTER 42
JACK

NO MORE THAN fifteen minutes after the first call, we get a second to the same location. The computerized voice begins dispatching the details.

"Attention Engine 12, Ladder 3, Rescue 5 – respond to a residential structure fire, possible arson related to domestic dispute. Address: 2214 Maple Hollow Road. Caller reports house fully involved, one victim possibly trapped inside, suspect seen fleeing the scene on foot. Law enforcement en route. Use caution. Time out: 02:41."

My feet freeze just before I can take a step down the stairs. Anderson runs past me, but I grab him by the shirt. "Did it just say Maple Hollow Road?"

"Yeah," Anderson says, looking at me confused, until we both hear the details again. Our eyes lock when we hear the street address. "Isn't that—"

I rush down the stairs, barreling into whoever is in my way. Adrenaline and pure terror overwhelms me, taking over my muscle memory as I gear up, my vision going blurry as I run to the truck.

"Jack!" Anderson yells to me, but it sounds like he's underwater. "Jack!" he says again, this time closer.

"What?" I bark.

"We need your orders," Anderson says among the movement of everyone gearing up and getting into the truck, and I can see his worried features trying to hide beneath a look of calm.

I shake my head, needing to keep a level-head. I exhale. "This is a potential arson with a victim inside—move fast and stay sharp. Ladder 3, you're on primary search; Rescue 5, back them up and check for extension. Engine 12, get water on that structure and secure a line for interior." My voice is tense and loud, and the crew watches me carefully as I turn to get in the truck.

Once we're all loaded up, we pull out into the evening, the low sun casting a warm glow over the horizon, but I can't focus on anything except for what the fuck happened.

An active fire at Rumi's house—is she home? Is Ava? What about Evee?

So many scenarios run through my brain, and it feels harder and harder to breathe with each one.

I can't freeze.

I can't make a mistake.

She needs to be okay.

"It's my girlfriend's address." I look into the eyes of each member of my crew as the truck speeds down the road, my heart on the verge of exploding.

We can't make a mistake.

Understanding dawns on their faces just before each one looks at me with determination in their eyes.

As the truck nears Rumi's neighborhood, I see the rising column of dark, churning smoke above the rooftops, flickering orange light mixing with the approaching sunset.

"Watch for structural instability and be alert for the suspect. PD's en route," I order.

And I hope for the suspect's sake that one of the others finds them—there's no telling what I'll do if I do.

As we approach the scene, I'm supposed to repeat orders and oversee the processes, but when I see the house of the woman I love up in flames, I don't hesitate.

Forgetting any protocol or way of handling these situations, I run directly to the front door—fuck any and all training and conditioning. I don't even waste time grabbing my SCBA or a mask.

"Hasting!" I hear from behind me, from multiple voices of the crew, but I don't care. I trust them to do what needs to be done, the same way I'm doing exactly what I need to do.

Kicking the door down, making a promise in my head to Rumi that I'll fix it again, I enter the house, finding it completely filled with thick, choking smoke. Glowing embers and flickering flames cast eerie shadows over the place I've gotten to know so well, and the heat is so intense that it distorts my vision.

A sense of urgency takes over as I hear the structure groan, and I have to rely on my familiarity with the house to make my way through it with how low visibility is, my arm in front of my face to decrease the amount of smoke I inhale.

Moving through the entryway, I enter the kitchen where I find a body slumped on the ground, blood coming from their head. My heart rate spikes, my stomach plummeting before I realize it's a body I don't recognize.

Who the fuck is this?

I reach down, feeling for a pulse, and it takes a second, but I find one on the man. Looking around, I see Evee's empty high chair and a big pot forgotten on the floor, so I act quickly, throwing the man over my shoulder and making my way to the sliding back door.

And that's when I see her.

Covered in black soot, laying on her side in a fetal position, wrapped around a tiny, fragile body, I see Rumi.

Carrying the man I found in her kitchen out the glass door, I set him down on the grass of the gated backyard before I gather Rumi and Evee in my arms. Evee's eyes are swollen from the smoke and from crying, but she's awake and responsive, her small whimpering my own personal hell. Her cries turn to wails as I hold her against me in one arm, picking up Rumi in the other, and my body threatens to crumple when I see her face.

Her eyes are completely swollen shut, her lip gashed with a cut that's still bleeding, her neck bruised with what look like handprints, streams of blood coming down her face.

I yell so loud that my throat starts to strain, already burning from all the smoke as I run to the gate door, hoping someone on the crew hears me.

"There he is!" I hear Anderson yell before him and two other guys from the crew run over to me, their masks down, oxygen on their backs.

"You didn't even grab your tank, Jack," Anderson says, as he approaches, his voice muffled behind his mask, but I see the relief on his face when he sees Rumi and Evee in my arms. "Thank fuck," he mutters before opening the gate door for me, just as I hear ambulance sirens approaching.

"There's another victim. A man. I found him in the kitchen," I rasp, refusing to let go of Evee or Rumi, even as the two guys on the crew reach for them to help me.

"I thought they said the suspect was on foot."

I think of Rumi's injuries, the ones that couldn't have come from the fire. "I think he never made it out of the house," I say as I walk a wailing Evee and an unconscious Rumi to the street where three paramedics are pulling out a gurney.

"We've got two victims—female, 25, pulled from the back-yard, unconscious with smoke inhalation and burns to the arms and legs, swelling to the face, bruising on her neck. Infant, 15 months old, was found next to her—conscious, breathing, but needs to be assessed. Both need oxygen and rapid transport."

One of the paramedics grabs Evee from me to assess her, and I help the other two load Rumi onto the gurney. My eyes burn as I look down at her, but it's not from the smoke.

She looks so pale, so vulnerable—the only reassuring thing about her is the slow rise and fall of her chest.

"She needs to be okay," I whisper to myself. I take off my glove to run a hand through her hair, a tear falling from my eye as I look at her, hoping I wasn't too late and wishing that we weren't in this situation again.

The paramedics try to wheel her to the ambulance, but I hold it tight, looking between the two of them as I say again, "She needs to be okay."

I look down at Rumi one more time, taking my helmet off to lean down and press a gentle kiss to her forehead, my chest cracking more and more the longer I look at her injuries.

The injuries that could only be from one person.

The person who is going to wish he died in the fire after I'm done with him.

When I pull back, I hope to see those pretty blue eyes looking back at me, but I don't think she'd be able to open them right now even if she tried, not with how swollen her face is.

"You riding with us?" one of the paramedics asks.

I feel a hand on my shoulder, and I turn to find Anderson. "Go," he says. "We got it from here."

And I believe him.

Following the gurney to the ambulance, I hop in, taking off my gear and grabbing Evee from the paramedic, holding her close while they load Rumi up.

"She's going to be okay," I whisper to Evee. She looks at me, recognition falling over her little features, and her head falls into my shoulder as we drive to the hospital.

CHAPTER 43
RUMI

I THINK I was hit by a bus.

Actually, there's no way. That would hurt less than this.

I try to open my eyes, but it feels like they're sewn shut. I move my hands around, feeling for something to tell me where I am, but the movement makes me tired, and darkness takes over before I even realize I was awake in the first place.

———

"I shouldn't have left that day." The soft voice lures me from sleep. I try to open my eyes, but it's still too hard, so I keep them shut as I listen. "You were right. Going to see Jett was stupid, and now look what happened."

Ava.

She's crying. I hate when she cries, and I want to reach for her. I try, but it's like my body won't listen. Then, I feel her hand wrap around mine. I try to hold hers back, but I can't. "I'm so sorry, Rumi."

I want to open my eyes and tell her that it's not her fault.

But I don't even know what she's apologizing for.

Where am I?

Where's Evee?

But before I can remember what got me here, sleep takes over once again.

———

"Rumi?" I hear the voice, low, gruff, and instantly familiar. "I don't know if you can hear me, but I need you to be okay." Jack's words are strained, emotion heavy in his tone, and I feel his hand wrap around mine, his lips pressing against my skin.

I'm okay, I want to tell him, but just trying to open my eyes feels like the toughest feat right now. I want to squeeze his hand, let him know I'm here, but it's like my body isn't connected to my mind.

"Ava and I have been taking turns with Evee at my house," Jack continues. I wish I could see him—his dark, wavy hair, his green eyes, his tan skin, his smile that always goes to one side of his face. "And whoever isn't with her is here."

How long have I been out?

"My mom and Emerson have been helping out too, visiting you or Evee as much as they can."

His voice cracks, and I wish I could make the pain I hear in his voice go away. "I miss you, pretty girl." He presses his forehead to where he holds my hand in both of his. "Come back to me," he whispers. "Please."

The events that lead me here come rushing back—Trevor, the fire, getting me and Evee out. I remember it all, even the moment that Jack found us. I heard the sirens, knew he would come, knew he would save us, and that's when I finally closed my eyes, only for them to be impossible for me to open now.

It takes all my strength, but I finally see the bright lights of the hospital room, my eyes slowly adjusting after being closed for who knows how long. Then, I use whatever's left to squeeze Jack's hand, his head shooting up to look at me, his green eyes glossy.

More memories begin to flood my brain.

But not from the fire.

Sirens.

Lights.

Voices.

Then just one.

"She needs to be okay."

Jade green eyes looking down on me.

Ones I've never seen before.

"She needs to be okay."

A gasp escapes my lips, remembering the few moments I woke up after my accident last year, just before I was loaded into the ambulance.

"Rumi baby," he says in disbelief before sitting up to wrap his arms around me, gently pulling me close to him.

"It was you," I manage to say though the pain in my throat, my voice cracked and soft.

"What?" Jack leans back to look at me, eyes roaming all over my face. "What was me?"

"You saved me," I rasp.

"From the fire? Yeah, the station got a call, and I—" he stops when he sees me shaking my head.

"From the accident." I watch as confusion turns to understanding. "I remember. You told the paramedics I needed to be okay."

Jack swallows, squeezing my hand as he continues to hold it in his. "I was on my way back to Milwaukee when I came across your car. It was the first time I used any of my training in months." He shakes his head. "I saw you, in your nightgown, pregnant and alone, and I made sure you hung on until the ambulance came."

His voice is thick with emotion, and I feel my eyes water.

"Why didn't you tell me?" I ask.

He shakes his head. "I honestly don't know." He lets out a humorless laugh.

My mind drifts back to the night I took care of him when he was sick, when he talked about my eyes. "Is that what you were talking about when you said you found me?"

Confusion spreads across his face. "When?"

"When you were high on a 102 fever," I tease, and his lips twitch. I know he's resisting the urge to tell me he wasn't *that* sick, but only one of us remembers him pouring his heart out that night. "You told me that when you found me, you knew you were going to be okay. That you saw it in my eyes."

"I told you all of that?" he asks, and I don't have to glance at his neck to know that he's embarrassed.

"It was cute," I reassure him, managing to squeeze his hands tighter, and we both laugh.

Shaking his head, his smile softens as his jade eyes meet mine. "I was in such a dark place, Rumi, but it's true. I saw your eyes, saw your strength, saw *you*, and I held on to it. For months following the accident, after turning around and heading back to my grandpa's cabin like a coward, I thought of you. I thought of you making it through and finding whatever happiness you were on your way to find that night."

"I found it," I say, and Jack's gaze lifts to mine. "I found *you*."

CHAPTER 44
RUMI

IT DOESN'T TAKE LONG for sleep to take over once again, but this time I fall asleep holding Jack's hand, feeling him at my bedside, eager to wake up to find him—and Evee who he promised to bring by to see me—again.

The next time I wake up, I feel more awake and less like I'm on borrowed time before my eyes close against my will.

My room is filled with relieved smiles and happy tears of Ava, Emerson, and Jack who's holding Evee, her arms wrapped around a stuffed animal I've never seen before—a bunny in firefighter gear.

Emerson is the first to notice I'm awake. "There she is."

Ava turns around, coming over to sit on my bed. "You're awake."

I look at Jack, and he immediately brings Evee to me.

"Hey, firefighter," I say, as he sets Evee down gently on my lap, pressing a kiss to my forehead. "And hi, lovebug," I coo, feeling tears prick my eyes seeing there's not even a scratch on her, that she's perfectly okay. She looks up at me, showing off her new toy and babbling "mama". I hug her close to me until she starts to squirm. "How long have I been out?"

"Four days," Ava answers, a tear falling down her cheek before she quickly wipes it away. "I'm so sorry, Rue."

"It wasn't your fault. You couldn't have known what was going to happen." Holding Evee with one arm, I open my other to her as best I can.

"I should've been there," my best friend whispers as she settles in my embrace.

I let out an exhale. "What were you thinking, Av?" I ask into her hair, the copper strands tickling my nose.

She shakes her head. "I don't know." I feel Emerson and Jack watching us carefully but quietly, giving us both this moment "Going to see Jett was stupid and immature, and I only did it because I thought I needed something familiar," she says, but it all comes out muffled against where her head presses against my shoulder. "I should've never talked to you that way though. I think I just knew you'd tell me the things I needed to hear but didn't want to," she admits.

I take in her words, knowing exactly how she feels and how hard it must be for her to admit it. And because of that, it's impossible to not forgive her. "You really like Anderson, huh?" I ask her with a smile, and she lets out a laugh that ends with a sniffle as she lets her tears fall. "It's okay, Av. I'm okay."

"How the fuck are you okay?" Emerson asks, sitting on the other side of my bed, and I love that I can leave it to her to treat me as normal as possible even in this situation. "He told me the gist," Emerson says, jutting a thumb behind her toward where her brother stands next to my bed, "but seriously? What the fuck happened?"

"My ex-boyfriend found me," I answer. Ava sits up, settling on the side of my bed opposite from Emerson.

"Is that who you thought you saw when you were leaving Hey Honey's?" Emerson asks, and I feel both Ava and Jack shoot daggers my way—their protectiveness thick in the air.

I nod sheepishly. "I didn't think it was possible, so I

chalked it up to just seeing things. Turns out, he figured out where to find me through the local child support branch that sent the court-ordered paternity test, and he just happened to be stopping at Lenny's when he spotted me at the shop."

"What a shitty coincidence," Emerson says, blowing out a breath. "So then what? He followed you home?"

I nod my head. "I let him in by mistake, thinking it was Ava." I reach for my best friend's hand, squeezing it once to remind her that none of this was her fault. "Then, he attacked me from behind, knocked me out, and threatened me when I came to."

The fear threatens to come back, but I can feel the support of the people I love the most in the room, reminding me of where I am and that I'm safe.

"But how did the fire start?" Ava asks. "Jack told us the official report says a dishtowel got caught in a lit burner, but that can't be the whole story."

"I tried to escape, grab Evee and run after throwing a pot of boiling water at him, but it just pissed him off. He threw me to the ground and kept throwing punches until I passed out. Luckily, I woke up when I smelled the smoke and heard Evee wailing. I think Trevor thought I was dead and was going to set the house on fire to cover his tracks."

I can still taste the smoke mixed with the anger I felt at the realization that not only was he leaving me here to die, but Evee too. The thought allowed me to muster up enough strength to stand up despite all the pain radiating through my body, my eyes barely opening enough to see a foot in front of me.

"With the fire growing, Trevor was distracted, so I grabbed the pot that had ended up next to me on the ground, and I aimed for his temple."

The same way I did the night I left.

"Badass," Emerson says, giving me a look of approval.

I can't help the small smile that forms on my lips. "Somehow, I got up before he could realize what happened and grabbed the pan again. Then I don't know how many times I hit him." I rest my chin on Evee's head. "When I saw he was finally out, I grabbed Evee and managed to get us outside. I just couldn't get far, not with my injuries."

I look down at my exposed arms, seeing the various shading of bruises all along the skin. I can't even begin to imagine how the rest of my body looks, not to mention my face.

"I got us as far into the backyard as I could, and then I heard the sirens and figured the firefighters would take care of the rest," I look over to Jack who watches me carefully.

"Damn," Ava says, her voice cracking. "I'm just so glad you're okay."

"Me too," Emerson echoes, no trace of tears in her eyes, but she puts her hand on my knees and squeezes.

"Me three," I hear from next to me, and the three of us look at Jack.

Jack clears his throat, and Ava and Emerson exchange a knowing glance with one another, quickly offering to go get some food and take Evee for a walk before making their swift exit.

Jack sits at the edge of my bed, reaching to brush a hair from out of my face.

"I don't even want to know how I look right now," I say with a dry laugh.

"You look beautiful."

I cock my head, and it makes him chuckle.

"You do, while also looking like you've been through hell." His smile is soft and sad, but I'm just happy to see one.

It must have been so scary for Jack, getting the call for the fire at my house, especially with what happened to Bennett and his PTSD and anxiety when it comes to those types of calls.

"It must have been pretty hard for you too," I tell him.

Jack shakes his head, grabbing my hands in his. "When I heard the address, I didn't hesitate." His eyes bore into me. "I knew you were in that fire, and I knew I had to get you out. That's all that mattered."

My mouth parts. "You were the one to find us."

"And I'd do it again without question," he answers. He explains how he found Trevor first and was in the process of getting him out when he found Evee and me outside.

A moment passes before I ask, "What happened to Trevor?"

Jack lets out a sigh. "He got away too easily in my opinion —and lucky my crew handed him over to the cops rather than let me deal with him." His voice is hard, and I can see his shoulders tense. "He's facing attempted murder, arson, and trying to destroy evidence which hopefully will land him in prison for a very long time."

"That sounds pretty bad," I admit.

Jack scoffs. "For what he did to you? To Evee? He deserves to rot in the ground. I know it's my job to help people, but I just can't help but think if I knew it was him—" He pauses, shaking his head.

"I'm just happy we're okay," I tell him, squeezing his hand. Jack is a better man than Trevor will ever be, and Jack being the one to save Trevor's sorry excuse for a life shows that.

Looking at the man in front of me, the man who saved me in more ways than one, I feel the words on the tip of my tongue, the ones I don't want to go any longer without saying, not wanting Jack to go any longer without knowing.

I think falling in love with Jack was inevitable, since the moment our paths crossed.

Somehow, the universe brought us together when we needed each other most, and I don't want to know what it's like living a life not loving Jack as hard and as loud as I possibly can.

I'm about to tell him just that, but he beats me to it. "I love you, Rumi."

Tears blur my eyes, and I think a part of me knew this moment was coming from the first time I saw those jade green eyes. "I love you, Jack."

CHAPTER 45
JACK

RUMI IS FINALLY CLEARED to leave the hospital, and I had been dreading this day since she woke up.

Not because I didn't want her to heal and go home but because the fire left nothing salvageable, nothing left to go home to.

Both her and Ava lost almost everything in the fire, anything that they didn't have on them or in their car.

Ava handled the news fine, just thankful that Rumi and Evee were okay, but I was worried Rumi wouldn't feel the same.

She's worked so hard to get to where she is, and everything in that house stands for the life she made for herself after leaving Minneapolis.

And now, it's all gone.

But I should've known she wouldn't care, that the tangible stuff didn't matter to her, that it's all replaceable.

I'm not scared of starting over, firefighter, she told me when I broke the news that the house and all of her things couldn't be saved.

Emerson offered the girls to stay with her, having already chatted with Ava about possibly moving in—knowing about my plan to ask Rumi to move in with me the day of Trevor finding her—but I convinced Rumi to stay with me.

"I could get used to living in your clothes," Rumi says from her spot on my couch. Her hair is damp and brushed back, having showered when we got home from the hospital. The bruises on her face and neck are fading, the cut on her lip almost healed from the wound Trevor inflicted almost a week ago, but the skin around her eyes is still pretty swollen.

Her feet are in my lap as we watch one of Evee's favorite movies. She's barely staying awake on her mom's chest, and I want to show them both the surprise I have planned before she falls asleep for the night.

"I need to show you two something," I say softly and then gently move Rumi's legs off me, so I can stand.

"Right now?" Rumi asks, surprised, and I hide my smile at the slight annoyance in her tone.

"Yes, pretty girl. Right now." I lift Evee from Rumi's chest, her arms stretching before rubbing her eyes with her palms as she looks at me with droopy eyes.

Rumi stands, still moving a little stiffly from the injuries to her side along with the bruises on her arms and legs, and anger stirs in my gut. I tamp it down, keeping my face neutral, wishing there was more to do than just wait for that fucker to get what he deserves.

I interlace my hand with hers and lead her down the hall to one of the bedrooms, the one I've been working in the last two weeks—since the last night Rumi was here.

I was driving myself crazy when I wasn't at the hospital with Rumi. When Evee slept in the Pack 'n Play, I worked in here, wanting it to be perfect for when I finally got to ask Rumi the question that's been heavy on my mind since the first night she spent here.

Opening the door and turning on the light, I lead Rumi into the nursery I put together with the help of Emerson. Deciding to do a jungle theme with rainbow accents, I wanted it to capture the children's book Rumi is writing, *The Rainbow of Emotions*, and her main character, Callista the Chameleon. I know the book is her dream, but I also know that she is writing it with Evee in mind. With Emerson's help, we were able to create a space that is perfect for her.

Rumi's hands go to her mouth as her eyes take in the room, and I wrap my arm around her, pulling her into Evee and me.

Knowing Rumi lost all of Evee's things in the fire too, I might have gone a little overboard with replacing it all.

But I couldn't help it.

These two deserve the entire world, and I vow to do everything in my power to give it to them.

"Do you like it, Evee girl?" I ask her, bouncing her in my arms. She's more awake now as her eyes roam the space.

I wanted the nursery to feel like you were walking into Rumi's book, the sage green walls wrapping the room in warmth, the hand-painted vines and animals Emerson did to make the space feel even more playful. A rug in the shape of a rainbow in the center of the room ties everything together, and the wooden crib is filled with rainbow-striped pillows and every stuffed animal I could find at the store.

"Okay, well we're going to have to find another place for those if we want Evee to have any room to sleep," Rumi says with a laugh, her eyes glistening as she turns to me. "I didn't realize how closely you were listening when I told you about all my ideas for the book."

I look down at Rumi, watching as she wipes her eyes, a smile on her face as she notices frames lining the walls. "Oh, those are for the book pages. Thought it would be a nice touch."

"Jack," she breathes, looking up at me. "I can't believe you did this."

I press a kiss to the top of her head. "Well believe it, baby.

You and Evee deserve the best, and I plan on spending my life giving it to the two of you."

We both look around the room in comfortable silence, only Evee's claps and squeals filling the air, and I notice Rumi looks at the wooden plate above Evee's crib—it's blank for now, only because I didn't know her middle name.

"Oh, Emerson is going to finish that, but I need Evee's middle name. We wanted to put both on there. And I wasn't sure if you'd want it to say 'Evelyn' or 'Evee'."

Rumi rolls her lips together, like she wants to say something but doesn't know how.

After a moment, she finally says, "Her middle name is Jade. Evelyn Jade." It comes out as some sort of admission, but I'm not sure why.

"Okay," I say carefully. "I'll let Emerson know."

Rumi shifts her weight back and forth on the balls of her foot. "I didn't realize it until recently, but I named her after you."

There's no way I heard her right. "What?"

Rumi lets out an exhale. "The night of my accident, I saw you but I didn't remember. Or, I thought I didn't. But, when the nurse asked me for her name, I knew it was going to be Evelyn. I had that name picked out for most of my pregnancy, but I was between a few middle names." I nod my head, watching her as she looks at Evee and then to me. "But for some reason, I knew her middle name was Jade. And now, I know why."

"Why?" I ask.

"Because of your eyes. Some part of me remembered them, remembered how they looked at me, how they made me feel like everything was going to be okay, that I was safe."

"Evelyn Jade," I whisper, absorbing Rumi's words.

She named her daughter after *me*.

She remembered *me*, remembered that I saved her.

But she was truly the one to save me.

EPILOGUE

RUMI

"COME ON, LOVEBUG," I say to Evee as I get her dressed. She's moving and grooving, having taken her first steps only a few weeks after we moved in with Jack last year. Now at two, we can't let her out of our sight for more than a second before she's wreaking havoc somewhere. "We can't be late."

"Are my girls almost ready?" I hear as Jack peeks in through Evee's bedroom door.

It's been a year since the fire and a little less than that since Evee and I officially moved in with Jack.

And it's flown by.

Between Trevor's trial, and publishing my children's book, it feels like so much time has passed. Yet, at the same time, it feels like the year has passed in a blink of an eye.

"Da-da," Evee squeals as Jack walks in and begins putting Evee's shoes on as I finish her hair. She's dressed in a light pink dress that perfectly matches the tie Jack has on.

"Ava just texted asking where we are," Jack says, as I fasten the bow to the bun on Evee's head. "We have five minutes to get to Hey Honey's before we're considered late."

"It's my party," I argue. "I can be late if I want to."

With the release of my second children's book, *Feeling Every Color*, and my first one making USA TODAY's Bestselling Booklist, Ava wanted to throw the release party she never got to throw last year because of everything that happened.

"You know this one is a long time coming," Jack says, picking up Evee and heading out the bedroom door before I can respond. He whispers something to her, but I can't make out what it is.

"Where's the fire?" I ask him, following him out of the bedroom. "Since when are you in such a rush to be on time?"

"Don't worry about it," he says, turning to give me a smile before pressing a kiss to my lips. "Let's go, pretty girl."

"Okay, but—" I stop, mid-step, seeing the living room lit only by candles in the shape of a heart, Jack standing in the center holding Evee in one arm.

"Come here, baby," he says, and I will my feet to move, stepping into the large heart, my own heart so incredibly full it feels like it could burst.

"A year and a half ago, I couldn't even look at a burning candle without feeling like I was suffocating. For so long, since losing Bennett, I constantly felt like I was walking through smoke, inhaling it with every breath—until I found you. You are my breath of fresh air, my peace, my solace, my everything."

He hands Evee to me, and I can practically feel the way she's buzzing with excitement. Her curious eyes and rosy cheeks are on full display as she looks between her dad and me. I notice she has something in her hand, but I don't have time to register it because Jack gets down on one knee.

"Rumi, Evee," he says, looking to each of us as he says our names. "You two are my world, my universe, and I wake up every day with purpose because of the both of you. You two make me want to be the man I know I'm capable of being— the man my best friend knew I was capable of being—and I truly believe he put the two of you in my path, helping me find two more of my soulmates."

I feel tears well in my eyes as Jack reaches a hand towards Evee, and she places whatever she's holding in his palm. That's when I notice it's a little white velvet box.

Holding it up to us, Jack opens the lid, revealing a gold ring with a solitaire pear-shaped prasiolite stone, the color perfectly matching his jade green eyes.

My tears fall as I nod my head before he can even ask the question, knowing I don't want another minute to pass with his arms not around me, his lips not on mine, his ring not on my finger.

But before he asks me anything, he turns to Evee, looking at her softly, with so much love in his eyes. "Can I marry Mommy?" he asks her, and she immediately nods her head with a huge smile on her face, one with almost all her teeth.

Jack turns to look up at me, and I let the tears of happiness fall.

"Rumi baby, will you marry me?"

"Yes," I whisper, and Jack slides the ring on my finger, standing up and kissing me hard as he holds us both closely. "Yes," I say again and again against his lips.

Pressing my forehead to his, I look into those eyes.

The ones that I fell in love with.

The ones I named my daughter after.

The ones that saved me.

ACKNOWLEDGMENTS

Did I think I'd ever be saying I started a SECOND book series? Absolutely not. But here we are, and I am so proud to say I did it.

Jack and Rumi popped into my head one day and haven't left since. I started with a hot, grumpy, sad firefighter and wanted to challenge myself to write a FMC similar to my past FMCs in some ways but unique in others. Rumi is a culmination of some of the most amazing women in my life, and she has quickly become one of my most favorite characters. Her story is one I hope is meaningful to those who need it most.

Thank you to my amazing alpha readers—Hannah and Chrissy. You truly helped me get this book off the ground. Thank you for loving Jack, Rumi, and Evee as much as me. And of course, thank you to my Elle-Bell for being there from the very beginning. Elizabeth, you already know that there's no such thing as a Katy Michele book that you are not a part of.

A huge thank you to my beta readers. Your feedback, comments, and love for Jack, Rumi, and Evee meant the world to me—I hope you all know that you're stuck with me from now on. Expect a message from me when I'm ready for you all to read book two!

Thank you to my wonderful editor, Ellie (@byellierich) for EVERYTHING. I have you to thank for turning this mess of a manuscript into the book that it is. You are also stuck with me from now on.

To my real-life found family, thank you for always

cheering me on and supporting me. You all have no idea how much you inspire me—your love, friendship, and the memories we share are all written throughout these pages.

To my husband. Max, thank you for being my biggest fan, cover designer, social media manager, and the person I can ramble on and on about when I'm stuck in my head. You are truly the best thing that has ever happened to me, and I am so lucky to be loved by you. I will forever have endless inspiration when it comes to writing love stories, and that is all thanks to you.

Finally, to my readers. To the ones who have been here from the beginning and the ones that have found me along the way. Thank you for taking a chance on me, for loving these characters that mean so much to me, and for making my dreams come true.

So happy you're here.

ABOUT THE AUTHOR

Katy is the indie author based in Milwaukee. Her favorite trope is forced proximity, and she is a firm believer that found families are the best families.

Lover of all things romance, pop punk, tattoos, anime, rainy days, matcha, and her husband, Katy's purpose for writing is to remind readers that you are deserving of the love you read about.

When she's not writing, you can find her reading, or adding to her never-ending TBR.

instagram.com/authorkatymichele
tiktok.com/@authorkatymichele
threads.net/@authorkatymichele
goodreads.com/katymichele
amazon.com/author/katymichele

ALSO BY KATY MICHELE

Giving Me Butterflies

Crash & Burn

Back to You